"CAPTIVATING . . . [AN] IRRESISTIBLE NOVEL."
—*THE SEATTLE TIMES*

"Like its high-flying subject, *Circling the Sun* is audacious and glamorous and hard not to be drawn in by. Beryl Markham may have married more than once, but she was nobody's wife."
—*ENTERTAINMENT WEEKLY*

"Markham's life is the stuff of legend. . . . McLain has created a voice that is lush and intricate to evoke a character who is enviably brave and independent."
—*NPR*

"BOLD, ABSORBING FICTION."
—NEW YORK *DAILY NEWS*

"[AN] ELOQUENT EVOCATION OF BERYL'S DARING LIFE."
—*O: THE OPRAH MAGAZINE*

"Paula McLain has such a gift for bringing characters to life. I loved discovering the singular Beryl Markham, with all her strengths and passions and complexities, a woman who persistently broke the rules. She's a rebel in her own time, and a heroine for ours."
—JOJO MOYES, author of *ME BEFORE YOU*

"By the last pages, readers will hate to say goodbye to such an irresistible narrator."
—*THE MIAMI HERALD*

Praise for *Circling the Sun*

"[Paula] McLain will keep you from eating, sleeping, or checking your e-mail—though you might put these pages down just long enough to order airplane tickets to Nairobi. . . . What's certain is that the reluctantly earthbound armchair reader will cherish this gift for the hidden adventurer in all of us."

—*The Boston Globe*

"Paula McLain brings Beryl to glorious life, portraying a woman with a great many flaws that seem to result from her zest for life and inability to follow the roles expected of women in the 1920s and '30s."

—*St. Louis Post-Dispatch*

"With a sharp eye for detail and style to spare, Paula McLain captures the nuances of complex relationships, the rigidity of social conventions, and the wide skies and breathtaking vistas of Africa."

—Christina Baker Kline, author of *Orphan Train*

"Set in 1920s Kenya, this fictionalized history of the beautiful, high-flying aviator Beryl Markham is as luminous as its headstrong heroine. An exhilarating ride."

—*Family Circle*

"Paula McLain is yet another twenty-first-century woman who can write rings around the hypermasculine men who dominate so much of American fiction."

—Liz Smith

"Dynamite. . . . Beryl Markham and her circle lived fascinating lives in a place that provided adventure and excitement—and Paula McLain has written a brilliant novel capturing it all."

—*Parry Sound North Star*

"McLain's latest showcases her immersive command of setting and character. . . . [She] paints an intoxicatingly vivid portrait of colonial Kenya and its privileged inhabitants."

—*Publishers Weekly* (starred review)

"Bravo to [McLain] for now fictionalizing the grandly adventurous, passionate, and scandalous life of British East African Beryl Markham. . . . McLain sustains a momentum as swift and heart-pounding as one of Beryl's prize horses at a gallop as she focuses on the romance, glamour, and drama of Beryl's blazing life, creating a seductive work of popular historical fiction."

—*Booklist* (starred review)

"Captivating . . . [an] intriguing window into the soul of a woman who refused to be tethered."

—*Library Journal* (starred review)

"A full-throttle dive into the psyche and romantic attachments of Beryl Markham . . . Ernest Hemingway, who met Markham on safari two years before her Atlantic crossing . . . proclaimed her 1942 memoir *West with the Night* 'bloody wonderful.' Readers might even say the same of McLain's sparkling prose and sympathetic reimagining."

—*Kirkus Reviews* (starred review)

Praise for *The Paris Wife*

"A beautiful portrait of being in Paris in the glittering 1920s—as a wife and as one's own woman."

—*Entertainment Weekly*

"[Paula] McLain has brought Hadley [Hemingway] to life in a novel that begins in a rush of early love. . . . A moving portrait of a woman slighted by history, a woman whose . . . story needed to be told."

—*The Boston Globe*

"*The Paris Wife* creates the kind of out-of-body reading experience that dedicated book lovers yearn for, nearly as good as reading

Hemingway for the first time—and it doesn't get much better than that."

—Minneapolis *Star Tribune*

"Compelling . . . Fascinating. [McLain] manages to catch the aura of the time."

—*London Free Press*

"McLain has skillfully brought these literary characters from the past to life. She was helped by the fact that she was using familiar, historical people, but she has also re-created a world that is enthralling and real. . . . It's all so realistic that it's easy to forget this is a work of fiction."

—*The Waterloo Region Record*

"Marvelous."

— *Edmonton Journal*

"Exquisitely evocative . . . This absorbing, illuminating book gives us an intimate view of a sympathetic and perceptive woman, the striving writer she married, the glittering and wounding Paris circle they were part of. . . . McLain reinvents the story of Hadley and Ernest's romance with the lucid grace of a practiced poet."

—*The Seattle Times*

"A novel that's impossible to resist. It's all here, and it all feels real."

—*People*

"Powerful and devastating . . . McLain pulls off a delicate balancing act, making the macho Hemingway of myth a complex and sympathetic figure."

—*USA Today*

"*The Paris Wife* is simply a sweet love story with surprising emotional impact."

—*Chicago Sun-Times*

"Provocative . . . an imaginative homage to Hadley Richardson Hemingway."

—*The Washington Post*

BY PAULA McLAIN

CIRCLING THE SUN

CIRCLING THE SUN

A NOVEL

Paula McLain

 ANCHOR CANADA

Copyright © 2015 Paula McLain
Anchor Canada paperback published 2016
Map copyright © Laura Hartman Maestro
Reading group guide © 2016 Penguin Random House LLC

Anchor Canada is a registered trademark.

Library and Archives Canada Cataloguing in Publication

McLain, Paula, author
        Circling the sun / Paula McLain.

ISBN 978-0-385-67723-3 (pbk.)

        I. Title.

PS3563.C385C57 2016   813'.54   C2015-901918-4

Circling the Sun is a work of fiction. Names, characters, places and incidents are products of the author's imagination or are used fictitiously. Any resemblance to actual events or locales or persons, living or dead, is entirely coincidental.

Book design by Dana Leigh Blanchette
Title-page and part-title images: © *iStockphoto.com*

Printed and bound in the USA

Published in Canada by Anchor Canada,
a division of Random House of Canada Limited
A Penguin Random House Company

www.penguinrandomhouse.ca

10 9 8 7 6 5 4 3 2

Penguin
Random House
ANCHOR CANADA

For my family—with love
and thanks unending—
and for Letti Ann Christoffersen,
who was my Lady D

"I learned to watch, to put my trust in other hands than mine. And I learned to wander. I learned what every dreaming child needs to know—that no horizon is so far that you cannot get above it or beyond it. These I learned at once. But most things came harder."

—BERYL MARKHAM, *West with the Night*

"We must leave our mark on life while we have it in our power."

—KAREN BLIXEN

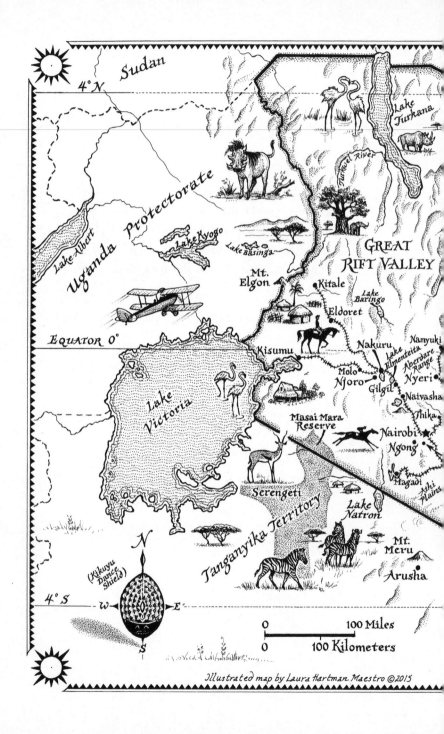

Illustrated map by Laura Hartman Maestro ©2015

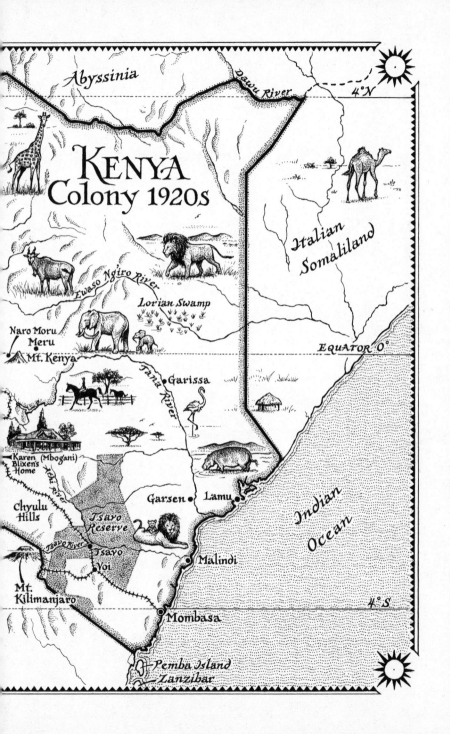

CIRCLING THE SUN

PROLOGUE

4 September 1936

Abingdon, England

The Vega Gull is peacock blue with silver wings, more splendid than any bird I've known, and somehow mine to fly. She's called *The Messenger,* and has been designed and built with great care and skill to do what should be impossible—cross an ocean in one brave launch, thirty-six hundred miles of black chop and nothingness—and to take me with her.

It's dusk when I board her. Storms have hunched over the aerodrome for days, and what light there is now is stingy and wrung out. Rain beats on the Gull's wings in timpani, and the wind gusts sideways, and yet I'm told it's the best weather I'm going to get all month. I'm less worried about weather than weight. The Gull's been fashioned with a special undercarriage to bear the extra oil and petrol. Tanks have been fixed under the wings and to the cabin, where they form a close-fitting wall around my seat with petcocks I can reach with two fingers to switch over the tanks mid-flight. I've been instructed that I should let one run completely dry and close it off before opening the next, to avoid an airlock. The engine might freeze for a few moments, but will start up again. I will have to rely on that. I will have to rely on a good many other things, too.

All over the tarmac puddles stretch out the size of small lakes, their surfaces whipped white. There are fierce, unremitting head-winds, and low brooding clouds. Some journalists and friends have gathered for my take-off, but the mood is undeniably dark. Everyone who knows the real nature of what I'm about to do has tried to convince me not to. Not today. Not this year. The record will still be there when the weather turns more favourable—but I've come too far to turn back now. I stow my small basket of food, tuck the flask of brandy into the hip pocket of my flight suit, and wedge myself into the cockpit, snug as a skin. I have a watch on loan from Jim Mollison, the only pilot who's ever attempted this particular feat and lived. I have a chart that traces my route across the Atlantic, Abingdon to New York, every inch of icy water I'll pass over, but not the empti-ness involved or the loneliness, or the fear. Those things are as real as anything else, though, and I'll have to fly through them. Straight through the sickening dips and air pockets, because you can't chart a course around anything you're afraid of. You can't run from any part of yourself, and it's better that you can't. Sometimes I've thought it's only our challenges that sharpen us, and change us, too—a mile-long runway and nineteen hundred pounds of fuel. Black squadrons of clouds muscling in from every corner of the sky and the light fading, minute by minute. There is no way I could do any of this and remain the same.

I steady my position and lean into my stick, roaring past the on-lookers with their cameras, and then the series of markers towards the single red flag that means the point of no return. I have a mile of runway and not an inch more. And she might not make it, of course. After all the planning and care and work and mustering of courage, there is the overwhelming possibility that the Gull will stay fixed to the earth, more elephant than butterfly, and that I'll fail before I've even begun. But not before I give this moment everything I've got.

After five hundred feet of runway, her tail comes up, ponderously. I urge her faster, feeling the drag of gravity, the impossible weight of her, feeling more than seeing the red flag growing nearer. Then the rudder and elevator finally come to life, swinging her nose up, and she's left the earth—arrow straight. A butterfly after all. We climb the dimming sky and the rain over green-and-grey-chequered Swindon. Ahead lies the Irish Sea, all that dark, dark water ready to grip and stop my heart. The smeary twinkling that is Cork. The hulking black of Labrador. The constant sobbing of the engine doing the work it was built for.

My nose bouncing, I drive hard through the wet spatter, thrusting into the climb and the shudder of pressing weather. The instincts for flying are in my hands, and the practical work of it, too, and then there is the more mysterious and essential thing, how I'm meant to do this and always have been, to stitch my name on the sky with this propeller, these lacquered linen wings, thirty-six hours in the dark.

It was two years ago when the challenge first came up, in the noisy, cedar-panelled bar of the White Rhino in Nyeri. There were tournedos of pepper-flecked beef on my plate, blanched asparagus spears, each as narrow as my smallest finger, and deep-stained claret in all our glasses. Then a dare thrown out like a last course from JC Carberry. *No one has managed the Atlantic solo from this side, England to America, not man or woman. What do you say, Beryl?*

Two years earlier, Mollison had fallen short in a similar water-jump, and no one had done much more than imagine the aeroplane that could accomplish the distance, but JC had more money than he could ever spend and the spark of a Magellan or a Peary. And there it was: the boundless ocean, thousands of miles of icy virgin air, a clear frontier, and no plane. *Want to chance it?*

JC's eyes were like agates. I watched them glitter and thought of how his beautiful wife, Maia, should be there in white silk with perfectly marcelled hair, but she had died years ago in a simple flying lesson near Nairobi, on a day with no wind or weather. She was the first air tragedy that hit close to us, but not the last. Many other dear ghosts were glinting from the past, winks of light playing along the rims of our wineglasses, reminding us of how reckless they'd been and how magnificent. I didn't really need reminding. I hadn't forgotten those ghosts for a moment—and somehow, when I met JC's gaze, I felt ready to pull them even closer. *Yes,* I said, and then said it again.

It's not long at all before the last bits of light rinse from the ragged edge of the sky, and then there's only the rain and the smell of petrol. I'm flying at two thousand feet above sea level and will be for nearly two days. Dense clouds have swallowed the moon and stars—the dark so complete I have no choice but to fly on instruments, blinking away fatigue to peer at the dimly lit dials. I have no wireless, so the sound and force of my engine and the wind blowing back against my nose at forty knots are soothing. The gurgle and sway of petrol in the tanks are soothing, too, until four hours into my flight, when the engine begins to falter abruptly. It sputters and whistles, then gives out. Silence. The needle of my altimeter begins to spiral downwards with shocking speed. It puts me into a kind of trance, but my hands know what to do even as my mind remains muffled and still. I only have to reach for the petcock and switch over the tank. The engine will start again. It will. I steady my hand and make my fingers find the silver toggle. When I do, it clicks reassuringly, but the engine doesn't budge. The Gull keeps losing altitude, eleven hundred feet, then eight hundred. Lower. The clouds around me part briefly, and I can see terrifying glints of water and foam. The waves reach up and the fathomless sky pushes down. I flip the toggle again, trying not to shake or panic. I've prepared for everything as well as I can, but is anyone truly ready for death? Was Maia when she saw the ground flying up to meet her? Was Denys, that awful day over Voi?

A bolt of lightning crackles near my left wing, bright as Christmas trimmings, electrifying the air—and suddenly I have the feeling that all of this has happened before, perhaps many times over. Perhaps I've always been here, diving headlong towards myself. Below me, heartless water lashes, ready for me, but it's Kenya I'm thinking of. My Rift Valley—Longonot and the jagged rim of Menengai. Lake Nakuru with its shimmering pink flesh of flamingos, the high and low escarpments, Kekopey and Molo, Njoro and the Muthaiga Club's glittering lawn. It's there I seem to be going, though I know that's impossible—as if the propeller is slicing through years, turning me backwards and also endlessly forward, setting me free.

Oh, I think, hurtling down through the dark, blind to everything else. *I've somehow turned for home.*

PART ONE

1

*B*efore Kenya was Kenya, when it was millions of years old and yet still somehow new, the name belonged only to our most magnificent mountain. You could see it from our farm in Njoro, in the British East African Protectorate—hard edged at the far end of a stretching golden plain, its crown glazed with ice that never completely melted. Behind us, the Mau Forest was blue with strings of mist. Before us, the Rongai Valley sloped down and away, bordered on one side by the strange, high Menengai Crater, which the natives called the Mountain of God, and on the other by the distant Aberdare Range, rounded blue-grey hills that went smoky and purple at dusk before dissolving into the night sky.

When we first arrived, in 1904, the farm wasn't anything but fifteen hundred acres of untouched bush and three weather-beaten huts.

"This?" my mother said, the air around her humming and shimmering as if it were alive. "You sold everything for this?"

"Other farmers are making a go of it in tougher places, Clara," my father said.

"You're not a farmer, Charles!" she spat before bursting into tears.

He was a horseman, in fact. What he knew was steeplechasing and foxhunting and the tame lanes and hedgerows of Rutland. But he'd seen paper flyers hawking cheap imperial land, and an idea had latched on to him that wouldn't let go. We left Westfield House, where I was born, and travelled seven thousand miles, past Tunis and Tripoli and Suez, the waves like great grey mountains swallowing the sky. Then through Kilindini Harbour, in the port of Mombasa, which smelled of sharp spices and drying fish, and onto the snaking train bound for Nairobi, the windows boiling over with red dust. I stared at everything, completely thrilled in a way I hadn't remembered feeling before. Whatever this place was, it was like nothing and nowhere else.

We settled in and worked to make our situation liveable, pushing against the wildness while the wildness pushed back with everything it had. Our land had no visible borders or fences, and our huts lacked proper doors. Silky, banded colobus monkeys climbed through the burlap sacking covering our windows. Plumbing was unheard of. When nature called, you walked out into the night with all the things that wanted to have at you and hung your derrière over a long-drop, whistling to keep your fear away.

Lady and Lord Delamere were our nearest white neighbours, a seven-mile hack through the bush. Their titles didn't save them from sleeping in the typical mud-and-thatch rondavels. Lady D kept a loaded revolver under her pillow and advised my mother to do the same—but she wouldn't. She didn't want to shoot snakes or her dinner. She didn't want to drag water for miles to have anything like a decent bath, or to live without company for months at a time. There was no society. There was no way to keep her hands clean. Life was simply too hard.

After two years, my mother booked a passage back to England. My older brother, Dickie, would go too, since he had always been frail and wouldn't weather Africa for very much longer. I had yet to turn five when they climbed aboard the twice-weekly train to Nairobi with steamer trunks and handkerchiefs and travelling shoes.

The white feather in my mother's helmet trembled as she kissed me, telling me I should keep my chin up. She knew I'd be fine, since I was such a big strong girl. As a treat, she would send a box of liquorice allsorts and pear drops from a shop in Piccadilly that I wouldn't have to share with a soul.

I watched the train recede along the still black line of the track, not quite believing she would actually go. Even when the last shuddering car was swallowed up by distant yellow hills, and my father turned to me, ready to go back to the farm and his work; even then I thought the whole thing was a mistake, some terrible misunderstanding that would all get sorted at any moment. Mother and Dickie would disembark at the next station, or turn around at Nairobi and be back the next day. When that didn't happen, I kept waiting all the same, listening for the far-off rumble of the train, one eye on the horizon, my heart on tiptoe.

For months there was no word from my mother, not even a dashed-off cable, and then the sweets arrived. The box was heavy and bore only my name—*Beryl Clutterbuck*—in my mother's curlicued script. Even the shape of her handwriting, those familiar dips and loops, instantly had me in tears. I knew what the gift meant and couldn't fool myself any more. Scooping the box into my arms, I made off to a hidden corner where, trembling, I ate up as many of the sugar-dusted things as I could stand before retching into a stable bucket.

Later, unable to drink the tea my father had made, I finally dared to say what I feared most. "Mother and Dickie aren't coming back, are they?"

He gave me a pained look. "I don't know."

"Perhaps she's waiting for us to come to her."

There was a long silence, and then he allowed that she might be. "This is our home now," he said. "And I'm not ready to give up on it just yet. Are you?"

My father was offering a choice, but it wasn't a simple one. His question wasn't *Will you stay here with me?* That decision had been made months before. What he wanted to know was if I could love this life as he did. If I could give my heart to this place, even if she never returned and I had no mother going forward, perhaps not ever.

How could I begin to answer? All around us, half-empty cupboards reminded me of the things that used to be there but weren't any longer—four china teacups with gold-painted rims, a card game, amber beads clicking together on a necklace my mother had loved. Her absence was still so loud and so heavy, I ached with it, feeling hollow and lost. I didn't know how to forget my mother any more than my father knew how he might comfort me. He pulled me— long limbed and a little dirty, as I always seemed to be—onto his lap, and we sat like that quietly for a while. From the edge of the forest, a group of hyraxes echoed shrieks of alarm. One of our greyhounds cocked a sleek ear and then settled back into his comfortable sleep by the fire. Finally my father sighed. He scooped me under my arms, grazed my drying tears with a quick kiss, and set me on my own two feet.

2

Mwanzo is the word in Swahili for "beginnings." But sometimes everything has to end first and the bottom drop out and every light fizzle and die before a proper beginning can come along. My mother's going was like that for me, though I didn't realize it straight away. For a long time, I could only feel confused and hurt and terribly sad. Were my parents still married? Did my mother love us or miss us? How could she have left me behind? I wasn't ready to go to my father with these questions. He wasn't all that soft as fathers go, and I didn't know how to share such private and wounded feelings.

Then something happened. In and beyond the Mau Forest on our land, several Kipsigis families lived in mud-and-wattle huts surrounded by high thorn *bomas*. Somehow they saw what I needed without my asking. One of the elders swept me up, murmuring a string of charmed words, and tying a cowrie shell ceremoniously to my waist. It swung on a leather thong and was meant to resemble the closed cowrie shell between my own legs and to ward off evil spirits. When a Kip girl was born, they did this. I was the white daughter of their white bwana, but something unnatural had happened that needed setting to rights. No African mother would ever have thought to abandon a child. I was healthy, you see, not maimed or weak. So they stamped out that first start and gave me another as Lakwet, meaning "very little girl."

I was thin and knock-kneed with unruly white-blonde hair, but my new name and place soon helped to toughen me. Running up and down our hill to the Kip village, my feet quickly turned to leather. Portions of our land that had frightened or intimidated me before became as familiar as the zebra skins that covered my bed. When the daylight bled away, I would climb under the skins and watch the houseboy pad soundlessly into my room on bare feet to light the hurricane lamp. Sometimes the sudden flare and hiss sent skinks in the hut walls flitting into hiding, the sound of them like sticks against straw. Then came the changing of the guard as the daylight insects— hornets and mason flies—tucked into mud nests in the rounded walls, and the crickets woke, sawing in a rhythm only they knew. I would wait an hour or more like this, watching shadows twist over the furniture in my room, all made of paraffin boxes and all the same until the shadows rounded and changed them. I listened until I couldn't hear my father's voice any more, and then I'd slip out of an open window into the inky dark to join my friend Kibii around a low spitting fire in his hut.

Kibii's mother and the other women drank a murky tea made of bark and nettles and spun out their tales of how everything had come to be. I learned most of my Swahili there, more and more eager for stories ... how the hyena had got his limp and the chameleon his patience. How the wind and rain had once been men before they failed at some important task and were banished to the heavens. The women themselves were wizened and toothless, or supple as polished ebony, with long-muscled limbs under pale *shukas*. I loved them and their tales, but I wanted more to join Kibii and the other *totos* who were becoming warriors, young *morani*.

The role of girls in the village was entirely domestic. I had a different position—a rare one, free from the traditional roles that governed Kibii's family set and also my own. At least for the moment, the Kip elders allowed me to train with Kibii: to throw a spear and hunt warthogs, studying stealth as Kibii did from *arap* Maina, his father, who was head warrior in the village and also my ideal of strength and fearlessness. I was taught to fashion a bow and take down wood pigeons and waxwings and vivid blue starlings, and to snap a rhino-hide whip and wield a knotted wooden throwing club with deadly accuracy. I grew as tall as Kibii and then taller, running just as swiftly through the tall gold grasses, our feet floured with dust.

Kibii and I often went out walking into the dark, past the freshly scythed grass that marked the edge of our farm and the damp higher grasses that brushed wetness up to our hips, past the Green Hill and the edge of the forest, which took us in and in. There were leopards there at night. I'd seen my father bait them with a goat while we crouched on top of the water tank for safety, the goat beginning to quake when it smelled the cat, my father zeroing his rifle and hoping he didn't miss. There was danger everywhere, but we knew all the night sounds and their messages, cicadas and tree frogs, the fat, ratlike hyraxes, which were actually the distant relatives of elephants. Sometimes we heard the elephants themselves crashing through brush in the distance, though they dreaded the scent of horses and didn't come too near unless provoked. Snakes in holes vibrated. Snakes in trees could swing down and cut the air like rope or make only the lowest rub of smooth belly against smooth-grained mahogany.

For years there were these perfect nights with Kibii, and long slow afternoons made for hunting or for riding, and somehow—with machetes and ropes and feet and human salt—the wilderness gave way to proper fields. My father planted maize and wheat, and they flourished. With the money he made, he found and bought two abandoned steam engines. Bolted down, they became the beating heart of our gristmill, and Green Hills the most vital artery in Njoro. Soon, if you stood on our hill and looked out past the terraced fields and head-high maize, you could see a line of flat oxen-drawn wagons bringing grain to our mill. The mill ran without stopping, and the number of our workers doubled and then tripled, Kikuyu, Kavirondo, Nandi, and Kipsigis men, and Dutchmen, too, cracking their whips to drive the oxen. The iron sheds came down, and a stable went up, then several more, the newly built loose boxes filling with cut hay and the finest thoroughbreds in Africa, my father told me, or anywhere in the world.

I still thought about Mother and Dickie sometimes when I lay in bed before sleep, listening to the night noises push in from every direction, a constant, seething sound. They never sent letters, at least not to me, so trying to picture their life was a trial. Our old house had been sold. Wherever they had finally settled, the stars and trees would be very different from what we had in Njoro. The rain would be, too, and the feel and the colour of the sun in the afternoons. All the afternoons of all the months we were apart.

Gradually it became harder to remember my mother's face, things she had said to me, days we had shared. But there were many days ahead of me. They spread out further than I could see or wish for, the way the plain did all the way to the broken bowl of Menengai, or to Kenya's hard blue peak. It was safer to keep looking forward—to move my mother to the far edge of my mind where she couldn't hurt me any more, or to imagine, when I did think of her, that her going had been necessary. A kind of forging or honing, my first essential test as Lakwet.

This was certain: I belonged on the farm and in the bush. I was part of the thorn trees and the high jutting escarpment, the bruised-looking hills thick with vegetation; the deep folds between the hills, and the high cornlike grasses. I had come alive here, as if I'd been given a second birth, and a truer one. This was my home, and though one day it would all trickle through my fingers like so much red dust, for as long as childhood lasted it was a heaven fitted exactly to me. A place I knew by heart. The one place in the world I'd been made for.

3

The stable bell clanged, breaking open the stillness. The lazy roosters woke and the dusty geese, the houseboys and grooms, gardeners and herdsmen. I had my own mud-and-daub hut, a little apart from my father's, which I shared with my ugly and loyal mixed-breed dog, Buller. He whined at the sound of the bell, stretching from his nest at the foot of my bed, and then looped his square head under my arm and against my side so that I felt his cool nose and the wrinkled half-moons of scars on the top of his head. There was a thick, lumpy knot where his right ear had been before a leopard had crept into my hut and tried to drag him into the night. Buller had ripped open the leopard's throat and limped home covered in their mingled blood, looking like a hero but also nearly dead. My father and I nursed him back to health, and though he'd never been particularly handsome before, he was grizzled and half-deaf now. We loved him better for it because the leopard hadn't begun to break his spirit.

In the farmyard, in the cool morning air, Kibii was waiting for me. I was eleven and he a little younger, and we had both become part of the oiled machinery of the farm. There were other white children nearby who went to school in Nairobi or sometimes back in

England, but my father never mentioned that I might do anything like that. The stable was my classroom. Morning gallops started not long after dawn. I was there without fail, and so was Kibii. As I approached the stable now, he shot up into the air as if his legs were coiled springs. I'd been practising that sort of jump for years and could manage to go as high as Kibii, but to have the edge in competition, I knew I should do as little as possible. Kibii would jump and jump, outdoing himself, and grow tired. Then I would take my turn and outshine him.

"When I become a *moran,*" Kibii said, "I'll drink bull's blood and curdled milk instead of nettles like a woman, and then I will have the speed of an antelope."

"I could be a great warrior," I told him.

Kibii had an open and handsome face, and his teeth flashed as he laughed, as if this were the funniest thing he'd ever heard. When we were very young, he'd been happy to let me join his world, maybe because he felt it was all play-acting. I was a girl, and a white one at that, after all. But more and more lately, I felt him becoming sceptical and disapproving of me, as if he were waiting for me to give up trying to compete with him and accept that our paths would soon be very different ones. I had no such intention.

"If I had the right training I could," I insisted. "I could do it in secret."

"Where is the glory in that? No one would know your deeds belonged to you."

"*I* would."

He laughed again and turned towards the stable door. "Who will we gallop today?"

"Daddy and I are off to Delamere's to look at a brood mare."

"I will hunt," he replied. "Then we shall see who comes back with the better story."

When Wee MacGregor and my father's hack, Balmy, were saddled and ready, we set off into the morning sun. For a time, Kibii's challenge clouded my thoughts, but then the distance and the day took over. Dust billowed around us, creeping under our loose-tied hand-kerchiefs and into our noses and mouths. It was fine and silty, red as ochre or the brush-tailed fox, and it was always with us. So were the chiggers that were like flecks of red pepper, clinging to everything and holding on. You couldn't think about the chiggers because you couldn't do anything about them. You couldn't think about the biting white ants that moved in menacing ribbons over the plains, or the vipers or the sun, which sometimes pulsed so brightly it seemed to want to flatten you or eat you alive. You couldn't because these things were part of the country itself and made it what it was.

Three miles on we came to a small gully where the red mud had dried and cracked in a system of parched veins. A moulded clay bridge stood at the centre, looking pointless without water running on either side, and also like the backbone of some huge animal that had died there. We'd been relying on the water for our horses. Maybe there was water further along, or maybe not. To distract us both from the problem my father began to talk about Delamere's brood mare. He hadn't seen her yet, but that didn't stop him from winding her neatly up into his hopes for our bloodstock. He was always thinking of the next foal and how it might change our lives—and because he was, I was, too.

"She's Abyssinian, but Delamere says she's got speed and good sense."

Mostly my father was interested in thoroughbreds, but occasion-ally you could find a gem in more common places, and he knew this. "What's her colouring?" I wanted to know. That was always my first question.

"She's a pale gold palomino, with a blonde mane and tail. Co-quette's her name."

"Coquette," I repeated, liking the sharp edges of the word without knowing what it meant. "That sounds right."

"Does it?" He laughed. "I suppose we'll see."

———

Lord Delamere was D to me and to anyone who knew him well. He was one of the colony's first important settlers and had an unswerving sense for which bit of land would be most fertile. He seemed to want to take over the entire continent and make it all work for him. No one was more ambitious than D or more headstrong or blunt about the things he loved (land, the Masai people, freedom, money). He was driven to make whatever he touched or tried a success. When the risks were great and the chances were dim, well then, so much the better.

He told good stories, his hands and shoulders moving so wildly that his untrimmed red hair slashed back and forth across his forehead. When he was a young man, he'd walked two thousand miles through the Somali desert with one ill-tempered camel for company and found himself here, in the highlands. He fell instantly in love with the place. When he went back to England to drum up the funds to settle here, he'd met and married Florence, the spirited daughter of the Earl of Enniskillen. "She'd no idea I would drag her here by the hair one day," he liked to say.

"As if you *could* drag me," Lady D often answered, her eyes playful. "We both know it's typically the other way around."

After our tired hacks finally got the water they'd earned, the Delameres walked us out to the small paddock where Coquette was at pasture with a few other brood mares and a handful of foals. She was the prettiest to look at by far, compact and flaxen, with a sloping neck and well-made chest. Her legs narrowed into shapely fetlocks and pasterns. As we watched, she pitched her head and swung round to look at us straight on, as if she were daring us to find her less than perfect.

"She's beautiful," I breathed.

"Aye, and she knows it," D said cheerfully. He was thick bodied and always seemed to be sweating, though he was generally cheerful about this, too. He swatted at the salty trickle along his temple with a blue cotton handkerchief while my father bent through the slats of the fence to get a closer look.

I rarely saw a horse startle or run from my father, and Coquette was no exception. She seemed to sense immediately that he was in command of the situation and of her, too, though she didn't belong to him yet. She shook her ears once, and blew air at him out of her velvety nostrils, but held still as he examined her, running his hands along her crown and muzzle, and then more slowly fingering her withers and spine, looking for any bump or sway. Over her loin and rump he slowed again, his fingers doing their work. He was like a blind man feeling along each of her lovely back legs, the gaskins and stifle joints, hocks and cannons. I kept waiting for him to straighten or for his face to cloud over, but the examination went silently on, and I grew more and more hopeful. By the time he'd finished and stood facing her, his hands grazing over her forelock, I could barely stand the suspense. If he couldn't love her now, after she'd passed all of his tests, it was going to break my heart.

"Why are you parting with her then?" he asked D without taking his eyes off Coquette.

"Money, naturally," D said with a small snort.

"You know how he is," Lady D said. "The new obsession always chases out the old. Now he's on to wheat, and most of the horses will have to go."

Please please say yes, I thought in a fierce running string.

"Wheat, is it now?" my father asked, and then he turned away and strode back towards the fence, saying to Lady D, "I don't suppose you have anything cool to drink?"

I wanted to fling myself at Coquette's knees, to grab a handful of her pale mane and swing up over her back and ride away into the hills on my own—or home with her, latching her up in a hidden stall and guarding her with my life. She already had my heart, and she'd won my father over, too—I *knew* it—but he wasn't ever spontaneous. He kept his emotions locked away behind a wall, which made him a wonderful negotiator. He and D would be at this for the rest of the day now, sorting out the terms without stating anything directly, each carefully guarding what it would mean for him to win, or lose. I found it all maddening, but there was nothing to be done but make our way to the house where the men settled themselves at the table with rye whisky and lemonade and began to talk without talking and bargain without bargaining. I threw myself down on the carpet in front of the hearth and sulked.

Though the Delameres had more land and at least as many workers at Equator Ranch as we did at Green Hills, D hadn't made many improvements to their own living quarters, two large mud rondavels with beaten-earth flooring, rough windows, and burlap curtains for doors. Still, Lady D had filled the place with nice things that had been in her family for hundreds of years, she'd told me—a heavy mahogany four-poster bed with a richly embroidered quilt, pictures framed in gilt, a long mahogany table with eight matching chairs, and a hand-bound atlas that I loved to pore over whenever I visited. That day I was too anxious to look at maps and could only lie on the carpet and click my dusty heels together, biting my lip and wishing the men would get on with it.

Finally, Lady D came over and sat near me, settling her white cotton skirt out in front of her and leaning back on her hands. She wasn't ever fussy or prim, and I adored that about her. "I have some nice biscuits if you'd like."

"I'm not hungry," I said. I was ravenous.

"Your hair is wilder every time I see it." She gently nudged the plate of biscuits in my direction. "It's such a wonderful colour, though. A little like Coquette's, actually."

That got me. "Do you think so?"

She nodded. "I don't suppose you'd let me brush it?"

I was too out of sorts to enjoy sitting still and having my hair fussed over, but I let her do it. She had a silver-handled brush with beautiful soft white bristles that I always liked to run my fingers over. There was nothing feminine in our house any more, no silk or satin or perfume or jewellery or powder puffs. The brush was exotic. While Lady D worked, humming a little, I fell on the biscuits. Soon the plate was nothing but buttery crumbs.

"Where'd you get that fierce-looking scar?" she asked.

I looked down at the jagged worst of it poking from beneath the frayed hem of my short trousers—a long rippled wound that went halfway up my thigh. It did look pretty rough. "Wrestling *totos*."

"*Totos* or bushpigs?"

"I trounced one of the Kip boys and threw him over my shoulder onto the ground. He was so embarrassed he waited for me in the forest and slashed out at me with his father's knife."

"What?" She made an alarmed noise.

"I had to go after him, didn't I?" I couldn't keep the pride out of my voice. "He looks far worse than I do now."

Lady D sighed into my hair. I knew she was concerned, but she didn't say anything else for the moment, and so I gave myself up to the tug of the brush and the way it rubbed against my scalp. It felt so good I was half asleep when the men finally stood and shook hands. I jumped to my feet, nearly landing in Lady D's lap. "She's ours?" I asked, rushing at them.

"Clutt bargains like a hyena," D said, "just latches on and doesn't let go. He nearly stole that mare from under me." As he laughed, my father laughed, too, and clapped him on the shoulder.

"Doesn't Beryl look pretty?" Lady D asked. She came up behind me and rested one hand on the top of my head. "I wondered if I'd find a nest of titmice tangled up behind one of her ears."

Reddening, my father cleared his throat. "I'm not much of a nursemaid, I'm afraid."

"Nor should you be," D barked in his defence. "The girl's fine. Just look at her, Florence. She's as strong as a mule."

"Ah, yes. We all of us want mules for daughters, don't we?"

The whole exchange was good-natured, and yet it gave me a strange topsy-turvy feeling. When we started for home again, an hour later, after the money and the details of Coquette's delivery were sorted, I could tell my father was unsettled, too. We rode in silence as the red sun inched lower and lower in the flat sky. In the distance, a dust devil churned like a dervish, whirling into a patch of flame trees and unhousing a fat band of vultures. One flew past, his shadow crawling over us so slowly it made me shudder.

"I'll admit it all gets away from me sometimes," my father said when the vulture had gone.

I could guess at what he meant from the way Lady D had blanched at my scar and general upkeep. I knew "it all" meant me, his daughter.

"I think we're doing all right," I said, and reached to pat Wee MacGregor's neck. "I don't want anything to be different."

He said nothing as the sun continued its descent. This close to the equator, we had almost no twilight. Day turned to night in minutes, but they were lovely ones. Around us the yellow grasses stretched and moved like the sea, sometimes dipping into antbear burrows and pig holes, or lifting towards the knuckled spires of termite mounds, but never truly ceasing. There was a powerful illusion that the bush didn't end—that we could ride for years like this, carried by the grasses and the sense of distance, on and on for ever.

4

When Coquette arrived, she was the darling of the farm. Since we didn't have any horses with her golden colouring, all the *totos* wanted to be near her and to touch her. She seemed to glow and bring good luck, and for several months everything went smoothly as she settled in and my father began to think and scheme over which horse should service her for the best possible result. Breeding is the most serious of matters for a horseman. Even before I could read I knew that every thoroughbred could be traced back to three original Arabian and Oriental sires from the seventeenth and eighteenth centuries, paired with a handful of very specific English dams. The long line of genealogy was lovingly and painstakingly laid out in *The General Stud Book*. Over dinner we would open the book and consult from it, along with the thick black ledger that kept a record of our own bloodstock—the old and new testaments of our bible.

After weeks of talking it through, it was decided that Referee would service Coquette when she came into season. He was a light chestnut Arab and compactly built at fifteen hands, with good hoofs, wide-open shoulder angles, and perfectly straight legs. He had a stride so even it seemed to eat up the ground in front of him effortlessly. We talked about the new foal a lot—the one that would come eleven months from the date of successful breeding, with his sire's swiftness and his dam's shimmering coat and graceful movements. He didn't seem remotely imaginary to me. Our talking had already brought him to life.

One long, airless afternoon I was drumming up names for the foal and saying some out loud to Kibii as we sat under the wattle tree near the edge of the wide yard. Beyond the bluish ring of shade, the earth was like hammered metal and wicked as metal, too, or live cinders if you dared to walk on it. We'd spent the morning at gallops and then helping oil dozens of bridles, until our fingers cramped. Now we were drained but also restless, needled by the heat.

"What about Jupiter, or Apollo?" I suggested.

"He should be Jackal. This is a better name for a colt."

"Jackals are so ordinary."

"Jackals are clever."

Before I could correct him, a tower of smoke came chuffing into view.

It was the noisy train from Nairobi, a dozen crude carriages that bumped so hard along the track you expected one to fly off or smash to pieces. Kibii twisted to look out over the slope. "Is your father expecting a horse?"

I didn't think my father was expecting anything, but we watched him come rushing out of the stable, smoothing his hair and tucking in the tails of his shirt. He squinted down the hill against the sun and then quickly made his way to our new Ford wagon and cranked the moody engine. Kibii and I didn't ask if we could join him, just trotted over and began to climb into the back.

"Not this time," my father said, barely looking up from his task. "There won't be room for everyone."

Everyone? "Are guests coming, then?"

Without answering, he climbed behind the wheel and pulled

away, pummelling us with clouds of rosy dust. Within the hour, we heard the buggy chugging back up the hill and caught glimpses of white. A dress. A hat with ribbons, and to-the-elbow gloves. This was a woman in the car, a beautiful one with a pile of glossy hair the colour of raven feathers, and a fancy lace-trimmed parasol that didn't look as if it had seen a day in the bush.

"Beryl, this is Mrs. Orchardson," my father said as they stepped out of the buggy. Two large trunks towered behind in the boot. She wasn't here for tea.

"I'm so happy to finally meet you," Mrs. Orchardson said, quickly looking me up and down.

Finally? I think my mouth fell open and stayed like that for a good long minute.

When we got inside the main house, Mrs. Orchardson looked around at everything with her hands resting lightly on her hips. Though my father had designed it simply, the place was solid, and a vast improvement from the hut it once was. But Mrs. Orchardson had never seen anything of that. She strode back and forth. There were cobwebs at all the windows, and the hearthstones were covered in layers of thick soot. The oilcloth on our table hadn't been changed in years, not since my mother left. The narrow charcoal cooler we stored butter and cream in smelled rancid, like muck at the bottom of a pond. We'd grown used to it like everything else. The walls were hung with bits and bobs from hunting adventures—leopard pelts, lion skins, long, corkscrewing kudu horns, an ostrich egg the size and heft of a human skull. There was nothing fine or very posh in sight— but we'd been all right without niceties.

"Mrs. Orchardson has agreed to be our housekeeper," my father explained as she pinched off her gloves. "She'll live here in the main house. There's plenty of room."

"Oh," I said, feeling punched in the windpipe. There was a room that could be used for sleeping quarters, but it was filled with tack and paraffin and tins of food and any number of things we didn't want to see or deal with. The room meant we didn't really *need* a housekeeper. And where would guests stay now that this woman, who was not a guest, had come to change everything?

"Why don't you go out to the stables while we get settled here?" my father said in a tone that left no room for wriggling.

"How nice, then," Mrs. Orchardson said. "I'll get the tea ready."

All the way across the yard, I fumed. The world was squeezing in on me, narrowing to the sudden fact of Mrs. Orchardson and what she might mean to do or be. When I returned, she had changed into a simple skirt and shirtwaist, and tied a clean white apron over the top. Her sleeves were rolled up to the elbow. A lock of her silky hair fell over her forehead as she refilled my father's cup, the kettle steaming in her hands. My father had settled into our one comfortable chair, his feet up on a low table. He was gazing at her familiarly.

I blinked at them both. I hadn't been gone an hour, and she had already taken over the room. The kettle was hers. She'd scrubbed the oilcloth. The cobwebs were gone and might have never existed at all. Nothing would need much coaxing or breaking in. Nothing seemed ready to resist her.

I was to call her Mrs. O, my father said. Over the coming days, she unpacked her steamer trunks and filled them again with things from the house—dusty hunting spoils, odd trinkets or bits of clothing my mother had left behind. It was all part of her plan to run a "tight ship"—two of her favourite words. She liked order and soap and the day sliced up into manageable portions. Mornings were for book learning.

"I have to be at gallops," I told her early on, feeling fully confident that my father would take my part.

"They'll make do without you for the time being, won't they?" she said matter-of-factly while my father made a dry, throttled sound deep in his throat and quickly left the house.

Within a week she'd convinced my father that I needed to wear shoes. A few weeks more and I'd been trussed up in an English frock and hair ribbons instead of a *shuka,* and told not to eat with my hands. I was not to kill snakes or moles or birds with my *rungu,* or to take all my meals with Kibii and his family. I was not to hunt warthog or leopard with *arap* Maina but to have a proper education and learn the King's English.

"I've let you run too wild and you know it," my father said when I went to him, asking to be left alone. "It's all for your own good."

He *had* let me run, but it had been wonderful. These new restrictions amounted to a conventional life, and we'd never had anything of the sort.

"Please . . ." I heard myself begin to whine, but then stopped short. I had never been a wheedling or complaining child, and my father wasn't going to bend anyway. If I really *could* do something about Mrs. O, I would have to work it out on my own. I would show her I wasn't a bit of cobweb in the corner, something to be wiped or straightened, but a rival worth her notice. I would learn her ways and habits, and track her closely until I knew what she was and how to best her, and what precisely it would take to steal my good life back.

5

Coquette was nearing her foaling date. She'd grown rounder and more barrel-like, the new life inside her pushing out against her flesh, those long limbs already trying to stretch and find their way. Somehow the effort of creation had dulled her golden coat. She looked tired and listless and rarely did more than nibble at the sheaves of lucerne I brought her.

For me, the foal couldn't come soon enough. Thinking about him was how I got through hours of Latin in pinching shoes. One night, I was fast asleep in my hut when I felt Buller rouse beside me. The grooms had come awake in their bunks. My father was awake, too. I recognized the timbre of his muffled voice and dressed quickly, thinking only of Coquette. She was twenty days early, which usually meant a weak or sickly foal, but it might not. My father would know what to do.

Out in the yard, the glow from several hurricane lamps rinsed out through the cracks in the stable door. High overhead, ribbons of stars swirled like milk, and a sickle moon lay hard and bright on its side. The night insects seethed away in the forest and from everywhere, all around, but the stable was quiet. Much too quiet, I knew, before I even came close to Coquette's box, but I couldn't guess why until I saw my father stand up. He strode to meet me, stopping me in my tracks. "You'll not want to see this, Beryl. Go back to bed."

"What's happened?" My throat closed around the words.

"Stillborn," he said quietly.

My heart fell, all my hopes silenced in an instant. Apollo wouldn't stand on tottering legs like a new giraffe. He wouldn't see the forest or the high escarpment, or race along the track with me bent over his shining neck. He wouldn't know Green Hills for even a day. But my father had never shielded me from the tough lessons of farm life. I forced back my tears and pushed ahead.

In the shadow-filled box, Coquette had dropped into one corner. On the ground behind her, the hay was matted where two grooms knelt, trying somehow to tidy up. The tiny foal was there, slick in part of its bag, but also wasn't. Its eyes were gone and most of the facial muscles, the flesh eaten away in a jagged blackness. Its belly yawned open, the entrails devoured—which could only mean the giant siafu ants had come. They were black warriors with huge bodies, and they ate quickly and terribly, as one thing.

"She foaled him so quietly no one heard her," my father said, coming to put an arm around my shoulder. "He might have been dead already, I don't know."

"Poor Coquette," I said, turning into his shirt and pushing my forehead against the bones of his chest.

"She's sound," he said. "She'll be all right."

But how could she be? Her foal was gone. The ants hadn't touched anything else, either—just made for this one soft and helpless thing and then disappeared into the night. *Why?* I thought again and again, as if there really were someone who could answer me.

The next morning, I couldn't stand even the thought of lessons and fled the house, out past the paddocks to a narrow path that twisted steeply down the hill. When I reached the Kip village my lungs burned and my bare legs were covered with welts from the thornbushes and elephant grass—but I already felt better for being there. I always had, even when I was too young to lift the latch on the fence. The thornbushes that knitted the fence together were as high as the shoulders of large oxen and kept everything protected from the dangers of the bush—the low-lying huts and prized oxen, the shaggy bleating goats and blackened cooking pots over licking flames, and children.

That afternoon, a string of *totos* were playing a training game with bows and arrows, kneeling in the hammered dust, each trying to get closest to a target made of tied-together leaves. Kibii was at the centre of the line, and though his black eyes glanced towards me with curiosity, he went on with the game while I squatted down nearby. Most of the *totos* were very good with a still target. The arrows were fashioned out of whittled twigs with barbed points that stuck fast when they reached their target, as they were meant to. I watched them, wishing, as I'd done so many times before, that I'd been born a Kip. Not one of the girls, with their endless cooking duties or their burdens of baskets, water, food stores, babies. The women did all the carrying and the hoeing, the weaving and ploughing. They cared for the animals, too, while the warriors hunted or prepared for the hunt, oiling their limbs with rendered fat, plucking small hairs off their chests with tweezers kept in pouches around their necks. These *totos* kneeling on the ground would one day aim not at gourds but bush-pig, steenbok, lion. What could be more thrilling?

When everyone had mastered one level, one of the older *totos* took another smaller target, also made of leaves but rolled into a round gourd shape, and pitched it into the air away from his body. The arrows flew—some landing but most not. There were gibes and ridicule for those who missed most disastrously, but no one gave up. Again and again, the youth pitched the gourd into the air, the *totos* releasing their arrows, until everyone had succeeded. Only then was the game finished.

When Kibii finally trotted over and sat beside me, I told him what had happened to the foal. He was still holding his curved bow and handful of slender arrows. He pushed the tip of one into the stiff earth and said, "The siafu are a plague."

"What good are they? What god would make such a thing?"

"It's not for us to know," he said with a gentle shrug.

"We do wonder, though." I looked at him and swallowed once, hard, feeling certain that I wasn't going to cry here, not in front of Kibii, and glad for it. Softness and helplessness got you nothing in this place. Tears only emptied you out. I stood up and straightened my shoulders and then convinced Kibii he should let me have a try with his bow.

My father had said Mrs. O would be our housekeeper, but even from the first day she behaved like something more. Like his wife, or like my mother. She had opinions about everything, and most particularly my stubbornness. Within a few months she had had enough of trying to be my governess. My father was going to hire one from town. "Emma shouldn't have to struggle to keep you at your desk, Beryl," he told me. "It's not fair."

I felt heat prickle along the tops of my ears. "I don't need a governess. I'll do the lessons."

"It's already done. This is for the best—you'll see."

A horrible woman named Miss Le May was found for me, and then another when a dead black mamba happened to turn up in Miss Le May's bed. All told, three governesses failed as well as a handful of tutors, and my father finally seemed to give up on the idea. No more tutors appeared on the horizon, and I began to believe I had won and felt pleased with myself for battling so well.

At the end of October, I turned twelve. Not long after, my father arranged for us to go away for a few days, just the two of us. Though the trip was for business and had nothing to do with me, I was glad to be invited along, since the alternative would have been to stay at home alone with Mrs. O.

We headed for Nairobi by train to settle some dealings my father had there with the bank. When we were finished in town, we went north to Kabete Station to visit my father's friend Jim Elkington on his ranch at the edge of the Kikuyu Reserve. As we rode, I sang out bits of Swahili and Bantu tunes. *Twende, twende kupigana,* went one warrior's song I loved. Let us go, let us go, to fight. When I tired of my own voice, I asked my father to tell me stories. In general, he was close-lipped, hoarding his words as if he were afraid someone would make off with them, but he was different when we rode. He seemed to like to talk then.

He would tell me the Greek myths he remembered from his time at school, the Titans and heroes and various gods, thrilling depictions of the underworld. At other times he spoke of the generations of tribal wars between the Masai and Kikuyu, fierce battles and cunning, night-time victories, or about how to hunt and to survive. To shoot a charging elephant, you stood your ground and aimed between its eyes. If you missed the brain, you wouldn't live to attempt your shot again. For a puff adder, you backed away as soundlessly as possible, a few inches at a time, trying not to let your heart persuade you into panicking. For the deadlier black mamba, you ran flat out. A man could always outrun a mamba, but would never survive a fully landed strike.

The day we rode out to Kabete Station, my father's mind was on lions. "A lion has more natural intelligence than most men," he said, pushing his bush hat back off his forehead with a fingertip. He wore khakis for riding—a light cotton shirt, trousers the colour of sand, and boots that would have had a high polish in the English countryside but here were rinsed with layers of red silt. "He also has more courage than a man, and more determination. He'll fight for what belongs to him, no matter the size or strength of his rival. If the rival has a drop of cowardice in him, he's dead already."

I wanted him to go on talking, all the way to the Elkingtons' and even further. If I just listened hard enough, I thought I might one day know everything he did. "What if two equal lions battle for territory, or for a mate?"

"They'll each size up the other, testing the odds. A lion is more cautious on equal footing, but even then he won't back down. He has no fear, you see, not as we understand it. He can only be exactly what he is, what his nature dictates, and nothing else."

"I wonder if this can be true of the Elkingtons' lion," said Bishon Singh, our Sikh groom. He had journeyed with us to care for the horses and rode just behind with my father's man, Kimutai.

"That damned animal makes me nervous," my father answered. "I don't mind telling you. It's unnatural for a wild creature to be kept like that."

"I like Paddy," I said, remembering how I'd once seen Jim Elkington rub him like a cat. "He's a good lion."

"Which only proves my point," my father said, while behind us Bishon Singh clucked his agreement. "You can take a cub from the savannah as they have, and raise it like a pet if you like. In a cage, as some do, or running free like Paddy. You can feed it fresh meat so it never learns to hunt and brush its coat so it carries a human smell wherever it goes—but know that what you've done is twist something natural into something else. And you can never trust an unnatural thing. You don't know what it is, and it's baffled, too. Poor damned animal," he said again, and blew air up towards his nose to clear away some of the dust.

The Elkingtons' house had leaded-glass windows and a pretty veranda that backed onto absolute wilderness, a thousand miles or more of untamed Africa. There was a feeling, as you sat and ate your nice sandwich or had your tea, that you were on the slowly tipping edge of nothingness and might fall forward at any moment, and that if you did, it was possible that nothing would know you'd ever been there at all.

Jim Elkington was round and red faced and even tempered. His wife wore a straw boater and white blouses she kept crisp and civilized looking, somehow, even with a rawhide whip tucked into her belt. The whip was for Paddy, who roamed about the property as if he owned it. In the clearest sort of way, he did. Who would challenge him, after all? He'd been like a puppy once, thick pawed, wrestling Jim on the lawn, but now he was full grown, his ruff of mane black tipped and glossy. The whip was only a prop.

The last time I had seen Paddy, Jim Elkington had fed him a string of skinned rabbits on a pike as we watched. The lion rested flat with his paws crossed, full shouldered and rust coloured with black lips and jowls. He had enormous golden eyes and seemed aware of the picture he made as he let the dainties come to him. There was a wrinkled place above his perfectly square nose, which made him look puzzled or even a little amused by us.

As we settled our horses, I didn't see Paddy, but I could hear him off somewhere, maybe miles away, roaring. It was a tortured sound and also a little mournful, stiffening the fine hairs on the back of my neck. "He sounds lonely," I said.

"Rot," my father said. "More like a howling banshee."

"I don't hear it any more," Mrs. Elkington said, and then led us to her tea: small, nice-smelling ginger cakes, dried fruit, potato dumplings in crisped skins that were eaten with your fingers, and good China tea in a pot. Jim had made a pitcher of cocktails with rye whisky and crushed lemons. He stirred the pitcher with a glass rod, rare ice tinkling like crystal teardrops.

The veranda was airless that day, and the conversation stultifying. I sighed and picked at a second ginger cake until my father finally gave me a look and a nod—*Go on, then*—as he and Jim rose to go towards the stables. Mrs. Elkington tried to ply me with a dice game, but I made off as quickly as I could, flinging my shoes and stockings into the grass and hurrying across the long yard.

I went out into the open country running fast, just to feel myself do it. Their land was much like ours, with dry grasses, dusty green and gold, and the rolling plain studded with thorn and flame trees or sometimes a single fat baobab. Away in the distance I could see the cloud-softened crags of Mount Kenya and thought of how wonderful it would be to run there, a hundred miles away. Of how proud my father would be when I returned, and how Kibii would be sick with jealousy.

Ahead of me there was a low hill with gooseberry bushes on top. I made a beeline for them, only half noticing a place in the grass where something large had slept recently, crushing the stems all around into a curved pressed-down mould. I had my eyes on the hill and didn't think of anything else or know that I was being watched as I ran, stalked from behind like a young gazelle or kongoni.

I picked up speed, scrambling over the rise, and that's when I felt a force of air push at me, hot and meaty. The blow was like a steel pipe aimed at the muscles of my back. I went down hard, face-first in the grass, my arms coming up instinctively to protect myself.

I didn't know how long Paddy had been watching me. He'd smelled me first—possibly before I'd left the veranda. Maybe he'd only been curious about my girl-smell, or maybe he'd started hunting me then. It didn't really matter, because he had already overpowered me.

Paddy's jaw closed on my thigh above the knee. I felt his dagger teeth and his wet tongue. The strangely cool feel of his mouth. My head swam as I smelled my own blood, and then he released me to bellow. It was everything I'd heard from the veranda and more—a vibrating black cave of noise that swallowed the earth and sky and swallowed me, too.

I closed my eyes and tried to scream, but only released a puff of air. I felt Paddy's mouth again and knew I had no chance at all. He would eat me here or drag me off to a glade or valley only he knew of, a place from which I'd never return. The last thought I remember having was *This is how it feels, then. This is what it means to be eaten by a lion.*

6

When I came back to myself, Bishon Singh was carrying me in his arms, his face bent over mine. I didn't want to ask about Paddy and where he'd gone, or to know how hurt I was. Blood dripped from a long gash along my leg onto Bishon Singh's white cotton tunic.

My father had been with the horses, but when he came running he held me close, crushing me to his chest. It was like being rescued—rescued again, really, because that had happened already.

Bishon Singh had seen me run past him as he tended our horses in the Elkingtons' stable. When he came up the hill Paddy was already standing on my back, his mouth stretched wide, lips rimmed in black, teeth slick with saliva. He roared again, the sound nearly stopping Bishon Singh and the six or seven grooms that came running up behind him, all of them trying to make their bodies appear larger and their voices boom. Then came Bwana Elkington rolling his huge frame, flicking the long *kiboko* whip out in front of him like a cresting wave, the tip electrifying the air.

"The lion did not like being disturbed," Bishon Singh said. "But bwana lashed the whip hard again. He rushed at Paddy and screamed, striking him with the whip over and over, and finally Paddy had had enough. He lunged at his master so quickly there was nothing for Bwana Elkington to do but race to the baobab. He flew up that tree and Paddy roared like Zeus himself. Then he was gone."

The wound running from my calf muscle to the top of my thigh burned as if I were holding it over flames. I could feel each of the deep, raw claw marks from where Paddy had stood on my back, and the smaller punctures on my neck, under my blood-soaked hair. After the doctor was called, my father went into the other room and talked in sharp whispers to Jim and Mrs. Elkington about what should be done about Paddy. A little while later, a *toto* came running in from a nearby farm saying that Paddy had killed a neighbour's horse and dragged it away.

Jim and my father loaded up their rifles, ordering the grooms to ready their hacks while I felt a swirl of emotions. Paddy was on the loose now. Part of me worried he could come back to the farm and attack someone—anyone. Another part of me felt awful for Paddy. He was a lion, and killing was what he'd been *made* to do.

The doctor gave me laudanum, and then stitched me up with a hooked needle and thick black thread. I lay on my stomach while Bishon Singh held one of my hands, his thin steel bangle rocking up and down his arm, his white turban wrapped around and around, who knew how many times, and the end tucked invisibly somewhere, like the fabled snake that swallows its own tail.

"The whip shouldn't have been more than a gnat for Paddy," Bishon Singh told me.

"What do you mean?"

"What is a whip to a lion? He must have been ready to let you go. Or perhaps you weren't ever meant for him."

I felt the tug of the needle, a pushing and pulling, as if just that part of my body were caught in a small current. His words were another kind of current. "What am I meant for then?"

"How wonderful that question is, Beru." He smiled mysteriously. "And as you did not die on this day, you have more time in which to answer it."

———

I stayed with the Elkingtons for several weeks, while Mrs. Elkington brought me nice food on a bamboo tray—candied ginger, devilled eggs, and chilled juices. She had her kitchen *toto* busy making me fresh cakes every day, as if that would somehow make up for what Paddy had done—and for the fact of him now, roaring sullenly and sometimes monstrously from a wooden pen behind the main paddock.

They'd finally caught him four days after he escaped and brought him back bound. When Mrs. Elkington told me he was behind bars, it was meant to reassure me, but it also turned my stomach. I had tempted Paddy by running in front of his nose, and now he was suffering for doing something that was natural for him. It was my fault—but there was also the matter, when I lay in my narrow bed at the Elkingtons', of Paddy's howling. I clamped my hands over my ears, relieved that he was locked away. Relieved and also sick about it. Safe and also guilty.

When I could finally travel by cart to Nairobi, and then home to Njoro by train, it was as though I'd finally been released from a prison of my own. One made of Paddy's awful noises. But I didn't truly stop thinking about Paddy or dreaming terrible dreams about him until I was able to tell Kibii what had happened. He and some of the other *totos* sat as still as posts while I drew every detail out, my story growing longer and more harrowing, and me growing braver, steelier, a hero or warrior instead of something that had been hunted and only narrowly rescued.

Every Kipsigis *moran* in training had to hunt and kill a lion in order to earn his spear. If he failed, he would live in shame. If he succeeded, nothing could be more magnificent. Beautiful women would sing his name, and his deed would pass into history, in verses his own children would learn and act out in games. I had always been wildly jealous that Kibii could look forward to so much daring and glory, and couldn't help but feel a little satisfied, now, that I had survived something he hadn't yet faced. And the truth was, no matter how I embellished or shaped the story of what had happened with Paddy, it *had* happened, and I had lived to tell the tale. That alone had a powerful effect on me. I felt slightly invincible, that I could come through nearly anything my world might throw at me, but of course I had no idea what lay in store.

"Emma and I think you should go to school in Nairobi," my father said a few weeks after I had returned home from the Elkingtons'. His tented fingers rested on the dinner table.

I jerked up to look at him. "Why not another governess?"

"You can't run wild for ever. You need schooling."

"I can learn here at the farm. I won't fight any more, I promise."

"It's not safe here for you, don't you see?" Mrs. O said from her chair. Her untouched tableware gleamed, mirroring back chips of red light from the hurricane lamp, and it struck me all at once that all of this was happening because I had never found a way to properly best her. I had grown used to her ways. I'd been distracted by foals and gallops and hunting games with Kibii. But she hadn't grown used to me.

"If you mean Paddy, that should never have happened."

"Of *course* it shouldn't have!" Her violet eyes narrowed. "But it did. You seem to think you're invulnerable, running around half naked with those boys, out in the bush where anything could get you. *Anything.* You're a child, though no one around here seems to know it."

I clenched my fists and brought them down hard on the edge of the table. I yelled all sorts of things and pushed away my plate and sent my tableware clattering to the floor. "You can't force me to go," I finally cried, my throat hoarse, my face hot and swollen feeling.

"It's not up to you," my father said, his mouth stern and unyielding.

The next morning I woke at first light and rode to Equator Ranch to see Lady D. She was the kindest and most reasonable person I knew.

She would have some sort of solution, I believed. She would know what to do.

"Daddy seems set," I began to rant before I was halfway through the door, "but he's only going along with Mrs. O. She told him that I'm going to be torn to ribbons by another lion if I keep going like this, but she doesn't really care. I'm in her way. That's really what it is."

Lady D led me to a comfortable place on her carpet and let me spit out everything without stopping for breath. Finally, when I had settled down a little, she said, "I don't know Emma's reasons, or Clutt's, but I for one will be proud to see you come back a young lady."

"I can learn what I need to learn here!"

She nodded. She had a way of doing that, warmly, even when she disagreed with every word you said. "Not everything. One day you'll think differently about education and be glad for it." She reached for one of my hands, gently pried it from my lap, and turned it over in hers. "Proper learning isn't just useful in society, Beryl. It can be wonderfully yours, a thing to have and keep just for you."

I probably scowled at her or at the wall because she gave me a look flooded with incredible patience. "I know this feels like the end of the world," she went on, "but it isn't. So much will happen to you. *So much*, and it's all out in the world ahead of you." Her fingertips moved in slow circles in the centre of my palm, lulling me. Before I quite knew it, I began to nod off, tucking in beside her, my head on her lap. When I woke a bit later, she got up and asked the houseboy to bring us tea. Then we sat at her table, thumbing through the giant atlas I loved, the page falling open to a broad map of England, green as a jewel.

"Do you think I'll ever go there?" I asked.

"Why wouldn't you? It's still your home."

Running my fingertips over the page, I traced the names of towns that were both foreign and familiar, Ipswich and Newquay, Oxford, Manchester, Leeds.

"Does your mother ever write to you from London?" she asked.

"No," I said, feeling a little disorientated. No one ever mentioned my mother, and life was so much easier that way.

"I could tell you things about her if you ever want to know."

I shook my head. "She doesn't matter now. Only the farm does."

Lady D looked at me for a long moment, seeming to mull this over. "I'm sorry. It's not my place to pry."

A short while later, D blustered in, kicking off dust and talking to himself. "My favourite girls," he cheered.

"Beryl's had a bit of a day," Lady D warned him. "She's going to go off to school soon, in Nairobi."

"Ah." He settled himself gruffly in a chair opposite me. "I wondered when that would come up. You'll be grand at it, girl. Really you will. I've always said you were as sharp as a tack."

"I'm not so sure." I made a half-hearted attempt to finish my tea, which had grown cold.

"Swear you'll come and see us whenever you can. You have a home here, too. You always will."

When I said goodbye, Lady D walked me out to the stable and put her hands on my shoulders. "There's no girl quite like you, Beryl, and you're going to do well in Nairobi. You'll do well anywhere."

It was nearly dark when I reached the farm, and the mountains were an inky blue and seemed to shrink and flatten against the distance. Wee MacGregor crested our hill, bringing us to the edge of the paddock, and I saw Kibii heading off towards the path to his village. I thought of calling out to him, but I'd had enough difficult talking for one day, and didn't know how to tell him I would be leaving soon. I didn't know how to say goodbye.

7

Over the next two and a half years I did my best at school—though my best was hardly up to scratch. I ran away half-a-dozen times, once hiding in a pig hole for three days. Another time I sparked a rebellion that had most of the school bolting onto the plains after me on their bicycles. That got me sacked, finally. My father met my train looking cross but also relieved, as if he understood that sending me away was never going to work.

But the farm wasn't at all the place I had left. The world wasn't the same, actually, and the war had made certain of that. We had heard all the biggest bits of news at school, about the archduke's assassination, about Kaiser Wilhelm and how nations we'd scarcely heard of had banded together to fight one another. For British East Africa, war meant stopping the land-greedy Germans from taking everything we believed was rightfully ours. Large portions of the protectorate had become battlefields, and men everywhere—Boers and Nandis and white settlers, Kavirondo and Kipsigis warriors—had left their ploughs and mills and *shambas* to join the King's African Rifles. Even *arap* Maina had gone off to fight. During one of my school holidays, Kibii and I stood together at the top of our hill to watch him march off to join his regiment. He held his spear high in one hand and his buffalo-hide shield in the other, and carried himself straight and proud as he walked down the dirt track. He was sent hundreds of miles away, to the border of German East Africa, and handed a rifle in place of his spear. He didn't know how to use a gun, but of course he would master it. He was the bravest and most self-assured warrior I knew, and I was sure he'd come home with stories, and perhaps enough gold to buy a new wife.

But before the end of that summer holiday, a messenger came running onto our farm one afternoon, and he told us what had happened so far away. *Arap* Maina had fought as bravely as he could, but he had died in that distant place and was buried where he fell, without his tribe or family to honour him. Kibii's face revealed nothing when we heard the news, but he stopped eating and grew thin and angry. I didn't know how to comfort him or what to think. *Arap* Maina hadn't even seemed *mortal,* and now he was gone.

"We should find the man who killed your father and plunge a spear into his heart," I told him.

"It's my duty to do this, the moment I become a *moran.*"

"I'll come with you," I told him. I had loved *arap* Maina like my own father and was ready to go anywhere and do anything to avenge his death.

"You are only a girl, Lakwet."

"I'm not afraid. I can throw a spear as far as you can."

"It's not possible. Your father would never part with you."

"I won't tell him then. I've run away before."

"Your words are selfish. Your father loves you, and he is alive."

My father meant the world to me. When I was away, I had longed for him every bit as much as I had for the farm, but the war had worked its changes on him, too. When he met my train, his face was so drawn and serious I barely knew how to say hello. We motored up the long hill, and he explained that nearby Nakuru was now a garrison town. The racecourse had become a remounting and transport depot for the troops. Our horses had been conscripted into service, leaving our stables and paddocks more than half empty, but it didn't matter since all the race meetings were suspended for the duration.

As soon as we reached the crest, I could see the difference for myself. Hundreds of our workers had gone off with only the clothes on their backs and any weapons they had—guns or spears or bush knives—and some confused idea of glory or honour. The empire had called, and so now they were soldiers of the Crown. It was possible they would be back soon, but for the moment, it was as if someone had turned Green Hills over like a box and shaken its contents out onto the hard ground where they'd blown away.

In the main house, Mrs. O had made a meal for my homecoming and dressed for it. She was as tidy and pressed as ever, but there were strands of silver along her temples, and fine lines around her eyes, and I found I was seeing her in a new way. My bunkmate for most of the time I was at school was a girl named Doris Waterman—though she liked to be called Dos. Night after night, she'd lean down from her bunk over mine to whisper things, her straight brown hair falling around her face in a curtain. She told me she was an only child and that her father owned a string of shops in town. He also owned the New Stanley Hotel, which was an important gathering place for anyone coming through Nairobi. Anything that happened there, or anywhere nearby, Dos seemed to know.

"Mrs. Orchardson?" she'd said quizzically when I mentioned her in passing. "Is her husband still in Lumbwa?"

"What? She's not married. She's been living with my father for years."

Dos made a clucking sound at my innocence and then proceeded to tell me how, years before, Mr. Orchardson, who was an anthropologist, had taken a Nandi woman for a lover and that she had become pregnant.

I was shocked. "How do you know that?"

She shrugged, still half-tipped over the bunk. "Everyone knows. It's not something that happens every day."

"So Mrs. O came to us? To escape her situation there?"

"Njoro wouldn't be far enough from Lumbwa for me. It's so humiliating. And now she and your father aren't even married."

It was as if there'd been clouds over my eyes, puffy and purely white. I hadn't known anything about the world of adults or the number of thorny things that could happen between men and women. I hadn't been paying attention, but now the clouds fell away in an instant, leaving the hard facts. My father must have known about Mr. Orchardson and the Nandi woman and either not cared or not given in to worrying about what the connection meant for him. Their current living arrangement was more scandalous than I ever imagined, for she was still married. Perhaps my father was, too. I'd never given the matter much attention, but I did now, feeling that their relationship was another thing that had grown infinitely more complicated in a very complicated world.

"When will the war end?" I asked my father. "At school everyone kept saying how the fighting is just preventative." Bright sunlight glinted through the glazed windowpanes on the simple tea service and the oilcloth and hearthstones and cedar panels. Each object was the same as it had been—but the air all around felt different. I was different.

"They do say that, don't they? And yet the casualties keep mounting. Twenty thousand in Africa alone."

"Will you go off to fight?" I had a hard time keeping my voice steady asking it.

"No—I promise I won't. But D has joined up."

"When? Why? Surely there are enough men already."

My father and Mrs. O exchanged a meaningful look.

"Daddy? What's happened? Has D been wounded?"

"It's Florence," Mrs. O said. "She fell very ill not long after your last visit. Her heart gave out."

"There was nothing wrong with her heart! She was always as fit as a horse."

"No," my father said slowly, with great care. "She'd actually been ill for years. No one knew but D."

"I don't understand. Where is she now?"

My father looked at the backs of his hands. The colour had drained from his face. "She died, Beryl. Six months ago. She's gone."

Six months? "Why did you keep it from me?"

"We didn't want to tell you in a telegram," my father said. "But I don't know. Maybe we were wrong to wait."

"She was a wonderful woman," Mrs. O said. "I know you loved her very much."

I could only look at her numbly. I pushed my chair back and made my way to the stable in a sort of trance, feeling undone. How many dozens of hours had I sat on Lady D's carpet, drinking her tea and soaking up her words, never knowing she was ill or even weak? Maybe I hadn't known her at all, not really, and now she was gone. I wouldn't ever see her again. I'd never even said goodbye.

In the shabby stable office, I found Buller napping and dropped to my knees, rubbing my face against his brindled coat. He was completely deaf now, and because he hadn't heard me he was startled—but also happy. He sniffed me everywhere and licked my face, wriggling all the way to his tail. When he flopped to the beaten earth again, I lay my head on him, looking around at my father's things—his desk with the thick black studbook, his riding helmet and crop, a plate full of pipe ash, yellowed newspapers, and the calendar on the wall. There should have been important dates circled in red. The stable should have been alive with activity, but it was as still as a Nandi burial ground. I had finally come back for good, and yet Green Hills barely felt like home any more. Would it again?

After a while my father came in and looked at us there on the floor. "I know she meant the world to you." He paused. "This is a lot to come home to, but sooner or later it will all get sorted."

I was desperate to believe he was telling the truth, that the worst of our troubles were behind us, that everything that had tumbled into chaos could still be set right again. I wanted that as much as I had ever wanted anything. "The war won't last for ever, will it?" I asked him, my voice catching.

"It can't," he replied. "Nothing does."

PART TWO

8

When the March rains fell over the plains and the ragged face of the escarpment, six million yellow flowers cracked open all at once. Red-and-white butterflies, the ones that looked like peppermint sticks, flashed in twists against the sparkling air.

But in 1919, the rains didn't come. Not the soaking April storms when one inky cloud could levitate for hours spilling everything it had, and not the short daily November rains that winked on and off as if they ran on a system of pulleys. Nothing came that year, and the plains and the bush all went sand coloured. Everywhere you looked seemed to shrink and curdle with dryness. Along the banks of Lake Nakuru, the waterline receded and collapsed, leaving powdery green mould and strange curls of dried lichen. The villages were silent, their herds emaciated. My father scoured the horizon line like every other up-country farmer within a hundred miles of Nairobi and saw no smudge of cloud anywhere, or even a single shadow on the sun.

I was sixteen now and full of restless feelings. In his study, I watched my father cup his chin solemnly and stare into his ledger with hooded, bloodshot eyes. Scotch before breakfast, neat.

I leaned over the back of his chair to tuck my chin between his neck and shoulder. He smelled like hot cotton, like the sky. "You should go back to bed."

"I haven't been to bed."

"No, I suppose you haven't."

The night before, he and Emma (I had taken to calling her that since I'd come home) had been invited to a small evening party in Nakuru, racing types, I suspected. I didn't understand how Emma kept herself up so well on the farm. Though lined and softened, her skin was still fair. She was slim, and her clothes moved well when she walked—a thing I might have managed to pull off if I'd stayed at school with the other girls instead of here, in the middle of the bush, in slacks and dusty knee-high boots.

"You really could make more of an effort, Beryl," Emma had said before they left for Nakuru. "Come to town with us."

I was better off at home. After they roared down the dirt track in Daddy's Hudson, I tucked in by the cedar-wood fire to read, liking and needing the quiet. But not long after I'd gone to bed, they were home again, whispering fiercely to each other as they crossed the yard from the car. He'd done something or she thought he had, their voices growing louder and more tense, and I wondered what had set them off. Sometimes things in town could turn volatile if Emma felt snubbed. She'd long been living openly as my father's common-law wife, but as I grew older I saw things that had been invisible to me before, like how even if she and Daddy seemed ready to throw off the usual conventions or at least ignore them, the colony at large couldn't. Many of the neighbouring farmers' wives had effectively shut Emma out. Even in town, as I'd learned from Dos, the arrangement was seen as disgraceful, no matter how much time had passed, no matter how conservative they seemed in other ways.

But if tensions from the outside world stirred the pot at home, at least Emma seemed ready to drop any nonsense about my needing a governess or schooling. Her efforts now were aimed at my manners and appearance—such as they were. She was forever trying to get me to wash more, to wear a frock instead of trousers. Gloves were essential if I ever wanted to keep my hands nice, and didn't I know that any proper young lady wore a hat outdoors?

She also seemed more insistent than ever that I shouldn't spend time with Kibii or any of the young men from the Kip village. "It was bad enough when you were children, but now ... well, it's not seemly."

Seemly? "I don't see what all the fuss is about."

"Emma's right," my father agreed. "It's just not done."

Though I continued to fight both of them on principle, the fact was I rarely saw Kibii now. When I came back to the farm from Nairobi, he began to walk three paces behind me when we went to the stables together for gallops.

"What are you up to?" I asked the first time I noticed him doing it.

"You are the memsahib. This is what's proper."

"I'm the same as I *have* been, you ninny. Stop it."

But we were neither of us the same as before, and I felt that as clearly as I saw the changes in my body when I undressed at night, the rounding and lengthening of my new curves. Kibii's arms and legs were muscled where they'd once been soft and boyish, and his face had hardened, too. I felt myself drawn to him, the polished look of his skin, and the strong length of his thigh beneath his *shuka*. He was beautiful, but when I tried to touch him casually, testing the waters, he flinched.

"Stop, Beru."

"Why not? Aren't you even a little curious?"

"Don't be stupid. Do you want to get me killed?"

When he stormed off, I was left feeling stung and rejected, but deep down I knew he was right. Neither of our worlds would have permitted that sort of touch between us for a minute, and the situation could have quickly become terrible for both of us. But I missed Kibii. Things had once been so simple and good between us, when we weren't afraid of anything, when we'd hunted in perfect lockstep. I remembered running for miles looking for an occupied warthog hole with *arap* Maina, and then stooping to crinkle paper outside the mouth of its den. This was what you did to call out the pig, the noise working to aggravate the animal in some way I didn't understand but rarely saw fail. Kibii and I did everything *arap* Maina asked of us and came home with the body of a large boar slung between us like a fleshy hammock. The hair on its haunches was like crisp black wire. Its mouth was frozen and clenched in death, bearing an expression of stubbornness I admired. My end of the stick bit heavily into my hands and felt exactly right. This was what the pig weighed, what the day weighed.

My God, how I wanted to live like that again! I wanted to see *arap* Maina, to follow him soundlessly through jagged elephant grass, to laugh with Kibii lightly over anything or nothing. But he was nearly fifteen now. When his circumcision ceremony arrived, he would become the warrior he was always meant to be. In all the time I'd known him, he'd never stopped dreaming of and longing for that day, but somehow, as I'd listened to him over the years, I'd managed to ignore how the ceremony would take away the boy I knew for ever and also the fierce warrior girl who had loved him. It already had. Those children were gone.

9

*O*n his stable office, my father folded his ledger and reached for a drink though he'd only recently finished his morning coffee. "You're going to run Pegasus today?" he asked me.

"A mile and a quarter at half speed. His head's been a little low. I thought I'd try the chain snaffle."

"Good girl," he said, but his eyes were flat and detached as I ran through the rest of the morning's duties—which of the horses were on gallop day, which were resting or in tendon boots, the feed ordered, deliveries scheduled. Since I'd failed at boarding school, this was my life. He organized the breeding and ran the farm, and I was his head boy. I wanted to be indispensable, but I would settle for being useful.

The groom, Toombo, had brushed Pegasus's coat to a lacquer and now boosted me into the saddle. At two, Pegasus was massive already—a notch more than seventeen hands. I was tall, too—nearly six foot now—but I felt like a leaf in the saddle.

In the yard, the morning was as clear as glass—the same as the last ten or twenty or a hundred mornings. We passed under the large wattle tree where a pair of grey-whiskered vervets chattered from one of the lower branches. They looked like two old men with their leathery black hands and thin, disappointed faces. They'd come down from the forest or escarpment looking for water, but our cisterns had run desperately low, and we had none to offer.

Over the hill, the dirt track stretched down and away through broadly terraced fields. In better days, our crops had spread around us in every direction, rich and green. When you walked through the chest-high maize, your foot would sink into the moist earth up to your ankle. Now the leaves curled and cracked. The mill still ran continuously, grinding *posho* that then waited in canvas bags to honour our contracts. Grain-filled rail carriages still streamed away from our station at Kampi ya Moto towards Nairobi, but no one was getting rich from any of it. My father had borrowed against chits at high interest and then borrowed more. The rupee was plummeting like a grouse full of bird shot. Where it was now, no one really knew. The creditors seemed constantly to change their minds, and my father's debts slid up and down a ladder almost daily. But our horses had to eat. They needed crimped oats, bran, boiled barley—not bleached patches of lucerne. My father had built his bloodstock from love and gut instinct and the thick black studbook with lists of names going all the way back to sires like magnificent princes. These were the finest horses there were. He wasn't going to let anyone or anything take an inch more without a fight, not after he had worked so hard.

When Pegasus and I reached the open track, we paused and settled, getting our bearings, then I opened him up. He charged out like a coiled spring, lengthening along the flat grade, thrusting through the rhythms of his stride—fast and perfect, close to flying.

I had foaled him myself when I was fourteen and home for a spring holiday—watching Coquette's trembling labour and overjoyed that I could be there for it. Coquette had delivered healthy foals every few years since the terrible birth of Apollo and the coming of the siafu ants, but I still didn't want to leave her side for a moment and took to sleeping in her loose box for the last few weeks. When the foal finally came, I broke open the slick, translucent birth sac with my hands and gently tugged him by his small perfect front hoofs into the loose straw bed. I nearly shook with happiness and relief. It was the first time I'd ever been midwife on my own, and there'd been no mishaps. My father had trusted me and didn't come into the stable at all until dawn as I held Pegasus in my arms, a bundle of wet heat and bony folded limbs.

"Well done," he said from the stable door. He seemed to know that even the dusty tip of his boot in the loose box would lessen what I'd carried off without him. "You brought him to life. I suppose he's yours now."

"Mine?" I'd never owned anything or thought I should—happily grooming, handling, feeding, and worrying over my father's animals for years. But somehow this miraculous animal belonged to me: a bit of grace I hadn't even known I was desperate for.

When Pegasus and I finished our run, we made for home the long way, around the northern perimeter of the valley where it furled out in an unbroken sweep. A neighbour had recently snapped up the adjoining parcel, and I saw signs of him now. Newly set fence posts stood as straight as matchsticks where there'd been only open land and unmarred emptiness. I traced the line they made and soon reached the farmer, hatless and barrel-chested, with a spool of wire over his shoulder. He was stringing it with a hammer and claw and staples, the muscles of his arms going taut as he drew the wire hard against the post and secured it. He didn't stop working until Pegasus and I stood five feet from him. Then he smiled up at me, his collar dark with fresh perspiration. "You're trampling my pasture."

I knew he was joking—there was no pasture yet, or much of anything finished—but I could tell it *would* all be marvellous one day. You could see it in the way he'd set the posts so well. "I can't believe your house is up," I said. He'd made it look more suited for town than the bush, with a shingle roof instead of thatch and real glass at the windows.

"It's nothing like your father's place." He'd already guessed who I was then. Shielding his eyes with the back of his arm, he squinted up at me. "I met him years ago, when I was laid up near here with the Madras volunteers."

"You were wounded?"

"Dysentery, actually. My whole troop had it. Loads of men died."

"That sounds awful."

"It was." The smallest hint of a Scottish brogue rolled from behind his tongue. "But there were a few pleasures. One day some of us went off hunting down in the Rongai Valley, and you were there. A good-looking native boy was with you, too, and you were both crack shots." He smiled, flashing neat square teeth. "You don't remember me."

I scanned his face—the squared-off jaw and strong chin and cornflower-blue eyes—looking for something familiar. "Sorry," I finally admitted. "There were so many soldiers around then."

"You've grown up."

"Daddy says I might never stop growing. I passed him a while ago."

He smiled and continued to look up at me in a way that made me wonder if there was something else I was meant to say or do. I couldn't imagine what. All I knew of men beyond farm life and work were the warm, confusing thoughts I sometimes had late at night now, about being touched or taken, thoughts that could make my cheeks hot even when I was alone in my hut.

"Well, it's nice to see you again." He reached for his spool of wire without moving his eyes from mine.

"Good luck," I told him, and then nudged Pegasus away, glad to be leaving him there with his fence posts, to be turning for home with the sun at my back.

"I met our new neighbour," I said at dinner that night, sawing at a slab of Thomsons'-gazelle steak with the tip of my knife.

"Purves," my father said. "He's done a lot with that land."

"This is the ex-captain you were telling me about, Charles?"

Emma asked from her end of the table. "He's a good-looking fellow. I saw him in town."

"He's a hard worker, I'll say that."

"What did you think of him, Beryl?"

I shrugged. "He's all right, I suppose."

"It wouldn't kill you to make more of an effort socially," she said. "Do you know *anyone* your age?"

"My age? He has to be thirty."

"Farm life is going to harden you, you know. You think you'll be young and beautiful for ever and that you'll have plenty of chances, but it doesn't work like that."

"She's only sixteen, Em," my father said. "She has plenty of time."

"That's what you think. We're not helping, keeping her out here with no company. School didn't do a thing—not that she was there long. She's wild. She doesn't know how to make conversation."

"Why are we talking about manners and society, when there are real problems to think about?" I pushed my plate away in frustration.

"One day you *will* want to attract a man," Emma said, glaring at me pointedly. "Your father and I have to prepare you for that."

"Emma thinks you should have a coming-out party," he explained, cupping the heavy base of his scotch glass.

"You've got to be joking. Out *where*?"

"You know perfectly well these things are done, Beryl. Even here. It's important to be known in society and to develop some grace. You might not think it matters now, but you will."

"I have all the society I need here," I said, meaning Buller and our horses.

"It's one night, Beryl."

"And a new dress," Emma added, as if this were any kind of draw.

"We've already made arrangements with the hotel," my father said with finality, and I knew it had been settled long before.

10

*N*airobi had grown in leaps since I was there at school. Ten thousand people now perched on the scrubby verge of the Athi Plains with the tin-roofed shops and public houses and the noisy and colourful bazaar. Even this much civilization was a wonder. The town had been formed accidentally when the Uganda railway was being forged between Mombasa and Lake Victoria in 1899. A flimsy headquarters went up, then an anchovy-tin shack the workers had dubbed "the Railhead Club," then more shacks and tents, and when the railway finally moved on, a town was left in its wake.

But even then, no one guessed how important the railway would become for the British Empire and the whole of the continent. Building the route was expensive, and maintaining it even more so. Colonial officials concocted a scheme to draw white settlers to the area by offering parcels of land for nearly nothing. Retired soldiers like my father and D received additional land as part of a pension. And this was how the colony went up, man by man, farm by farm, with Nairobi as its steadily beating heart.

By 1919, there was a Government House with a ballroom on Nairobi's central hill, a racetrack, and three good hotels. To reach town, we only had to board the train and travel one hundred and thirteen miles through dusty bush and red murram mud and papyrus swamp. A full day spent on the sooty, lurching iron contraption so I could stand in a rented room at the New Stanley Hotel, in a frock the colour of egg custard.

The frock was probably very pretty. Emma had picked it out and insisted it was perfect—but the stiff lace crimped too high on my neck and gave me a rash I couldn't scratch at. There was a crown of roses, too—tight yellow-pink buds sewn together in a circlet. I kept looking in the mirror, wondering if I looked right and hoping I did.

"What do you think, really?" I asked Dos, who stood behind me in her slip, pulling pins from her bobbed brown hair.

"You're lovely, but stop scratching, will you? Everyone will think you've got fleas."

Dos was still a student—currently at Miss Seccombe's in town—and we had almost nothing in common. She was curvy, brown, and tiny in her blue lace frock, good at conversation and the usual pleasantries, easy in the company of others. I was rail thin, a head taller than Dos, even in flat shoes—and far more comfortable talking to horses and dogs than people. We were as mismatched as two sixteen-year-old girls could be, but I was still fond of Dos and glad she was here.

At 10:00 p.m. sharp, according to a silly British custom, I gripped my father's arm on the stairs. I only ever saw him in dusty khakis and sun helmet, but his dark tails and white shirtfront looked natural on him, reminding me of the life he'd led before, in England. There, I would have been formally presented to the king at court, in a procession of other well-born young women in pearls and gloves and ostrich feathers, curtsying my heart out. In this far-flung colony, where sovereignty was a flag and a notion and sometimes a few rousing verses of "God Save the King" that had everyone in tears, I was brought out to a hotel ballroom full of ranchers, former soldiers, and Afrikaners, all soaped clean and half-pickled. A five-piece band played the lilting opening to "If You Were the Only Girl in the

World," the cue for my father and me to take our turn on the dance floor.

"I'm going to step on your toes now," I warned.

"Go on, then. I won't make faces and give you away."

He danced beautifully, and I did my best to keep up, concentrating on his grey wool tailcoat, which smelled faintly of the cedar chest it had been pulled from the day before. I had to hunch a bit to keep from towering over him, and this made me feel more awkward than I already did.

"You know, they don't hand out manuals for the tough stuff," he said as the band slowed. "I haven't always known what to do as a father, but somehow you've turned out all right."

Before I could really take in what he'd said, or make the moment last, he stepped away in one move, passing my right hand to Lord Delamere.

"Look at you, Beryl. Pretty as a filly," D said.

He had come out of the war looking older by a dozen years. There were deep lines around his eyes, and his hair had gone white in a bad bout of fever, but he'd come through. I rarely saw him now. He still owned Equator Ranch but had moved on to another ranching operation south and east of us, on the chalky shores of Lake Elmenteita.

"Florence should be here," he said against my shoulder. "She would have been so proud."

I felt a sharp plunging sensation from the tender way D had said her name and told him I still thought about her every day. "It's not fair she's gone."

"Not a bit." And then he kissed my cheek before smoothly passing me on to the next in line.

It took me several dances to clear the dip in my mood, but the fellows partnering me didn't seem to notice or mind. For an hour or more I was spun in a press of warm shaved faces, strong hands and damp ones, good dancers and ones with clumsy sidesteps. I tasted champagne on the back of my tongue as a lone trumpet swooned the verses I knew but didn't sing:

A Garden of Eden just made for two
With nothing to mar our joy
I would say such wonderful things to you
There would be such wonderful things to do
If you were the only girl in the world

And then there was Jock—Purves, as my father called him—looking a good deal cleaner than he had done twisting fence wire and more handsome now that we were nose to nose. When he spun me close, I smelled shaving powder and gin, and though I didn't have the slightest bit of experience with men or swooning, I could tell by Dos's look, as we came past her table again, that it was high time I learned.

There were lots of men like Jock in town—discharged soldiers who'd taken their Settlement Allotment and snatched up acreage, trying to reinvent themselves in a purposeful way—but few were as handsome. He was strong-looking and squared off everywhere, shoulders and jaw and chin. This was what a man was supposed to be, I thought, if you could build him from scratch and break him in like new land.

"Is your fence still standing?" I asked him.

"Why wouldn't it be?"

"Any number of things." I laughed. "Starting with marauding elephants."

"You think I'm funny."

"No . . ." I let my voice trail off.

"A certain kind of man comes to Africa and builds fences. Is that what you think?"

"How should I know?" I threw out. "I'm only sixteen."

"You were never sixteen."

He was flattering me, but I didn't mind much. I'd had three glasses of champagne by then, and everything was beginning to seem wonderful—Jock's dark jacket under my hand, the band in an alcove opposite the bar. The tuba was a golden blur. The horn player seemed to be winking at me. And then there were the other partnered girls sailing by us in silk dresses, gardenias tucked like stars into their hair.

"Where did all these girls come from? I've never seen half of them."

He glanced around. "You outshine them."

Out on the farm, there'd been no occasion to flirt. I hadn't learned how to try to draw a man in, so I simply said what I thought, even though it stamped me as insecure. "Emma says I don't paint well."

"All that rouge and face powder has to come off at some point. Maybe it's better you don't." We danced for half a minute in silence, and then he said, "These town girls all come from the same box of sweets, anyway. I think I'll marry you instead."

"What?" I breathed, caught off guard.

He grinned, his teeth neat and shiny and square. "You *are* wearing a white dress."

"Oh." I leaned back in his arms and felt my head go woozy.

Sometime later I went to sit near Dos at one of the cloth-draped tables. Her chin was propped up on one of her hands. A gin fizz foamed in the other. "He's lovely," she said.

"You dance with him then. He makes me nervous."

"He hasn't looked at me twice."

"How do you know?"

She laughed at me. "Really, Beryl. You're so thick."

"Why *wouldn't* I be?" I glared at her. "It's all so stupid anyway. Half the fellows have sweat pouring off them, and the other half look right over my shoulder as if I'm not there. Well, at least the ones who're tall enough."

"I'm sorry," she said, softening. "I was only teasing. You'll learn."

I made a face at her and pulled at the neck of my dress. "Want a smoke?"

"You go. It might be my only chance for a little male attention."

"You look grand."

She smiled. "I'll look better with you outside."

———

On the street, it was dark in the way only Africa can be. I took a deep breath, tasting dust and eucalyptus, and moved past the smeary lights of the veranda. In the small park across the road, smooth clay had been spread like a dusting of confectioners' sugar, and a dotted line of dwarf gum trees newly planted for effect. This was Nairobi trying to civilize itself, but a greater emptiness stretched out beyond it, ready to swallow every last stitch of all of us. I loved that about Africa and hoped it would never change. Strolling, I felt the dark tug at me, and a pleasant itch to be out of my dress, out of my skin even.

"You look like Diana," an English voice said, startling me.

A man stood in the street behind me in a well-fitting evening jacket and trousers, both white as the moon. "I'm sorry?"

"Diana the huntress," he clarified. "From the Romans." He was drunk, I realized, but still pleasant for all that. A fat bottle of wine sloshed against his leg, and when he smiled I saw he had a wonderful face, at least in the dark. "I'm Finch Hatton . . . or maybe I'm Virbius."

"More Romans?"

"That's right." He looked at me more closely, tipping his head. He was taller than I was, when so very few men were. "You look as if you've been to a party."

"So do you. This one's for me." I pointed my chin in the direction of the hotel.

"Your wedding party?"

I laughed. "My coming out."

"Good, then. Never marry. Dianas don't, as a rule."

He stepped a little nearer, and I could better see his face under the rim of his dark bowler. His eyes were large and heavily lidded. His cheekbones were strong, and his nose was sharp and fine. "Do you feel ready for society, then?" he asked.

"I'm not sure. Can anyone tell you when you're grown up?"

Another man came around the corner near the hotel and was walking towards us with purpose. He carried himself like a prince, too, and had a thick, combed moustache, reddish hair, and no hat. "Denys, finally," he said with a dramatic sigh. "You've led me quite a chase." He bowed at the waist in a way that was probably meant to be funny. "Berkeley Cole at your service."

"Beryl Clutterbuck."

"Clutt's daughter?" He peered at me. "Yes, I catch the resemblance now. I know your father from the race meetings. There isn't a man who's better with horses."

"Miss Clutterbuck and I have been discussing the perils of marriage."

"You're drunk, Denys." Berkeley clucked, then turned to me. "Don't let him frighten you."

"I'm not a bit frightened."

"See?" Denys said. He tipped the wine bottle into his mouth, and then brushed stray drops away with the back of his hand. "Have you ever seen stars like this? You can't have. They don't make them like this anywhere in the world."

Above our heads, the sky was a brimming treasure box. Some of the stars seemed to want to pull free and leap down onto my shoulders—and though these were the only ones I had ever known, I believed Denys when he said they were the finest. I thought I might believe anything he said, in fact, even though we had just met. He had that in him.

"Do you know any Keats?" Denys asked after several minutes of stillness. Then, when I was clearly confused, "It's poetry."

"Oh, I don't know any poetry."

"Berkeley, give us something about the stars."

"Hmm," Berkeley mused. "How about Shelley?

"Wrap thy form in a mantle gray,
Star-inwrought!
Blind with thine hair the eyes of Day;
Kiss her until she be wearied out,

Then wander o'er city, and sea, and land,
Touching all with thine opiate wand . . ."

"'Kiss her until she be wearied out,'" Denys repeated. "That's the best bit, isn't it, and Berkeley does it so well."

"Wonderful." My father had read the classics to me by firelight sometimes, but that had felt like school. This was more like a song, and also like being alone in the wild with your thoughts. Somehow it was both at the same time.

While Shelley's words still hung there, Denys began to recite something else, quietly, as if only for himself:

"This is thy hour O Soul, thy free flight into the wordless,
Away from books, away from art, the day erased, the lesson
   done,
Thee fully forth emerging, silent, gazing, pondering the themes
   thou lovest best.
Night, sleep, death and the stars."

The words were so natural for him they took no effort at all. You couldn't learn that, no matter how much you tried. Even I recognized it, feeling a little small. "That's Shelley again?"

"Whitman, actually." He smiled at me.

"Should I be embarrassed not to have heard of him? I told you I don't know anything about poetry."

"It only takes practise, you know. If you really want to learn, do it. Take some poetry every day."

"Like your quinine for malaria," Berkeley added. "A measure of good champagne helps, too. I don't know what it is about Africa, but champagne is absolutely compulsory here."

Without any further ceremony, Denys tipped his hat to me, and then the two men moved off down the road, turning a corner and passing out of sight. They might have been headed to another party, or to white steeds waiting to whisk them off to an enchanted palace. I would have believed a magic carpet as well, or any storybook ending. They were that lovely, and now they were gone.

"Are you drunk?" Emma said when I went back inside.

"I might be."

She pursed her lips tightly, fed up, and moved off just as Jock was stepping towards me.

"I've been looking for you everywhere," he said, taking my arm.

Without saying anything I reached for the champagne flute he held and downed it in one go. It was a dramatic gesture, but there were bits of verse still swirling in my head like the milky trails of stars. There was the picture of two beautiful men in white jackets at the untamed edge of town, and the idea that the world was far bigger than I'd ever imagined and that all sorts of things would happen to me. Things already were happening to change my life for ever, even if I didn't quite know what they meant. There was only the promise for the moment, as exhilarating as the feeling of champagne fizzing and dancing on my tongue. *Compulsory,* Berkeley Cole had called it.

"Let's have some more of this," I told Jock, lifting the glass. And then, as we made our way towards the bar, "Do you know any poetry?"

11

A few weeks later, my father and I met the train from Nairobi at Kampi ya Moto Station, down the hill from our farm. The engine settled and breathed hard in place, like a small dragon home from war. Smoke chuffed and streamed out behind, marring the flat sky, while half-a-dozen men bent in two alongside the sooty freight cars, readying a wooden ramp. Six of our horses were returning home victorious from the Turf Club in town—including Cam, Bar One, and my Pegasus. Cam had taken the cup and a hundred-pound purse, but now, as we stood on the short platform and waited for Emma to come round with the Hudson, my father didn't want to talk about our winning runs. He wanted to talk about Jock.

"Do you like him at all?" he asked, looking up the hill into the sun.

"I suppose he's all right. He'll make that farm work."

He chewed lightly for a moment at the corner of his lip. "He will." And then: "He's serious about you."

"What?" I spun on him. "We've only just met."

He smiled wryly. "I'm not sure that's a detriment in marriage."

"Why is everyone so keen to find me a husband? I'm too young for all of that."

"Not really. There're plenty of girls your age who've been dreaming about husbands and families for years. You'll want to be taken care of one day, won't you?"

"Why? We're doing all right as we are."

Before my father could say anything more, the silly klaxon punched through the air over the hill. We heard the low metallic clanking of the motorized buggy, and as it nosed into view, I saw Emma at the wheel, bouncing on the hard leather seat. She pulled up to us, idling. "Where's your hat, Beryl? You'll get freckles in this sun."

I wasn't sure how our success in Nairobi could dissolve so quickly, but that night at dinner my father was silent and remote, while Emma came forward, peevish about the soup. It was a thin broth with turbot and potatoes and small coins of leeks.

"The fish is off. Don't you think, Charles?" She pushed her bowl away and raised her voice to call the houseboy, Kamotho. When he appeared in his white coat and small velvet fez, Emma told him it should all go back.

"And we'll eat what, bread and butter?" My father put up a hand to stay the confused Kamotho. "Leave it alone, Emma."

"*Now* you care what I do? That's rich." Her words clattered in the air above the table.

"What is this all about?" I finally brought myself to ask.

My father looked pained. He asked Kamotho to leave us, and as the boy slunk off gratefully, I wished that I could join him. I didn't want to hear what came next. "It's the damned rupee," he finally said, squeezing one of his hands in the other. "I went to bed last week owing five thousand and now it's seventy-five hundred, with eight per cent interest on all of it. I can't climb out this time."

"He's taken a training post in Cape Town," Emma pronounced coldly. "The farm is finished."

"What?" I felt myself rocking dangerously off centre.

"Farming's a gamble, Beryl. It always has been."

"And Cape Town isn't a gamble?" I shook my head, barely able to grasp what was happening.

"They love horses there. I'll make a fresh start. Maybe the change will be lucky."

"Lucky," I repeated flatly.

In my room that night, I turned the lamp lower and lay there feeling stunned. Shadows came creeping and sighing over my bed, the posts still hung with beads and pouches of feathery animal bones. It gave me a kind of vertigo thinking about how quickly my whole life could shift away from under me. Our stables were still filled and perfectly run—eighty-four matchless animals that had won my father a golden reputation and strings of solid wins. In the morning, the stable bell would ring and everyone and everything would wake as they always had. The mill would turn, the horses would canter and stamp in the paddock and churn loose hay in their boxes—but none of it was real any more. We lived on a ghost farm.

12

When the moon climbed above the camphor trees beside my hut, light streamed in through the open windows, yellowing the tops of the shelves and boxes. I dressed quickly in trousers and moccasins and a long-sleeved shirt and then headed out into the cool dry night. There was to be a *ngoma* that night, as there always was for full moons—a tribal dance of the young Kikuyu men and women, up the high embankment at the far edge of the forest. I headed there with Buller at my heels, listening for anything that might want to do me harm and thinking about my father.

Earlier that night, I'd found him behind his paper-strewn desk working on the lists he'd begun to collect of interested buyers for the horses. The surrender in it seemed to have cut new lines around his brown eyes.

"Is Emma going along to Cape Town?" I asked him.

"Of course."

"Will I go?"

"If that's what you want."

Gooseflesh prickled the back of my neck. "What else would I do?"

"Stay here and make your own start as a farmer's wife, I suppose."

"Marry Jock?" My words came out in an unsteady rush.

"It's clear he's ready to settle down, and he wants you."

"I'm only sixteen."

"Well"—he shrugged—"no one's forcing you. If you want to come along, we'll be starting all over from the beginning, working for someone else."

He returned to his lists and I studied the top of his head, the skin pale pink and vulnerable-looking under his thinning brown hair. Had I heard a hesitation in his voice? He said it was up to me, but something in his tone seemed to be nudging me gently away from Cape Town. "Does Emma not want me to go?"

"Honestly, Beryl." He glanced up from shuffling his lists, looking exasperated. "I have so much to worry about at the moment. This has nothing to do with you."

I went off to bed then, but I hadn't slept much or been able to think about anything else. Maybe my father's hard choices *didn't* have anything to do with me, but they were upending my life all the same and forcing me to make hard choices of my own, ones I had hoped never to make.

Before I was even halfway up the steep ridge, I heard the *ngoma*. Drums set the air vibrating and rang through the ground under my feet as if something were tunnelling powerfully in every direction at once. Smoke rose in a coil above the ridge, then high-licking flames and cinders. Finally I was on level ground and could see the dancers, alive with movement, and the encompassing circle of those who watched, too young or too old to join in. At the centre of the beaten ring of earth, the fire danced, too, giving off a singed smell and painting a lustre on limbs and faces. The young women had smooth-shaved heads dressed with strings of beads. More beads swept in long looping chains over the tight leather strappings of their clothes. They weren't much older than me, but they looked older dressed like this, and as if they knew something I didn't, and possibly never would.

A few of the young men wore the long white skins of serval cats on leather thongs around their waists. When the skins swung under their buttocks, the dots and dashes of the animals' coats shone as if alive, then flicked between their legs as they pitched forward and back with the steps. The tribal chief bent back his neck and made a screeching caw I felt everywhere. The men called out and the women responded, cry and mirroring cry, high and looping, filling the sky and slicing it open. Films of sweat caught the light and the vibrating skins of the drum. My breath quickened. My heart seemed to leave my body as the verses and refrains gathered speed like a great wheel. And just when the song reached its highest pitch, I looked across the blazing circle and saw Kibii.

We had always come to these *ngomas* together as children, staying late and walking back home through the forest afterwards, Kibii full of judgements about how the dancers could have been more graceful or more passionate. Now the two of us were rarely alone, and I couldn't remember the last time we'd been easy with one another. As the firelight painted shadows on him, I saw how much older and different he'd become. Instead of his usual *shuka,* he wore a finer one, knotted high on his left shoulder and gathered at his waist with a beaded belt. There were black and white bands of monkey fur around both his ankles, and at his throat hung the hollowed claw of a lion. He was angled away from me, and his profile was a prince's, as it had always been, but with steelier edges. Finally he turned. His black eyes found mine over the licking flames, and my heart jumped. He was a *moran* now. That's what had changed—he'd become a man.

I backed away from the circle, feeling hurt. We hadn't been close for a long time, but I still couldn't believe that Kibii could cross the most momentous threshold of his life without my hearing a whisper of it. I scanned the area for Buller, wanting to be gone as quickly as possible, but didn't see him. I made off anyway, and had reached the edge of the ridge, readying myself for the steep descent, when I heard Kibii calling my name. The moon beamed down at the tangle of brushy plants and grasses that hid my feet from me. Even if I hurried, I knew he could easily catch me again—so I stayed.

"They say your father is leaving Njoro," Kibii said when he'd reached me. "Is it true?"

I nodded. "For Cape Town." I didn't want to say anything about the money troubles. It was too shameful.

"There are plenty of good horses there, or so I have heard."

"You've become a *moran,*" I said, wanting to talk of anything else. "You look very fine." Moonlight showed the pride on his face, but there was something else, too. I realized he didn't know how to be near me any more.

"What will you do now?" he asked.

"I don't know, actually. I've had a marriage proposal."

I thought he would be surprised or show some reaction, but he only shrugged as if to say *of course,* and then spoke a native phrase I'd heard before: *A new thing is good, though it be a sore place.*

"Are you ready for marriage?" I challenged him, not liking the authority and confidence in his voice. As if he'd already sorted out every piece of the puzzle that had made a muddle of my life.

He shrugged again—*why not?* "I will go into the world first. The *ndito* in my village aren't meant for me."

"The world is a big place. Do you know where you'll go?"

"My father told me of many places he travelled to—north as far as Kitale, south to Arusha, and to the slopes of Donya Kenya. Perhaps I will begin by walking where he has walked."

Arap Maina's last steps had been very far from here. I suspected Kibii was thinking of that place, too, though he hadn't named it. "Do you still mean to find the soldier who killed *arap* Maina?"

"Perhaps," he said. "Or perhaps I'll learn the difference between a boy's dreams and a man's." He paused, and then said, "When I marry, my father will live again in my sons."

He sounded so arrogant, so sure of himself. It made me want to challenge him or put him right. I said, "The man who wants to marry me is very rich and strong. He lives near here. He built his house in three days."

"A proper house or a hut?" he wanted to know.

"A real house, with shingles and a pitched roof, and glass windows."

He was silent for a moment, and I was sure I'd finally impressed him. "Three days," he said at last. "There is no wisdom in such hurrying. This house will not stand long."

"You haven't seen it." My voice rose with irritation.

"How can that matter?" he said. "I would ask him to build another dwelling, just for you, and to take more care." He turned away, dismissing me, and said, partly over his shoulder, "You should know I have a *moran*'s name now. I am *arap* Ruta."

All the way back to the farm I smarted, running over the clever things I should have said to him, things that would wound him and make him feel as small as I did now, and as outmatched. *Arap* Ruta indeed. I had known him since he wasn't any taller than a bushpig, and now he'd become worldly and wise after one night's ceremony? A sharp knife and a cupful of curdled bull's blood to drink?

As my thoughts buzzed and grated against one another, I realized that if Ruta had even the slightest notion of how scared I was about the coming changes, I would die.

But I *was* scared, and full of confusion. Cape Town was a world away, and my father was going to be busy and worried there, focused on pleasing new owners and stable managers. I could trail him, trying to stay out of the way, or throw my lot in with Emma to set up house. What a thought that was.

England was another choice, too, I supposed, or might be if I were another sort of girl. I might have considered writing to my mother to see if there was room for me with her and Dickie—but England seemed even more foreign and distant a world than Cape Town in a way, and she had never once tried to reclaim me over the years. Asking for her help now would cost me too much and open the door for all the old hurt again. No, never that—which left Jock.

I didn't know the slightest thing about marriage, and the only happy union I'd ever seen modelled was D and Lady D, a foggy memory well behind me. The farm and our horses had always seemed better things to hitch my fate to. I hadn't even let myself imagine something else, but that was all dissolving now, moment by moment. I barely knew Jock and didn't know why I'd caught his attention in the first place, other than that I hunted well and he liked the way I looked. But marrying him would mean I could stay here in Njoro, seeing the same hills and distances, living the same sort of life. Did Jock fancy himself in love with me? Could I learn to love him?

Everything was so murky suddenly. And it seemed even more unfair that while my future whirled sickeningly, Ruta's was rolling out exactly as he'd always dreamed. For ten years or more he and I had played at besting each other, practising fearlessness, stretching for more. The games had prepared Ruta for his future, and should have prepared me for mine, too. The manoeuvres had become riskier and more difficult, but maybe each was the same when you got down to it. Jumping had taught me how to jump, hadn't it? I only had to look at Ruta to know he wasn't a child any more. Neither was I.

The next afternoon, after I'd practised the pronouncement over and over in my hut, so I could sound certain of myself, I told my father I was going to stay in Njoro.

"Good." He nodded and tented his fingers, studying me. "I think that's best. Jock's sensible and not afraid to dirty his hands. I know he'll take care of you."

"I can look out for myself, too," I bluffed, my pulse thudding in my ears. I had to pause and steady myself to say the next thing. "Can I keep Pegasus?"

"You earned him fair and square. He's not mine to take back." He rose to get himself a drink. The peaty odour of scotch flickered up and stung my nose.

"I'd like one of those."

He looked at me, surprised. "You'll have to go for water."

I shook my head.

"All right," he said. "I guess you've earned that, too." He handed me the rounded heavy glass, and we sat in silence as the sun retreated.

I'd had wine and champagne, but this was different. It made me feel older.

"We've had a good run here, haven't we?" he asked.

I nodded, unable to reach words for anything I felt. I looked into my glass, letting the scotch burn through me.

13

Once I decided to say yes to Jock, everything moved with shocking speed. Our clothes were ordered, the priest engaged, paper invitations sent flying far and wide. Emma had very clear ideas about my dress—pearl-trimmed ivory satin with embroidered rosettes and thistles on the train—and since I had no taste myself, I agreed to all her choices. Orange blossoms and long silk ninon for the veil, slippers so thin and fine I couldn't imagine them lasting beyond the day. When gifts began arriving—a silver cake stand, filigreed napkin rings, a cut-glass bud vase, various cheques written out to Mr. and Mrs. Purves—they were carefully put away in one corner of the house, while things belonging to Daddy and Emma were packed in crates and settled in other corners. It was dizzying to see the farm dissolving as my future was being planned, but I also understood it couldn't be any other way.

Jock and I didn't spend more than a few moments alone in the weeks of hurried preparation and manoeuvring. When we were, he squeezed my hands tightly in his and told me how happy we were going to be. He talked about the changes and expansions he would make to our farm. How ambitious he was for our future. How prosperity was surely just around the corner. I latched on to Jock's dreams, wanting to feel reassured. Hadn't Green Hills started with nothing long ago? Our new farm would grow and become wonderful, just like that. I had to believe it was possible even as I waited to feel more for Jock himself.

"*You're* a fast worker," Dos squealed when I told her the news. "The last I heard he made you nervous."

"He still does a bit," I confessed, "but I'm trying not to let on."

"It's not as if we have so many options here," she said. "I'll be a farmer's wife one day, too, I imagine. At least he's dashing."

"You think it's all right, then, that I'm not in love with him?"

"You *will* be, silly. At least you'll stay here where you belong—and he'll take care of you. Even if your father wasn't moving to Cape Town, he couldn't look out for you for ever." She smirked. "Or so mine tells me every chance he gets."

We were married at All Saints on a sun-shocked Wednesday in October, two weeks before my seventeenth birthday. The legal marrying age was eighteen then, but my father thought I was old enough, and that seemed good enough for me. At the church, I walked on his arm, keeping my eyes on Jock to hold me in place, as if I were going into battle with him. It did the trick until I reached him and the starch-collared reverend, and then my heart began to gallop. I worried that everyone could hear it, that they all knew or guessed that I had no love for this man. But love was dubious, too, wasn't it? It certainly hadn't done much good for my mother and father, or Emma and my father, for that matter. Maybe being practical was one way to ensure I ended up differently from them? I hoped so as I gripped Jock's hand, finding the breath to say *Yes* to the reverend's long string of difficult questions, and then, *I will.*

Jock had a pal from the King's African Rifles who came to stand up for him—the tall and smart-looking Captain Lavender, with bright eyes and a cowlick that swept a wing of golden hair onto his forehead. It was Lavender who drove us to the Norfolk Hotel in

Jock's yellow Bugatti. He sped through the streets of Nairobi, throwing me across the leather backseat towards Jock, so that I nearly bruised myself against his clenched thighs. It had to mean something that he was so strong, I told myself. He would be able to hold me up and direct the forces around my life when my father was gone. I clamped on to that hope and didn't let it go as we stepped out and onto the long run of wooden steps to the hotel, everyone smiling for us, my dress and veil arranged like fondant, our picture taken for the papers and for all time.

One hundred guests were herded into the dining room, which was dressed as finely as the place could muster. The event had flushed out the up-country—the farmers who'd become soldiers, then farmers again. D was there, his hair long and wild under a ribboned helmet. A scabbard swung out from his belt, whacking at the air as he turned and tried to kiss me. He had given us a generous cheque and let me know, a little sentimentally, that if I ever needed him I had only to call out and he'd be there. His promise touched me and made me feel a little steadier as I carried myself from guest to guest, holding the yards of silk ninon in my hands so I could walk without tripping.

Under buttery gravy, there was the ubiquitous tommie steak with buttons of potatoes and pearled onions. My father was paying through the nose for the champagne, so I drank as much as I could, every time it came round. When I danced later, my feet were slightly numb and tingled as I backed across the parquet, led by D and every farmer who could scoot away from his wife. Finally I reached my father. He looked dashing that night, but also sad. There were long lines around his mouth, and his eyes seemed tired and far away.

"Are you happy?" he asked.

I nodded into his shoulder and squeezed him more tightly.

In the wee hours, Lavender chauffeured us again, this time to the Muthaiga Country Club, to a square room lit with a single crystal lamp. A broad bed swam with chenille.

Jock and I didn't know each other. I felt that now, seeing the dense shape he made in the room and wondering, in a dizzy way, how it would be when we lay down. I was drunk and glad for that when Jock's hands tugged at my buttons. His tongue flicked around the inside of my mouth, both sour from the wine. I tried to match him, to be good at it—to catch up with what was happening. His mouth was hot on my neck. His hands dropped to push here and there along my body. We fell to the bed, and there was an absurd moment when he tried to squeeze between my legs, my long narrow skirt resisting him, and me trying to help. I laughed and realized instantly that was the wrong thing.

What did I know about sex? Nothing except what I saw in our paddocks or had heard from Kibii about the games young Kip boys and girls played in the dark. I'd no idea what to do or how to arrange myself to be taken—but I did know that something meaningful had changed. Jock had been hard—I'd felt the stiff knot of his groin against my leg and hip—but that was gone now. Before I knew what was happening, he rolled off me and onto his back, his arm coming up to shield his eyes as if there were a glaring lamp in the room instead of shadows.

"I'm sorry," I finally said.

"No, no. I'm just done in. It's been a long day." He rose on his elbow to give me a smacking kiss on the side of my cheek, and then turned away again to settle his pillow under him, punching it into place.

I studied the lines of his neck and shoulders, my mind whirring. What had I done or not done? Was it that I'd laughed at him—at us? As I lay there feeling stunned and confused, Jock began to snore lightly. How could he sleep at such a moment? It was our wedding night, and I was alone.

I kicked my way out of my dress and then washed my face in the basin, stripping off the paint and the waxy lipstick, being careful not to look in the mirror. I had packed only a flimsy nightgown, something Emma had found in a lace shop, and it was cold against my skin. Back in bed, I stretched out next to Jock's hulking form. He made a solid mountain, seeming to take up even more space now that he was unconscious. He breathed on gutturally, dreaming his unknowable dreams while I lay there in the dark, willing myself to sleep.

The next morning at Nairobi Station we climbed aboard the train that would take us to Mombasa, and then onto the ship that would ferry us to India for our honeymoon.

I was Beryl Purves—and still a virgin.

14

*I*n Bombay the air was full of spices and the crying sitars of street musicians. White bungalows crowded the lanes, with peeling shutters that closed at the hottest part of every day and then opened again at night when the sky went red and deep purple. We stayed with Jock's aunt and uncle, in their compound below the posh Malabar Hill. Jock's parents and two of his three brothers were there, having come to see if I was up to snuff. I wanted to have a long look at them all, too—the new family I'd won, as if in a lottery.

On the voyage, Jock had told me how his family had moved to India from Edinburgh when he was a boy, but I found it hard to remember details of landholdings and business mergers when I stood and looked at them—a band of ruddy, high-boned Scots in a silky brown Indian sea. Jock's mother was the pinkest of all, like a flamingo in bright silk. She wore her auburn hair in a high coil that was being quietly taken over by strands of pure white. Jock's father, Dr. William, was a version of Jock, with strong-looking hands and bright blue eyes that winked at me, trying to put me at ease, as his wife asked a string of questions that weren't really questions.

"You're very tall, aren't you?" she kept saying. "Unnaturally so, don't you think, Will?"

"I don't think I'd go so far as to say un*natural,* darling. . . ." His brogue tipped the ends of his sentences up expectantly. I always thought he was about to say something more, but then he didn't.

Jock patted my knee nervously. "It means she's healthy, Mother."

"Well, she's got plenty of sun, hasn't she?"

Later, when Jock and I were alone in our room dressing for dinner, I studied myself in the full-length looking glass. I wasn't used to frocks and stockings, or the strapped high-heeled shoes that were the fashion then. My stocking seams wouldn't line up straight. My new underthings, bought in Nairobi with Emma's instructions, pinched at my waist and under my arms. I felt like an impostor.

"Don't fret," Jock said. He sat on the bed, tightening the elastic on his braces. "You look fine."

I reached behind me to adjust the stockings again. "Your mother doesn't like me."

"She just doesn't want to lose me. That's how mothers are." He'd spoken the words so lightly, but they stung. What would I know about it?

"She looks down her nose at me," I said.

"Don't be silly. You're my wife." He got up and came to take my hands, giving them a strong, reassuring squeeze—but as soon as he let go, his words clattered to the floor. I didn't feel old enough to be anyone's wife, or that I knew enough or had lived enough, or understood the essential things. I didn't know how to say any of this to Jock, either. That I was afraid of the promises we'd made. That late at night as I lay beside him in bed I felt lonely and numb, as if some part of me had died.

"Please kiss me," I said, and he did, and though I leaned against him and tried to meet the kiss and to take it in, I couldn't quite feel it. I couldn't feel *us.*

———

I had never spent so much time by the sea, and hated the way the air thickened with salt and sat on my skin and made me always long for a bath. I was far more comfortable with dust. Here, moisture puddled on everything and seeped into the walls, swelling the windows shut. Black spores of mould grew on the walls of the houses, ageing them like a skin.

"It seems wrong," I said to Jock. "Bombay is drowning, when at home we'd kill for even a little of it."

"It's not as if India has stolen Njoro's rain. And we are here. Try to enjoy it."

Jock seemed to like playing the role of tour guide at first, proudly showing me the bright bazaars smelling of curry and onion chutneys; turbanned, swaying sitar players; the polo fields and the Turf Club, which was so rich and manicured its gleaming grass put ours in Nairobi to shame. I held his hand and listened, wanting to forget all about the trouble at home. We were newlyweds, after all—but when evening came things fell apart. We'd been married for several weeks now, and I could count on one hand the number of times we'd actually had sex. The first had been on the voyage to India. I'd been seasick for much of it, particularly when we launched away from land at the Gulf of Aden and headed out into the Arabian Sea. The horizon stretched and pitched, when I could stand to look at it.

Before the nausea set in, we had managed to make love on my narrow bunk, but the whole thing was such a tangle of elbows and knees and bumping chins, I barely knew the thing was happening before it was over. Afterwards, he kissed my cheek and said, "That was lovely, sweetheart." Then he crawled out of my bunk and into his, while I was left feeling just as lost and confused as I had been on our wedding night.

Jock's drinking didn't help matters. At four o'clock every afternoon when we were in Bombay, we met the rest of the family on the veranda for cocktails. There was a ritual to it, I learned very quickly, every feature played out to the letter, how much ice went in, how much lime, the air filling with a tangy zest that I felt at the back of my throat. Jock's uncle Ogden was pink faced, and always at the gin before anyone but Jock, settling in his chair under the jacaranda tree and dark, forever-noisy jackdaws.

"These birds have become our personal housekeepers in India," Ogden explained with a strange note of pride, gesturing to a flock in the courtyard. "If not for them, the streets would be overrun with rubbish."

I watched one delicately pluck at the carcass of a mouse, then peck at a hillock of pale-pink sand. "What's he doing?" I asked.

"Cleaning his gullet," Ogden explained. "A bit like rinsing your mouth after dinner."

I studied the bird, and then two others swooping in to fight over a smear of crushed mango on the stones, pecking with sharp beaks at each other's throats, ready to fight to the death. Somehow they made me sad and long for home more than I already did. Too much was new about India, and the days had no anchor. Jock might have fallen for the bold girl I was when I was fourteen, but he didn't really know me any more than I knew him. We were strangers, and also together nearly all the time. I kept telling myself it would be easier when we were at home on our own farm, with work to do. It had to be.

One night at the Purveses', the table was set with a feast that hardened and grew cold because Jock's mother had tipped back so much gin she'd forgotten the cook had called us in long before. She listed in the darkening courtyard and finally leaned into a potted palm and closed her eyes. No one else seemed to notice or care.

"Let's go up to bed," I said to Jock.

"What?" He tried to fix his bloodshot eyes on my face, lip-reading.

"I'm exhausted," I said.

"I'll be right behind you."

I walked past the dining room with a table full of thickened and filmed-over curries, the servants too afraid to clear them away. In the bathroom, I climbed into the soaking tub lined with painted tiles. One was of a tiger, though age had faded his stripes to a tired beige. Somewhere in India, real tigers roamed, hungry and roaring as

Paddy had once roared. It was an awful thought, but in a way, I knew I would rather be wherever the tigers were, or even back in the muddy pig hole I'd spent several nights in the time I'd run away from school. At least then I had known what I was up against. I lowered myself into the stinging water and waited there for Jock until it ran cold, then filled it again. Finally I went to bed and curled up on the apricot silk sheets, shaking a little.

Dear Dos, I wrote on a picture postcard the next day, *Bombay is beautiful and glamorous. We've been to the Turf Club nearly every day where Jock and the other members are showing me how polo is really done. You should see it all one day.*

I looked at the words I'd written, knowing I ought to be telling her, or someone, how miserable I felt, but didn't know where to begin. And what would it change anyway? I chewed on my pen, thinking of what I might add. Finally, I signed my new married name and left the card to be posted.

15

*W*e were nearly four months in Bombay, and when we returned, British East Africa didn't exist any more. The details of the armistice had finally been settled, and the protectorate dissolved. We were Kenya now, after our tallest mountain—a proper colony, with the graveyards to prove it. Africans and white settlers had died in the tens of thousands during wartime. Drought had stolen thousands more, and so had the Spanish flu. Disease tore through towns and villages taking the thinnest and smallest, children and young men, and new wives like me. Demobilized farmers and herdsmen came home in despair, not knowing how they might begin again.

I felt much the same way. At Green Hills, I expected to find my father and Emma packed and on the verge of departure. That had been part of my plan—to spend the worst of the dismantlement in Bombay—but the farm hadn't even been sold yet. My father hadn't made a move.

"I'm going to eke things out here as long as possible," he tried to explain. "If I can win a few more races, I might draw better buyers."

"Oh," I said, while inside my chest, everything shifted and slid. I had run headlong into marrying Jock, believing there wasn't any other way—but now it was clear I would have had another full year to think it all through. A year to stay at home and ease into the idea, getting to know Jock better, or perhaps—just perhaps—for some other thing or choice to show itself. I felt ill even thinking about it. Why hadn't I waited?

"You and Jock want to come for dinner?" my father asked lightly, but this too seemed like a slap. I would never be more than an invited guest now. My home was elsewhere.

The next few months were among the hardest of my life. Jock's farm had nearly the same views as Green Hills, and the same feel to the air—but I couldn't quite convince myself I belonged there.

The sun went down early in our valley—never a moment after 6:00 p.m.—and by the time it set, every night, no matter what else was happening, Jock had washed and was inside at our bar cart, doctoring a whisky. When we were still in Bombay, I told myself his drinking was a family affair that belonged to those nights, like the jackdaws and the tang of tamarind, but once we were home Jock kept up the same pace on his own. After dinner was cleared away, he'd smoke and pour a second. There was something tender and almost loving in the way he cradled the glass, as if it were his oldest friend, the thing that would always get him through—but through what exactly?

I rarely knew what Jock was thinking. He worked hard, as hard as my father ever had, but the greater part of him was turned in on himself, as if there were a fixed screen just behind his eyes and no way to get through it. My father hadn't exactly been emotional. It was possible that all men were difficult to read, but I had to live with Jock through every long evening, and the silence was often deadly. And if I tried to talk to him or, God forbid, ask him to take it easy on the whisky, he'd lash out.

"Oh, sod off, Beryl. It's all easy for you, isn't it?"

"What is?"

But he waved me off, turning away.

"If there are pressures ...," I said quietly, guessing my way towards him.

"What would you know about it?"

"I wouldn't. I don't." I waited for him to fill in the gaps, but he didn't seem to know how. I certainly didn't, either. I kept wishing Lady D were still here to give me encouragement or advice—or even Dos elbowing me in the ribs and saying, *Go on then, you have to talk to him. Try harder.* Left to my own devices, I'd poke the fire or find a book, or turn to the training ledger, going over the next day's lists. I buried my head in work and tried not to give my doubts any air—as if that would silence them. But it wasn't just Jock I doubted. There was furniture all around us. There were accounts to keep and meals to prepare, and beds to make and kisses to be had. *This is marriage,* I kept telling myself. People everywhere did this every day. Why, then, did it feel so strange and wrong for me?

Some nights I would try to close the distance and make love to Jock. In our room under the mosquito netting, I would slip my leg over his broad hip and search out his mouth in the dark. His tongue was warm and limp, whisky flavoured. I pushed on anyway, manoeuvring my way deeper into the kiss, straddling his waist while he kept his eyes closed. I kissed them and pushed up his cotton shirt with my hands, moving lower, my lips brushing the thick hair on his chest, circling his navel. I breathed along his belly, and he released a small groan. His skin was salty and warm, and he was responding to my kisses a little at a time. I hovered over the top of him, cupping him gently with my hand, and then, hardly daring to breathe, lowered myself onto him. But it was too late. Before I had even begun to move, he softened inside me. I tried to kiss him, but he wouldn't meet my eyes. Finally, I pulled down my nightgown and lay beside him, humiliated. He must have been humiliated, too, but he wouldn't let me in.

"I'm sorry I'm no good, Beryl," he said. "I've just got too much on my mind."

"What? Tell me."

"You wouldn't understand."

"Please, Jock. I really do want to know."

"Running this place is a huge burden, you realize. If we fail, it will be my fault." He let loose a sigh. "I'm trying my damnedest."

"I am, too."

"Well then, that's all we can do, isn't it?" He kissed me chastely with dry lips. "Good night, sweetheart."

"Good night."

I tried to fall asleep then, but as he breathed deeply, already off in a separate world, I was filled with a childish longing for my bed at Green Hills. I wanted to be in my old hut with the paraffin-box furniture and the shadows I knew by heart. I wanted time to reverse and leave me in a place I recognized. I wanted to go home.

"I wish I knew what to do about Jock," I told Dos in town a few months later. She was busy with school and harried, but I'd coaxed her into meeting me at the Norfolk for tea and sandwiches. "I thought sex would be the easy part."

"I wouldn't know anything about it. There aren't any boys at Miss Seccombe's. The ones I meet at dances push and prod, but it doesn't really go anywhere."

"Nothing does with us, either; that's what I mean. And we never talk about it. I feel so in the dark about everything."

"Does he not like to do it then?"

"How should I know?" I watched Dos divide the crusts of her sandwich away from the good bits—pale butter and chopped ham—thinking how lucky she was to have only exams to worry about. "Don't you sometimes wish we were still thirteen?"

"God, no." She pulled a face. "You don't, either."

"It was so much simpler, though." I sighed. "Jock has lived twice as long as I have, and he's fought in a war. He should know things and take charge, shouldn't he?" I sighed again, feeling exasperated. "It's what men *do*."

"I'm hardly an expert." She shrugged. "And I don't really know Jock."

"Come stay with us for a while," I urged. "I need someone on my side, and it could be fun, too. Like the old days."

"I've got exams, remember? And when they're done, I'm off to Dublin to stay with my mum's family for a year. I've told you all about it."

"But you *can't* go away. You're my only friend."

"Oh, Burl. Maybe things aren't as bad as they seem." But she didn't get any further. I surprised us both by bursting into tears.

Over the months that followed, though I wasn't involved any more, I watched my father win the Naval and Military Cup, the War Memorial Cup, the Myberg-Hiddell, and the prestigious East African Standard Gold—and yet very few good buyers came sniffing around. News had already begun to leak out that Green Hills had gone belly-up. It didn't seem to matter that my father had been a pioneer in the colony, with a gold-flocked reputation; the same newspapers that had once touted his victories were full of gossip about the bankruptcy. Several editors speculated about the causes, and the *Nairobi Leader* even published a jeering little poem:

They speak of a trainer named Clutterbuck
Who enjoyed the most absolute an' utter luck,
Now he's turning his tables,
And selling his stables,
In fact he is putting his shutter up.

My father seemed to take it on the chin or pretended to, but I was mortified to see our failings at Green Hills so publicly exposed. I wanted everyone to remember what was marvellous about our farm, how it had been built up from nothing at all, how happy we'd been there. But after sixteen years of impossibly hard work and high standards, now all anyone wanted to talk about was its failure. Green Hills had become a dark joke, and my father a cautionary tale, someone to pity.

The auction process dragged on for several gruelling months. Buyers came, haggling over the price of wheelbarrows and pitchforks and riding tack. Like a puzzle box emptied out on the floor and picked over by strangers, the outbuildings were dismantled piece by piece and stick by stick—the groom's cottage, the stables, and the house. The horses were sold off at alarming bargain prices that made my stomach twist—all but sixteen that Jock and I were to hold on to until the right price could be fetched, and Pegasus, of course.

"You can't let Cam go for less than five hundred pounds," my father reminded me the day he left. I had travelled as far as Nairobi to see him off. At the railway station, livestock was being loaded and unloaded with commotion and clouds of red dust. *Totos* dragged or carried trunks and boxes twice their size. One wrestled with a swooping yellowed ivory tusk as if he were dancing with it, while Emma fussed with her hat.

After years of pelting me with advice and restrictions, Emma had nothing left to say now. Nor did I. I could barely remember why I had fought her so much. She seemed just as lost as I was. Squeezing my hand once, she hurried up the three sooty steps to the carriage, and that was that.

"Let us know if you need anything," my father said. His hands worked over the brim of his hat, turning and turning it.

"Don't worry. I'll be fine," I said, though I wasn't at all sure that was true.

"One day you might want to train for other owners, maybe even for Delamere. You've got the right base and you've the instincts."

"Get my trainer's licence, you mean? Has a woman done that?"

"Maybe not. But there aren't any rules against it."

"I could try. . . ." I let the words trail away.

"Take care of yourself and work hard."

"I will, Daddy."

Neither one of us had ever been good at voicing our feelings. I told him I would miss him, and then watched him board his train, the back of his shoulders defiantly straight under his jacket. His departure had been months and months in coming, and still I wasn't nearly ready. Did he know how much I loved him? How sick and raw I felt to have lost all we'd shared?

A red-jacketed porter hurried by me with a heavy steamer trunk, and I felt a rushing up of memory. At four, I had stared at the shrinking train that carried my mother away, black smoke rising, distance between us stretching by the moment. Lakwet had learned how to bear her loss—how to live in the world her leaving had changed, and find good things, and run hard, and grow stronger. Where was that fierce girl now? I didn't feel any whisper of her stirring in me. I also had no way of knowing how much I was yet supposed to weather—when my father might return, or even *if* he would.

The soot-black engine groaned in readiness. A sharp whistle pealed, and my heart turned over sickeningly. Finally, I had no choice but to walk away.

Almost as soon as I arrived back at Njoro, it began to rain for the first time in over a year. The sky went black, splitting open with a deluge that didn't want to stop. Five inches fell in two days, and when the storm had finally cleared, and our long drought had ended, the land went green again. Flowers sprang across the plains in every colour you could think of. The air was thick with jasmine and coffee blossoms, juniper berries, and eucalyptus. Kenya had only been sleeping, the rain said now. All that had died could live again—except Green Hills.

16

In all my years of living in the bush, I had never caught malaria or any other of the terrible fevers or plagues. Now I was felled by something just as serious though more difficult to name—an illness of the spirit. I didn't want to sleep or eat, and nothing made me happy. Nothing made sense. Jock, meanwhile, bustled around me, full of plans for our farm and for us. He had bought up my father's gristmill, one of the last things to go at auction, and had got it for a song. Though he seemed delighted by the deal, I could barely stand to think that we were profiting from my father's failure; that our holdings were being built on the bones of Green Hills.

All I could do was turn my attention to the horses. I found a black ledger exactly like the one my father had used and began to mark down everything that happened in the stables every day—the exercise sessions and feeding schedules, the wages of the grooms and equipment to be ordered. I set up a small office in one corner of the stable the way my father had done—just a tiny desk and a lamp and a calendar on the wall with the date of the next race meeting circled boldly. Each day I rose before dawn to be at morning gallops—but it wasn't enough. More and more a bell tolled through me. It woke me up early and sometimes in the still middle of the night, sending a cold chill up over the surface of my skin. *What have I done? Can I still mend this? Can I free myself?*

Most days, Jock and I were at cross-purposes. The harder I worked, the more he behaved as if I were taking something away from him. He had assumed I would only want what he wanted, I imagined, that I would be happy to throw myself at his aims instead of my own. Sometimes, after he'd had a few too many, I would hear the phonograph start up, and the first lilting bars of "If You Were the Only Girl in the World." Jock had bought the record not long after we were married, saying he wanted a keepsake of our first dance. I had thought the gesture sweet, but when he played it now it was to drive home the fact that I wasn't the girl he thought he'd married. I wasn't, of course, and I didn't know what to do about it either.

Pulling on my robe, I went out into the main room, where he was deep into his cups, humming along with the words, sharply off tune.

A Garden of Eden just made for two
With nothing to mar our joy
I would say such wonderful things to you
There would be such wonderful things to do

"You're going to feel like hell in the morning. Turn that off and come to bed."

"Don't you love me, Beryl?"

"Of course," I said quickly, woodenly. The truth was that when I measured Jock against my father or *arap* Maina, the men I admired most, he came up disastrously short. But not everything was his fault. Somehow I had thought I could marry a perfect stranger and have it all magically work out. Like the house we lived in, my promises to him had gone up far too fast to be sound. I had lunged at a choice, and it had been the wrong one. "Have some coffee or come to bed."

"You don't even try to deny it." The song finished and the recording hissed. "You care more about that dog," he said, and got up to move the needle back to the beginning.

Almost overnight, Buller had become ancient and arthritic. He was blind as well as deaf and moved as if he were made entirely of brittle glass. My father would have shot him and been right to do it. I couldn't, and waited with him instead, sometimes lowering my face to rest just above his gnarled head and telling him things he couldn't hear, about how brave he'd been and still was.

"He's *dying*," I said to Jock, my voice beginning to break. But even at the edge of death, Buller was showing more courage than I was. For most of a year I had been hiding behind my hasty decision, trying not to think about the future or the past. Both were here in the room with us, and the terrible bell was beginning to toll again. I knew it wouldn't be silent until I thrashed my way out of the mess I had made, no matter how awful that was. There was no other way.

"I want to go and work for Delamere," I said quickly, before I could change my mind or take it back. "I can learn to train there. My father suggested it before he left and I think it's a sound move."

"What? We have our own animals. Why go somewhere else?"

"It isn't just the work, Jock. *Nothing's* right between us. You know it as well as I do."

"We're just beginning. Give it time."

"Time won't do a thing. You should have a proper wife, one who wants to care for you and have a dozen children and all of it. That's not me."

He turned with the drink in his hand, and I could see the hard edge inside him, its silhouette as clear and sharp as if he were his own faraway mountain. I had caught him off guard. "You *don't* love me, then." He said it coldly and cleanly.

"We don't really even *know* each other. Do we?"

His lips pressed hard together, flat and white, before he spoke. "I've never given up on anything in my life. It's not how I do things. How would it look?"

"How would it look? *Honest,* for one thing. Isn't it better to own up to things?"

He shook his head almost imperceptibly, small quick movements. "I'd be a laughing stock in town . . . made a fool of by a girl. My family would be horrified. Humiliated. We actually have a name to protect, you know."

This was an obvious dig against my father and the bankruptcy scandal, but I couldn't let it stop me from plunging ahead. "Blame it all on me then. I don't care. I don't have anything left to lose."

"I'm not sure that's true."

When he stormed off to bed that night, I still didn't know where we stood. I slept in front of the hearth, tossing back and forth, feeling alternately too cold and too hot. I thought we would have it out in the morning, but the row lasted for three days. Whatever he was sorting out, it seemed to have less to do with losing me than with the sullying of his reputation, and how the colony might perceive his failings. I understood that. He had married me because it was time to marry, and that was all. His family had expected it of him, to complete the picture of a settled and prosperous life. He certainly wouldn't let them down now. He was too proud and had always managed to take control of any wayward detail in his life—deep-rooted tree stumps in the field, boulders where a garden should go. He came at every obstacle with muscle and gumption, but he couldn't simply strong-arm me. Or could he?

On the third evening, Jock finally sat down across from me, his eyes flat as chips of flint. "This isn't something you can bury in the sand and forget about, Beryl. Go and work for Delamere if that's what you're going to do, but you'll go as my wife."

"We'll be pretending then? For how long?"

He shrugged. "Don't forget you need me, too. Your father's horses are half mine now, and you can't care for them on a pauper's salary."

"You'll hold my horses ransom? For God's sake, Jock, you know how much they mean to me."

"Then don't test me. I don't want to look like a damned fool, and you can't afford to buy me out." His voice was like a stranger's, but it was possible we'd never stopped being strangers, both of us. Either way, I doubted if I would ever be able to reach him again. "You've been making such a stink about honesty," he went on. "Is this honest enough for you?"

17

*W*hen I rode away from Jock's farm a week later, I took nothing that I couldn't tie onto the back of my saddle—pyjamas, a toothbrush and comb, a second pair of slacks, a man's shirt in heavy cotton. For Pegasus I carried a thick rug and brush, several pounds of crushed oats, and a small, tarnished blacksmith's knife. It felt wonderful to be riding out in the bush and travelling so lightly, but I was also leaving much unsettled behind me. It was a devil's bargain I had struck with Jock. He owned my freedom, and the only way I could wrest it from him was by getting the licence. That came first, and then hard work and a chance, just a chance, at winning. Everything would have to fall into place perfectly—a terrifying thought—for me to ever be fully independent. I would have to hope for that, and give it every-thing I had.

Soysambu lay at the edge of the Rift's great undulating fold, in one of the narrower regions of the highlands, between Elmenteita and Lake Nakuru, where Delamere's stock had ten thousand acres to graze in relative comfort and safety. D had turned to sheep mostly—Masai ewes with deep brown coats so heavy and knotted they were almost unrecognizable as sheep. At Equator Ranch a decade before, his debut lambing had turned out only six surviving animals of four thousand ewes. Undaunted, he had burned through more of his inheritance (eighty thousand pounds, some claimed), replaced his stock, learned his hard lessons, and was now the most successful large-scale rancher in all of Kenya.

Not everyone admired him. In town or at the track, many people gave D a wide berth, trying to avoid an argument or a lecture about "the Indian problem." He was louder than anyone about how we needed to sever our ties with that country once and for all. He was also land greedy and full of bluster, and impossible to argue with—but Lady D had always seen what was good in him, and I did, too. He worked harder than anyone I knew—twelve or sixteen hours a day, out with his herd along the rolling hills. He was passionate and indomitable, and in the time I'd known him—my whole life, really—he'd only ever been kind to me.

"Beryl, dear," he barked when I arrived. He had broken down his rifle and was polishing the butt with tender precision. His long hair was a thicket. "So you want to be a trainer like Clutt, do you? I can't imagine it will be an easy life."

"I'm not after an easy life."

"Maybe not." He looked at me plainly. "But I've never seen anyone near as young as you with a proper English trainer's licence. And I expect I don't have to tell you you'll be the only woman."

"Somebody has to be the first at everything."

"You wouldn't be running away from Jock, would you?" His eyes had softened. I found I had trouble meeting them. "I was married for a very long time, you remember. I know how tricky things can get."

"Don't worry about me. All I need is a clear job to do. I don't want any special treatment either. I'll bunk in the stables like everyone else."

"All right, all right. I won't pry and I won't coddle you, but if you ever do need anything I hope you know you can come to me."

I nodded.

"I can be a sentimental old bastard, can't I? C'mon, let's get you settled."

D showed me to a small wooden cottage beyond the far paddock. Inside, there was a camp bed and a scarred wide-planked floor, and a single hurricane lamp hanging on a wall peg. The room wasn't much bigger than the stall Pegasus was sleeping in, and it was cold, too. He told me the terms of my stay—*indenture* was more like it—and where and to whom I'd report the next day.

"You said no special treatment," he said, eyeing me as if he expected me to turn and run on the spot.

"I'll be fine," I promised him, then said good night. After he left, I built a small fire, boiled bitter coffee, and then ate tinned meat, cold, with the tip of my knife. Finally I curled up in the narrow bed, chilly and still a little hungry. I looked up into the shadows on the ceiling and thought about my father. He had written me only a few sparse letters since he'd moved to Cape Town, barely enough words to fill a teaspoon, let alone the yawning gap he'd left in my life. I missed him awfully, like someone who'd died—and yet just now, in my cold cot, I felt strangely close to him. It was *his* life I was reaching for in coming here, and if I couldn't have my father back, exactly, maybe not ever, I could have the rightness of looking in the same direction, of stepping into his shadow with my own. I didn't know a thing about marriage or men—that had been proven well enough. But I did know horses. For the first time in a long time, I was exactly where I should be.

18

$\mathcal{B}$it burrs. Tongue-tying. Saddling for exercise and saddling for races. There was shoeing and bandaging, conditioning and equipment. I had to learn to read track surfaces and stakes sheets, and calculate weight allowances. I had to know the diseases and ailments forward and back—bowed tendons and splints, foundering, bucked shins, bone chips, slab fractures, and quarter cracks. Thoroughbreds were glorious and also fragile in very specific ways. They often had small hearts, and the exertion of racing also made them susceptible to haemorrhaging in the lungs. Undetected colic could kill them—and if it did, that death would be on me.

There were things to look for in the conformation of the animal, the head, the legs, the chest, and many other things you couldn't see, which were even more important. Each animal was its own written-out book or a map to study and then memorize, decisions made accordingly. To really know everything that went into this life would take for ever, and maybe not even then. The sheer scale and impossibility of that lent purity to my days at Soysambu. I walked from my cottage to the paddock, to the stables, to the track, and back to my cottage to read charts and tables until my eyes gave out.

In exchange for Pegasus's stall and my own bunk, D gave me two horses to train. They were both past their prime, dull eyed and recalcitrant, but I was trying to prove myself. I would have to treat them like royalty. I laboured over their exercise and feeding schedules, filling notebooks, trying to meet them on their own territory, and to find or understand something untapped in them, something no one had yet seen.

Dynasty, a six-year-old mare, had a case of girth gall—tender blisters and raw chafed skin along her belly—that needed special care. Her groom had tried every kind of tack on her, but the sores never completely healed. He seemed embarrassed about this.

"You're cleaning the tack well," I told him. "I can see that . . . and it's not too stiff. You've taken good care of her."

"Yes, memsahib. Thank you."

I crouched to get a better sense of the sores—some well scabbed over and some fresh—and then stood to have a good look at all of her.

"It might just be the way she's made," I told the groom, pointing. "See how her shoulders are tight and square. She doesn't have much breathing room here, behind the elbows, so the girth squeezes close. Don't put any tack on her for at least a week—no riding at all—just a lunge line for exercising. You also might try some of this." I reached for a small vial in my pocket, a mixture of oils my father and I had always used with our horses, and which I had been tinkering with on my own, trying to perfect it. "To condition the skin."

When I turned to leave the groom to his work, I saw that D's ranch manager had been watching us. His name was Boy Long, and he was exotic-looking for these parts, with jet-black hair and a single gold hoop in one ear. His particular flair made me think of a pirate. "What's in the tincture?" he wanted to know.

"Nothing unusual."

He looked me up and down. "I don't believe you, but you can keep your secret."

A few days later I was standing along the paddock fence watching the groom lunge Dynasty when Boy came along. Already the mare had begun to heal, and her coat shone. Though Boy only leaned beside me for a while, watching and saying nothing, I felt his attention on me as much as on the horse.

"I thought D was crazy when he told me he'd hired a girl," he finally said.

I shrugged, not taking my eyes off Dynasty. She was moving well, not at all tenderly. "I've been doing this all my life, Mr. Long."

"I can see that. I like to be proved wrong every now and again. It keeps me on my toes."

Boy was good at his job, I soon learned. He oversaw the workers on both sides of D's operation, the horses and the sheep, and seemed always to know what was going on, and even what was about to happen. One night I awoke to a commotion outside my cottage and the smell of fire. I dressed quickly and stepped out to find that a lion had been spotted in the paddock.

The night was cold and I felt it gripping around my heart as I thought of a lion slinking full-shouldered and tawny through the compound, past my thin door. "What was taken?" I asked Boy. He stood surrounded by grooms holding torches and hurricane lamps. An oiled rifle was cocked open over his arm.

"Nothing. I got there in time."

"Thank God. You were awake, then?"

He nodded. "I had a feeling I should be. Do you ever get that sense?"

"Sometimes." I'd felt nothing tonight. I'd been sleeping like a baby. "Did you hit him?"

"No, but I'll have one of the grooms sit up to make sure he doesn't come back."

I returned to my cottage and tried for sleep again, but a nervous feeling had lodged itself in my shoulders and my neck, and my mind wouldn't quiet. Finally I gave up and walked to the stable to find a bottle we kept on hand in the office. Boy was there, having already found it himself. He poured for me and I thanked him, and said goodnight.

"Why not stay?" he asked. "We can keep each other company." His words were offhand, but his look made it clear what he meant.

"What would my husband think about that?" I asked him. I didn't want any of the men on the ranch to get the idea that I was available, particularly not this one, with his glinting earring and his bold eyes.

Boy only shrugged. "If you were really worried about your husband, you'd be at home, wouldn't you?"

"I'm here to work." But that didn't satisfy him. His dark pupils stayed fixed on mine in a disbelieving way until I said, "The situation isn't simple."

"It rarely is. I have someone, too, you know. Back in Dorking. She isn't built for the heat."

"Doesn't she miss you?"

"I don't know," he said. In two smooth moves he'd set down his glass and crossed the distance between us. He reached to either side of me, his hands cupping the wall, and leaned nearer until I could smell rye whisky and smoke, his face inches from mine.

"This isn't a good idea."

"Nights can get pretty long here." He bent his mouth to my neck, but I flinched away, my shoulders unyielding. "All right," he finally said, "I get the picture." Then he smiled at me lazily and let me slip out of his arms.

When I went back to my cottage and lay down, closing my eyes, the lion wasn't on my mind any more. I'd never met anyone as direct as Boy. It was unsettling and also a little thrilling to imagine wanting and being wanted so simply, without any claims of love or strings of collapsing promises. Men were a puzzle to me, even after a year of marriage. I knew nothing about love, let alone being anyone's lover— but for now even a kiss from Boy was a dangerous idea.

———

Though Kenya was vast, there was surprisingly little privacy in our colony. Everyone seemed to know everyone else's business, particularly when it was personal. I'd always been able to steer clear of all of that, being too young and inexperienced for anyone's serious notice, but now I'd married a notable landowner and was meant to behave accordingly. And so it was that every few weeks, on a Saturday morning, I went home to Njoro to be a wife.

D taught me to drive and lent me the ramshackle wagon he used to haul cargo back and forth from the toolsheds and dip sheds. I preferred the view from horseback, but I learned to like and even crave the speed of the auto, and how it felt a little dangerous whipping along the narrow dirt road, whanging over deep potholes, my teeth rattling, dust in my hair. There were mud bogs to watch out for, and places where I knew if anything happened to strand me I could be in real trouble, but it was also exhilarating—especially in the first dozen or so miles. The nearer I grew to Njoro, though, the more strongly I felt Jock's hold on me. I didn't belong to myself. I hadn't since I decided to say yes to his proposal, but now the reality of that sank in more deeply and seemed to stretch larger as I struggled with it, like a bog or a patch of quicksand. Njoro had always been my home, the place I loved best. Now the effort it took to spend even a few civil days a month in the same house as Jock, for the benefit of neighbouring farmers and anyone else who might be watching, was ruining it for me.

When I pulled up in D's wagon, I nearly always got a chaste kiss on the cheek. We'd have a drink on the veranda and discuss what had happened on the farm while I was away, the servants milling around us, always happy to see me home. But as soon as night fell and we were alone, the mood turned chilly fast. Jock never tried to touch me sexually—that had never worked for us anyway, not even in the beginning. But every question he asked about my work at D's and my plans felt proprietary.

"Is D looking out for you?" he wanted to know. "Making sure you don't get into trouble?"

"What do you mean?"

"You always had your own rules about things. Like that boy you ran around with when I first met you."

"Kibii?"

"That's right." He tipped his cocktail glass back and pulled the whisky along the rim through his teeth. "You were always a bit of a savage here, weren't you?"

"I can't think what you're implying. And anyway, you seemed to admire my hunting with Kibii when we first met. Now I'm a savage?"

"I'm only saying that what you do reflects on me. The way you were brought up out here, running around with God knows who doing God knows what . . . and now you're off at D's, a woman alone surrounded by men. It smacks of trouble."

"I'm *working,* not taking dozens of lovers."

"I'd hear of it in an instant if you were," he said flatly. His eyes flicked away and returned. "You've already put me in quite a position."

"I've put *you* in a position? Just give me the damned divorce and let's have done with it."

Before he could answer there was a rustling just inside the house, and our houseboy, Barasa, came onto the veranda, ducking his head to show us he'd not meant to disturb us. "Does bwana want the evening meal served here?"

"No, in the house, Barasa. We'll be in directly."

When the boy had gone, Jock looked at me pointedly.

"What?" I asked. "The servants won't tell tales."

"No," he said. "Usually not. But they always know the score, don't they?"

"I don't *care* what anyone knows."

"Maybe not, but you should."

We ate our meal in strained silence, all of the furniture seeming to lean heavily in from the walls. The servants were very quiet as they came and went, and it was awful to sit there, wanting to scream but saying nothing. Jock was terrified I was going to embarrass him—or embarrass him further. That was all he seemed to think of now as he flexed and cautioned me, running thick strands of wire around the charade of our life together. He'd always been good at fences. I had known that from the beginning, but I hadn't guessed how desperate I could feel bound up inside one.

When I could finally excuse myself to the small guest bedroom where I was sleeping, I felt chapped and raw and prodded at. I barely slept at all that night, and the next morning, though I generally stayed for lunch, I bolted for the wagon at first light.

Back at Soysambu, Jock's warnings and expectations continued to wear on me, but only in weak moments, when I let myself think of him. Most of the time I could wrestle my worries about my own life clear away to focus on my horses and each day's training schedule. I tethered myself to morning gallops and feed lists and details of grooming. Dynasty and Shadow Country, my two charges, were both coming along well, but there was always the chance I could take them further still; bring them even closer to perfect form. Puzzling over their care was how I got to sleep each night, how I turned off my own doubts and fears as simply as blowing out the lamp. The work was what mattered. It alone would get me through.

When the day of my exam finally arrived, D drove me to Nairobi. Over the roar of the engine, we talked about the upcoming race meeting, the Jubaland Cup, weighing the stakes and the possible competition. We didn't speak of the exam itself or the way my nerves had climbed up into my shoulders and neck, or how I was missing my father something terrible and wishing to God he could be there. We didn't talk about Jock and how I *had* to succeed that day to be free of him. There wasn't room for a whisper of remorse or self-doubt, and so even when I turned up for the test and saw the proctor's small, dismissive eyes, I didn't falter. He was the marshal of the Royal Kenyan Race Association, and his office was hot and airless. As he glowered at me from behind his broad desk, I could guess what he was thinking. Women weren't trainers, not in Kenya or anywhere else. I wasn't yet nineteen years old, either. But I had learned to thrive when others assumed little or nothing of me—like when Kibii or the other *totos* in the Kip village looked down their noses, goading me to stretch for more. I was still a child to the marshal, no doubt, as well as female—but if he assumed I'd fall short, that was enough to quiet the last of my worries and make me jump higher, try harder, and prove him wrong.

When my exam results arrived several weeks later, I took the simple envelope off where I could be alone with it, my heart gunning, and broke the seal. Inside, instead of a dreadful notice telling me I'd failed, there was an official document, typed and signed. MRS. B. PURVES had been granted an English trainer's licence, good until 1925. I ran my fingertips over my name and the date, the leaping scrawl of the secretary who'd endorsed it and all the corners and creases. Here was a stamp of legitimacy, my ticket to compete in a circle I'd observed for most of my life, straining towards the action from my father's side. If only he could be here now. I longed to hand him the notice and hear even a few measured words about how proud he was of me. And he would be proud. I had rounded a new corner and could finally see a swath of territory I had only been able to dream about and guess at before. But it was a lonely, lopsided feeling—missing him even as I flared with hope, wanting him there fiercely though that was impossible.

That night D had his cook prepare a dinner to celebrate: thick gazelle chops that had been cooked over an open fire, preserved peaches in syrup, and an almond-scented blancmange custard that tasted like clouds. He played his favourite song, "All Aboard for Margate," again and again, refilling my brandy glass until the entire evening seemed to tip pleasantly on one edge.

"You're the best I've seen in a while," D said as he wound up the gramophone for yet another encore. "Pure and natural instinct is what you have."

"Thanks, D."

"Aren't you *pleased,* girl? You're probably the only eighteen-year-old female horse trainer in the world!"

"Of course. But you know I've never been the type to do a jig."

"Then I'll do one for you. The papers will want your name, of course. Everyone will be talking about it."

"If we win, they will. If we don't they'll say it's because Delamere was daft enough to let a green girl run his horses."

"We've got six weeks to worry about that. A bit more, actually." He glanced at the mantel clock. "Tonight, we're going to get stinking."

19

$\mathcal{B}$efore sunrise on the opening day of the Jubaland Cup, I walked out of the Eastleigh stable in Nairobi and past the grandstand. The etched shape of Donyo Sabuk was scored onto the pale morning sky, and the big mountain, Kenya, shimmered silvery blue. Sometimes in the long dry season, the soil hardened into long cracks and gouges under the sod, wide enough to grab hold of a speeding hoof and drag it off-centre, destroying tendons. That wouldn't happen today, though. The turf appeared flat and fast to me. The post had a fresh coat of white paint with two jaunty black stripes, making it look like a buoy fixed and still in a bright emerald sea.

Though the morning was smooth and still, soon thousands would fill the arena and the grandstand. Race days were magnetic things, drawing not just from Nairobi but all the nearby villages—millionaires and scrapers-by, the best-dressed ladies and the simpler ones, too, everyone poring over the racing forms, searching for a sign. There was money to be made on betting, but that had never interested me. Even as a girl, I had only wanted to press into the rail next to my father, far from the noise of the crowd in the stands, the owners in their elite boxes, the betting booths where who knew how much money changed hands. Races weren't supposed to be pageants or cocktail parties. They were tests. Hundreds of hours of training came down to a few breathless moments—and only then would anyone know if the animals were ready, which would rise and which would stumble, how the work and the talent would match up to carry this horse through, while that one would be left wearing dust, the jockey ashamed or surprised or full of excuses.

There was plenty of room for magic in any race, too, for chance and for grit, for tragedy, if an animal went down, for unexpected reversals at the tape. I had always loved all of it—even what couldn't be controlled or predicted. But there was a new urgency now that I was on my own, and so much more was at stake.

Reaching into the pocket of my trousers, I pulled out a telegram my father had wired back from Cape Town when I sent word of my licence. Already the sheet of pale-yellow paper was soft from my fingers, and the letters had begun to fade: WELL DONE STOP ALL FINE HERE STOP WIN SOMETHING FOR ME! All sorts of magic happened on race day. But if I'd had the power to conjure anything, it would be for him to suddenly appear out of the crowd to stand next to me for those thunderous, dizzying minutes. That would mean so much more than winning—more than anything.

A few hours later, when Dynasty danced onto the track, I felt my pulse jump. Her coat gleamed. Her steps were high and springing and confident. She didn't look like the six-year-old mare D had turned over to me months before, but like a queen. All around her, the other contenders were being led or ponied to the starting post. Some had running martingales to curb swinging heads; some were in tendon boots, while others wore blinker hoods to keep them on the straight and narrow. Jockeys soothed or prodded with crops as their horses skittered backwards into the barriers, jumpy and wild eyed, but Dynasty glided right through the chaos as though none of it involved her.

The starter's hand climbed, then went still; the horses struggled in their places at the post, desperate to do what they had come for. The bell sounded, the horses breaking in a hiccup of colour and movement, twelve singular animals blurred and transposed. A clean and bolting start.

A quick bay gelding—the favourite—vaulted out first, the field loose around him, all of them drumming up the turf. The front-runners took the rail, the sounds of their hoofbeats rumbling viscerally. I felt them in my joints, like the drums of childhood *ngomas,* taking my heart for a ride. As the group barrelled down the home straight, I don't think I breathed. Dynasty was there, gunning for the rail, all control and finely tuned muscle. Our jockey, Walters, wasn't pressing or fighting her, just letting her go. She gained rhythm stride by stride, melting through the pack, sailing just above the bright turf. Walters floated, too, the blue-and-gold silks he wore butterfly light over the curves of Dynasty's back.

In the grandstand, the cries of the crowd grew louder and shriller as the field pulsed for the far rail. The animals were like a storm moving whole, and then breaking, every strategy falling away, all caution gone. In the last few furlongs, nothing mattered but legs and length. Dynasty sailed through the final contenders and gained on the favourite, who seemed to stand still for her alone. She ran as if she were flying. As if she were dreaming the win, or winning in someone else's dream. Then her nose was at the tape. The crowd exploded. She'd done it.

I had done it, too. Tears stung the corners of my eyes as I looked around for someone to embrace. A few of the other trainers came over to pump my hand, saying words that would have meant everything to me if they'd come from my father, and then Jock was suddenly at my elbow.

"Congratulations," he said, leaning into my ear. The pressure of his fingertips led me through the bodies around us. "I knew you could win it."

"Did you?"

"Your talent's never been in question, has it?" I tried to ignore him, but he went on. "This will be good for business."

Just like that, the flush of pride and gratitude I'd felt after Dynasty's win winked out of me. He was pouncing on my success. When Dynasty was led into the winner's enclosure and one of the newspapermen asked for my name and a photo, Jock stepped in to spell out *Purves* carefully. His hand stayed on my elbow or the small of my back like an immovable tether, but none of it was about me. He was only thinking of what greater notice meant for the possibility of new grain contracts or additions to our bloodstock.

Later it would come to me how this win meant more for him than me, strangely. As Dynasty's trainer, I would receive a percentage of her prize money. If I one day managed to get her placed regularly, I might glean a good-enough salary to win financial independence, but that was a distant dream. Jock still had plenty of leverage as he loomed at my side, cheerfully considering his own gain as my husband and my keeper. It was shocking how quickly we'd become adversaries.

"Do you suppose there will one day be female trainers in England?" one of the newspapermen asked.

"I haven't given it any thought," I said. I posed for the photo, wanting to elbow Jock hard in the ribs—to send him right out of my circle and my light. Instead, I smiled.

D had always known how to celebrate. That night, as the liquor ran freely, he made red-faced elaborate toasts and took to the dance floor with any number of smartly dressed women while a five-piece band played whatever he asked, bribed by good champagne.

The Muthaiga Club was the very best Nairobi had to offer. Three miles from the centre of Nairobi, it was an oasis, with pebbled walls pink as a flamingo's feather. Behind them, club members felt they'd earned the right to be there, to be waited on deferentially at one moment and surrender all restraint the next. You could bask by the tennis courts with your tall glass of gin and chipped ice, stable your best horse, whack glossy croquet balls over glossy bits of trimmed lawn, hire a European chauffeur to take you around, or simply get good and drunk on one of the blue-screened terraces.

I loved the club as much as anyone—the sitting rooms all done in dark hardwood flooring, the loose chintz-covered sofas and Persian carpets and framed hunting spoils—but I was still out of sorts. Jock had remained clamped to my side so completely I couldn't enjoy myself for a moment. It was only when D came over with a nice bottle of aged whisky to share with Jock that I was able to bolt for the bar in the other room, slinking along the wall to escape notice.

The bodies on the dance floor were frenzied, as if everyone worried the night might pass before they'd reach their portion of happiness or forgetting. Race days always whipped everyone up into this state, and as the party had been going on for most of the day, the waiters and porters all looked exhausted from trying to keep up. When I got to the cocktail bar, the queue was several bodies deep.

"You could wither away waiting for gin here," the woman just in front of me warned. She spoke with a clipped English accent and was tall and slim, wearing a deep-green Ascot gown and a matching ostrich-feather hat. "Thank God I planned ahead." She reached into a small jet-bead handbag and pulled out a silver flask, handing it to me.

I thanked her and fumbled with the tiny silver stopper while she smiled.

"Good show today, by the way. I'm Cockie Birkbeck. We met at a race meeting years ago. I'm actually distantly related to you, on your mother's side."

The mention of my mother instantly unsettled me, as it always had. I took a healthy sip, feeling the fire in my nose and throat, and passed back the pretty flask. "I don't remember meeting you."

"Oh, it was ages ago. You were a child then and I was . . . younger. Don't you *despise* this dry climate? It splits and shrivels everything, and gives you ten years for every two."

"You're beautiful," I said plainly.

"Aren't you a lamb for saying so? I'll bet you're still wishing that you were older, particularly in the world you're in, elbowing around with burly men in the paddock?" She laughed and then tapped the shoulder of the man in front of her. "Can't you speed things up, Blix? We're languishing here."

He turned and gave her a grin that was somehow youthful as well as hungry-looking. "That sounds vaguely sexual."

"Everything's vaguely sexual for you."

He winked. "Don't you love that about me?" He was stocky with a thick neck and squared shoulders, and his round face still had something of the schoolboy in it, though he must have been thirty or more.

"Bror Blixen, this is Beryl Clutterbuck."

"It's Purves now, actually," I said awkwardly. "I'm married."

"That *does* sound serious," Cockie said. "Well, not to worry. You're in very capable hands here." She clasped one of my arms and one of Blix's conspiratorially.

"Dr. Turvy has sent a prescription," Blix said, "and medicinally speaking, I'd say we're in the clear."

"Dr. Turvy?" I laughed. "Is he your private physician?"

"His *imaginary* private physician," Cockie said, shaking her head. "But I'll say one thing for Turvy. He always does come through."

As we found a corner near the dance floor and settled ourselves, I watched the swirl of bright faces and hoped Jock would be entertained enough by D's liquor to give me a few more minutes of peace. Blix had the waiter bring three silver buckets and three bottles of pink champagne. "So none of us have to share if we don't want to," he said.

"It's his leonine territorialism," Cockie explained. "Our Blix is a marvellous hunter. It's because he has their instincts."

"It's better than *working,*" he agreed. "I'm just back from the Belgian Congo. Up in the Haut-Uele, there are legends about elephants with four tusks. They have special names for them there and any number of stories about the mysterious powers they possess. A wealthy client of mine had heard about them and offered me double my usual rate if we saw one. We didn't even have to shoot it, he said; he only wanted to see one in his lifetime."

"And did you see one?"

He gave me a funny look and took a long pull on his glass. "She doesn't know how to listen to stories, this one."

"You have to let him draw it out, darling. Otherwise he doesn't look half so brave or interesting."

"Exactly so." He winked at her. "We were out for three weeks—in the Ituri Forest, along the sticky marshes of the Congo. Sometimes you can go for months without seeing elephants, but we saw several dozen, and three or four of them great hulking males with ivory dragging the ground. They were perfect specimens, I tell you, but all two-tuskers. Meanwhile, my client was growing restless. The longer we stayed in the bush, the more certain he was that there was no such thing, and that we were out to hoodwink him and take his money."

"You *are* there to take his money, Blickie darling."

"Of course, but honestly. Or as honestly as possible." He grinned. "The elephants do exist. I've seen photographs of them slain. So had the client, but being out for so long does funny things to you. I became more and more dodgy to him by the hour, and he did everything but accuse me of wanting to kill him in his sleep. One day he simply had enough and called the whole thing off."

"A month out for nothing?" Cockie exclaimed. "These people are getting more absurd all the time."

"Yes, but richer, too, and there's the rub. The money makes you think anything's worth it. But we'd taken fifty porters with us. They had to be paid somehow, and I was worried he'd lost his sense entirely and wouldn't foot the bill when the time came." He shook his head. "Anyway, we were on our way back when we spotted the strangest thing. A lone bull, off by himself, at the edge of a lake, sleeping with his head on a giant anthill and snoring like nobody's business."

"The four-tusked phantom," I guessed.

"Something even stranger." Blix smiled his most winning boy's smile. "A three-tusker—the only one ever sighted, as far as I know. The left tusk had grown double, you see, from the same socket, at the root. It was the most extraordinary thing."

"He must have been in ecstasy."

"The client? You'd think so, but no. 'It's deformed,' he kept saying. *Of course* it was deformed . . . some sort of hereditary malformation, probably. But he was so put off he didn't even want to photograph it."

"You've got to be joking," Cockie said.

"No. That's just it." He flicked the side of his glass to make his point. "They want things only *so* wild. Real nature terrifies them. It's too unpredictable."

"Well, I hope you got your money," Cockie said.

"I nearly didn't," he said. "But then we became mysteriously lost on the way back to town, with very little water."

"I'll bet." Cockie laughed. "You do tell wonderful stories, darling."

"Do I? I'll go and get more of them for you if you like." He gave her a familiar look, the two of them locking eyes in a way that told me if they weren't lovers yet, they would be very soon.

"I'll just go and freshen up," I said.

"Send the waiter, will you? I don't want to run dry here."

"Does Dr. Turvy send a new prescription every time," I asked, "or will the old one do?"

"Ha, I like this one," he said to Cockie. "She's got real potential."

My plan was to return to Eastleigh without anyone noticing, but I wasn't halfway to the door before I spotted Jock barrelling towards me, his eyes glassy. "What's the big idea, Beryl?" he barked. "I've been looking for you everywhere."

"I just slipped out for some air. Where's the crime in that?"

"We're in town. How does it look if I'm twiddling my thumbs

waiting for you and you're nowhere to be found?" He reached for my arm, his grip not at all subtle.

"I haven't done anything wrong. This was *my* day, after all." I twisted out of his grip, noticing that several people around us were glancing our way curiously. It made me feel braver. Surely the attention would make him back down.

"Lower your voice," he warned, but I'd had enough. As he reached for my arm again, I wrenched myself free and nearly flattened Boy Long in the process. I hadn't even seen him.

Glancing between Jock and me quickly, gauging the situation, Boy said, "Is everything all right here?"

"We're fine, aren't we, Beryl?" Jock said.

I had never loved him, it was true, but now I couldn't remember even liking Jock. I was only exhausted, all the way through me. "Go to bed."

He stared me down. I think he was surprised I was standing up to him.

"You heard her," Boy said. "Time to call it a night."

"This isn't any of your business." A knot along Jock's square jaw twitched. His mouth had hardened into a line.

"Your wife happens to work for me, so I'd say it is."

I was sure Jock was going to lunge for Boy. He was much the taller and broader man and could have wrecked Boy without trying—but some tide inside him turned, like a switch going off, and he thought better of it for the moment. "You should be careful, Beryl," he said icily, without taking his eyes from Boy's face. Then he stormed away.

"Charming," Boy said when Jock had gone, but I could hear that his voice wasn't entirely steady.

"Thanks for sticking your neck out for me. Can I buy you a drink? I could do with one."

We went to the bar for a bottle and some glasses, and then took them out onto one of the low verandas. Over the textured pink wall, I could make out the ghost of the croquet lawn where brightly painted wickets curved into the grass at intervals, and the post sat waiting for someone's shiny mallet. People passed in and out of the main door, porters and bellmen in white gloves, but we were almost entirely in shadow.

"I never thought I'd get married," I told Boy as he poured for us. Scotch spilled into the squat glasses with reassuring lapping noises. "I should have left well enough alone."

"You don't need to explain."

"I'm not sure I could anyway."

As we sat in silence for several minutes, I watched his face and hands. Both were mottled grey and soft-looking in the dimness. His earring was the only thing glinting, as if it caught the light from some other time or place.

"I've stopped trying to understand people," he said. "Horses and sheep make a damned sight more sense."

I nodded. It had always been the same for me. "Do you think I'm silly to want this? Life as a trainer, I mean?"

He shook his head. "I see you trying to be tough skinned, but that makes sense. As a woman you'll have to work twice as hard for everything. I'm not sure I could do it." He lit a cigarette and drew on it, the end flaring red in the dark. When he released the held smoke, he looked at me. "I think you're rather brave, actually."

Was I brave? I hoped so. I gazed back at him, his thick ivory bracelets, the native-looking piece of bone on a leather thong around his neck, his shirt the colour of the sea when everyone wore khaki. He was such a character, really, but he was here. And I knew he wanted me. I had a split second to consider what I was doing before I reached for his cigarette and put it out against the pale-pink wall. He leaned into me, opening my mouth with his, his tongue smooth and hot. I didn't think of resisting him or about anything else. One of his hands grazed the front of my blouse. The other slipped between my knees with a warm pressure I couldn't help responding to. A hunger for touch, for *this,* seemed to be coming up from the bottom of me. Maybe it had always been there, sleeping like an animal. I had no idea. I ran my hand along his thigh, twisting into him, and pressed my lips and teeth against his neck.

"You're dangerous." He whispered it.

"You mean Jock?"

"And you're awfully young."

"Do you want to stop?"

"No."

We didn't talk any more that night. Somehow, the feel of his skin and his mouth on mine didn't have anything to do with the rest of my life. They had no cost and no consequences—or so it seemed to me. Night sounds climbed the cool air beyond the veranda wall, and all thought of caution slipped away.

20

*I*t was late when I got back to Eastleigh. I fell into my cot feeling too chafed and hard kissed to sleep, but I did sleep. Just after dawn, I rose to do my work as ever. There was another race to prepare for, and the things that had happened with Boy and, before that, with Jock had to be swept off to the side of my attention. I wouldn't have known what to do about them anyway.

Jock didn't turn up until after my second horse, Shadow Country, had run and came a respectable third. Instead of appearing the way he had the day before, stepping into my limelight, he waited until after the clamour had cleared and then approached me as if nothing at all were amiss between us, trailed by Cockie Birkbeck and a slight, dark-haired fellow who wasn't a bit like Bror Blixen. He turned out to be her husband, Ben.

If I gave Cockie a curious look, she didn't seem rattled. Instead, she congratulated me on the day's race, and then Jock explained that Ben was thinking about getting more seriously into horses and suggested the four of us get a drink.

I was still waiting for the other shoe to drop, for Jock to grab hold

CIRCLING THE SUN · 129

of me again, to threaten or warn me, or for him to do something—
anything—to suggest he had somehow learned about Boy Long. But
it seemed this moment was all about business.

"When Ben finds the right horse, you should train him," Jock said
when we were settled with cocktails at a watering hole.

"If Delamere will spare you," Ben added. "I'm also keen on your
part of the country. There's a plot of land near your place I've had my
eye on."

We set a date for the couple to come out and have a look at Njoro,
and then Cockie made it clear that all this business talk was dull, and
we two girls excused ourselves and moved to a table of our own.
When we'd settled out of earshot, she said, "Sorry if Blix and I scared
you away last night. It's not often we're alone. Being married to other
people will do that." She made a face and took off her cloche hat, pat-
ting her honey-coloured hair. "We met when he took Ben and me on
safari. Blix always seduces the wives if he's given enough time. He
likes them trembling with fear, I suppose . . . at the precipice of mortal danger." She raised a feathery eyebrow. "I don't think he counted
on keeping me, but that was almost two years ago."

"That's a long time for things to be so intricate. Does Ben sus-
pect?"

"I think so, not that we have the bad taste to talk about it. He's got
his own entanglements, too." She gave me a complicated smile.
"You've heard the joke, haven't you? *Are you married or do you live in
Kenya?*"

"That's funny." I shook my head. "And sort of awful, too." Only
the day before, Cockie's dark joke wouldn't have included me, but
now it did. "Is love always such a mess, do you suppose?"

"Maybe not everywhere, but the rules are different here. It's sort of
assumed you'll have dalliances or go crazy . . . but discretion still plays
an essential part. You can do anything as long as the right people stay
shielded. And the funny thing is, that doesn't always mean your
spouse."

I absorbed her words slowly, a sobering sort of schooling on the ways of a world that had always resided somewhere else, for other people. "And you'll carry on like this?"

"You say it as if I'm doomed. It's not as bad as all that." She reached for the bottle on the table between us and freshened our drinks. "Ben isn't hard to manage, but Blix's wife, Karen, likes the title too much to part with it. He's made her a baroness." She sighed. "The whole thing has got rather *baroque*. Karen and I are friends, or were, in any case. Blix asked her for a divorce and told her he was in love with me, probably thinking it would soften the blow." She shook her head. "Now she won't speak to me."

"Why would anyone fight to stay married if they knew the other desperately wanted to leave?" I was thinking of Jock, of course.

"I don't pretend to understand any of it," Cockie breathed, "but Karen seems determined to test Blix at every step."

I had never been good at sharing my thoughts and feelings the way she was doing so easily, but her openness made me want to try. I also wanted her advice . . . some bit of wisdom that might help see me through my present tangle. "I was too young to get married," I told her, glancing behind me to make sure Jock and Ben were still distracted by each other. "Now I'm trying to pull away, but Jock won't hear of it."

"That must be hard," she said. "But honestly, if I hadn't had the bad luck of falling in love, I can't say I'd be keen for a divorce, either."

"You wouldn't want to be free, just on your own?"

"To do what?"

"Live, I suppose. Make your own choices or mistakes, without anyone telling you what you can and can't do."

She shook her head as if I'd said something absurd. "*Society* does that, darling, even if there isn't a strapping husband on hand. Haven't you learned that yet? I'm not sure anyone gets what they want. Not really."

"But *you're* trying now." I felt exasperated and a little confused. "You sound cynical, but you're in love with Blix."

"I know." Her forehead wrinkled prettily as she frowned. "Isn't that the silliest thing you ever heard?"

When I returned to Soysambu the next day, and for weeks afterwards, I continued to puzzle over what Cockie had said, wondering what her situation and bits of guidance actually meant for me. By her estimation, an affair was as de rigueur for the colonists as quinine tablets were for fever—a way to weather or temporarily forget marital unhappiness. But Boy wasn't really an affair, was he? What he offered was purer and more animal than what Cockie was embroiled in with Blix, or so I was telling myself. Besides, it felt wonderful.

After a year of fumbling and embarrassing encounters with Jock, I was finally learning what sex was, and that I liked it. Boy would come into my cottage at night and wake me by roughly pressing against me, his hands everywhere before I was fully conscious. He had none of Jock's tentativeness, and I found I wasn't shy with him, either. I could move any way I liked and not spook him. I could turn him away and not hurt his feelings, because feelings had nothing to do with any of it.

One night he found me alone in the stable and led me to an empty loose box without saying a word. Turning me over onto a hay bale, his hands came around to the waist of my cotton shirt and tugged it open roughly. My ribs rocked against the bale and my teeth caught on bits of hay. Afterwards, he stretched out naked without a flicker of modesty, his arms crossed behind him. "You don't seem like the same girl who snubbed me for several months running."

"I don't know what sort of girl I am any more, to tell the truth." I rested one of my hands on his chest, lightly stroking the thatch of springy dark hair. "I grew up with the Kips. For them, sex doesn't get all tangled up with guilt or expectations. It's something you do with your body, like hunting."

"There are people who'd tell you we're exactly like the animals. Same appetites, same urges. It's a nice idea."

"But you don't believe it?"

"I don't know," he said. "Someone always seems to get hurt."

"It shouldn't have to be like that. We have our eyes open, don't we?"

"Of course we do. Your husband's still in the picture, though. Does he have his eyes open?"

"Now you're trying to rub my nose in it."

"I'm not," he said as he easily pulled me on top of him. "How could I be?"

The following Saturday when I went home to Njoro, Ben and Cockie's car stood in our yard with luggage strapped to the boot. I parked D's wagon behind it and rounded the veranda to see them sitting comfortably at our rattan table in the shade, having cocktails with Jock.

"We've saved you some ice," Cockie said. She wore a loose silk dress and a hat with sheer netting that fell to the bridge of her nose. She looked lovely in it, and I was happy to see her. Her and Ben's company would make my time in Njoro much more bearable than usual.

Jock fetched me a drink—a scarlet-laced Pimm's with fresh lemon and orange peel over chipped ice, pretty as a picture—but he had an odd look on his face, and he didn't try to give me his usual perfunctory peck on the cheek.

"Everything all right?" I asked.

"Yes." He didn't meet my eyes.

"You've really done wonders with the place," Ben said. Before turning to ranching, he had been a major in the King's African Rifles, and there was something military about him still, a precision and a clipped composure. With neatly trimmed dark hair and fine, straight features, he was considerably better-looking than Blix—but I already guessed he didn't have Blix's humour or his sense of adventure.

"Jock is the miracle worker," I conceded. "There's nothing he can't plough or hammer into place."

"Except maybe my wife." He said it easily, almost cheerfully, as though the barb were harmless. Ben and Cockie laughed, and I tried to join them. I'd never been good at reading Jock, and certainly wasn't now that we were living apart.

"We've just bought the parcel next door," Cockie said. "We'll have to play bridge at the weekends. I adore cards," she went on. "Though Ben here would rather eat knives."

Barasa came to refill our ice bucket, and we all had another while the sun rose a little higher in the sky—but I couldn't shake the distinct feeling that something was off with Jock. Maybe he was punishing me for the scene at the Muthaiga when he'd stormed away half pissed. Maybe the whole façade of our arrangement was finally starting to wear and crack. Whatever was happening, Cockie clearly felt it, too. When the four of us headed over to admire their new property before dinner, she clasped my elbow, letting the men get well ahead of us.

"Is there something you want to tell me?" she asked quietly.

"I don't know," I said. I didn't. But by the time we settled before the fire later that evening, things became clearer as they unravelled. Jock drank too much at dinner, and his eyes took on a troubling sheen. I recognized this as a kind of warning—the first stone along the path to a good row—and hoped he would think twice with the Birkbecks here.

"How will you follow up your success for the next race meeting?" Ben asked from the sofa while the fire made cheerful crinkling noises. "Care to share some of your secrets?"

"When I train your horses, I'll share *all* of them," I said.

Ben laughed thinly. It seemed he'd felt the tension in the room, too, and now was trying to plot a strategic way to safely steer us back on course. He rose and made a sweep of the room. "I say, Jock, but this is a beauty." He meant the broad smooth Arab door that Jock had bought for the house not long after we were married. Like the phonograph, it was a sign of prosperity, and Jock was proud of it. The wood of the door was a rich puzzle of knots, with an overlay of carvings the artisan had painstakingly worked into the surface.

"It's lovely," Cockie said. "Wherever did you find it?"

"Lamu," Jock said. "I've been thinking of improving it, though."

"What?" She laughed. "It's a relic, isn't it? You wouldn't really touch it."

"I might." He slid over the last word strangely, his tongue too thick and uncontrolled. He was drunker than I thought.

"Let's have a game." I reached for the deck of cards, but Jock wasn't listening. He strode out of the room only long enough for Cockie to give me a questioning look and then came back again with a wooden mallet he'd found in the kitchen. It was a kitchen tool, meant for tenderizing meat, but he was beyond caring about proper uses. While we watched, he dragged over a chair and climbed on top of it to pound a small copper peg into the upper-right-hand corner of the door with the mallet, hammering away.

"Every time my wife has an indiscretion I'm going to add a nail," he said to the door. I couldn't see his expression and couldn't bear to look at Cockie or Ben. "It might be the only way we'll be able to keep track."

"Good God, Jock," I cried, horrified. Somehow he'd learned about Boy, then, and this was how he was exacting revenge, with an all-out scene in front of new friends. When he whirled round with the mallet, it balanced in his hand for a moment like a *rungu* club, his eyes glittering. "Get down."

"Just one by my count, is that right?" he asked me, and then turned to Ben. "Unless you've had her, too."

"Stop!" I yelled as Cockie's face went deathly white. One of Jock's knees buckled, and he tipped off the chair, tumbling to the floor. The mallet flew away from him, whipping over my left shoulder, and bouncing with a thudding clatter off the window casement. Thank goodness for instincts. I had ducked at precisely the right moment. Another few inches or portion of a second and the mallet would have cracked me on the head. Then we really would have had a story.

As Jock scrambled to find his feet again, Ben hurried to Cockie, and they made for the other room just as Barasa arrived.

"Please help bwana to bed," I told him, and soon I could hear them in the other room, a thump of shoes and shuffling of bedclothes. When I found the Birkbecks, they told me they were heading back to town. I was mortified. "At least wait till morning," I said. "It will be safer then."

"We're nothing if not intrepid," Cockie said gently. She signalled to Ben to go and pack their things and when he'd gone said, "I don't know what you've done, darling, but I can tell you there are things men don't want to know. And with us here, too . . . I suppose he had to show you he was still in charge."

"You don't mean to say he was justified in acting that way?"

"No." She sighed. But it seemed as if she was saying precisely that.

"I'm a disaster at marriage, and now at infidelity, too?"

She laughed soberly. "None of this is easy, I know. You're so young, and everyone makes great lurching mistakes sometimes. You really will work it out one day. For now, though, you've got to eat humble pie."

I walked them out, and after their Ford's quavering headlamps had passed from sight, I was alone with the Southern stars. How had I got here, exactly? The shadowy Aberdares were the same as they had ever been and the forest sounds, too, and yet I wasn't. I'd forgotten myself. I'd let one dodgy, fearful choice roll into another, somehow thinking that through this twisting and sticky route, I could still arrive at freedom. *Arap* Maina would have clucked and shaken his head to see me. Lady D would have gazed at me with those wise grey eyes of hers and said—what? That I had to eat humble pie? I didn't think so. And what of my father? He had raised me to be strong and self-sufficient—and I wasn't that now. Not by a long shot.

From somewhere nearby, a hyena whined, high and breathy, and another answered. The night pushed at me from all its edges. It seemed I could either walk into Jock's house and close the door and continue with this nonsense, or I could plunge out into the dark with no map for what happened next. Jock could come after me in a full-blown rage for smearing his name. Friends and neighbours might slowly and subtly turn away or snub me for breaking rank, the way they had with Mrs. O. I might never see my horses again or might go completely broke trying to find my way without Jock's support. I could fail in so many ways but, even so, there was no choice really.

When I went into the house again, I turned down all the lamps and padded to my room in the dark. Soundlessly, I packed my few things quickly and was on my way before midnight.

21

"Do you think Jock will come after me?" Boy asked when I recounted the whole story back at Soysambu. "Now that he knows about us?"

"Why would he? His whole argument has been about keeping up appearances and avoiding gossip. If anything, he'll make my life harder or dig in more about the divorce."

We were in my cottage after dark. It was a cool night, and as I warmed my hands against the chimney of the hurricane lantern, Boy's face remained clouded over with his thoughts. He seemed unsettled and out of place, though he'd been in my room dozens of times. "And what about us?" he finally asked.

"What do you mean? We've had a few laughs, haven't we? I don't see why anything should change."

"I only wondered." He cleared his throat and pulled the Somali blanket more snugly around his shoulders. "There are women who'd be expecting a fellow to step up and get serious at some point."

"Is that what you're worried about? I can't seem to get rid of the husband I've got, and anyway, what I'd really like to know is how it feels to be on my own. Not someone's daughter or wife, I mean . . . but my own person."

"Oh." It seemed I'd surprised him. "There isn't a lot of that kind of thinking around here."

"Of course there is," I told him, trying to draw a smile. "It's just usually a man who's doing it."

Now that I wouldn't have to keep up the ruse of weekend wife, I had more time and energy for my horses and was ready to give them my all. The St. Leger was an event for three-year-olds and Kenya's most illustrious stakes race. D had a few promising contenders, but the best of the lot was Ringleader, a satin-black and high-stepping gelding. He was a real horse, and D was offering me a chance to train him. But he'd "got a leg," as they say in horse speak. Before he'd come to Soysambu, he'd been overtrained, and his tendons had become sensitive, with a tendency to swell. With plenty of care and patience, though, he could still come back. He'd need soft, forgiving soil—so I took him down to the shore of Elmenteita and did all his galloping there along the moist edge while nearby herds of eland looked on curiously, and hordes of flamingos stirred over the lake's surface and settled, squawking the same alarm over and over.

Late one afternoon, I was coming back from a training session there, my clothes and hair flecked with bits of dried mud, when I ran into Berkeley Cole again. It had been two years since my coming-out party, that night he and Denys Finch Hatton had recited poetry for me in blindingly white coats, both of them with manners like something out of a book about knights and gallantry. Now he'd driven over with a few other settlers to meet D about some recent political nonsense. I happened to find him out for a smoke, leaning against a length of fence railing as the last of the sun vanished behind him. His collar was loose and his auburn hair hatless and slightly windblown. It was almost as if someone had sketched him there.

"The last time we met you weren't long out of pigtails," he said after we'd recognized each other, "now you're all over the papers. Your Jubaland was impressive."

I felt myself squirm slightly under his praise. "I didn't ever wear pigtails, actually. Couldn't sit still long enough for them."

He smiled. "It hasn't seemed to hurt you much. And you've married?"

Not knowing quite how to describe my current state, I hedged. "In a manner of speaking." In the several weeks since the terrible scene with the Birkbecks and the Arab door, I hadn't heard a peep from Jock. I'd written to him making it plain that I wanted a divorce and wouldn't back down, but he hadn't answered me. Maybe that was all right, though. It was a relief simply to be in our separate corners.

"In a manner of speaking?" Berkeley's mouth twisted in a way that was both wry and slightly paternal. But he didn't press me further.

"What's D getting you wrapped up in?" I gestured towards the house. From the booming of D's voice, things sounded fairly volatile.

"I'm afraid to know all of it. Vigilance Committee guff."

"Ah. Maybe you'd better run."

D had formed the committee a few months before, part of a new effort to combat the old problem of just who had a right to Kenya, and why. White settlers had always been keen on self-rule, which amounted to something more like total domination of the territory. They saw Indians and Asians as outliers, to be fought off with sticks, if necessary. Africans were fine as long as they remained clear about their inferior state and didn't want too much land. But recently the British government had issued the Devonshire White Paper, a series of declarations meant to beat back the white settlers' greedy demands and restore something like order in the colony. We had a new governor, Sir Robert Coryndon, and he was taking the White Paper awfully seriously. Though he was as British as could be, from his starched collar to his gleaming oxfords, he was pro-Asian and pro-African, a loud and fearless champion for both groups, where the previous governor had been malleable and cheerful and benign. Because things had swung in the white settlers' favour for so long, they could only be enraged now and think of how to fight back, even if that involved force. Not surprisingly, D was the fiercest among them.

"I'm actually relieved I've been out of the country for most of this past year," Berkeley explained. Then he told me how he'd been in London seeing a slew of doctors for his heart.

"Oh no. What did they say?"

"Nothing good, I'm afraid. The damned thing's been troubling me for years."

"What will you do now?"

"Live until it gives me away, of course. And drink only the best champagne. There's not time for anything else." His face was delicate and sensitive-looking, like a well-bred cat's. He also had rich brown eyes that seemed to want to laugh at the idea of sadness or self-pity. He flicked away his cigarette and cleared his throat. "I'm throwing myself a birthday party next week," he said. "One of the many ways I'm whistling past the graveyard these days. I'll bet you're a grand whistler, aren't you? Please come."

Berkeley had settled on the lower slopes of Mount Kenya in Naro Moru. He'd built a broad stone bungalow right up against the curves of the mountain, so it seemed to belong there and nowhere else. There were paddocks full of well-fed sheep and a winding river surrounded by thorn trees and twisting yellow witch hazel. Kenya's crags loomed over everything, looking deeply black up close, full shouldered and imposing and also perfect, somehow, exactly what Berkeley should have looking after him, I thought.

D came along to the party as well. When we motored up, a drove of automobiles crisscrossed the lawn and drive. Berkeley was out on the veranda in a smart white tailcoat, humming snatches of a tune I didn't recognize. His colour was high and he seemed to be in the peak of health, though I guessed that, like his lovely suit, it was put on. It probably mattered a great deal to him to appear to be the perfect host and dazzlingly well, too, no matter how things really were or felt beneath the surface.

"Your river is gorgeous." I leaned through a cloud of clean-smelling hair tonic to kiss his cheek. "It was gleaming with fish when we crossed it."

"Glad you're keen on the trout. I couldn't get a proper goose for dinner." He winked. "Now come get some champagne before Denys swills it all."

Denys. Though I'd only met him briefly on the street in Nairobi, for some reason my heart jumped at the sound of his name. We crossed the veranda and entered the main room of the house, which was full of people and the sound of laughter. And there he was in a languid slouch against the wall, hands in the pockets of his nice white trousers. He was as tall as I remembered, and just as lovely to look at.

"Beryl Purves," Berkeley said, "you've met the honourable Denys Finch Hatton."

I felt my face go warm as I reached for his hand. "Long ago."

"Of course." He smiled, the lines around his eyes deepening. But his tone was so light, it wasn't clear if he remembered me at all, even vaguely. "Nice to see you."

"Denys has been at home, in London, for far too long," Berkeley said.

"What will you do now that you're back in Kenya?"

"That's an excellent question. I might do some land developing. Tich Miles thinks we can form a legitimate company." He smiled as if *legitimate* were a pleasant surprise in this context. "And I've been dying to do some hunting."

"Why not?" D broke in. "The world is clamouring for more great white hunters."

"You should know." Denys laughed at him. "You invented the term."

"Yes, well, I never guessed who'd come galumphing over to Kenya hungry for trophies. Two or three times a month some rich banker shoots himself in the leg or offers himself up to a lion. It's absurd."

"Maybe that sort deserves what they get," I said. "If they don't have the slightest idea what they're up against, I mean, or even what it means to kill an animal . . ."

"You're probably right," Denys agreed. "I've only hunted for myself so far. I'm not sure I'd have the patience for clients."

"What's wrong with farming?" Berkeley wanted to know. "It's a good deal safer without bloody hyenas or what have you trying to nibble off your face in the middle of the night."

"Safer," Denys repeated. He had the look of a schoolboy, suddenly, ready for a prank. "Explain the fun in *that*."

Denys seemed a few years younger than Berkeley, somewhere near thirty-five, I guessed, and just as well born. In my experience, these sorts of men usually launched into Africa lured by virgin territory, big game, or a sense of adventure. They were the sons of British aristocrats who'd been sent to the very best schools and given every advantage and freedom. They came to Kenya and used their birthright fortunes to buy up thousands of acres. Some were serious at putting down roots and making a life here, like Berkeley, while others were playboys who had grown bored in Sussex or Shropshire and were looking for a bit of trouble. I didn't know which Denys was, but I liked looking at him. He had a wonderful face, a little pink from the sun, with a sharp strong nose, full lips, and heavily lidded hazel eyes. There was an ease and a confidence in him, too, that seemed to pull the room towards him, as if he were its anchor or axis.

After I had walked away, sipping at my drink and listening to bits of gossip here and there, a clutch of pretty women appeared to swoop down on him, most of them polished to a sheen. They wore nice frocks and stockings and jewels, and had hair that behaved. I could see they were all drawn to him—but that wasn't exactly surprising. I was too.

"You should have a look at my new horse," Berkeley said, stepping up to me with a fresh cocktail. "I think he's Derby material."

"Wonderful," I agreed automatically, and before I knew it, we'd collected Denys and headed to the stable, where half a dozen horses were turned out in their loose boxes. The one we'd come to see was

Soldier, a big and rangy dark bay with a white moon for a blaze. He wasn't as proud-looking or fiery as the thoroughbreds my father had always loved, but I found him handsome in a rough way and was instantly intrigued. "He's a half-breed, then?" I asked Berkeley as the three of us approached the stall.

"Part Somali pony, I think. Not highborn, but you can see he's got spirit."

Opening the gate, I moved towards Soldier the way I'd learned as a child, gently but firmly. My father had passed his touch with animals on to me—or maybe I'd been born with it. Soldier felt my authority and didn't shy or even step back as I passed my hands over his back and rump and hocks. He was sound and strong.

From his place at the gate, I felt Denys watching me. The skin along the back of my neck prickled from the attention, but I didn't look up.

"What do you think?" Berkeley asked.

"He's got something," I had to concede.

"What's he worth to you?"

As broke as I was, I knew I shouldn't even pretend to bargain, but it was in my blood. "Fifty quid?"

"I spent more than that on the champagne you've been drinking!" Though he and Denys both laughed, I could tell Berkeley loved to haggle, too. "You should see him run. Let me get one of the grooms to take him out for you."

"Don't bother," I told him. "I'll ride him myself."

It didn't take me five minutes to borrow trousers and change. When I came out of the house, a number of people had gathered on the lawn, and though Berkeley laughed to see me in his clothes, I knew they fitted me well and that I didn't have to feel embarrassed about riding in front of this well-born crowd. Being on horseback was as natural as walking for me—perhaps more so.

I nudged Soldier away from the onlookers, and soon forgot everything else. Behind Berkeley's paddock, a dirt lane led past a few tin-roofed farm buildings and down a slope to a small clearing with bits of scrub. I rode over and eased Soldier into an extended trot. His back was wide and his sides were as rounded and easy as a comfortable chintz-covered chair. It wasn't clear that he could really run, but Berkeley had insisted on it, so I nudged him faster. Instantly, his hind and forelegs quickened. In a canter, his stride was fluid and powerful, and his neck relaxed. I'd forgotten how much fun it could be to ride a new animal—to feel power climbing up into my hands from the leather reins and into my legs through Soldier's body. I urged him even faster and he stretched from his centre, his muscles in balance, beginning to fly.

Then, quick as a string breaking, he froze. Midstride, his forelegs plunged down stiffly, and I swung forward over his withers like a cracked whip. Before I could recover, he reared and twisted sideways, whinnying with a sharp cry. I was in the air. Thrown hard on my side, my teeth jarred against my tongue. I tasted blood as my hip exploded with pain. Beside me, Soldier squealed and reared again. I flinched, knowing he could crush me, but a moment later, he bolted cleanly away. Only then did I see the snake.

About fifteen feet from where I lay, it was coiled over itself like fat black ribbon, and it was locked on me. When I startled, the top part of its long body shot up elastically, with dizzying speed. Its pale-striped neck widened into a kind of cape. It was a cobra, I knew. We didn't have them in Njoro, and I had never seen this type exactly, with zebra-like colouring and an arrow-shaped head, but my father had told me many types of cobra could stretch their body length in a single strike. Some could spit venom, too, but most snakes didn't want a confrontation.

A twisted piece of mahogany lay only a few inches from my hand. I would try to reach for it and brandish the stick out in front of me to block a strike, if one came. I readied myself, watching the movement of its head. The hard, glassy eyes were like small black beads. Hovering, the snake trained on me, too, its pale tongue darting and tasting the air. I steadied my breathing and, as slowly as I could manage, sent my hand out towards the stick.

"Don't move," I heard suddenly from behind me. There'd been no footsteps, at least not that I could hear, but the cobra reared up even higher. Half its body flared from the ground, its belly glazed with yellowish slashes. Its hood breathed open. This was the only warning as it whipped forward. I pinched my eyes shut, my arms flying over my head as I scrabbled backwards. At the same moment, a shot rang out. The charge hit so close I felt it vibrate through my skull. My ears rang. Even before the explosive sound had cleared the air, Denys strode forward and shot again. Both shots landed, the second one catching the snake in the neck so that it jumped sideways. Bits of flesh spat into the dust with bright splashes of its blood. When it was still, he turned to me coolly. "Are you all right?"

"I think so." When I stood, pain erupted through my side and along my hip. My knee was throbbing and didn't want to take my weight.

"That type doesn't shrink from trouble, you know. It's good you didn't do anything stupid."

"How did you even find me?"

"I saw the horse come back alone and thought, 'I'll bet she doesn't fall for no reason.' After that, I just followed the dust."

He was so calm, so matter-of-fact. "You sound as if you do this sort of thing every day."

"Not every day." He smiled crookedly. "Shall we go back?"

Though I probably could have managed on my own, Denys told me I should lean on him. Against the side of his body, I smelled his warm cotton shirt and his skin—and felt how solid and sound he was. And he'd been so clearheaded when he took aim. He hadn't thought about anything else, only acted. It wasn't often I'd seen that level of self-possession in a man.

We came to the house all too soon. Berkeley rushed out, mortified and alarmed, while D knitted his eyebrows together paternally.

"What the hell do you think you're doing, risking my best trainer?" he shot at Berkeley.

"I'm fine," I told them both. "There was hardly anything to it at all."

Denys downplayed the moment, too—almost as if we had agreed on it without speaking. He said nothing of his own bravery and behaved as if the whole ordeal were commonplace. That impressed me, and how for the rest of that day we didn't mention what had happened again. But the memory lent a palpable charge to the hours, as if there were an invisible length of string or wire between us. We talked of other things, how much he still thought about his years at Eton, how he'd found Kenya by chance in 1910, meaning to settle in South Africa instead.

"What was it that drew you?" I asked him.

"About Kenya? Nearly everything. I think I'd always been looking for an escape route."

"Escape from what?"

"I don't know. Any tight-fitting definition of what a life should be, I suppose. Or what I should be in it."

I smiled. "*Should* isn't a word that suits you, is it?"

"Worked that one out already, did you?"

"It's never been one of my favourite words either." Our eyes met for a moment, and I felt a spark of perfect understanding. Then Berkeley sailed up, and the two friends started talking about the war. How they'd enlisted in a scouting party near the border of German East Africa and Kilimanjaro.

"We weren't very glorious, I'm afraid," Denys said, sketching it in for me. "Most of our casualties came from tsetse fly and bush-rat stew."

It was almost a kind of dance, how funny and clever these two were together—lighter than air. Before long we were all a little drunk from the champagne we'd been swilling, and it had got quite late. "Let's take a few bottles over to Mbogani," Denys said suddenly to Berkeley. "The baroness is on her own tonight."

Baroness? The word jangled. Cockie Birkbeck had used it in the Norfolk the day she'd told me about Blix's situation and his wife.

"I can't leave my own party," Berkeley said. "It's too late anyway, and you're in no state to drive."

"I *have* a mother, thank you very much." Denys turned his back on Berkeley and fixed on me. "Want to go for a ride into the country, Beryl?"

Berkeley shook his head, warning me off. I stood there for a moment, wondering how serious Denys was, and whether they were in fact speaking of Blix's wife. But before I could begin to sort it out or say a word, Denys strode over to the bar, wrestled three bottles of champagne into his arms, and was on his way out of the door. Berkeley laughed. I was dumbstruck.

"Good night," Denys sang back over his shoulder before passing out of sight.

"Shall we have one more nip and turn in?" Berkeley asked.

I still hadn't caught up. "What just happened?"

"Merely Denys being Denys," he said mysteriously, and reached for my hand.

22

D and I stayed over at Berkeley's that night—camping out on thick rafts of Somali-made quilts with a handful of other tipsy guests. Every time I rolled over, I felt the sore place on my hip, and Denys's image flickered up like a new ghost. But when it was time to leave the next day, he still hadn't returned. Somehow that made me even more curious about him. The moment with the cobra might have worked to cement us in a strange way, or maybe Denys was just nicer to look at and more confident than almost any man I'd ever met. Either way, I was already thinking of how good it would be to see him again.

"You'll let Denys know I said goodbye?" I asked Berkeley as D went off to fetch the wagon for us.

"Hmm?" He gave me a curious look. "Please tell me you haven't fallen for Finch Hatton, too, darling."

"Don't be silly." I felt myself flush. "I like him, that's all."

"Is that so?" He stroked his moustache. "I've never known a woman who could resist him. They fall for him by the dozens, but he never seems to fall for anyone."

"No one?"

He shrugged. "Desperately sorry about the business with the horse, by the way. You won't hold it against me, I hope."

"Of course not. I'd buy him if I could, but Jock holds the purse strings and I'm trying to be done with all that. With marriage, I mean. I haven't quite known how to talk about it."

"I've been wondering what's going on between the two of you, what with your working for D and all." His voice was kind, not judgemental, as I had feared.

"It's not so common for women in the colony to stray far from their duties, I suppose."

He shook his head. "Send word if you need anything. Or whistle," he added, smiling.

"I will," I assured him. And then D roared up with the wagon, and we were away.

Ringleader's training was coming along bit by bit. He had the right breeding to win and the right nerves, too. If only his legs would heal properly. I continued to exercise him along the mud-soft shoreline of Elmenteita, liking the time to myself as well. Even with the flamingos it was far less chaotic there than at the ranch. I always felt myself grow calmer as I connected to Ringleader's movements, his stride, and also to the rich landscape around us. The lake formed a shallow basin that opened up to green savannah in every direction. Low and knobby hill formations sprang up here and there, and the swooping lines of the mountain called the Sleeping Warrior. Its reflection was often painted perfectly on the flat surface of the lake and studded with flamingos at rest like a fan of bright jewels. It was beautiful country, and though none of it moved me as much as Njoro did, Soysambu was beginning to grow on me, and even to feel like a place where I could happily stay.

One day after I had run Ringleader to the edge of his gallop, encouraged by his growing strength and confidence, I saw a car coming overland from a few miles away, pointing as straight at Soysambu as the crow flies. I didn't know who might be bold enough to leave the main road. It had rained on and off for several days, and the tyres were kicking up pellets of mud, sending a large group of eland zigzagging off over the bush. When the vehicle drew nearer, I recognized Denys.

His machine was built like a rhinoceros, with heavy mud-painted tyres. I tethered Ringleader so he wouldn't startle and went on foot to meet him as he came round the lake. The ground around the shore had gone boggy, and as his car idled, the tyres sank slowly into the muck. Denys didn't seem remotely concerned.

"The road not fine enough for you today?" I asked him.

"You never know who you'll run into this way." He cut the motor and pushed off his hat, squinting up at me. "I saw you flying along the shore when I came up over the rise. I didn't know it was you, but it was beautiful to watch. Thrilling, actually."

"My horse is really starting to come along. I felt something new in him today. Maybe that's what you saw." Free of his helmet, Denys's sparse brown curls were matted with sweat. Small flecks of mud had spattered along his forehead and cheekbones, and I felt an inexplicable urge to brush them off with my fingertips. Instead, I asked him where he was going.

"D's sounded the alarm for one of his meetings. Apparently Coryndon has done something unforgivable, as the committee sees it. D's all set to tie him up and throw him in a cupboard."

"Kidnapping the governor is at least as reasonable as all of D's other ideas."

"I try to stay out of it mostly. But today was such a nice day for a drive."

"Mud and all?"

"The mud especially." His hazel eyes sparked, catching the light for a moment before he resettled his hat, preparing to leave.

"Perhaps I'll see you in town some time," I told him.

"I'm not often there any more. I've recently moved out to Ngong, to stay with my good friend Karen Blixen."

Surely he meant Blix's wife, the mysterious baroness. "Is that right?"

"She's wonderful. Danish. Runs a coffee farm all on her own while Blix is off stalking his rhino. I don't know how she pulls it off, but she does." His voice chimed with obvious admiration. "I imagine you've met Blix. There aren't many pretty women who escape him."

"Yes." I smiled. "That was my take on him, too." It was hard to know what Denys was actually saying about the baroness. Was he living with her, as if they were husband and wife? Or were they merely close companions, as he and Berkeley were? There was no way to ask directly, of course.

"The farm is so much nicer than town," he went on, "and the air is champagne. It's the altitude, I think."

"Sounds like something Berkeley would say," I remarked.

"I suppose it does." He smiled again. "Come and visit us some time. We love to have company . . . and Karen has a small house sitting empty on her property just now. You could stay as long as you like. Come with a story, though," he said, cranking the engine. "It's one of our requirements."

"A story? I'll have to drum one up then."

"Do that," he said before he roared away.

23

A few weeks later, D called me in from the paddock and handed over a telegram addressed to me. I assumed it was a rare bit of news from my father—or perhaps some sort of demand from Jock—but the envelope had a smeared return address from London. Turning away from D, I broke the sticky seal with a sharp twinge of dread. DEAR BERYL—I read—HARRY HAS DIED AND THE BOYS AND I WILL RETURN TO THE COLONY STOP WOULD YOU PLEASE LOOK FOR LODGINGS?— WE DON'T KNOW ANYONE AND MONEY IS DEAR STOP MOTHER.

Mother? That word alone felt like a slap. I'd pushed her memory away long ago, as far as I could, but it lurched dizzily to life now. My eyes raced over the few sentences again. My throat was as dry as dust.

"Everything all right?" D asked.

"Clara's returning to Kenya," I said numbly.

"Good grief. I thought she'd vanished for good."

"Apparently not." I handed him the flimsy paper, as if it would explain anything. "Who's Harry?"

"Harry?" He was quiet for a moment, reading, and then he sighed heavily and raked his hands through his hair. "Let's have a nip of brandy, shall we?"

It wasn't easy to drag the whole story out of D, but the drink worked to pry him open a little, and me as well. After an hour I had the gist of it. Harry Kirkpatrick was a captain my mother had met in her second year in Kenya, at a dance in Nairobi after a race meeting. Their involvement was meant to be a secret, but those kinds were hard to keep. By the time she left for London with him, Dickie in tow, the scandal had blazed through the colony.

"Obviously she married him at some point," D said, "though I can't say when. We fell completely out of touch."

"Why didn't anyone tell me the truth?"

D cupped his brandy glass, thinking, and then said, "It might have been a mistake. Who's to say? Everyone wanted to protect you from the worst of it. Florence was the loudest of all. She insisted it would only make everything worse."

I thought of the day I'd pored over the map of England in Lady D's atlas, and her saying she could tell me things about my mother if I wanted to know. Had she planned to invent a tale, a doctored version of the truth? Or had she begun to feel it was time I understood what had really happened? It was impossible to do more than guess now.

"So the whole story about how *hard* things were for Clara, that was just rubbish?"

"Your mother *was* terribly unhappy, Beryl. Green Hills was in shambles then. It took every drop of energy Clutt could give it. I think that's why she latched on to Kirkpatrick. Perhaps she saw him as her only way out."

"But she had responsibilities," I spat. "She should have been thinking of us, too." *Me,* I meant—for Dickie had been fine, he'd been chosen. "What was this Harry like anyway?"

"Handsome, as I remember, and very attentive to her. She was a beautiful woman, you know."

"Was she?" My father had managed to hide or throw out every likeness, every last reminder—particularly once Emma came along. He had rooted Clara out of our lives so well she might never have been there at all, and I saw why. She'd gone off with another man, hurting and embarrassing him, very much as I had done with Jock; but for us there were no children to think of. "Why couldn't he have told me the truth?"

"Your father did what he thought was best. Sometimes it's difficult to know what that is."

I swallowed back rising tears, hating the fact that my mother could make me cry—that she still could, after all these years. But my feelings wouldn't be tamped down. They flooded over me, so far past my control that I had to wonder if I'd only *imagined* surviving Clara's leaving when I was a girl. What if the strength and invincibility I'd felt then—feats of daring, leopard hunts, and rides over the savannah on Pegasus, my ears roaring with speed and sharp freedom—were only the thinnest layer of straw over a gaping hole? Either way, I felt bottomless now. "Am I really supposed to be nice and to show her around? As if nothing whatever has happened?"

"Oh, Beryl, I don't know what to tell you. She has her faults like the rest of us, I suppose." He came over and clamped my shoulders with work-reddened hands. "You'll do what's right for you."

If D felt certain that I'd make my way towards clarity, I had my doubts. Clara's telegram continued to sting, wrenching me back through time. It was so strange to be learning only now why she had left the colony, the crux of the story buried for decades. And though it didn't surprise me that my father had hidden the truth and his feelings and forged ahead with life on the farm, I couldn't stop wishing he had told me. She'd left me, too, after all. Her going had changed everything, and now she was returning? It didn't make sense. Why would she think she could find her feet in Kenya, a place she couldn't get away from quickly enough? And how had she summoned the nerve to ask for my help? How was any of this my responsibility?

Angry and baffled, I was more than tempted to tell Clara to find her own way around—but she wasn't the only one I had to consider. She hadn't mentioned Dickie in her cable, though her casual reference to "the boys" meant she and the captain had had children together. Now those boys were fatherless and about to be dragged into an utterly foreign world. What would they think about that?

As I struggled with Clara's plea, Denys suddenly came to mind. He had mentioned the baroness's land and empty house less than a week ago. He'd meant it for me, for a friendly visit, but I couldn't help but be struck by the opportunity, and by the perfect sense of timing. Though I still hadn't entirely sorted out that I *wanted* to help Clara, her need and this solution seemed mysteriously matched up and sorted out already, as if the whole situation had been on its way for years and years. As if we were all being drawn together by unseen hands. It nearly felt inevitable.

I told Boy and D that I would be away for a few days, and went to saddle Pegasus, feeling better than I had in some while. I still didn't have the slightest idea of what it would mean to have Clara back in the colony and in my life, but I was on my way to see Denys again, and perhaps tell him a story. It was a warm afternoon, I was on a strong and beautiful horse, and I had a plan.

24

Karen Blixen's farm lay twelve miles west of Nairobi, along a rut-ted road that climbed steadily. The altitude was thousands of feet higher than Delamere's or Jock's, and the climbing forest cut sharp ridges into the pale sky. A long valley swung to one side of the road, strung through with carpets of orange lilies, the kind that grew up wild everywhere after it rained. The air was sweet with them, and also the white-flowering coffee plants, which smelled like jasmine. Everything seemed to sparkle, just like champagne. Denys had been right about that.

Though I was fairly sure the baroness would at least consider let-ting the house to my mother—it was sitting empty, after all—I felt a twinge or two about coming unannounced. Settlers were spread out so widely in Kenya that visitors were generally welcomed however and whenever they popped up. But I didn't know if Denys had yet mentioned me to her, or what their relationship was exactly. My curi-osity had been simmering about them both, and I felt a sense of antic-ipation—of being on the verge of something interesting.

The substantial bungalow was built of grey stone with a pitched and tiled roof, and sturdy-looking gables. A long porch swept all the way around the house, as did a wide, groomed lawn. Two large deer-hounds sunned in the grass as I rode up, blue-grey and whiskered, with lovely pointed muzzles. They didn't bark or seem troubled by me, so I dismounted and let them have my hands to smell.

I looked up as a woman came out of the house. She wore a simple white housedress and was slenderly built, with very fair skin and dark hair. Her face was most striking for its angles, and for her eyes, deep set under feathery brows. Her gaze and her sharp fine nose gave her the look of a pretty hawk. I felt myself squirm, suddenly embarrassed.

"I'm sorry, I should have wired you," I said, giving her my name. "Is Denys around?"

"He's out on safari, actually. I don't expect him for at least a month."

A month? But before I could feel deflated or more awkward about where to begin, she went on to say that Denys had spoken of me, and that she'd been keen for some company. "I haven't spoken to anyone but the dogs for days, it seems." She smiled and her features softened. "I've just got some new records for my phonograph, too. Do you like music?"

"I do, though I'm not very educated about it."

"I'm trying to learn more myself. My friends tell me my taste is too old-fashioned." She pulled a small face and sighed. "Let's see to your horse then."

Karen's house reminded me of my childhood visits to Lady D at Equator Ranch. It was the quality of her things, the civility in the smallest details. Inside the broad front door, richly coloured carpets ran over the mahogany parquet, connecting the rooms and warming them. There were silky wood tables, plump chintz-covered sofas and overstuffed chairs, thick draperies at every window, flowers in vases and flowers in bowls. She had shelves and shelves of finely bound books. As I looked at them, I felt very aware of my spotty education. I ran my hand along a row of their spines. My fingertips came away with no dust. "Have you really read them all?" I asked.

"Of course. They've saved my life many times over. Nights can drip like molasses here, especially when good friends have gone away."

I wondered if she meant Denys, but she didn't elaborate. Instead, she showed me to a small guest room so I could wash, and then we met again on the veranda for tea. Her houseboy, Juma, held the china pot and poured for us, white gloves flapping around his thin black wrists. He passed a plate of biscuits and sweets with a formality I hadn't seen in many servants, not in these parts.

"I've come to ask a favour," I told her when Juma had gone. "But maybe you've already guessed that."

"You've come to stay then?" Her accent rolled and swooped. Her dark eyes were pretty, but I found myself squirming under them a bit. She seemed to watch rather than simply look at things.

"Not exactly. My mother is returning to Kenya after many years away. I thought your house might do if it's still empty. She'll pay you a fair price, of course."

"Why, yes. There hasn't been anyone in it for so long. It will be nice to have her here, and for you, too."

"She's not actually . . ." I had no idea how to explain it all. "We don't know each other that well."

"I see." Again her dark eyes fixed on me, making me want to fidget in my chair. "It's very kind of you to help her in that case."

"I suppose so," I said, not wanting to say more. Above her house on the ridge, five deeply blue hills cut a rising and falling line. They drew my eye back and forth.

"Aren't they wonderful?" Karen said. "I love them indecently." She held up her fist to model how the shape of the ridge was like the knuckles of her hand. "There's nothing like them in Denmark. Nothing like any of what I have here." She drew a slim silver case from her pocket and lit a cigarette, shaking out the match and plucking a thread of tobacco from her tongue, all without taking her eyes from my face. "Your browned skin looks so wonderful with your hair, you know," she finally said. "You really are one of the most beautiful girls I've seen in these parts. And I read about your racing successes in the Nairobi paper. That can't be an easy life for a woman, and the society isn't terribly gentle here, is it?"

"Do you mean the gossip?"

She nodded. "It's such a small town, Nairobi. So provincial—which is funny considering how vast Kenya is. You'd think we were all crouched up next to one another, whispering between windows, instead of hundreds and hundreds of miles apart."

"I hate it. Why do people hunger to know every nasty thing? Shouldn't some things be private?"

"Does it trouble you that much, what others think?" Her face was sharply and darkly beautiful—and her deep-set onyx eyes had an intensity I hadn't seen very often. She was older than me by ten or fifteen years, I guessed, but her attractiveness was hard to ignore.

"I just feel a bit over my head sometimes. I think I was too young to get married."

"If it were another man, the right man, age might not be an issue. The rightness of the match changes everything."

"You're a romantic then."

"A romantic?" She smiled. "I never thought so, but lately I don't know. I've come to think differently about love and marriage. It's not a proper philosophy. I don't want to bore you, in any case." She fell quiet for a moment, and a small speckled owl glided towards her from an open window on the porch, as if she'd called it silently. It settled on her shoulder. "This is Minerva. She always turns up for company . . . or maybe it's the biscuits."

25

The name of Karen's farm was Mbogani, meaning "house in the woods." Out past her wide lawn, frangipani trees bloomed yellow-white and deep pink. There were palms and mimosa trees, stands of bamboo and thorn trees and banana groves. Six hundred acres of the lower slopes of the ridge had been groomed and tiered for bright green coffee plants. Another portion of her farm was native forest, more was rolling, fragrant grassland, and still more was home to Kikuyu *shambas,* native squatters who tended cattle and goats and grew their own maize and pumpkin and sweet potato crops.

We walked along a trampled footpath through shoulder-high plants and tangled vines to Mbagathi, the house she would be offering Clara. It was only a small bungalow with a tiny veranda, but there were plenty of windows, and around the back stood an arbour and clustering mimosas to keep things cool. I tried to imagine my mother there, resting in the shade, but found I couldn't conjure her at all without a shiver of anxiety.

"Bror and I lived here first," Karen explained, "just after we were married. I'm still very fond of it."

"I met your husband once in town. He's charming."

"Isn't he?" She smiled a complicated smile. "It's kept me from strangling him any number of times."

Inside, there were three small bedrooms, a kitchen, a bathroom, and a sitting room furnished with lamps and a leopard-skin rug. The sofa was like a bed squeezed into one corner, forming a cozy nook. She showed me a pretty French clock on the mantelpiece, a wedding present. Dusting the top of it with her sleeve, she said, "No doubt you've heard whispering about my marriage as I have yours."

"Only a little."

She shook her head doubtfully. "Ah well, it doesn't matter. No one really knows how it is with anyone else. That's the truth. That's our only real retaliation when the gossip starts to churn."

I thought of the humiliating jokes and rumours that came with the final days of Green Hills, and how they had seemed to ruin even what had been good. "Maybe that's the secret to surviving all sorts of trouble, knowing who you are apart from it, I mean."

"Yes." She picked up the clock, turning it over in her hand as if to remind herself of its significance. "But like many things, it's so much easier to admire that stance than to carry it out."

We left Mbagathi for a tour of her factory, where dozens of Kikuyu women raked through long, narrow tables of coffee cherries that were drying in the sun, going from red to chalk white.

"This whole structure burned to the ground last January." She plucked up a coffee cherry and rolled it between her palms until the skin split and fell away. "One of God's little cruelties. I thought it would finish me off at the time, but here I am still."

"How do you manage? Farming is so difficult."

"Honestly, I don't know, sometimes. I've risked absolutely everything, but there's everything to gain, too."

"Well, I admire your independence. I don't know many women who could do what you've done."

"Thank you. I have fought for independence here, and freedom, too. More and more I find they're not at all the same thing."

It began to rain on our way back. By the time we reached the edge of Karen's lawn, we were slick and streaming, our boots caked to the knees with red Kikuyu mud. Laughing at the sight of each other, we came around the veranda, beginning to loosen our wet things. There sat Blix, unshaven and covered with dust. He'd raced ahead of the rain, apparently, and now had an uncorked bottle of brandy at his side.

"I've arrived just in time. Hello, Beryl. Hello, Tanne, dear."

Karen said, "I see you've made yourself comfortable."

"It is still my house."

"So you keep telling me."

Their teasing had a wicked edge, but under the surface there was more. Some part of whatever had stitched them together was still alive and well. That was obvious even to me.

Karen and I went in to change, and when we reappeared, Blix had settled himself more comfortably and was smoking a pipe. His tobacco smelled exotic, like something he'd found only by belly-crawling through the far reaches of the continent. "You look well, Beryl."

"So do you. Dr. Turvy must be earning his keep."

"He's got you enlisted in that silly game?" Karen turned to Blix. "Where have you been this time?"

"Uganda and then back through Tanganyika with a Vanderbilt—after rhinoceros. I nearly lost him, actually."

"The Vanderbilt or the rhino?"

"That's funny, darling. The Vanderbilt. Two lethal-looking males charged straight at him. The man's very lucky I had the right gun on me." He turned to me. "A rhino isn't something you want in your back yard. It's like a massive snorting locomotive encased in unconquerable hide. When threatened, it will crash through anything, even steel."

"Weren't you afraid?"

"Not really." He smiled. "I had the right gun."

"If you sit at the Muthaiga Club long enough," Karen said, "you'll hear any number of hunters making their kills again. The stories grow bigger and more harrowing with every telling. Bror is the only one I know who makes mountains into molehills instead of the other way round."

"Except for Denys, you mean," Blix corrected.

"And Denys. Yes." She didn't seem remotely flustered at hearing Denys's name roll from her husband's lips. And Blix had said it so easily I couldn't imagine that Denys was Karen's lover. Still, the whole dance was fascinating. "Did you see him out there?" she wanted to know.

Blix shook his head. "They say he's gone west, into the Congo."

"What's that country like?" I asked him.

"Very, very dark." He sipped at his brandy. "They have every kind of snake there, and some say cannibals."

"Are you trying to scare me?" Karen narrowed her eyes.

"No, inspire you. Tanne scribbles stories all the time, did you know, Beryl? She's quite good, actually."

"I'll tell you one by the fire some night." She waved away his praise. "I'm more of a storyteller than a writer in any case."

"Denys mentioned you loved stories here."

"Oh, we do," she insisted. "And Bror is awfully skilled at them as well. Perhaps he'll play Scheherazade for us tonight."

"If I don't have to pretend to be a virgin," he said, and we all laughed.

That evening we had dinner on the veranda. The Ngong Hills went plum coloured and almost hypnotically still as Blix treated us to more tales from his Vanderbilt safari. One rolled easily into the next. He had dozens and dozens of them and didn't fall silent for more than a few minutes at a time as Karen's cook, Kamante, brought us a string of dishes. There was lightly breaded chicken in a cream sauce, roasted vegetables with herbs, a corn pudding studded with mushrooms and thyme, ripe cheese, and oranges. Blix kept our glasses filled, and by the time we reached the final course, I was floating because of the wine, and also surprised at how very much I liked these two. There wasn't anything simple about them, and I preferred that, and trusted it. My life wasn't simple either.

When a hooked moon had risen into the sky, and we'd had our pudding and our Calvados and our coffee, Blix said good night and began his journey back to town.

"Isn't he a little too tight to be driving?" I asked her.

"I don't think he can drive any other way." She was silent for several minutes, looking out into the dark. "He's asked me for a divorce. That's why he came."

I knew from Cockie he'd asked more than once, but also that it would be cruel to let on. "Will you give him one?"

She shrugged. "How would it be to have two Baronesses Blixen in the colony? There's not room, you see. One would be elbowed out and forgotten."

"I can't imagine anyone forgetting you," I said. I wasn't flattering her. I truly couldn't.

"Well, we shall see."

"How is it you've managed to stay friends?"

"We were friends before we were anything else. It was his younger brother Hans I was taken with. This was long ago, in Denmark. Bror became my confidant when Hans married another." She paused and shook her head so that her long silver earrings tinkled.

"Younger brother? He couldn't have offered you a title then?"

"No. Only love." She smiled darkly. "But it wasn't to be. And then Bror thought of this, a new start in Africa. If only it hadn't brought a mountain of debt."

"Do you still love him?"

"I wish I could say no. But Africa sets you up to feel things you're not prepared for. I came to believe we could have everything . . . children, devotion, fidelity." She shut her eyes and opened them again, the pupils flaring black. "Maybe he's not capable of loving just one woman. Or perhaps he is, but not me. He was never faithful, not even in the beginning, and that's what I keep coming back to, how I thought I knew what I had bargained for when I married Bror, when actually I had very little idea of any of it."

I took a bolstering swallow of Calvados. "You could be talking about my marriage. That's just how I feel."

"And will you get *your* divorce, do you think?"

"I hope so. I'm afraid to apply any pressure just now."

"We're all of us afraid of many things, but if you make yourself smaller or let your fear confine you, then you really aren't your own person at all—are you? The real question is whether or not you will risk what it takes to be happy."

She was referring to Jock, but her words made me think of other things, too.

"Are *you* happy, Karen?"

"Not yet. But I mean to be."

26

Through a series of telegrams, everything was settled with Clara very quickly. The house was going to be perfect, she insisted, and fell over herself to thank me. But even this much intimacy felt confusing. I hadn't had a mother for more than sixteen years, and didn't have the slightest idea how to behave with her, even on paper. I struggled with every line, wondering how affectionate I should be, or how aloof. I had no practise with any of this—there wasn't even a word for what we were now, not mother and daughter, but not utterly estranged. It was bewildering.

In one message from Clara, I learned that my brother, Dickie, had been in Kenya for many years and was currently up north in Eldoret, jockeying for a good stable there. I couldn't quite believe it. Dickie had been here, in my world, without my being aware of it? What did it mean? Would we all somehow come to know one another as a family again? Did I want that? Was it even possible?

I was still tumbling with conflicting feelings when Clara arrived at the tail end of May. As I set off to meet her at the Norfolk Hotel in a motorcar I'd borrowed from D, my hands shook and my throat felt full of knots. Sweat sprang up under my arms and behind my knees like a bout of mysterious fever. It was all I could do not to run for cover when she and the boys came down and met me in the tea room. I had tried to remember what she looked like, wondering if I'd even recognize her, but I needn't have. We had the same face, with identical high cheekbones and foreheads, the same pale-blue eyes. Looking at her gave me a strange, lurching feeling—as if I were meeting myself as a lost ghost—and I was glad the boys were there to pull me out of the sensation. They were seven and nine, blond and clean and combed and shy at first. They half hid behind their mother as she took me in her arms. Unprepared, I bumped her hat with my elbow and pulled away, feeling stung and confused. I didn't want her embrace, but just what did I want?

"How was the voyage?" I managed.

"The waves were bigger than anything," Ivan, the older one, said.

"Ivan was sick all over the side of the boat," Alex broke in proudly. "Twice."

"It was a trial," Clara confirmed. "But we're here now."

We moved to a narrow table, where the boys fell on plates of biscuits as if they'd been caged. "You really are *too* beautiful," Clara exclaimed. "And married now, I understand."

I didn't know how to answer her, and so only nodded.

"Harry was the joy of my life." Clara's mouth trembled. Her eyes silvered with tears. "You've no idea how hard it's been, with the debts and the uncertainty. And now I'm alone again."

As she dabbed at her tears with a handkerchief, I stared at her, feeling slightly stunned. For some reason, I thought she might try to explain herself or apologize. That she might ask regretfully about Clutt, or want to know how things had really been for me. But she was very much caught up in her own sad story, this recent one, as if there weren't any other.

"Mbagathi is beautiful," I said, making an effort to plunge ahead. "The boys will love it there. They can run around to their hearts' content, and maybe even go to school. The baroness has found a teacher for the Kikuyu children on her land."

"You really have been my saviour, Beryl. I knew I could count on you." She sniffed loudly. "Isn't your sister marvellous, boys?"

I was their sister, and also a stranger, a fact that didn't seem to rattle them as much as it did me. Ivan ignored Clara completely. Alex glanced up with his lips covered in biscuit crumbs, and then dived back in.

Two hours later, I drove them away from the hotel, the boys spitting over the open sides of the borrowed car into the dust. Clara chided them distractedly, and then said, "I just can't get over how much Nairobi has changed. It's a proper town now. You should have seen it back then."

"Well, you've been gone a long time."

"In those days you couldn't walk for the goats. A postal office no bigger than a can of beans. No proper shops. No one to talk to." She swatted at the still-spitting boys with her handkerchief, and turned around. "I just can't get over it."

She didn't seem embarrassed to be speaking of the past with me. She didn't seem to remember I *was* a part of her past in the colony, in fact. Though maybe that was best, when I thought about it—if we could treat each other more impartially, as if there were nothing to apologize or make amends for. As if nothing had been lost. Then perhaps there might not be any further pain ahead. I hoped not as I squeezed the steering wheel with my gloved hands, pointing us out of town on the rutted road and towards Mbogani.

It had been more than a month since my last visit to Karen's. I went to the main house first. Karen was up the slope at the factory but heard the motor and came running, her hair windblown, a fingerprint of coffee dust on her cheek. There was no sign of Denys anywhere. Perhaps he was away still—or again.

"I'm sorry I look a fright." Karen extended her hand to Clara. "Today we're busy with a harvest."

"Beryl explained all you do here on the ride out. I admire what you've taken on. And your house and lawn are so beautiful." Clara swept around in an appreciative circle.

"You'll want some tea—or sandwiches?"

The boys perked up at the mention of more food, but Clara shushed them. "We've had our tea."

"I'll ride out to the house with you then. Let me just change my shoes."

We motored along the winding road to Mbagathi while the sweet-smelling trees pushed in at us through the windows of the car.

"Oh, it's quaint," Clara said when we arrived. "We'll be very snug here."

"You'll be staying for a while, too, Beryl?" Karen asked.

"I hadn't thought." I stalled, wondering how comfortable I'd be. Clara was a stranger, and a complicated one at that.

"But of course you must. We haven't caught up properly." Clara turned to the boys, who were already down in the dust watching a Hercules beetle towering forward with a twig in its staglike pincers. "Tell her we need her."

"Yes," Ivan said. Alex grunted, never taking his eyes from the beetle.

"It's settled then."

Karen lent us her cook and her houseboy, and left my mother with the names of several Kikuyu *totos* who would be there the next day ready to work if Clara would have them.

When she left, Clara said, "I wouldn't have whispered a word while the baroness was here, but the house *is* a little simple, isn't it?"

"I suppose so. No one's lived here for a while."

"It's much smaller than I imagined."

"There are three bedrooms, and you are three."

"Not for tonight," she clarified.

"But I can sleep anywhere. I'm not fussy."

"That's a wonderful skill, Beryl. You always were the toughest of us."

I flinched, involuntarily, and rearranged myself in my chair. "Dickie's been jockeying, you said?"

"Yes, and very good at it. Do you remember how he could ride?"

I nodded vaguely.

"I know he'd want to be here now, but he hasn't been feeling well. He never had a strong constitution, as you know."

I remembered so little . . . skinned knees when the farm was raw and full of obstacles. Him kicking me once, hard, in my side as we fought over a toy. But even that was too much, in a way. It would have been simpler to have forgotten every last stitch.

"He's going to send money as soon as he can, naturally," she went on, her eyes beginning to well up again. "Forgive a silly woman, Beryl. Forgive me."

That night, I tossed and turned on the sofa near the hearth, feeling unsettled by Clara, her strange combination of neediness and amnesia. I found myself wishing that I hadn't answered her first telegram or that she hadn't thought to send it. But we were here now, stuck in a curious limbo.

Sometime past midnight, long after the fire had died away, it began to rain. I heard the pattering getting louder, and then Clara appeared, kneeling at my side. She wore a nightgown and robe, and held a guttering candle. Her feet were bare and her hair tumbled down her back, making her look very young. "It's pouring."

"Try to ignore it. We get lots of rain at this time of year."

"No, I mean inside." She dragged me to one of the smaller rooms where the boys were huddled together in one bed while a seam in the roofline dripped water down on the blankets. The water was coming straight at them, but they barely had the sense to get out of the way.

"Let's move the bed," I suggested.

"Right," Clara said. She never would have thought of it on her own. That was clear. The boys clambered down, and Clara and I pushed the bed to the other wall.

"It's wet here, too."

The second bedroom was a bit drier. We found buckets in the kitchen and moved them around, catching the drips, then went from room to room, trying to find the safest place for the furniture. "It's hopeless," Clara said, throwing up her hands.

"Only a little rain." I sighed. "You boys don't mind, do you?" But they seemed just as fragile suddenly. Alex had a rumpled bear, a teddy bear, after Roosevelt. He tugged at its ear and looked ready to hide in a cupboard.

"We'll just have to get through the night," I suggested. "Tomorrow we'll see if workers can repair the roof."

"I think it's driest here," my mother said of the couch. "Do you mind if the boys and I have your place?"

"Not at all." I sighed again.

"Thank you. And it would be lovely if we could have a fire, wouldn't it, boys?"

The wood was damp and smoked and took a real effort to get going. When I finally did, I was too exhausted to move the beds again. I fell into the first one I came to and curled up in the damp sheets and tried to sleep.

It rained buckets all the next day. By mid-afternoon, Clara was at her wits' end. Karen had come to try and make things suitable, but the downpour wouldn't stop, and the rain got through everywhere. Finally she moved Clara and the boys into the main house.

"I really am sorry for your trouble," Karen said again and again.

"It's not your fault," Clara assured her, gathering damp bits of her hair into hairpins. But something in her tone told me she *did* hold Karen responsible—or perhaps me instead. I suppose it wasn't a great surprise to see she had very little gumption or resilience, and yet it made me sad for her. How dreadful it would be if everything toppled you and you folded in. Rain, for instance, not to mention the loss of a husband. She was so pitiful I shouldn't have been irritated with her, but I couldn't help it. By dinnertime, I was too fed up with the whole situation and bolted for Soysambu and my horses—for work, which was never mysterious and never failed to soothe me.

"I'll be back at the weekend," I said, and rode off in D's motorcar through thick and spattering red mud.

27

By the time I arrived at Mbogani three days later, Clara had already bolted. She'd hired a car to come and take her and the boys back to Nairobi, leaving only a brief note to apologize for the inconvenience.

"I *did* take care to get the house cleaned up and ready for them," Karen said. "Rain is rain. What could I have done?"

"I hope she left you some money at least."

"Not a rupee."

I was horribly embarrassed. "Let me pay you something."

"Don't be silly. It's not your doing. You can stay and cheer me up, though. I've been lonely."

Late that night the rain began again. This could happen in May and often did—seismic, drenching storms that went on and on, turning the roads into gullies, and gullies into impassable torrents.

"You can't go back in this," Karen said the next morning, looking out through the open veranda at the streaming grey sheets.

"D will be wondering about me. I may have to risk it."

"He's a reasonable man . . . occasionally, anyway. You can't very well swim home."

Before we'd finished talking, a young Somali boy ran up to the house, nearly naked, with red mud splattered up to his slender hips. "Bedar is on his way," the boy announced. "He will be here soon."

Bedar was Denys, obviously. I could read on Karen's face how happy the news made her as she brought the boy inside and insisted he bathe and change and eat something hearty before returning.

"Denys's servants are utterly devoted to him," she told me as she dabbed with a cotton cloth at the wet footprints the boy had left on her tiles. There were servants everywhere, but clearly she liked to work with her hands, and to be useful. "They respect him as if he were one of them. I think they'd lie down in a lion's mouth if he asked them."

I felt her guard lowering a little and inched my way closer. "How did you become friends?"

"At a shoot we threw several years ago. He arrived with Delamere and then came down with a terrible fever and had to stay. I had about given up on finding anything like good company here, but then there he was." She looked up from her work. "Honestly, I'd never met such an intelligent person before. It was the loveliest surprise of that whole year."

"Even with a fever?"

"Yes, even so." She smiled. "But then I went away home, and after that he did, and it's only lately that we're back to our friendship, you see. I feel very fortunate." She stood up and wiped her hands on her apron. Beyond the open door the sky was thick and low and the rain went on and on. "I'll have one of the boys fetch your horse if you'd like. Unless you'll reconsider."

I thought of the slick miles to Soysambu, and then of Denys's hazel eyes and his laughter. I wanted to see him again, and also to know how he and Karen were together. "I may have to," I told her. "It's not going to stop."

All that day Karen stayed focused on Denys's imminent arrival, dreaming up dinner menus and getting her servants to polish the house from top to bottom. Finally, Denys's Somali boy came running into sight again, and Denys himself followed not long after, wet to the skin but somehow cheerful. He rode up, unflappably, while his equally undaunted Somali man, Billea, walked.

"It's a little embarrassing to be held up by rain when you've managed quite well," I confessed after we'd said our hellos.

"I haven't told you about the bits where my horse was up to his neck." He squinted at me, and then took off his hat, water pouring from the brim. "Besides, it's nice to see you."

Karen whisked him away deep into the house to get comfortable before dinner while I took myself into the library, suddenly nervous. I wasn't sure why, but as I tried to page through a pile of Thackeray novels and travel books Karen had set aside for me, I found myself reading the same snatches over and over again, holding on to nothing, while from her perch nearby, the little owl Minerva swivelled her head and looked at me with great, round unblinking eyes. She was the size of a feathered apple, with a glossy beak like the tip of a buttonhook. I went over to her and tried to show her I was a friend, petting her with one finger as Karen had done, and finally she seemed convinced.

Maybe my feelings were only bald insecurity, I thought, looking again at the thick stack of books. Denys and Karen were each so intelligent . . . and together they might make me feel a fool. Would it have killed me to stay at school for a few years and glean some knowledge that had nothing to do with horses or farming or hunting with Kibii? I had been so anxious to be back at home, thrusting myself at what I knew, that I couldn't imagine any part of book learning that might be useful. Now it was probably too late. I could try to soak up a few titbits from the Thackeray and possibly sound clever at dinner, but that would be acting a part, trying to be some version of Karen. *"Stupid,"* I said, irritated with myself, while Minerva stretched out one striped yellow claw. For better or worse, I was who I was. It would have to do.

———

Denys was starved for talk after so many weeks in the bush. During the meal of scented tomato water, blanched tiny lettuces, and turbot in a hollandaise that melted on the spoon, he told us how he'd come back through the North Country. Near Eldoret, he'd stopped at some property he owned and had seen and heard evidence of tourists hunting wild game from their motorcars and leaving the carcasses to rot.

"My God." I had never heard of such a thing. "It's slaughter."

"I blame Teddy Roosevelt," he said. "Those photographs of him straddling slain elephants like some sort of buccaneer. It came off too glamorous. Too easy."

"I thought his hunting was a scheme to collect specimens for museums," Karen said.

"Don't let the museum piece fool you. He was a sportsman through and through." Denys pushed his chair back from the table and lit a cigar. "It's not Roosevelt that gets to me so much as what he started. These animals shouldn't die for nothing. Because someone gets drunk and loads a rifle."

"Perhaps there could be a law one day," Karen said.

"Perhaps. But in the meantime, I hope I don't run into one of these joyriders, or I won't be responsible for my actions."

"You're trying to hold on to paradise." Karen's eyes simmered in the candlelight, intense and deeply black. "Denys remembers too well how unspoiled things were in the early days," she told me.

"So do I. It's hard to forget."

"Beryl's mother was here for a short time," Karen explained to Denys and then said, "I thought she was going to be a tenant at Mbagathi."

"Oh," he said. "I assumed your mother had died."

"It's all right. You wouldn't be very far off. She went away when I was very young."

"I couldn't survive without my mother's love," Karen said. "I write to her every week, on Sunday, and live for the letters she sends. This week I'll tell her about you and say you look like the *Mona Lisa*.

Would you ever let me paint you? You'd make a wonderful picture, just as you are now. Lovely, and also a little lost."

I flushed at her description, feeling pried at. She spoke so frankly, but it was her eyes, too, and how nothing seemed to escape her. "Those things don't really show on my face, do they?"

"I'm sorry, try not to mind me. People interest me so much. They're such wonderful puzzles. Think of it. Half the time we've no idea what we're doing, but we live anyway."

"Yes," Denys said. "Searching out something important and going astray look exactly the same for a while, in fact." He stretched and resettled himself like a rangy tomcat in the sun. "Sometimes no one knows the difference, especially not the poor damned pilgrim." He winked at me, almost imperceptibly. "Now how about a story? No supper without a tale."

I'd been thinking of what I might tell them and had finally settled on Paddy and that day at the Elkingtons' farm. Wanting to hold their attention, I described everything I remembered from the beginning, and slowly—the ride out to Kabete Station and my father's speech about lions. Bishon Singh and his endless turban, the gooseberry bushes and the sizzling crack of Jim Elkington's *kiboko*. After a while, I forgot that I was trying to draw Denys and Karen in and became engrossed myself, almost as if I'd forgotten what was going to happen and how it all turned out.

"You must have been absolutely terrified," Karen said when I'd finished. "I can't think many have lived through such a thing."

"I was, yes. But later I came to see it as a kind of initiation."

"I'll bet it was important for you. We all have those moments—though not always so dramatic." Denys paused, looking into the fire. "They're meant to test us and change us, I think. To make plain what it means to risk everything."

The room grew quiet for a time. I thought of what Denys had said and watched the two of them smoke in silence. Finally, Denys pulled a pocket-sized volume from inside his brown velvet jacket. "I found a small gem in a bookshop when I was in London. It's called *Leaves of Grass*." He opened to a dog-eared page and held it out to me, saying I should read for us.

"God, no. I'll butcher it."

"You won't. I thought of this one particularly for you."

I shook my head.

"You do it, Denys," Karen said, saving me, "in Beryl's honour."

" 'I think I could turn and live with animals,' " he read aloud,

"they are so placid and self-contain'd,
I stand and look at them long and long.
They do not sweat and whine about their condition,
They do not lie awake in the dark and weep for their sins. . . ."

He recited the words simply, not at all theatrically, but they had their own gravity and drama. The poem seemed to be about how naturally dignified animals are and how their lives make more sense than those of humans, which are cluttered with greed and self-pity and talk of a distant God. It was something I'd always believed. He finished with this passage:

"A gigantic beauty of a stallion, fresh and responsive to my
      caresses,
Head high in the forehead, wide between the ears,
Limbs glossy and supple, tail dusting the ground,
Eyes full of sparkling wickedness, ears finely cut, flexibly
      moving."

"It's wonderful," I said quietly. "May I borrow it?"

"Of course." He handed the little volume to me, light as a feather and still warm from his holding it.

I said good night and went off to my room, perching under a lamp to read over more of the poems. The house grew still around me, but after a while it occurred to me that I was hearing sounds coming from down the hall. Mbogani wasn't all that large, and the noises—though muffled—were unmistakable. Denys and Karen were making love.

I closed the book in my hands, feeling a small surge of adrenaline. I'd been so certain they were only close friends. *Why had I thought that?* Blix had said Denys's name so lightly that night he'd come here, but perhaps that only meant he'd come to accept Denys's place in Karen's life. In fact, the more I thought about it, the more obvious it seemed that these two would be drawn together. They were both beautiful and interesting, full of deep water, as the Kips would say. And no matter what Berkeley had said about Denys being elusive in love, he and Karen had an obvious bond. I could see that clearly.

I turned to the book again, leafing through to the animal poem Denys had recited for me, but the black type jumped. Beyond several walls, the lovers were whispering things to each other, their bodies blending with shadows, coming together and apart. Their affair had nothing to do with me, and yet I couldn't stop thinking of them. Finally, I turned out the lamp and pulled the pillow up around my ears, wanting only to go to sleep.

The next day the clouds parted and the sky went a deep fresh blue, and we went out on a small shooting expedition. Ostriches had got into the garden and plucked through most of the baby lettuces. There were dung and feathers everywhere as the birds lurched through the patch taking what they wanted.

Both Denys and Karen looked well rested and happy, when I had slept unpleasantly. Still, tired as I was, and slightly embarrassed by what I had learned the night before, Denys's confidence and ease impressed me, as they always seemed to.

"These birds have brains the size of coffee cherries," Denys explained, hoisting his slim-line Rigby effortlessly onto his shoulder. "If you aim wide, they'll often gambol right into the shot."

"Why not shoot into the sky?"

"It's somehow not enough. They need to feel the whizzing of the cartridge to panic properly." He sighted down the barrel and took expert aim. The group startled as one animal, and then went blundering off in a noisy scatter, awkward as unmanned wheelbarrows.

We laughed at them—it was impossible not to—and then made sure the fencing was secure again. After that we walked together to the top of the ridge to see Karen's view. Her deerhound, Dusk, led the way while I trailed a little behind, thinking about how lightly Denys wore his body. There wasn't the smallest twinge of self-consciousness in him. He knew how to stand and where to put his arms and his feet, and how to accomplish what needed doing—and never seemed to doubt himself or any part of the world he moved in. I understood why Karen was drawn to him, even if she still cared for Blix and appeared determined to remain his wife.

"Where did you get your keen eye?" I asked him when I'd caught up.

"On the golf links at Eton, I suppose." He laughed. "What about yours?"

"How do you know I have one?"

"Don't you?"

"I learned from the Kips on my father's land. You should see me with a slingshot."

"As long as I'm out of range." He smiled. "I'd like that."

"Bror taught me to shoot," Karen said as she fell into line with us. "At first I didn't understand why anyone would want to do it. But there's something sort of ecstatic in it, isn't there? Not bloodlust but a powerful connection you feel with all of life. Maybe that sounds cruel."

"Not to me. Not if it's done with honour." I was thinking of *arap* Maina, of his warrior's skill but also the way he had great respect for even the smallest creature. I'd felt that so strongly whenever I'd hunted with him, but also every time I'd walked beside him, as I was doing with Denys now. For some reason, being near Denys seemed to put me in touch with those years at Green Hills. Maybe it was because I saw a graceful and utterly competent warrior in him and was reminded of the warrior in myself, the bit of Lakwet I still carried with me.

By then we'd climbed above the coffee plants and thorn thickets and a narrow, twisting riverbed winking with quartz. The hill flattened out into a kind of plateau, and from there we could see straight down into the Rift Valley, its crags and ridges like pieces of a broken bowl. The rain had finally cleared, but a billowy ring of clouds rested over Kilimanjaro to the south, its flat top painted with snow and shadows. East and a little north, the Kikuyu Reserve drew itself out in a long rolling plain all the way to Mount Kenya, a hundred miles or more away.

"You can see how I wouldn't want to be anywhere else," Karen said. "Denys wants to be buried here."

"A pair of eagles have an eyrie somewhere nearby," he said. "I like the idea of them soaring nobly over my carcass." He squinted into the sun, his face brown and healthy, his long limbs throwing purple shadows behind him. There was a single line of perspiration running along his back between his shoulder blades, and his white cotton sleeves were rolled over his smooth, tanned forearms. I couldn't imagine him any other way but this: every inch of his body absolutely and completely alive.

"The Kikuyu put out their dead for the hyenas," I said. "If we could choose, I think I'd take eagles, too."

28

*O*n September, Ringleader ran for his life at the St. Leger and placed second without a waver or a flinch, no swelling, no whiff of his troubled history, as if he'd been reinvented. When I stood at the edge of the winners' enclosure and watched D accept his silver cup, I felt good about the work I'd done, that I'd read Ringleader correctly and saw what he needed to become great again—what he was meant to be.

Everyone had come to town for the race. Eastleigh was overrun with grooms and trainers, so D arranged to have a canvas tent put up on the lawn of the club for me, with my name on a stake out front. It wasn't glamorous. I had to stoop in half to climb inside, crawling through mosquito cloth, but Berkeley thought it might be fun to have a drink there. He turned up with a chilled bottle, and we sat outside the tent flap on stools.

As always, he was turned out in beautiful clothes, but he looked pale. Perhaps he'd grown thinner, too, but when I asked about his health, he brushed me off. "You see there?" he pointed to a small cottage not far away in a grove of eucalyptus trees. It was made of stucco, with a rounded door and its own miniature garden—like something from a storybook. "That's where Denys stayed for years . . . before he moved out to Ngong."

"You should have told me about Denys and the baroness. They're in love, aren't they?"

Berkeley's eyes grazed over mine. "Should I have? I thought you weren't interested." We fell silent for a few minutes as he refilled our champagne glasses. Swarms of bubbles crested into buttery-looking foam. "In any case, I'm not sure how long it will last."

"Because Denys can't be caught?"

"There's 'settling down,' and then there's Denys. He brought her back a ring from Abyssinia made of such soft gold it can be shaped to fit any finger. She's been wearing it like an engagement ring, missing the point, of course. Not that I don't love Tania"—he used Denys's pet name for Karen—"I do. But she shouldn't forget who Denys is. Trying to domesticate him won't work. It's certainly not the way to his heart."

"If the reins are too tight, why has he moved there?"

"He loves her, of course. And it makes some things easier." He combed his moustache with his fingertips absentmindedly. "She's had some fairly brutal headaches lately. Money trouble."

"You heard about the fiasco with my mother, I'm sure."

"Ah yes." He grimaced. "The widow Kirkpatrick and the leaking rooftop."

"I'm still so mortified."

"The rent on Mbagathi would only have been a drop in the bucket anyway." His eyes lit up for a brief moment at his own joke before he said, "Where do things stand with your mother now?"

"Damned if I know. She's in town somewhere, I heard. The whole situation is more and more bizarre. Why are people so complicated?"

He shrugged. "What would you hope for with her—if it could be anything you liked?"

"Honestly, I couldn't even say. To care less, maybe. She was away for so long, I didn't imagine she could still do harm, but now . . ." I let my voice trail off.

"My father died when I was young. We all thought it was rather fortunate at first. It simplified all sorts of things. But over time . . . well. Let's just say I've developed a theory that only the vanished truly leave their mark. And I still don't feel I've sorted it out. Maybe we never do survive our families."

"Oh, dear. And this is meant to cheer me up?"

Under his moustache, his lips stretched into a wan smile. "Sorry, darling. At least Tania hasn't held your mother's bad behaviour against you; I'm certain of it. I'm riding out there later for dinner. Come along."

I shook my head. "I'm thinking of turning in early."

"You have the energy of ten men and you know it." He fixed me with a prying look. "I think you're pining over Denys, and if you are, darling, he's—"

"No, Berkeley." I cut him off. "No warnings, and no more advice. I can fend for myself, thank you very much, and if knocks are coming my way, I'll find a way to take them, all right? I have a hard skull."

"You do," he conceded, "though I'm not sure anyone's is hard enough. Not when it comes to these sorts of things."

We finished the bottle, and he went off to Ngong while I lit the lamp and tucked myself into the cot in my tent, pulling the little volume of *Leaves of Grass* from my satchel. I had made off with it like a thief months before—and couldn't quite bring myself to give it back, not yet. Opening the book I read, *I think I could turn and live with animals.* What moved me about the poem, I realized, was that Denys had seen me in it. The self-sufficiency and free-spiritedness Whitman was celebrating, the connection to wild things and wildness— that was a part of me, and Denys, too. We recognized these things in each other, no matter what else was true or possible.

A breeze lifted the canvas flaps and stays. Through a triangle of mosquito netting, the night pulsed. There were a host of stars in the sky, all of them close and sharp.

29

In November, Karen hosted a shooting party and invited me to come and stay for a few days. Between Boy and Jock and a string of new, bewildering thoughts about Denys, part of me wondered if it was wise to accept—but I did.

When I arrived, Denys and Karen were playing host and hostess to a houseful of guests including Ginger Mayer, whom I'd never met before but had heard about from Cockie. Apparently she had been Ben's lover for ages, and somehow the two women remained friends. They were both on the lawn when I turned up, playing a game that looked something like golf and something like cricket, using squash racquets, croquet mallets, and even a riding crop. Ginger wore a flowing silk dress that she'd knotted between her legs to form culottes. She was beautiful, with crimped auburn hair and freckles. She and Cockie could have been sisters as they raced around each other to swat at the ratty-looking leather-seamed ball.

"I'm surprised to see you here," I said to Cockie when she came up to say hello. "I thought Karen wasn't speaking to you."

"She still isn't, not technically, but some sort of truce is in the works. Maybe it's because she's finally got what she wants." We both gazed over to where Karen and Denys stood on the veranda looking over dozens of bottles of wine, very much the master and mistress of the house. "How are things with Jock?"

"We're at a stalemate, I think. I've been trying to press for the divorce, but he won't respond. Not reasonably anyway."

"I'm sorry, darling. But it all has to get sorted soon, doesn't it? Even the worst things end . . . that's how we go on."

When she danced back to the game with her racquet, I went inside and saw that Karen had outdone herself. Candles and flowers were everywhere, and the table was set with her most beautiful china. Each surface and view had been choreographed, perfectly arranged to bring comfort, and also admiration. Karen might write and paint, but this was another kind of art, and she did it well.

"Is there some special occasion?" I asked her.

"Not really. I'm just so happy I don't want to keep it to myself." Then she went off to instruct Juma about some detail of the menu while I stood in place, reminded of something she'd told me months before—that she'd *meant* to be happy. I'd heard pure determination in her words, and here lay her quarry, as if she had chased and hunted it down. She'd gone full tilt in the derby of her life and won the grand prize.

When the dinner hour arrived, the houseboys donned white jackets and gloves and served seven courses for us, while Karen directed everything smoothly from the end of the table with a small silver bell. When I'd been here alone she'd worn simple white skirts and shirt-waists, but now she was in rich plum-coloured silk. A rhinestone band swept back her dark curls. Her face was heavily powdered and her eyes deeply shadowed. She made a stunning picture, but of course it wasn't me she meant to impress.

I'd brought one of the two dresses I owned for town, but it probably wasn't fine enough and I worried that it set me apart. That wasn't the only gap to bridge, either. Everyone seemed to know the same jokes and songs. Denys and Berkeley were Eton men, and there was a tune they sang over and over as the night went on, some sort of boating tribute that called for *rowing together, steady from stroke to bow,* with Denys singing loudest in a beautiful ringing tenor. Laughter and wine flowed freely, and I couldn't help feeling slightly outside of it all. I was the youngest guest by far and the most provincial. Karen had taken to referring to me as "the child," as in, to Ginger: "Isn't Beryl the loveliest child you ever saw?"

Ginger was seated to my left at dinner. All I really knew about her was what Cockie had told me, that she was Ben's paramour. She nudged ash from her cigarette into a cut-glass tray and said to me, "You walk like a cat. Has anyone ever told you that?"

"No. Is that a compliment?"

"But of course it is." She shook her head at me so that her red curls trembled. "You're not a bit like the other women round here, are you?" Her blue eyes were enormous and acute. Though I felt myself wriggling a little under her scrutiny, I also didn't want to back down.

"Is there really only one sort of woman?"

"It's catty of me to say, but sometimes there seems to be. I've just returned from Paris where absolutely everyone was wearing the same Lanvin gown and pearls. That stopped being fresh in about two minutes flat."

"I've never travelled," I told her.

"Oh, you absolutely should," she insisted, "if only so that you can come home and really see it for what it is. That's my favourite part."

After the table had been cleared, almost everyone gathered around the stone hearth on chairs or benches or great stuffed cushions. Karen draped herself in one corner like a piece of art, with a long ebony cigarette holder in one hand and a red glass goblet in the other. Denys sat close to her, and when I came nearer I could hear them discussing Voltaire. One rushed to fill the end of the other's sentence. They looked like the same person halved or twinned, as if they'd always been sitting just like this, leaning close, their eyes alive.

———

The next morning I rose at dawn to go shooting with the men. I bagged more ducks than anyone but Denys and got several claps on the back for it.

"If I'm not careful, you'll outshoot me," Denys said, shouldering his Rigby.

"Would that be terrible?"

"It would be marvellous, actually." He squinted into the sun. "I've always liked a woman who could aim well and ride better . . . the type who stands on her own two feet and keeps everyone on their toes. Other men can have the demure shrinking ones."

"Was your mother like that? Is that where you get your appreciation?"

"She was a strong woman, yes. And she might have made a great adventurer if she hadn't had so much to do."

"You're not keen on family life." It was a statement. He was becoming clearer and clearer to me.

"It's awfully small, isn't it?"

"Africa is the cure, then, the opposite of being boxed in. Has it ever failed you? I mean, can you imagine this place starting to pinch on you, too?"

"Never." He said it plainly, without a second thought. "It's always new. It always seems to be reinventing itself, doesn't it?"

"It does," I agreed. It was exactly what I'd wished I'd said to Ginger the night before, what I thought without quite being able to put my finger on it. Kenya was forever shedding its skin and showing itself to you all over again. You didn't need to sail away for that. You only needed to turn around.

When Denys strode off on those endless legs, I matched his pace in my muck-covered boots with a strong sensation that he and I were quite alike in several ways. I couldn't compete with Karen on the side of refinement and intellect. I would never be able to . . . but neither did she have what I had.

When we returned to Mbogani, two fine autos were in the yard, and two new sets of guests had arrived to join the party—Mr. and

Mrs. Carsdale-Luck, the wealthy pair who ran the top-notch horse farm called Inglewood up north in Molo, and John Carberry and his beautiful wife, Maia, who owned a coffee estate up north near Nyeri, on the far side of the Aberdares.

Carberry was an Irish-born aristocrat, apparently, but I would never have guessed. He was rugged-looking and lanky and fair, with a broad American accent he'd taken up, I was told, when he denounced Ireland and his heritage.

Karen introduced him to me as "Lord Carberry," but he pumped my hand cheerfully and corrected her, nearly drawling, "JC." Maia was fresh and lovely in summer-weight silk and lace stockings, with shoes that had her teetering above the dowdy, frumpish Mrs. Carsdale-Luck, who kept fanning herself and complaining of the heat.

"JC and I are off to America next week," Maia was explaining to Karen and Mrs. Carsdale-Luck. "We're going to finish my flight training there."

"How many hours have you logged?" Denys asked keenly.

"Just ten, but JC says I've taken to it like a duck to water."

"I'm dying to get up there myself," Denys said. "I was certified in the war, but then haven't had a chance to get back to it. Or a damned plane, for that matter."

"Come up in ours," JC said. "I'll wire you when we're back."

"Wouldn't you need a lot of training?" Karen asked warily.

"It's like riding a bicycle," JC said airily, and the two men strode off to examine a new rifle.

The aeroplane was utterly new for me. On the few occasions when I'd seen one high above, stitching a pale-blue sky with puffs of smoke, it seemed silly and wrong to me, a child's toy. But Denys was clearly drawn to flight, and so was Maia.

"You're not terrified you'll drop right out of the sky?" Mrs. Carsdale-Luck asked her incredulously, her hand still flapping around her damp face and neck.

"We all have to go some way." Maia smiled and a dimple appeared in her rosy cheek. "At least I'd make a proper splash."

30

Kekopey was an estate owned by Berkeley's brother, Galbraith Cole. It stood on the western edge of Lake Elmenteita, near a natural hot spring. In Masai, the name meant "the place where green turns white," and soda ash bubbled up steadily there to drift sideways, like snow. It caught in your throat and could sting your eyes, too, but the waters were supposed to be medicinal. People often bathed there, fending off snakes and scorpions. I wouldn't do that, not for any amount of hot water, but I happily rode to Kekopey with D for Boxing Day for a change of scenery, and because I thought it would be fun.

When we arrived, Denys and Berkeley were camped out with cocktails by the fire. Apparently they'd turned up in the middle of the night having hacked from Gilgil in the dark after their car broke down. Karen had stayed at Mbogani.

"We tried to mend the springs with rawhide first," Berkeley explained, "but it was too dark to see anything. Finally we loaded ourselves down with the ducks and got on with it."

"Fifty pounds of duck," Denys said.

"It's a damned miracle you weren't set on by lions," D said.

"That's what I was thinking," Berkeley said, "or trying not to."

As Denys said hello to us, he kissed me on the cheek. "You look well, Beryl."

"Doesn't she?" Berkeley said.

"Berkeley has a special sense about what women need to hear," Galbraith's wife, Nell, said. She was small and dark in the way Karen was, but without the powder and kohl, or the sharp intelligence.

"Beryl already knows she's beautiful," Denys said. "She was beautiful when she looked in her glass this morning. What could possibly have changed?"

"Don't be difficult, Denys," Nell chided. "All women like a little flattery from time to time."

"What if they didn't? What if they simply liked themselves and no one needed to bend backwards to flatter them? Wouldn't it all be simpler then?"

"We're only talking about compliments, Denys," Berkeley said. "Don't be so dramatic."

"I see his point," I said. "And honestly, how far will beauty get you anyway? What about strength? Or courage?"

"Oh dear." Berkeley laughed to Nell. "Now they're ganging up on me."

In the dining room, Nell had set up lines of filled champagne flutes. I drank a glass down quickly, feeling the bubbles sting my nose, and then took two back to Berkeley and Denys. "Champagne is absolutely *compulsory* in Africa," I said in my best impression of Berkeley.

He laughed, his eyes crinkling. "And all this time I thought I was talking to myself."

I shook my head. "Happy Christmas."

"Happy Christmas, Diana," Denys said softly, and the word flickered through me like a living thing.

For dinner, a suckling pig had been roasted over smoked wood, and there were other delicacies I hadn't seen in ages—cranberry relish and roasted chestnuts and Yorkshire pudding. I sat across from Denys, who couldn't seem to stop eating.

"I've got a special permit for ivory and will be three months out on safari after the New Year," he said. "I might line my pockets with these chestnuts."

"Poor Denys," D said.

"Poor Denys nothing. He's going to make a fortune," Berkeley said.

"Where are you headed this time?" I asked.

"To Tanganyika."

D said, "That's Masai territory."

"Yes. Not much there in the way of roads, but the game should be good if my lorry holds out."

"You might pack the rawhide, just in case," I suggested.

"Ha. Yes. I'll do that." And then he filled his plate again.

There were games after dinner and then smoking by the fire, and then brandy—all of it moving at two different speeds for me, stretching out like something frozen, and also half gone already. I couldn't properly explain it, even to myself, but I couldn't imagine leaving or missing the slightest opportunity to be near Denys. Something was gathering in me, pushing up from under my skin—a feeling I couldn't name.

When D got ready to leave I had three different excuses for why I had to stay. I don't think he believed any of them, but he fetched his hat and said his good nights, giving me only a last dubious look before heading off into the night. *I'm not doing anything rash,* I wanted to tell him, but of course that wasn't true.

It *was* rash to sit alone with Denys by the hearth after everyone had gone to bed, and to puzzle over how to get closer to him when he belonged to Karen. Rash and wrong, and yet it was all I could think about. A pair of charred logs smouldered in the grate. Reddish light caught the strong planes and ridges of his hands in a mesmerizing way.

"You talk about safaris as if something essential can be found there," I told him. "Maybe only there. I used to feel that way about my father's farm, near Njoro."

"Beautiful country."

"The very best."

"When I first started the safaris, you know, there weren't any lorries. The porters carried everything, and you had to cut your way through with a machete. There were grisly stories, too . . . about hunters and gun bearers being skewered or gored. One had his face taken off by the horn of a threatened buffalo. Another startled a lion up by Longonot and had his stomach ripped clean out. Everything was wilder, and the land was, too. Going out felt like gambling against a well-stacked deck."

"You can't really be wistful about gorings?" I smiled, and when he smiled back, the skin around his eyes creased and his lips curved higher on one side. I was beginning to be an expert on his face. I could have closed my eyes then and seen all of him just as clearly.

"The last time I went out, the client wanted four different kinds of wine at every meal. We had an icebox bumping along with us, too, and bearskin rugs."

"I wouldn't want any of that, just the stars, thank you very much."

"That's what I mean. If a client wants to be out in the bush, at least he should try and feel it. See it for what it really is. He wants the trophy, but what is it a sign of if he hasn't even really been there?"

"Will you take me out sometime? I want to see it . . . before it's all gone."

"All right. I think you'd understand it."

"I think I would, too."

Galbraith's pet serval cat came along looking for scraps or a good scratch. It rolled on the floor at Denys's feet, revealing the pale spotted ruff along its belly. The fire was almost cold now, and the night was slipping away. Denys stood up and stretched broadly, and I spoke quickly, on pure instinct.

"Can I stay with you?"

"Is that a good idea?" I'd caught him by surprise. "I thought you and Tania were becoming friends."

"I don't see what one has got to do with the other." It wasn't the truth, but I didn't know how to say what I really felt, that I wanted this night with him. One night, and then I would forget any hope of him for good. "We're friends, too, aren't we?"

His eyes met and held mine, and as blithe as I was being—or trying to be—I felt his look in my gut, turning everything inside out. I stood up. We were just a foot away from each other, and he reached out to touch my chin with the tip of his finger. Then, without answering me, he turned and walked down the hall towards his room. I followed him a few minutes later, and when I did, everything was so black I had to inch through the door he'd left open. I could feel the wooden boards under my bare feet, smooth and soundless, and how the cottony dark was like its own sort of animal all around me. Neither of us spoke or made a noise, but I sensed where he was and moved in that direction. Step by step I found him, feeling my way.

31

*W*hen I woke it was impossibly dark. Denys was next to me. His breath was still and even, and as my eyes adjusted, I could make out the long curve of his hip, one leg loosely thrown over the other. I had imagined our being together before—the crush of his arms and how he would taste—but I'd never worked out how it might be after, what we would say to each other, how it would change the way we were, or not. How stupid that was. I was in real trouble now, I realized.

He opened his eyes as I lay watching him. Everything stopped whirling for a moment and stood stock-still. He didn't blink or look away, and when he reached to pull me beneath him his movements were slow and deliberate. The first time had been rushed, as if neither of us wanted a moment to breathe or consider what we were setting into motion. Now time stopped completely and we stopped with it. The house was quiet. The night beyond the window had hushed itself as well, and there was only the fact of our two bodies rippled with shadow. We pressed to get closer, to push through something—but even then, I didn't think, *This is the love that will change my life.* I didn't think, *I don't belong to myself any more.* I only kissed him, dissolving, and it was done.

When Denys fell asleep again, I dressed without a sound, slipping out of the house and down to Galbraith's stables to borrow a horse. The horse might take a little explaining the next day, I knew, but not as much as my face when I wouldn't be able to hide what had happened. The pony was a sure-footed Arab, and though it was dark when we set out, I wasn't afraid. Within a few miles, pale light began to thicken to the east and then the sun rose clean and sharp, the same intense colour as the flamingos resting in the shallows of Elmenteita. As I came nearer the water's edge, I could see them beginning to stir as a group, as if they were all knitted together beneath the surface. When they fed, they fed in twos and threes, sieving the muddy water for one another, pulling along in S-shaped wading strides.

I'd seen this same picture hundreds of times, but today it seemed to mean something else. The lake was as still as a skin, as if this were the first morning of the world. I stopped to let the pony drink his fill, and when I mounted again I clucked him from a walk into a canter, and the flamingos rose and turned like a tide. They swept one way over the rim of the lake, all pale bellies and furled wings, and then twisted back as a single body, a gyration of colour that swept me up inside it. I had been sleeping, I realized. Since the moment my father had told me the farm was finished, I'd been asleep or on the run or both. Now, there was sun on the water and the sound of a thousand flamingos beating the air. I didn't know what would happen now. How it would be with Denys and Karen, or how all these snarled feelings inside me would be set to rights. I had no earthly idea of any of it, but at least I was awake now. At least there was that.

Four days later, D threw a New Year's party at a hotel he owned in Nakuru. Everyone came dressed in his or her very finest to ring out 1923 with bright paper horns and bring 1924 down from the place it waited, the newness of it like a length of unmarked cloth. The band members were promised caviar and all the champagne they could guzzle if they would play until dawn. The small parquet dance floor was a riotous mass of swinging arms and legs.

"How's your heart these days?" I asked Berkeley when we danced. He wore a bright red Christmas tie, but there were dark smudges beneath his eyes, and his skin was ashy.

"A little battered, but still ticking. How's yours?"

"About the same, actually."

We waltzed past a table where Denys and Karen sat talking, he in a brilliant-white suit, and she in yards of black taffeta that bared her pale shoulders. It made my chest hurt to look at them. I hadn't spoken to or even seen Denys since I had crept from his bed like a thief. I hadn't been in touch with Karen since her shooting party and didn't know how I would begin to behave normally with either of them. Normal was gone for good now.

When the song had finished, I excused myself to find a drink. It took me ages to push my way through to the bar, and by the time I had, Karen was there already. Her long ebony cigarette holder sculpted the space between us.

"Happy New Year, Beryl."

"Happy New Year." I leaned to kiss her on the cheek. Guilt surged through me in small waves. "How are you?"

"Up to my neck. My shareholders want me to sell the farm."

"Are things really that bad?"

"Nearly always." Her teeth clicked on the ebony holder as she pulled in smoke, releasing it slowly, revealing nothing. That was Karen. Her words were so full they made you think you knew everything about her, but it was a magician's trick. The truth was she kept her secrets closest when she said them outright.

I said, "Having Denys around must help." I was struggling to be natural.

"Yes, it means everything to me. Do you know I die a little whenever he goes away?"

I felt my chest tighten. Her poetic flair was the same as ever, but something in her tone made me wonder if she was warning me some-how, or staking her claim. I watched the angles of her cheekbones through the quivering smoke, thinking of how good she was at read-ing people. I was "the child" to her, but it was possible she sensed what had changed. That she tasted it on the air.

"Can you convince your shareholders to give you one last chance?"

"I've had it already. Twice, actually—but I'll have to do some-thing. I might marry for instance."

"Aren't you still married?" I managed.

"Of course. I'm just thinking ahead." She looked down her angu-lar nose at me. "Or perhaps I'll give up everything and move away to China, or Marseilles."

"You don't really mean that."

"Sometimes . . . it's a fantasy I have of beginning again. Surely you have one, too."

"Of leaving Kenya? I've never thought of that. I wouldn't be the same anywhere else."

"You might change your mind one day, though. If you're hurting enough." She fixed me with one of her looks, her eyes arrowing through me, and then she moved away.

For the next few hours I stood along the wall behind the band, piecing over what Karen had said and wondering if she knew what had happened with Denys. He certainly wouldn't risk coming over to talk to me, but part of me was glad of that. I wasn't sure what I would say to him, or what I even wanted. Everywhere I looked, complex pairings came together and slid apart again, like characters in a melo-drama. Lives tumbled. They changed in an instant . . . that's how quickly something could be newly begun, or finished for ever. Every now and then, those things didn't look so very different on the sur-face. They both cost a great deal, too.

It was nearly dawn when I left the Nakuru Hotel with D and Boy Long. I walked between them, relieved the night was finally over. I had only come face-to-face with Denys once that evening, in a mo-ment at the bar when our gazes had clicked and locked. Then Karen had put a hand on his shoulder, and he'd turned round, and that was that. Now I was deflated and bleary-eyed. That's probably why I didn't realize what was happening at first. How Jock appeared from nowhere and began lurching towards us from across the street, calling out words I couldn't understand. It jolted me even to see him.

"You were supposed to look out for her," he slurred at D. His eyes were wild, not quite focused on anything.

I felt Boy flare beside me. He made as if to charge Jock, but D stepped forward first, saying, "Let's talk like men and get you settled down."

"I won't be made a fool of," Jock spat, and before anyone could say another word, he sent one arm wildly through the air at D, landing just shy of him, while my blood went icy and thick. Somehow he'd learned about Denys—that's all I could think.

D ducked backwards, nearly losing his balance. I could tell he was rattled and probably panicked, too. Boy had had enough by then and made a move to grab Jock's arm, but Jock erupted, stepping out of Boy's reach and swinging out wide again. This time, his fist caught D on the chin with a sickening wallop. D staggered and went down on one knee, as if all the air had left his body. Boy scrambled for Jock, but he was windmilling punches now, bellowing something about getting satisfaction.

But even if my being with Denys had come to light, what did that have to do with D? Why on earth go after an old man, and an innocent one? Nothing made any sense, and Jock was so drunk he'd become wooden—flailing and rawboned and wild.

"Stop it!" I screamed. "It's D. D! Stop!" I pulled at him from behind, slamming into his back with my fists, but he threw me off easily. I landed hard and scrambled up again.

D had fallen to his side on the ground and lay crumpled there, his arms cradling his head, while Jock went after him again. Everything was happening so fast. "Stop, stop it!" I kept crying out, suddenly terrified that Jock would kill him.

I screamed at Boy to get help from the hotel, and he finally ran out with a handful of men who wedged themselves between Jock and D. They pinned Jock to one side of the building where he strained against their grip, his face purple with rage.

"You selfish bitch," he spat at me. "You thought you could rut around like a dirty whore and I wouldn't find out? That I wouldn't fight back?" With a great push, he flung off the arms of the men and then staggered away at a run, down the street and into the dark.

D was a ruin. We got him to the infirmary somehow, his eye sealing up by the moment, his mouth and nose dripping blood. A surgeon was called out of bed to treat him, and Boy and I sat for hours waiting as stitches were sewn and plaster applied. His arm had been fractured in three places, his neck sprained, and his jaw broken. When the surgeon described the extent of D's injuries, I buried my face in my hands, overcome with shame. My recklessness had lit the fuse in Jock. I should have known what he was capable of. This was all my fault.

"Will he be all right?" I asked the surgeon.

"With time. We'll keep him here for several weeks at least, I'd say, and once he's home he'll require a nurse."

"Anything he needs," Boy assured him.

When the surgeon had gone, I thought of Jock bolting off into the night and how he might get off scot-free. "We should go to the authorities anyway," I told Boy.

"D doesn't want this out in the open. He's protecting you . . . both of us, probably, but also himself. How would it look for the Vigilance Committee to have him seem so vulnerable to attack?"

"I suppose . . . it just doesn't seem right."

"Right and wrong don't always factor in cases like this."

"Don't they, though?" I asked him, thinking painfully, horribly, of how answerable I was to all of it.

When I was finally able to see D, I took in the horror of his purpled jaw and forehead, the braces and plasters, the blood snagging his white hair, the pain in his face. I took his hand. "I'm so sorry."

D couldn't speak, but he nodded ever so slightly. The whites of his eyes were bloodshot. He looked incredibly fragile and ancient, too.

"Is there anything I can do?" He merely turned away into his pillow.

As D stirred, his breath caught and he grimaced before his breathing fell into a steady pattern again. I watched the rise and fall of his chest for a long time, and finally I dropped into an uneasy sleep.

32

In the weeks that followed, gossip filtered to me at Soysambu from all over the colony. Apparently my exposure at the St. Leger had set tongues wagging about Boy again. Jock had got wind of it and figured he'd had enough. The details of my marriage were all common knowledge now. Maybe they always had been—but thankfully I didn't hear a whisper about my night with Denys. Somehow that secret was safely tucked away even if nothing else was.

D stayed in town, mending, while Boy was preparing to up sticks. He'd left his job at the ranch and booked a passage to England.

"I'm finally going to marry my girl in Dorking," he said, throwing bits of pirate-bright clothing into his duffel bag. "I feel a bit strange leaving you in the lurch."

"It's all right," I told him. "I see why you'd want to go."

Though he didn't look up from his duffel, I saw how he struggled with his pride. "If you ever need anything, I hope you'll search me out."

"In Dorking?" I looked at him sceptically.

"Why not? We're friends, aren't we?"

"We are," I said, and kissed him on the cheek.

———

After Boy had gone, my conscience continued to prickle and sting, keeping me awake at night. I had always told myself that leaving Jock and running around with Boy wasn't any worse than what anyone else did in the colony. But at Soysambu, there were now rumours among the ranch hands that Jock had threatened to shoot Boy if he ever saw him in town. That's why he'd run to Dorking.

I felt alone and overwhelmed and dearly wished my father were nearby. I needed the anchor of his presence and also his advice. Should I try to ignore the gossip, or was there something I could do to help it all blow over? And how would I begin to deal with Jock, when he'd become such a loose and desperate cannon?

When D came home, he was incredibly fragile and shaken. He would be in bed a full six months while he recovered.

"I feel terrible for what Jock did," I told him while the nurse settled his bedclothes and changed his bandages. I'd said it dozens of times, but couldn't seem to stop.

"I know." D had a plaster on one arm up to the shoulder. His neck was in a stiff brace. "The thing is, the community is protective of me. More than I am of myself."

"What do you mean?"

He asked the nurse to leave us for a moment and then said, "I've tried to keep your name out of it, but when the colony chooses to feel scandalized, it doesn't let up."

I felt a rippling of humiliation and also outrage, the two feelings twisted up in each other. "I don't care what anyone thinks of me," I lied.

"I don't have that luxury." He lowered his eyes to his hands on the neatly folded sheets. "I think you should stay away from the races for a while."

"And do what? Work is the only thing I have."

"People will forget eventually, but it's fresh now. They want your head on a stake."

"Why not Jock's head? He's the one who's gone mad."

He shrugged. "We're all very liberal until something shines a light on us. Somehow everyone understands a husband's jealous raging more than a wife's . . . indiscretions. It's not fair, but what is?"

"You're firing me then."

"I think of you as a daughter, Beryl. You'll always have a place here."

I swallowed hard. My mouth was dry as chalk. "I don't blame you, D. It's what I deserve."

"Who knows what anyone deserves? We like to play judge and jury, but we're all a rotten mess under our skins." He reached for my arm and patted it. "Come back when the fire dies down. And take good care of yourself."

Scalding tears threatened, but I fought them back. I nodded and thanked him, and then walked out of his room on shaky legs.

I didn't know where to go. My mother and Dickie were out of the question. Cockie was away in London visiting family. Berkeley was too worried about me, too perceptive, and I would never go to Karen now. I had betrayed her—that was the only way to see it—and if I still liked and admired her, no matter what I felt for Denys, well, that was a puzzle for me to work out on my own. In any case, I'd probably already lost her respect—and Denys's, too.

It was painful how much respect seemed to matter now that my life was under glass. It reminded me of Green Hills and the scandal around my father's bankruptcy. He had a tougher skin than I had, and the gossip hadn't really seemed to touch him. I wished again, fiercely, that he were here to guide me now. I felt shaken to the core, right down to my bones. All I could think of was getting away from the colony as quickly as possible, away from prying eyes and wagging tongues. Even Cape Town wasn't far enough. But what place was? I thought and thought, turning the problem over and turning out my pockets. I had about sixty pounds all told, almost nothing. How much would nothing get me? Just how far could I go?

33

Tinned chestnuts and sugared almonds in a window at Fortnum & Mason. Candy-striped cotton shirts and cravats and handkerchiefs dressing the shopfront mannequins on Regent Street. Lorry drivers standing on their horns, clamouring for the right of way. The sights and sounds of London were dizzying and overwhelming. And then there was the cold. I'd left Mombasa on a sultry day. Standing at the ship's rail, I watched Kilinidi Harbour shrink away, a warm wind blowing through my hair and thin blouse. In London, sooty snow clogged the cobbles. The walking was icy, and my boots were all wrong, and so were my clothes. I didn't own an overcoat or galoshes and had only one address in my pocket to guide me on my way—for Boy Long and his new wife, Genessee, in Dorking. In so many respects, it was odd to turn up at the home of my ex-lover, but after what we'd been through I believed him when he let me know I could lean on him. And I trusted him. That meant everything.

When I got to Dorking, it was a bit of a shock to see that Boy was a different character here. He'd left the pirate back in Kenya and wore houndstooth trousers and fitted shirts with braces and fine, polished oxford shoes. Genessee called him Casmere, not Boy, so I did, too.

Thankfully Genessee was warm and kind, and also tall. She graciously lent me some of her clothes so I could go out without being stared at or catching my death—and it was in her knitted suit with Boy's directions that I made my way by train to West Halkin Street in the fashionable Belgravia neighbourhood of London to search out Cockie.

It was late afternoon when I turned up at her house unannounced. I didn't know much about Cockie's family situation, but clearly there were resources somewhere. She was within spitting distance of Buckingham Palace, and the townhouse stood in a long, regal row of matching neighbours, all in a creamy stone, with black iron balustrades and deep front entrances. I screwed up my courage to knock at the grand door, but I needn't have. Only the maid was at home. She looked me over, coatless as I was, seeming to place me as some sort of poor relation. I stared at my dripping feet on the marble in the foyer and couldn't think of any message to leave. Finally I hurried back out into the cold again without even giving the girl my name.

I didn't want to go all the way back to Dorking, so I wandered around Hyde Park and Piccadilly Circus and Berkeley Square until my toes froze solid, then found a hotel in Soho that wasn't too dear. The next morning I went back, but Cockie was out again, at Harrods.

"Please wait," the maid said. "She's asked me to keep you here."

When Cockie finally arrived, just before lunch, she threw her bags down and lunged at my arm. "Beryl! I somehow knew it was you. How did you get here?"

"It's a terrible story." I took in her plump good health, her lovely skirt and shoes and draping fur coat caught with snowflakes. Except for the coat she hadn't altered much from the last time I'd seen her in Nairobi, and yet, for me, everything had changed. "Could we have a nip of brandy first?"

———

It took a long while before I could get the whole sordid affair out—in pieces—and even then there were bits of it I wouldn't touch. I didn't speak of Denys at all, or the way things with Karen had grown so uncertain. Thankfully, Cockie listened quietly, and held her worst faces for the end.

"Surely D will have you back when the waters are calm again."

"I don't know that he should. He's got a reputation to protect."

"Life is full of messes. Your mistakes aren't bigger than anyone else's."

"I know that . . . but the brunt of them didn't only fall on me. That's what's hard to live with."

She nodded, seeming to consider this. "Where's Jock now?"

"The last I heard he was running off into the night in Nakuru. I can't imagine he'll fight a divorce now."

"Maybe not. But as long as you're married, you can get financial support."

"What? Take money from him? I'd rather starve."

"Where else will it come from then?" She looked at my clothes, which were passable for country fare, but wouldn't see me through in Belgravia. "You can't have much."

"I'll find a way to work or something. Honestly, I *will* find my feet again. I always seem to."

No matter how much I tried to reassure her, Cockie was worried about me and keen to be a sort of guardian angel. I stayed with her for the next few weeks and let her take me along to parties and introduce me to the best sorts of people. She also gently tried to explain the way money worked in London. I'd never been savvy about funds and had only ever known the chit system. In Kenya, shop owners would give you credit for anything you needed, stringing you out for years even in lean times. But in London, apparently you didn't sign for anything unless you had the money to hand.

"If I had it, why would I sign?"

She smiled and sighed. "We're going to have to find you a handsome benefactor."

"A man?" I balked. I could barely stand the thought after the gauntlet I'd run.

"Think of them as sponsors, darling. Any man would be lucky to parade you around on his arm in exchange for some nice gifts. Jewellery preferably." She smiled again. "That might just get you through."

Cockie was curvy and a full head shorter than I was, so none of her things would do for me, but she took me shopping, and also over to a wealthy friend's to raid her cupboards. I was grateful she wanted to look out for me and to help me sort out my current state. But I didn't much feel like myself in London. In truth, I hadn't felt one hundred per cent right since the sea voyage from Mombasa, when nausea had kept me green to the gills and chained to my bunk below decks. The dizziness had lingered long after I had my feet on dry land—but once I'd arrived in Belgravia, it had faded and been replaced by general fatigue. I was reluctant to mention anything to Cockie, but she saw it for herself soon enough and began to canvass me about my symptoms.

"You might have the influenza, darling. People die from it over here. Go and see my surgeon."

"But I've never caught any kind of fever."

"Everything's different here, though. Please go, won't you? Do it for me."

In general I avoided modern medicine and had ever since *arap* Maina had told Kibii and me about the crazy *mzungu* doctors that took blood out of someone else's body to cure you. He had scoffed, waving his hand at the ludicrousness of white men, and Kibii and I had shuddered, thinking of someone else's sticky red life snaking through our veins. Could you even be yourself after something like that?

Cockie wouldn't hear my protests. She dragged me along to the surgery, where the doctor took my temperature, felt my pulse, and asked me all sorts of questions about my journey and recent habits.

Finally he declared me right as rain. "A little constipation at most," he said, and recommended cod-liver oil in a handful of doses.

"Aren't you glad you went, though?" Cockie asked in the cab back to West Halkin Street. "Now your mind will be at ease."

But it wasn't. Something still wasn't right with me, and it wasn't constipation. I thanked her and went back to Dorking again, keen for a rest from town and its pace. Boy and Genessee were just as warm and patient with me as they had been before—but there came a morning in my snug bed in Dorking when it all added up, the nausea and dizziness and fatigue. The way I was growing rounder under borrowed clothes. I tried to remember the last time I'd had my monthly bleeding and couldn't. I reached under the down quilt and rested my hands on my waist, which had thickened considerably over the last few weeks. I'd blamed that on buttered crumpets and clotted cream—but now the truth arrived all at once.

I lay back on the pillow feeling reality slide around me like a carousel. Birth control was a dodgy thing. Since the end of the war men could get hold of condoms, but they were stiff and crude, susceptible to breaking and tearing. Mostly the man pulled out before anything happened, or you tried to avoid the more dangerous times of the month, as I had done with Boy when we were still involved. But with Denys, everything had happened so quickly that I'd done nothing. Now I was in dire straits. If I'd been at home, I might have gone to one of the native women in the Somali village and asked for a tea made from pennyroyal or scale-leaf juniper and hoped that would solve the problem—but here, in England?

I curled more deeply into the bed and thought about Denys. It was cruel that one night in his arms had got me into such trouble. And I couldn't fool myself that he'd be happy to learn I was carrying his child. Family life was too constricting for him—he'd made that clear from the beginning. But where did that leave me? I was twenty-one with no husband to count on, no parents to speak of, not in practical terms, and thousands of miles from the world I knew best—my home. And time was not on my side.

Later that day, I made my excuses to Boy and Genessee, thanked them for all their kindnesses, and boarded the train back to London with a prickling dread.

Cockie's surgeon seemed surprised to see me again—and a little put out, actually. He'd sent me packing with my cod-liver oil, and here I was again like a cat at the door. But a few additional weeks had made the problem quite clear. As Cockie waited in a small sitting room, I lay back on his table and squeezed my eyes shut. He poked and prodded, and I took myself away, thinking of Njoro instead—the curving of our dirt track down the maize-gold hill, the flat, still sky, and morning heat trembling up from the dust. If only I could be home, I told myself, I could bear anything.

"You're several months gone," the surgeon told me when I sat up again. He cleared his throat and turned away while the whole room lurched.

"How did you miss it *before?*" Cockie nearly shouted when the doctor made his pronouncement again, in his private office. The room was drenched with dewy April light. There was a deep-blue ink blotter on his broad leather desk. Near my crossed ankles stood a bone-tidy rubbish bin that seemed never to have touched actual rubbish.

"It isn't an exact science."

"Five weeks ago you said she was constipated! You never really examined her. Now things are so much worse." Cockie continued to harass him, and I sat in my chair, as still as a tombstone. My vision blurred at the edges, as if I were looking down a long, indeterminate tunnel.

"Certain young women have been known to cross into France under these . . . circumstances," he said without quite looking at either of us.

"Is there time for France?" I asked.

"Perhaps not," he finally admitted. With a little more badgering he gave us an address, saying, "I never sent you. I've never seen you at all."

I knew only the sketchiest stories of the kind of place he meant, where women in trouble got "taken care of." I shuddered, terrified in the cab home from the surgeon's, panic like clenched metal pooled around my heart. "I've no idea where I'll find the money," I told Cockie.

"I know." She looked out the window, then sighed deeply and squeezed my hand. "Let me think."

As it turned out, there was almost no time to spare. Two days later, we drove to a little room on Brook Street. Cockie hadn't pressed me with questions, hadn't shown me anything but utter warmth and kindness, but in the cab I couldn't hold in the truth a moment longer. "The baby is Denys's," I said. Stinging tears burned trails down my cheeks and onto my borrowed collar.

"Denys's? Oh, darling. I had no idea how complicated things had got at home. You don't want to tell him first?"

I shook my head. "It's no use. Can you see him marrying me? And Karen hasn't the slightest idea about us. It would steal her happiness—Denys's, too. I couldn't live with myself."

Cockie let out a long exhalation, nodding, and then bit her lip. "I wish I could take some of the pain away for you or make something easier."

"No one can do that. And anyway, I brought it all on myself."

"Don't be silly, Beryl. You're still a child."

"I'm not, though," I told her. Not any more.

34

I recovered—if that truly is the word—in Dorking with Boy and Genessee. I told them I'd been downed by fever and let them park me in the sun near a sprawling plane tree. I drank gallons of English tea and tried to look at magazines, feeling grief stricken and sick at heart. Though my rational mind knew I had lunged at the only possible solution, that didn't comfort me in the least. Denys and I had created the promise, the essence, of life together, and I had wilfully destroyed it. That there had never been even a remote possibility that he would be happy about this pregnancy and want to make a life with me felt sadder still. The world didn't exist where I could show him how much I cared or what I truly wanted. I knew too much to even *dream* of such a place.

Several times each day I traced the curving stone wall slowly, all the way down the hill to the hedgerow and back again, trying to right myself, and yet stuck on the same difficult thoughts. Denys would never know this terrible secret, that I had carried his child. Karen wouldn't either, and yet we were all stitched together so deeply now, and in such a complex pattern, that I couldn't clear my mind of either of them. The light in Dorking was dappled, not piercing. There were goshawks cresting over the plane tree, not Ngong's magnificent eagles—but at the centre of my mind and my heart as well, I spent a good part of every day travelling home.

Strangely, the newspapers were full of Kenya, too. No matter how aggressively D's Vigilance Committee and others like it had fought, the Devonshire White Paper had taken full hold, and rumblings of African rights were growing louder. As for the Asiatics, it was now being touted that they might one day be counted in the electoral role and own land in the highlands. These were new and threatening sentiments on the wind, and though none of it would resolve at any time soon, even the notion of such change was shocking.

"You know," Cockie remarked when she took the train out to visit me at the end of May, "*The Times* goes on and on about how greedy we settlers are, how we've muddied up the colony they gave us and overrun everything. But they also have to print a map of Kenya every time they run a story. Otherwise, Londoners might not know it actually exists." She flipped the paper closed.

"It doesn't matter," I said, feeling numb. "No one can parcel up Africa or even defend it. It doesn't belong to anyone."

"Except the Africans, you mean."

"More than anyone else, I suppose. Or maybe we're all daft to think we can own even a stitch of it."

"Will you go home again? Is that what's on your mind today?"

"How?" I looked off across the meadow, where a goshawk moved slowly and beautifully in a flat plane, gliding along without seeming to move even a muscle. "If I had wings, maybe."

The stone wall that cut the rich green field was knee high and derelict in that English country way meant to be charming, toppled in places and crawling with mosses. I stood and walked slowly, tugging at a nest of dead leaves and crushing them to powder in my hands. That one night with Denys, at Kekopey, he had been tender with me and absolutely real. He'd looked into my eyes, and I had felt that he saw who and what I was at my centre. I understood him, too, that was the thing—and knew he couldn't ever belong to anyone. But that didn't help me now. My heart had been battered and kicked, and I didn't hold out hope that anything would offer a cure, anything except going home. I had to find a way.

In a little while, Cockie moved through the meadow to join me. Quietly, she sat on the edge of the wall.

"How did you ever get the money?" I asked her. "For the doctor."

"Why do you want to know?"

"I'm not sure. Tell me."

"Frank Greswolde."

"Frank?" He was an old friend from the colony—another horse owner my father had known well when I was a girl. Cockie and I had seen him the month before at a party in London, along with an entire clutch of London's showier well-to-do. He hadn't seemed all that interested in me, except to see how Clutt was—and I had no idea how he was.

"Frank has a good heart."

"He has deep pockets, you mean."

"Honestly, Beryl. A man can have both. When I told him—very discreetly—how in need you were, he insisted on helping."

"So this is what you meant by *sponsor.* What does he expect in return?"

"I don't think he has any ulterior motives. He probably only wants to go around with you when you're feeling up to it. There's nothing terribly wrong with that."

For her there wasn't; that was obvious—but I hated even the idea of being obligated to a benefactor, no matter what stripe or what he wanted in return. I wouldn't need *anything,* not if I could help it. I also didn't see another way, not immediately. "Let's go back to London then," I said. "I want to get on with it."

"Don't get Frank wrong, darling. I'm sure you can do whatever you like with him, or nothing."

"It doesn't matter in any case," I told her. "I've nothing left to lose."

PART THREE

35

The port of Mombasa was a snarled and fabulous thing, full of cargo vessels and fishing dinghies, their flat decks hung with curled, drying shark meat or buckets of eels. The arcing seafront pulsed with heat and trolleys and droves of oxen. Pink and yellow bungalows climbed the slopes of low hills, their pale-green tin roofs sharp against the colour of fat baobab trees, which were nearly purple. The smell of fish and dust and dung throbbed in the air like a loving assault as I leaned into the railing, watching my home country get nearer and wider, clearer and wilder. Around my neck rested a fat and glossy string of pearls. I wore a white silk dress that cut me right everywhere. Near my hand on the rail rested Frank's hand. It had a right to be there. I had become his girl.

"Should we stay in Mombasa for a few days?" Frank asked. "Or drive down the coast?" He stood next to me, his large belly touching the white painted railing. A porter had brought us each a glass of wine. He sipped his and faced me, so that I could see the puckering scar under his right eye, below a dark eye patch. He'd lost that eye shooting several years before, and though it gave him a hardened look, he wasn't hard. At least not to me.

"I'm ready for home," I told him.

"I suppose all the rumpus has died down. It's been six months."

"That's a lifetime in the colony," I said, and hoped I was right.

A gold ring sat on one of Frank's pinkie fingers, squat and square with a watery blue beryl stone. He'd got it in London and been excited to show me. "Pure beryl is colourless," he'd said then, "but this was the prettiest."

"It's like the African sky."

"So are you," he said.

But if Frank's words flared with romance, they didn't move me half as much as his loyalty did. That mattered more than anything—and also his belief in me. What I wished most for myself—to be back in Kenya and working—was what he wanted for me. From the moment Cockie had helped bring us together, Frank hadn't done anything but insist he could set me up with a stable full of horses. I could train for myself, beholden to no one, he promised, and so far he'd been true to his word. Before nightfall we would board a train that would take us to Nairobi. Then we would motor to Knightswick, Frank's cattle ranch at the base of the Mau Escarpment. There, I could begin to work and train again.

"Are you happy?" Frank asked as the ship eased into the harbour. It was a leviathan surrounded by bits of flotsam and colour and noise—the cacophony of Mombasa, curved palms and red sand, a high and pale-blue sky. The stevedores threw out the long ropes to the mooring, each gnarled length as thick as a man's leg.

"I am. You know, even the smells of home make me feel more like myself. The colours, too. If only I didn't have to see anyone, I think I'd be as right as rain already."

"We could head straight for Knightswick."

"That feels cowardly. Just stay nearby, will you?"

"Of course," he said, and squeezed my hand.

Two days later, we roared into Nairobi in Frank's Ford Runabout. The town looked the same as it had when I left—red dust streets

lined with tin-roofed shops and cafés, wagons loaded down with supplies, pale-green eucalyptus trees soaring up on slim, shedding trunks,
their leaves quaking in a light breeze.

Through the low pink gate of the Muthaiga Club, the drive curved
along a stretch of manicured green turf. We pulled into the portico,
and a white-gloved porter moved to open my door. My foot slid out
gracefully in its lovely shoe. My dress and stockings and hat were all
nicer than anything I'd ever worn at the club, and I felt that keenly as
we moved through the shade-darkened foyer. Frank had one proprietary hand on my elbow and was steering me towards the bar as if I
hadn't been there hundreds of times. Maybe I hadn't been. I'd shed at
least one skin since I'd left for London and maybe more.

"Let's see who's about," Frank said. He meant *his* friends. I didn't
know much about them except by way of gossip, and there was plenty
of that. They were all of the Happy Valley set, the beautiful rich who
hoisted themselves up on vast parcels of land near Gilgil and Nyeri,
where they could frolic or play at farming with little heed to the rules
or civilities that governed others. They had their own rules, or none
at all—which could happen when you had too much money and too
much time. They entertained themselves by borrowing one another's
husbands and wives and by smoking pounds of opium. Every now
and again, one would turn up in Nairobi half-naked and delirious.

Frank wasn't quite of that world, because he wasn't refined
enough—if that was the right word. He talked like a sailor and
walked with a limp. As I saw it, the very rich kept him around because he knew where to find the best cocaine. He carried some with
him always in a brown velvet bag. I had seen it come out in London
once or twice, though I never touched it. I wasn't curious about drugs
at all. Even the idea of not having my wits about me made me feel too
vulnerable. Frank respected that and didn't try to change my mind or
make me feel puritanical—at least in London. I wondered if things
would be otherwise now.

It was the middle of the afternoon. Glossy wooden blinds were
closed against the heat, making everything dark and slightly damp-

feeling, cavelike. Frank surveyed the room like a prospector but saw no one he knew. We had a drink anyway, quietly, keeping to ourselves, and then he took himself back into town, seeing to his affairs, while I set myself up in one corner of the dining room and had lunch and coffee. I'd let him go because no one had even tried to approach me or even seemed to recognize me in my new clothes. I began to feel I really *had* changed into someone else until Karen came in in a broad white hat and coloured scarf. She looked me over, passing through, and then stopped dead. "Beryl. It's you. You've come back."

I lay my napkin aside and stood to kiss her. "Did you think I wouldn't?"

"No, no." She blinked like an exotic cat. "I only wondered how. Everything seemed so hopeless when you left."

"It was." I cleared my throat and made myself meet her eyes. "I hope to never be that low again, actually. How's D?"

"Fully recovered—and irascible as ever. You know him."

"Yes . . . I hope I do still. Six months is long enough for smoke to clear, but also for a divide to stretch and grow. I miss him."

"No doubt he misses you, too." Her eyes dropped to my pearls and then to my fine new shoes. I could see she was full of questions about how altered I was, but I doubted she would ask them.

"Stay and have a drink with me."

"All right." She sat down and removed her hat, smoothing her hair, which had been cut in a shingle, the new liberated style. I'd seen it everywhere in London but had never thought Karen would bend to the moment's fashion. "Isn't it terrible?" She laughed. "I'm not sure why I did it." Then her expression changed, and she said, "What's happened with your divorce? Are you finally free?"

"Not yet." Cockie had urged me to write to Jock from Dorking, insisting on a divorce, but I hadn't yet heard anything back from him. "Did Jock face charges here?"

"Not for that." She looked serious, doubting.

"What then?"

"There was another incident recently. No one witnessed it, so it's difficult to know what actually happened, but Jock apparently ran his auto into another car in Nakuru. Then he went after the couple inside, as if it were their fault instead of his. Both cars caught fire."

"My God, was anyone hurt?"

"Thankfully, no. They held a trial for damages, but nothing was decided."

"No doubt he was drunk."

"One can only assume." She plucked at the end of her scarf seeming embarrassed, and we sat silently for several strained minutes. Then she said, "You really do look well, Beryl. If I ever paint you, you should wear white. It's very much your colour."

In my hand, my cocktail glass was cool and smooth. Flecks of foamed gin and egg white clung to the chipped ice. I had fled to get away from scandal, but it was still here, lying in wait. There were many other still-unsettled things, a web of difficult truths that hadn't been spoken and wouldn't be sorted. And yet I was glad to see Karen again. I had missed her company.

"Did everything turn out all right?" Frank asked when he returned. Karen and I had already said our farewells.

"I suppose so. But being in town does make me wary. It can't be long before gossip about us starts to burn through the outposts."

"There was gossip in London, too. People love to talk rot. They can't help themselves."

"Well, I'm sick of it." My gin was long gone. I stirred the dregs of it in my glass. " 'I think I could turn and live with animals,' " I said quietly.

"What's that?"

"Nothing . . . just some poetry I heard once." He shrugged and I pushed at the edge of the table with resolve. "I'm ready. Take me home."

36

*F*rank didn't have much of an interest in farming and hired out crop work so that he could spend his time shooting or visiting friends. His hunting cabin was ten miles from the main house at Knights-wick, in the Kedong Valley. He slept there most nights with his tracker, Bogo, returning to see me every few days. We'd have lunch or dinner, and then he'd lead me to the bedroom. After he watched me undress, he'd stretch me out on the bed. He loved to hear my breath catch, to see and feel my hips moving, my hands clutching the sheets. He seemed to enjoy giving me pleasure even more than he wanted release for himself, and I guessed it made him feel as if he were taking care of me. He was, in his way.

Frank never forced himself on me, but still I can't say I was ever attracted to him. He walked in an awkward, rolling way, like a trained bear, with squat square hands and feet, and his belly was round and taut as a drum. At dinner, his talk was coarse and gruff, but he never failed to ask me how I was feeling and what I'd been doing and thinking about. He'd tell me stories of the hunting he'd done or the rides he'd taken. He never asked me to accompany him when he went away, and that was fine with me. It was more than enough to have his company intermittently. When we had sex, I saw it as a kind of physical transaction. We were giving something to each other, even if it wasn't exactly affection. I squeezed my eyes shut, or trained them on the curled grey hairs on his chest, and tried not to think that he was as old as my father. He was kind. He cared about me. He wouldn't give up on me.

In the bureau in Frank's bedroom stood a pile of currency he had earmarked for me to buy horses, or whatever I liked. I often opened the drawer and looked at the stack of bills, feeling strangely removed from the world of commerce, where shillings made things happen. I'd been so broke for so long that I should have leapt at the chance, but I didn't. I was grateful to Frank and trusted that he meant well, and I wanted to be deeply engaged in training again more than I could say. But I wasn't ready for anything permanent with him, not yet. Something simply didn't feel right—so I rode Pegasus on my own or walked in the grounds in a pair of printed silk pyjamas that Frank had bought for me in Nairobi. His friend Idina Hay wore hers everywhere, even to town, and he thought I should look just as glamorous and indolent.

When we went to visit Idina at Slains, her estate near Gilgil, he begged me to wear them, swearing I'd feel more at home like that, but I put on the white silk dress instead, the one that Karen had told me was my colour, and stockings and heels and the pearls we'd found in a shop in Belgravia not long after Frank came into my life. I suppose I wanted Idina and her friends to see me as respectable, though I don't know why I cared.

We turned up at Slains on a hot afternoon in July. The estate sat like a rough-cut jewel on two thousand acres in the hills above Gilgil, right at the foot of the blue Aberdares. We bumped along narrower and narrower roads and finally came to the house, which was partly bricked and partly shingled, a puzzle of colour and texture that nonetheless managed to look inviting.

Idina and her husband Joss had built the house but rented the farm. He was her third husband, actually, and together the pair

looked as though they might have stepped out of a magazine. They
were fair-skinned and slim-hipped, and both wore their auburn hair
cropped and slicked to one side. He looked feminine, or she looked
masculine. Either way, they were radiant twins as they greeted our
car, followed closely by several servants in fezzes and long white
robes. The servants swept our bags away while the barefooted Idina
and Joss led us over the weedy hummocks to a place where an elaborate picnic was laid out. Another couple sprawled out on the grass on
a tartan blanket, both in straw hats and drinking whisky sours in
frosty glasses. For most people, a picnic meant dry sandwiches and
tepid water in canteens. Here there was an ice machine that ran on a
generator. It whirred like a valet at the ready. A gramophone played
rolling tendrils of jazz.

"Hello," cooed the slim, pretty woman on the tartan. She sat up,
cross-legged, and adjusted her hat. This was Honor Gordon and the
gentleman, Charles, was her new husband—a pale, dark, smart-
looking Scot who'd been cast off a few years before by Idina herself.
They all seemed good friends now, thoroughly comfortable with one
another and also with Frank, who drew out his brown velvet bag
before he'd finished his first drink.

"Oh, Frank dear," Idina said. "That's why we invite you. You have
the best toys."

"And a keen taste in women," Joss said, reaching for the bag.

"You are delicious-looking," Idina agreed. "Though I can't quite
imagine how Frank got his hooks into you. Nothing personal,
Frank." She cut her eyes at him, smiling. "But you aren't exactly Sir
Galahad."

"Frank's been a good friend," I said.

"What would we do without friends?" Idina lolled onto her back,
letting her legs swing to one side. Her sarong-like shift slid up past
her pale thighs.

"You're lily white!" Honor exclaimed. "Why don't you roast here
like everyone else?"

"She's a vampire." Joss laughed. "She has no blood of her own at all, only borrowed blood, and whisky."

"That's right, my lion," she purred. "It's why I'll be immortal."

"As long as you don't leave me alone," Joss said, and bent over a line he'd made with the cocaine on a tray. He had a rolled paper cone and gave a tremendous snort.

We lay there in the spotted shade until the daylight lengthened and turned gold, and then went to dress for dinner. The bedroom assigned to Frank and me was plush with rugs and throws and elaborately scrolled and painted antique furniture. The bed was massive, and folded silk pyjamas nestled on the two rounded pillows, gifts from Idina.

"I told you about the pyjamas," Frank said, stepping out of his corduroy trousers. His legs were thick and furred above the elastic of his socks. "They're all right, aren't they? You seem rattled."

"It's all just a little empty. Everything seems to be an entertainment for them—especially people. I don't really understand that kind of sport."

"Maybe if you drank more, you'd relax."

"I don't want to lose my head."

"No chance of that." He laughed. "You might have a better time, though."

"I'm fine," I insisted, wanting the matter dropped and the day over. I rolled down my stockings and manoeuvred out of my damp brassière just as the door opened without a knock. Joss stood there.

"Hello, darlings." A friendly and expansive smile painted his face. "Do you have everything you need?"

I felt my spine tighten and resisted the urge to cover myself. That kind of modesty would be shockingly priggish here. "Yes, thank you."

"Idina wants to see you before dinner, Beryl. She's just down the hall, last door on the right." He winked and went out again, and I gave Frank an exasperated look.

He shrugged and worked at the bone buttons on his pyjamas. I could tell he was drunk by the thick way he moved, and felt a flaring of old feelings, like a visiting ghost. Frank wasn't at all like Jock, but I didn't want to see him like this all the same. "You can't really blame him," he said.

"No? Maybe I'll blame you instead then."

"I see we're feeling feisty." He came round to where I stood and reached for me.

"Please, Frank." I pulled away.

"It's one dinner. We'll leave tomorrow if you like."

"Nobody works. I don't know what on earth they do with their time."

"If you have enough money you can play for ever, I suppose."

"Work does more than pay your way." My own intensity surprised me. "It gives you a reason to go on."

"You *do* need a drink," he said, turning to his mirror.

Idina's bedroom was three times the size of ours, with a sprawling bed loaded down with silky furs. A great gilt mirror hung above it. I'd never seen such a thing.

"I'm in here," Idina sang out from the bathroom. I found her there in an enormous jet-green onyx tub. She soaked in it up to her chin, the perfumed water leaking steam. "Those fit you perfectly." She nodded at the pyjamas. "Do you like them?"

"They're lovely, thank you." I knew I sounded stiff from the way she eyed me and reached for her smooth black cigarette holder, lighting a match with damp fingers.

"You didn't mind what I said earlier, about Frank?"

"It's fine. I'm just tired."

She drew in on the holder, and then blew out smoke in a cloud, never taking her eyes from me. "I wouldn't want to be blonde," she said, "but yours is lovely."

"It's horsehair." I lifted up a strand and let it fall. "It won't stay put no matter what I do."

"Somehow the effect works." She pulled on her cigarette again and then waved the smoke away. "Your eyes are good, too, like chips of blue glass."

"Do I get to go through all of your features now?"

"I'm praising you, darling. You seem to like it when *men* look you over."

"I don't—unless it's the right man."

"Do tell," she said with a laugh. "I'm *starved* for a little indiscretion."

"Maybe you should get into town more."

She laughed again, as if I weren't being a perfect bitch, and then said, "Whom are you in love with?"

"No one."

"Really? I thought it might be Finch Hatton." She arched an eyebrow, waiting for my reaction. I would rather have died than give her one. "Don't you think Karen is a little demanding for him? Poor Tania . . . how she sighs when he goes."

"I didn't know you two were even acquainted," I said, feeling a need to defend Karen.

"But of course we are. I adore her. I just don't think she's the one to hold Denys. There's nothing wild in her."

"No one admires only wildness." Somehow I couldn't stand to hear Idina make Karen out to be so small. She was many things, but not that. "They have a great deal to talk about."

"Do you think so? If you ask me, he's too good at being a bachelor. Why choose one when you can have a dozen?"

"He probably *can* have dozens." Heat tightened my throat. I hadn't spoken of Denys in a long time, and never to a stranger. "But it doesn't really cut both ways, does it?"

"Why not? Women can have plenty of lovers, too. Dozens upon dozens, as long as they're clever and don't crow about it."

"But it never plays out that way. Someone always knows."

"You're not doing it right then," she pronounced. With a swishing sound, she stood up. Slick water glazed her white-pink skin. Her perfect body was like art, or a carefully sculpted dish on a platter. She didn't even reach for the towel but simply stood there and let me look at her, knowing I would feel awkward turning away.

I flushed, resenting her and the life she lived. If she was the model for discretion and polish, I wasn't interested. "Maybe I don't want to do it right," I said.

Her eyes crinkled, but without any humour. "I don't believe you, darling. Everyone always wants *more*. Why else are we here?"

Dinner was served at a long low table near the fire. It was always cool at night in the highlands, but this blaze was also meant to be ornamental. It set the room glowing and Idina's cheeks, too, as she held court at the far end of the table. The wide hearth opened just behind her, glinting along the tips of her hair. Above her, a twisted set of buffalo horns stabbed out from a wooden plaque.

There was something about Idina that reminded me of a hunting kestrel or kite. It was her hard, bright eyes as well as her words—the expectation that everyone was just like she was, constantly hungry, with little concern for who might get hurt along the way, or how. I couldn't understand why Frank would want to spend time with this crowd. They were bored, naughty children with highballs and morphine and sex for their toys. People were toys, too. Idina had invited me into her bathroom to bat at me like a mouse, curious about whether I would freeze or run. Now she began a game, which was another version of the same manoeuvre. It was a parlour game where everyone contributed a line to a story that moved in a circle. The point was confession.

Idina launched us forward. "Once upon a time, before Kenya was Kenya, I hadn't even met my lion and didn't know how smitten and changed I would be."

"You *are* sweet to me," Joss said, beaming a little dementedly in the firelight. "Once upon a time, before Kenya was Kenya, I bathed with Tallulah Bankhead in a tub brimming with champagne."

"Didn't that tickle?" Charles scoffed. Idina didn't bat an eyelash.

"In the nicest way," he purred. "Now you, Beryl."

"I'm too drunk," I said, trying to avoid the game altogether.

"Oh, posh!" Joss cried. "You're dead sober. Play along, please."

"Can't we have cards instead? I don't understand the rules of this one."

"You need only to say something true about the past."

Only? The game was placid and tame and, yes, childish on the surface. But the point was to see if you could force the mouse you'd cornered to show you its insides. I didn't want to tell these people a single thing about myself, particularly from the precious past. Finally I said, "Once upon a time, before Kenya was Kenya, I put a dead black mamba snake in my governess's bed."

"Aha! I knew you had some nastiness in you!" Joss said.

"Remind me not to make you angry," Idina added.

"Show us what you do with *Frank's* black mamba." Charles cackled like an idiotic schoolboy, and everyone laughed along.

The game went round and round—on and on—and it seemed I would only be able to play, or even survive the night, if I did get drunk. It was difficult to catch up with this crowd. I had to make a real effort, and when I finally succeeded, I succeeded too well. The whisky made me maudlin, and for every confession I managed to reveal aloud, another unspoken confession thrummed through me and threatened to bring me down. *Before Kenya was Kenya, Green Hills was alive and my father loved me. I could jump as high as Kibii and walk through the forest without making a sound. I could bring a warthog out of its hole by crinkling paper. I could be eaten by a lion and live. I could do anything, for I was in heaven still.*

By midnight, when everyone had grown glittery-eyed and nearly delirious, Idina moved onto another game. She made us sit in a circle and blow a feather into the centre. Whomever the feather landed nearest would be our bedmate for the night. At first I thought she was joking, but when Honor blew her feather into Frank's lap, the pair simply got up and walked down the hall, Frank's back wide and square next to Honor's slim form, while no one so much as leered at

them. My head swam with the whisky. Everything tipped and receded in a tunnel effect. Sounds reached me with a slight delay. Now
Idina seemed to be laughing because Charles had got on his hands
and knees and was bringing the feather to her with his teeth.

"But I'm old hat for you, darling." She pretended to swat at him
with her cigarette holder. "You can't want me."

"It's all a blur." He laughed. "Show me again."

When the two had lurched off down the hall, I looked at Joss, feeling nauseated. I had drunk much too much. My tongue was thick
and coated in my mouth. My eyes felt heavy and dull. "I'm going to
bed."

His eyes were glassy and mirrorlike. "Isn't that the point?"

"No, really. I don't feel well."

"I have something for that." He stroked the inside of my thigh, his
hand like a pressing iron through the silk. He moved to kiss me and
I pulled away reflexively. When he looked at me again, his eyes had
come into focus more. "Frank said you might be a little cool at first,
but that I shouldn't give up."

"What?"

"Don't play the lamb, Beryl. We all of us know you've been
around."

I wasn't at all surprised by Joss, but if Frank had meant to throw
me to the wolves by bringing me here, he had another thing coming.
Without a word I stood and walked down the hall, but the door to
our room was closed. I banged at it with the flat of my hand. Only
laughter came back.

"Frank!" I shouted, but he wouldn't answer me.

The hall was dark, and all the other doors were shut tight. Not
knowing what else to do, I locked myself in one of the bathrooms and
sat on the floor, waiting for morning. I knew the night would be long
indeed, but I had things to remember ... things I wouldn't have
shared earlier, not for all the money in the world. *Before Kenya was
Kenya, I threw a spear and a* rungu *club. I loved a horse with wings. I
never felt alone or small. I was Lakwet.*

37

*W*hen we returned from Slains two days later, Frank immediately retreated to his hunting cabin and I made plans to leave him. There wasn't any panic in my actions. I packed slowly and carefully, filling my rucksack with things from my life before. Everything Frank had given me I left in the bureau—the money, too. I wasn't angry with him. I wasn't angry with anyone, I only wanted to find my own way, and to be sure of what I stood for again.

There were a few clues about what I might do next. Before I left London, Cockie had mentioned Westerland, a stable in Molo. Her cousin Gerry Alexander ran things there, and she thought the place might do for a second start. I had no idea if gossip about me had threaded that far north, or if Gerry was even in need of a trainer, but I trusted Cockie to help set me on the right path. First, though, I needed to go home.

After following the main road north to Naivasha, I headed east the least travelled way, straight into the open bush. Piled stones and gold grasses gave way to red dust and thorn trees, and unbroken savannah. The steady rhythm of Pegasus's plates rang out. He seemed to know we weren't going out for a casual ride, but didn't balk at any of it, not the terrain or the eerie quiet, not even when a mammoth bushpig charged from a ravine a hundred yards ahead, storming over the path on squat, split hooves, squealing its rage at being startled. Pegasus only bobbed his head once, then pushed on with steady, smooth legs.

Finally we began to climb again, and to see the greening rim of the Mau Forest at the escarpment's far side, dense trees and knuckled ridges, the land rolling out in the view I loved better than any other—Menengai, Rongai, the blue and furling Aberdares.

I found Jock inside just finishing lunch. I had wanted to catch him off guard and did, his face blanching before he pushed back from the table, twisting his linen napkin in his hand. "I can imagine why you're here."

"You didn't answer my letters."

"I thought maybe you'd change your mind."

"Really?" I couldn't believe him.

"No. I don't know. Nothing has gone the way I planned."

"I could say the same," I told him. Part of me felt an urge to drag out all the casualties in our long, weary battle, to name everything and let him hear just what he'd cost me. But I had done my part, too. The losses were on my head as well. "Please, Jock. Just say you'll give me the divorce. This has all gone on long enough."

He stood and went to the window overlooking the valley. "I should have found a way to make it work. That's what I keep thinking."

"When the papers are drawn up, I'll send them."

He sighed loud and long, and then faced me. "Yes. All right." His eyes met mine for a moment, and in those cold blue discs I finally saw—after all this time—a shadow of contrition, of real regret. "Goodbye, Beryl."

"So long," I said, and when I walked through the door, knowing I would never return, a great and old weight unfurled from my shoulders and lifted off into the sky.

———

I headed straight for Green Hills, where the tall grass had grown up thickly and what was still standing of the stables and main house had begun to tip irrevocably towards the earth. The mill was long gone and the fields overgrown, as if the land was taking it all back. I thought of the work my father had done, and the happiness we'd known—but I didn't feel empty for some reason. I had the pure sense that I couldn't ever truly lose the past, or forget what any of it had meant. To one side of the path that led into the forest, a high pile of stones stood marking Buller's grave. I stopped Pegasus and held his lead while I sat for a while, remembering the day I had buried him. I had dug at the packed earth until the hole was deep enough so that no hyena would find him. Not even a stone had shifted from the cairn. Buller was safe in his long sleep—his grizzled scars and his victories. No unworthy predator could ever touch him.

Winding down the hill, I traced the path to the Kip village and tied Pegasus to the thorn lattice of the *boma*. When I entered the compound, a young woman named Jebbta was the first to notice me. I hadn't seen her for years, not since we were both girls, but I wasn't all that surprised when she turned from where she stood in her yard to see a baby threaded around her hip, round as a gourd.

"You are welcome, memsahib. Come."

I approached her and then reached to touch the silky plait of the child on her hip, then the sheen of his shoulder. Jebbta had grown into a proper woman, with a woman's burdens. That was the way things worked in the Kip village. Nothing had changed there.

"Is this your only child, Jebbta?"

"The youngest. And your children, memsahib?"

"I have none."

"Are you not married?"

"No. Not any longer."

She tipped her head back and forth as if to say she understood, but she was only being polite. At the outdoor hearth fire, yellow flames licked up the sides of a black pot, the smells of the bubbling grain inside making me feel hungry in a way I'd forgotten. "I've come for *arap* Ruta, Jebbta. Is he nearby?"

"No, memsahib, he hunts with the others."

"Oh, yes. Will you tell him I was here and that I asked for him?"

"Yes. He will be sorry to have missed such a friend."

Molo was eighteen miles north and west from Njoro, and stood on a plateau at the top of the Mau Escarpment, ten thousand feet nearer the stars. The elevation made it dramatically different from home. Icy streams and rivulets ran through dense bracken; woolly sheep grazed on low, misted hillsides. I passed farms, but they were mostly pyrethrum crops, miles and miles of the white chrysanthemums that flourished in the highlands, their dried heads used as insecticide when ground into powder. They were striking now, the bushes snowy and rounded as drifts. It *did* snow in the highlands, and I wondered if I was ready for that.

The small village was a clustering of battered wooden houses and shops, tin roofs and thatched ones, cold hammered streets. It was a harder place than Njoro or Nakuru or Gilgil, and I saw instantly that it would be more difficult to love. At the first café I came to, I tethered Pegasus and went in to enquire about Westerland. With a very few questions, I learned what I needed to know, and more, too—that the neighbouring estate, Inglewood Farm, was owned by Mr. and Mrs. Carsdale-Luck, the stodgy couple I'd met at Karen's shooting party the year before. I hadn't developed any relationship with either of them in the handful of days we were thrown together, but as I made my way towards Westerland, I tried to think how I might stitch the two opportunities together. The scheme would take some fast talking, but I did have wins behind me. I knew my trade and could prove it; I would only need time and a little faith.

Cockie's cousin Gerry turned out to be a warm and level-headed fellow. Cockie had already sung my praises in a long letter, and he was ready to let me have a try with a two-year-old bay stud, the Baron, which he owned along with a silent partner, Tom Campbell Black. The Baron had yet to find his footing, but he had fire and plenty of guts, too. I knew I could do something with him and also with Wrack, a yearling stud sired by Camciscan, the star of my father's breeding roster from days long past. Wrack belonged to the Carsdale-Lucks, who had also agreed to take a chance on me. They had given me a nimble filly, too, Melton Pie, and a hut on their property and the use of one of their houseboys as a groom.

"With Camciscan's blood, Wrack is sure to have some winning in him," I promised the couple when they came to watch us work. George Carsdale-Luck smoked spiced cigars that made the paddock around him smell like cloves and Christmas. His wife, Viola, was forever perspiring even in Molo's chill, with always-damp collars and a host of paper fans. She stood at the edge of the track as I ran Wrack a mile and a quarter at half speed, and then said, as I paraded him by, "I haven't seen many women in this line of work. Aren't you afraid it will coarsen you?"

"No. I never think of that."

There was more than a whiff of Emma Orchardson in Viola. If I let her, I thought, she might go on to suggest I wear a hat and gloves, but my rough edges weren't going to matter a whit once Wrack hit a win and good money. I had only a few short months—just until July to get him ready for the Produce Stakes, which would be run in Nairobi. Until then, I would work hard and not let myself get distracted.

Throwing myself into training was easy to do in Molo. I rose before dawn, toiled all day, and fell into bed exhausted. Only sometimes very late at night did I let myself think about what might be happening at the Muthaiga Club, what joke Berkeley might be telling, with what in his glass, what the women wore dancing or at tea, and if anyone ever mentioned my name, even in passing. If it was a very long night, and sleep didn't come at all, I would let every guard down and think of Denys. Perhaps he was sloped in one of Karen's low leather chairs by the millstone table, reading Walt Whitman and listening to some new recording on the gramophone. Or in his storybook cottage at the Muthaiga, sipping at nice scotch, or off in the Congo, or in Masai country after ivory or kudu or lion, and looking up, just then, at the same tangle of stars I could see from my windows.

How close people could be to us when they had gone as far away as possible, to the edges of the map. How unforgettable.

38

One morning Pegasus and I rode out from Westerland to get supplies. I was hunched over the saddle in my buckskin coat, fingers cramping with cold, when I saw the canopy of a motorcar folded and propped, throwing back chilly light. A man stood bent over the engine, wearing dungarees and moccasins much like my own. There weren't many motorcars in Molo, which was as far behind Nairobi in time as Nairobi was behind London. It was a difficult place to get to, the steep escarpment wanting to wall you out. It was a hard place to break down, too, so I knew I should help if I could.

"Is there something I can do?" I called out from the saddle.

"What's that?" He straightened from behind the canopy, wiping oil-blackened hands on an oil-blackened bit of cloth. He was young, I saw, with a sweep of almost-black hair. His breath rose in puffs past thin lips and a dark, trimmed moustache.

"You've got yourself into a spot here."

"I haven't given up yet."

"You must know about engines then."

"Not really, but I'm learning. This one seems to want to challenge me—to see if I'm serious."

"I don't think I'd have much patience for that."

"You don't think this one tests you?" He pointed at Pegasus.

I laughed and climbed down from my saddle, holding on to the reins. "We test each other," I conceded. "But that's more the natural order. Men and horses have lived together for centuries. I sometimes think the autos will all break down and be abandoned and we'll find them like skeletons on the side of the road."

"That's a nice picture you're painting—but I predict it will go the other way. The auto is just the beginning. The tip of things. Men only want to go faster and feel freer."

"Pegasus is enough for me, thank you."

He smiled. "Pegasus, eh? I'm sure he's very fast, but if you ever went up in an aeroplane you'd swallow your words—and your heart as well, maybe."

I thought of Denys and JC and Maia—each of them alive with the talk of flight. Above us in the sky there was nothing at all, not even clouds. "What's it like?"

"Like breaking through everything that ever wanted to rein you in. There are no barriers up there—nothing to stop you from going on for ever. All of Africa stretches out under you. It doesn't hold anything back or want to stop you."

"I might guess you're a poet."

"A farmer, actually." He grinned. "I have a little plot up near El-dama. What do you do around here?"

When I told him, we quickly put two and two together. He was Gerry's silent partner, Tom Campbell Black; he owned part of the Baron. "You've got a fine horse," I told him. "I'm banking he'll win something big come July. Maybe then you can buy that aeroplane."

"Can I hold you to that?" He bent over the engine again and made a few last adjustments. "Mind your horse, I'm going to give it a crank." After half-a-dozen lurching wheezes, the engine clanked to life. I watched him fold the canopy and settle his tools in the boot while Pegasus stamped beneath me. He was cold. I was, too.

"Good luck to you," I called out over the noisy churning of the motor, and we both waved goodbye.

Within a few months, things in Molo took a turn without warning. One of the stable doors at Westerland had a rusty hinge, and Melton Pie got out late one night and panicked somehow. She ended up tangled in some wire fencing, her barrel and cannons badly torn. She would recover, but the veterinary bill was shocking. George and Viola were furious and wanted to pin it on me.

"How's a rusty hinge my fault?" I asked, when the two had me driven into a corner one night in their library at Inglewood.

"She was in your care!" George railed. "You should be overseeing *everything.*"

I looked at Gerry to back me up, but he only sat pinched in his chair, his neck flaring pink under the line of his trimmed beard. "Perhaps you could offer to pay half, Beryl," he finally offered.

"With what? I live like a pauper, Gerry. You know that. And besides, why should I pay for her care? That's an owner's place. I certainly won't get a penny when she wins."

"She's won nothing," Viola said flatly.

"You haven't given me time."

"I can't see how we can take the risk now," George pronounced, folding his arms over his tight-fitting vest.

And so the matter was settled, and not in my favour. I would have to pay the fees, somehow, and the Carsdale-Lucks were letting me go. They would give me a week to find another place to live and clear off their property. I went back to my cold hut that night feeling kicked and maligned. Gerry had assured me he wasn't going to pull the Baron away from me, but I would have to find more horses, and somewhere to live while I trained them. I sat up late, poring over my account books, wondering how I would come up with the money for Melton Pie, when I heard footsteps outside my hut. There was no bar on my door, and for a long moment, I froze. Was it George Carsdale-

Luck coming to ask for the cash on hand? Was it Jock, ready to announce that he'd changed his mind about the divorce? My heart clutched and thundered in my chest.

"*Hodi*," a man's voice called from just outside.

"*Karibu*," I said as I moved towards the door, still not recognizing the voice.

I pushed open the thatch door and saw a tall, well-muscled warrior with his *shuka* gathered over one shoulder. A curved sword rested in a leather scabbard swung low on narrow hips. His hair was shorn close but for one heavy plait that began at his forehead and cut over his clean scalp. His eyes were black and bottomless and when I saw them I wanted to cry. *Arap* Ruta had found me. He'd found me, even here.

I looked at his bare feet, the plaited thongs tied around dusty ankles. He'd walked from Njoro—pointing himself at me the way you might throw a single arrow at several hundred square miles. For all of Kenya's vastness, it was incredibly difficult to disappear into, even if you wanted to. There were so few of us that we left trails as clear as smoke signals. That Ruta had managed to find me wasn't a surprise, but that he had wanted to. I thought he had forgotten me.

"I'm so happy to see you, Ruta. You look well. How is your family?"

"There has been cattle sickness at home." He stepped into the patchy glow of my lantern. "It's difficult to feed many on little or nothing."

"How awful," I told him. "Is there something I can do?"

"Everything has changed. There is no work. I thought you might have a job for me to do."

He'd been proud even as a boy; as a man I guessed he was even more so, and that it hadn't been easy for him to come to me asking for a favour. "You're my oldest friend, Ruta. I would do anything I could to help, but I don't know if there *is* work just now."

He looked at me, trying to read my expression. "Your father was happy to have me in his stables. I haven't forgotten what I know about horses, and I still ride well. I could sit anything once."

"Yes, I remember. Will you come in?"

He nodded and brushed the dust from his feet, and then sat on a folding stool as I tried to explain. "Things have been difficult. One day there might be many horses to train, and plenty of money for everyone, but for now . . ." I let my words trail away.

"I am patient." His eyes were clear and black and steady. "When we win, you can pay me."

"But I don't know when that will be. The best chance I have is the Baron, at the Produce Stakes, four months away. I haven't begun to prove myself here yet."

"I believe we can win, memsahib."

"You do?" I couldn't help but smile. "I've been doing it all alone, but the truth is I don't know how much real faith I have any more."

"I've never seen you show fear. I am not afraid, either. I will send for someone to bring my wife. She will cook for us."

"It's a good plan, Ruta, but where will we put everyone?"

"We are serious and mean to win derbies. Surely room can be found."

I sat blinking, astonished by Ruta's optimism and by how simple it all sounded coming from him. Nothing *was* simple, of course—but there was a striking symmetry in Ruta's turning up here. We both needed the other very badly. That alone felt right. Perhaps we *could* win one day.

"Have some coffee. It's not very good, I'm afraid."

"You never had a gift for cooking," he said with a small smile.

"No, I never did."

At the tiny cedar-wood table, I poured for us. He told me of his wife, Kimaru, and his two-year-old son, Asis. I explained that my marriage had ended, knowing he wouldn't understand or approve in the least. For the Kips, wives were treated as property, and the power balance was inimitably clear. Men were the heads of households, and their women respected this, and them, as law.

"Bwana Purves was not your father," he allowed once I'd finished my story.

"No," I said. "Nor yours." Ruta might never fully grasp the choices I'd made, but we didn't have to agree on everything to help each other. He had his own reasons for the long journey from the valley floor to my hut in Molo. "You have no idea how much I've needed your help, my friend. I didn't know it myself until now."

"I'm glad I've come. But tell me, is it always so cold here?"

"I'm afraid it is."

"Then we will have to build a bigger fire, Beru."

"We will," I said. *We already have.*

39

Only fearlessness would do now, and with Ruta by my side, I could finally remember what that felt like. I boldly beat the bushes for horses to train, and by early April had a bright chestnut, thick-shouldered stud named Ruddygore as well as the Baron—and I had Wrack and Melton Pie back, too. The Carsdale-Lucks had sold them both to another owner who immediately trusted me a good deal more than they ever had. I was able to take them all with me when I left Molo for Nakuru—for this was how Ruta and I solved our housing dilemma. Molo was too cold and too forbidding, and so we made arrangements to lease space at the Nakuru racecourse, not far from Soysambu and territory I knew well. Ruta and his wife took over a small mud hut behind the main paddock. I had a bed on crates high up in the stands under a tented metal roof. There was a bale of hay for my bedside table, another bale for a chair, and yet I was immediately happy and at home there. Life seemed liveable again. Ruta and I had each other and a good race looming. What more was there?

I was most excited about Wrack. He'd had potential since the moment of his birth—perfect conformation and the very best lineage. But potential could turn or spoil, or even dissolve. The final shadings of any racehorse's training were the most important strokes in the whole process. In a few months I'd watched him grow from a wilful and arrogant colt into something magnificent. Every muscle under his rippling chestnut coat spoke of power and grace. His legs were pistons and his body bright. He was built to run, and to win, and he knew it.

Wrack was our ticket—Ruta's and mine. He would be the way we'd shoulder into this difficult world and make our mark.

One afternoon, a few weeks before the race meeting, I was in town sorting out a feed order and decided to drop in to D's hotel. It had been more than a year since the last time I was there, that traumatic night when Jock had gone for D and smashed him to pieces. It wouldn't have been hard to avoid the place altogether if I didn't want the memories or the chance of running into D, but I was finally feeling ready to face him again and see where we stood. I tied Pegasus outside, brushed off my moccasins, and swatted at my hair, wondering if I was even half presentable. Inside, it took a moment for my eyes to adjust to the light, but when I had my bearings, I saw that D wasn't in the room at all. But Denys was—stretched out long in his chair with a drink, his dusty hat beside him. I think I stopped breathing.

"You look well, Beryl," he said, when I'd made my way towards him, only half feeling my feet. "How have you been?"

There was already too much history between us, too many difficult choices. Losses I might never have words for. "Getting by," I managed to say. "What about you?"

"About fair." He blinked his hazel eyes, and as I took in the fact of him, I felt my heart shudder and spin as it always had when he was near. Perhaps it always would. "You were in London, I heard?"

"Yes." I reached for the top of a chair to steady myself.

"I was away as well, for my mother's funeral."

"I'm so sorry, Denys."

"It was her time, I suppose. Or maybe that's just what people say."

"And you're working now?"

"Yes. I took out my first professional client a few months back. A pretty good fellow ... American actually. He learned to use a machete and carried his own supplies."

"See? I knew you could train all these spoiled Teddy Roosevelts to be reasonable."

"I'm not so sure. Blix had one recently who insisted on bringing a piano along."

"Oh, Blix. I miss him." The words hung between us for a few moments like filaments or webbing. "How's Karen?"

"She's gone to Denmark to visit her mother, but by all reports she's well."

"Ah." I fell silent, reading his face again. He'd had a lot of sun, but under the healthy colour, I could glimpse a hint of exhaustion, or maybe it was worry. "And Berkeley?"

"Berkeley's taken a bad turn, I'm afraid. He was stuck in bed at Soysambu for a month when his heart nearly gave out there. The doctor told him not to move again, but he didn't listen."

"That sounds like Berkeley. Where is he now?"

"At home. I don't know how much time he has."

"Berkeley can't die. I won't allow it."

"Maybe you should tell him that soon, then."

I tried to force back my emotions while we rested in silence for a few minutes. Berkeley would *have* to be fine somehow, and what of Denys? Could we be friends again after all that had happened?

"Come out to Mbogani sometime," he said when I readied myself to leave. "I'll stand you a drink."

"I thought you said Karen's away."

"She is. You're always welcome, though."

"Oh" was all I could say. Then I stood and leaned in to him for a moment, brushing his smooth-shaved skin with my lips. "Good night, Denys."

The next day I rode to Solio, arriving near the cocktail hour. Knowing Berkeley, I half expected him to be out in the yard, a bottle of champagne in each hand, but he was confined to bed. It broke my heart to see him there, frail and bloodless, small-looking as a child.

"Beryl, you angel," he said when I handed him a fat cigar I'd brought him from Nakuru. "Light it for me, will you? I'm not sure I have the breath."

"I didn't know how bad things were. I would have come before."

"What do you mean?" he feigned. His colouring was so off even his lovely teeth seemed grey. His voice was weak. "Do you know the farm has never been more profitable? I'm just now getting the hang of things. Just in time." He tried to sit up, and I leaned over to help, gathering pillows to prop him up while his Somali servants looked on severely. "They're not sure you should be touching me," he whispered. "There aren't usually beautiful women in my bed."

"I don't believe that for a second. You're a prince, Berkeley. You really are the best of them."

"Except for minor bits of me." He gazed at the cigar I'd placed in his hand, the wraithlike curlicues of silvery smoke twisting higher before trailing away to nothing. "But I'll go out like the great poets, won't I, full of fire and deep soundings?"

"Don't go at all, you rat. Please don't."

He closed his eyes. "All right. Not today."

I found glasses for us and he told me where to search out the very best wine, at the back of a cupboard near his bed.

"It's Falernian, this bottle." He held it up to the light. "It's one of the few wines that's got the stamp of the ancient Romans. Some think it's the best wine in the world."

"You don't want to waste it on me, then."

"Poor beautiful Beryl. Are you sure you can't marry me? You could have my fortune when I die and raise scandals as my young widow."

"Poor beautiful Berkeley. You always talk such a good game, but tell me, who truly has your heart?"

"Ah, that." He coughed into his shirt cuff. "That's a very great secret." Through dark-fringed lashes, his brown eyes had a soft fire about them, as if he already knew what waited for him, past this life into the next. "Grab a book and read something out to me, will you? I'm feeling lonely for verse."

"I have something," I said quietly, and began to say out my Whitman lines, from "Song of Myself," the ones I had managed to keep close to me for years now. I didn't think I could look at him and go on, so I focused on his fine pale hands on the snow-white blanket, the pale-blue moons low on his clipped fingernails, the small nicks of scars, the failing veins.

When I'd finished we sat quietly for a while. He swirled the wine in his glass. "It's the loveliest colour of amber, isn't it? Like lions in the grass."

"Exactly like that."

"Now begin again, but more slowly this time. I don't want to miss anything."

I started again from the beginning while his breath grew more and more quiet, his eyes softening and then closing. There was a slight smile on his waxen lips, and his spiked lashes were like fragile ferns on his cheeks. How could I ever say goodbye? I couldn't, I wouldn't. But I kissed him before I left, tasting Falernian wine.

40

The long rains began, with towering storms moving through every few days, but the day of Berkeley's funeral was startlingly clear. He wanted to be buried at home, on the banks of his river, which carried, he had always sworn, perfect glacier water all the way from Mount Kenya. Along a bend that curved like a woman's waist and hip, the river water sang over black basalt stones and riddled layers of peat. At that place, we watched Berkeley go into the ground, while starlings and flycatchers rang bell-clear scales through the canopy.

Dozens of friends were there. Blix had come all the way from Somaliland, and still wore inches of pale-yellow dust on him. D's eyes looked sombre under his curving sun helmet, but once the final words were said and the earth mounded up over Berkeley's coffin, he came to me and gripped my hands lightly and didn't let them go for a long time. "I felt like a terrible shit for sending you away, you know," he said.

"You didn't have much of a choice," I said. "I saw that."

He cleared his throat gruffly, and shook his head, a long lock of his near-white hair leaping on his collar. "If you ever need anything, I want you to come to me. You're still so young. I've forgotten that sometimes. When Florence and I were your age, we didn't have enough sense combined to scratch our own backsides." He met my eyes and I felt whatever was left of my humiliation rinse away. I had learned some hard lessons, but they had been important ones.

"I will, D. Thank you."

From Berkeley's long shaded veranda, I heard the slow melodic strains start up from the gramophone. Denys stood over the flared cone and hissing needle, and D and I walked over together to join him.

"Don't you hate Beethoven?" D asked.

A faint pink blaze of feeling moved over Denys's high cheekbones. "Berkeley doesn't."

We stayed for a long time, toasting Berkeley's fineness and his life, lingering over every story of him we knew, until the sky thickened with grey-clotted clouds and the light began to fail. When nearly everyone else had gone, Denys said, "Come back to Ngong with me."

"I have Pegasus."

"I can bring you back for him."

"All right," I answered, as if this happened all the time, and I wasn't crumbling inside, full of confusion and lingering hurt, disappointment and desire, all of it swirling riotously through me.

On the drive, we talked very little. The threatening sky finally opened properly, and a slow, constant equatorial rain began. It rinsed over the window glass and pattered soft drums over the leather top. He didn't take my hand, didn't say a word about what he wanted, nor did I. There was so much unspoken terrain between us that we couldn't make our way to the simplest phrases.

When we drew close to Karen's farm, he veered off the main road early, towards Mbagathi, and I understood. He wouldn't be with me in her house, with her things looking on. That was their space together. We would have to make a place that was new and only ours.

Denys cut the engine, and we ran into the house, dripping, but it was wet there, too. More than a year had passed since my mother's strained visit and, if anything, the roof was even less reliable. The rain came in everywhere, and we ducked and dodged as we built a fire. It fretted and smoked, the wood damp. He searched out a bottle of good brandy, and we drank without glasses, passing the neck back and forth between us. Even with the rain and the hissing cedar wood in the hearth, I could hear us both breathing.

"Why didn't Berkeley ever marry?" I asked him.

"He did, in his way. There was a Somali woman in his household he was involved with for many years. They were devoted to one another."

"What, for years? And no one knew?"

"There's tolerance in the colony for certain things, but not for that."

It all made perfect sense now, how Berkeley had kept his distance from the women in the colony, how coy he always was when I questioned him about romantic entanglements. It made me happy to know he'd had love in his life, but what had it cost him? How heavy was the secret he kept? "Do you think there'll ever be room in the world for that kind of attachment?" I asked.

"I'd like to think so," he said, "but the odds don't look very good."

When the brandy was nearly gone, he led me to the small back bedroom and wordlessly peeled off my clothes, his lips on my eyelids, fingertips stroking the insides of my wrists. We lay down in a crush of warm limbs. He buried his face in my hair and neck, his movements so tender I could barely stand it. As desperate as I was for his nearness, I was haunted by the last time we were together, and all the days between. My heart galloped loudly. I worried it might burst.

"I don't know what this is between us," I was able to say, finally. "Maybe we'll never have anything beyond this moment." I touched him, the cage of his ribs and chest rising and settling with his breathing. Our shadows painted the wall. "But I do care for you, Denys."

"I care for you, too, Beryl. You're an extraordinary woman. Surely you know that."

Part of me wanted to lay everything bare then—to tell the truth about London. To ask him about Karen, and just how he made sense of it all for himself. But in another way I didn't believe anything would be solved by talking or explaining. We'd made our choices, separately and together, hadn't we? We were who we were.

Coming to my knees, I traced the hollows of his collarbones, cupping shadows, his broad neck and shoulders and forearms. I was memorizing him with my hands. "If you had another life to live," I asked him, "would you change anything?"

"I don't know. Maybe our mistakes make us who we are." He fell quiet for a few minutes, and then said, "The only thing I'm really afraid of is shrinking away from life, not reaching for the *thing* . . . you know?"

"I think so, yes." I rested my hand on his heart. Its soft drum sounded through my palm. It was true that many of the twists and turns that had led me to this room had been painful and costly, and yet I hadn't ever felt more fully alive. I was terrified, but I didn't want to run from him. I wouldn't . . . not if I could help it. "Denys?"

"Mmm?"

"I'm glad we're here now."

"Yes," he said against my lips, while above us the rain thundered on. The whole roof could have come down on our heads for all I cared. I was in Denys's arms. I would happily have drowned.

41

From the first trumpets to the roar and release of the grandstand, races are quick and ephemeral things. Ten horses galloping with everything they have in them. A mile and three-quarters, no time at all, and yet enough time—curled and poised and expanding like breath—for the race to be won and lost many times over.

At the Produce Stakes, Wrack went like the wind and like pure unfettered courage, thundering out in front the whole way. I kept him in my glasses, afraid to look away for even a moment. Ruta stood beside me, as still as a prayer, while the lead was stolen from Wrack, one hair's breadth at a time. He never relinquished anything, never stopped pulling. But at the tape, a quick-boned gelding took it and I finally breathed, deflated.

"Did you see how close it was?" Ruta said when the dust cleared and my heart had started again. "The next time he runs, Wrack will remember this and give more."

"I don't think it works that way for horses, Ruta." I was trying to collect myself, thinking of next time, too—if Wrack's owner, Ogilvie, would let us have him again.

"Why not?"

"I don't know. They don't have memories like we do. Every race is new for them."

But when we went to Ogilvie, he was far more inclined to side with Ruta. "Did you see how close that was? He'll win next time."

And he did.

For the remainder of 1925, my horses won and placed often enough so that Nairobi's close-knit racing world finally seemed ready to let me in, and to believe I belonged there. D asked me back to Soysambu, telling me, whether it was now or later, there would always be a place for me in his stables. Ben Birkbeck wrote to say he was keen to give me horses, and that I appeared to be on track to take over my father's reputation in the colony. At one of my events, I spotted my mother in a towering feathered hat, cheering me on. I hadn't seen her for over a year, and felt a jolt, stinging and complex. I still didn't know who she was in my life, or how to be anywhere near her without feeling waylaid. Maybe I never would.

"It makes me proud to see you doing so well," she said when she searched me out afterwards. "Congratulations."

I watched her sip at a carnation-pink cocktail and listened to her news. She was living up near Eldoret with Dickie and the boys, and trying to find some way to help Dickie make ends meet, but having very little luck.

"I'm sorry things are difficult," I told her, and was surprised to find I actually meant it. Maybe Berkeley had been right about family—maybe we never survive them, or anyone we love. Not in the truest way. My feelings for Clara were tangled at the root, unresolvable. Whether I liked it or not, I would always carry the ghost of her leaving. But it also didn't seem right somehow to walk away and ignore her need. "Is there something I can do?"

"We'll manage," she said, curiously stoic. She finished her drink and readied herself to leave, saying, "It *is* wonderful to see you're getting what you deserve."

———

With my string of wins, I could finally begin to pay Ruta what he was worth, and pamper his wife with new shoes and cooking pots. I could buy a proper bed for my tent under the stands, too, and put away money for a car—but I wasn't going to rest on my efforts or trust that the flush days would last.

I felt the same way about Denys. Every hour with him was sweet and stolen. I began to borrow a motorcycle of Karen's, to visit him when he was at Mbogani—and somehow the thrill of the motorbike beneath me, bouncing over the hard red dust, careening past deep potholes and stones, was like the sensation of being near him. Both were dangerous, both a bold and unforgivable form of trespass. Karen would have died a dozen times over to know I was at Mbagathi under the holey roof, in her lover's arms, while she was away in Denmark—but I couldn't think of that, or of her. If I did, I couldn't have any of it, and that would be so much worse.

Karen would be coming home soon. When Denys began to talk of a scouting trip he was going to take near Meru, I knew he was really saying this might be our last chance to be together. "You could ride over and join me."

There were logistics to sort out. I would ride to Solio, Berkeley's old farm. I could leave Pegasus there, and we would go on together in Denys's Hudson. When we returned, we'd be heading our separate ways.

We were set to meet in February. In the meantime, he was going off on a long safari with a wealthy client from Australia, and I was working on getting Wrack ready for the St. Leger, Kenya's premier race. With his recent successes, Wrack was the favourite, and I planned to put everything I had into making sure he would do all he was expected to and more.

On the afternoon I meant to head out to meet Denys, the sky opened with a crack and it began to rain as if it never planned to stop.

Ruta looked out of the stable door at the sheets of grey water. "You'll stay then, *msabu*?" He knew my plans; I kept no secrets from him and never had.

"No, I can't do that, but I'll delay. You don't approve of my being with Denys. I know that."

He shrugged and then sighed out a well-known native proverb. "Who can understand women and the sky?"

"I love him, Ruta." After everything, I hadn't admitted this yet, even to myself somehow.

His inky eyes cut through the dense pooling air and the drizzle. "Does it matter whether I approve or not? You will go to him anyway."

"You're right. I will."

All day I watched the rain and the rivulets of red-running mud. Finally, when there was a small break on the horizon, and I was able to see paler clouds and a sheer hint of sunlight, I tacked Pegasus and made off. Solio was on the far side of the Aberdares, thirty-five miles straight east. Under perfect conditions, I would have spared Pegasus and ridden around the mountain to the north. As it was, I was making such a late start that I thought to shear off hours by heading over the top on a small snaking trail.

That I was on horseback alone in the middle of the night didn't frighten me. I'd ridden in the dark before, without half so much provocation. Pegasus could get me there. He had always had wonderful instincts in the hills, as sure on his hoofs as a mountain goat.

At first we made good time. The weather had cleared, and the night air felt good on my skin. As the narrow route doglegged upwards, climbing steadily, town lights were sprinkled here and there beneath us. Merchants slept in cramped beds, and children bundled on the floor on cane mats, snug and sound. I could scarcely begin to imagine that kind of quiet life with Denys. Neither one of us was cut out for sameness or routine, the pinchings of domesticity—but there was this night and the next one. Pirated kisses. Sweet and terrifying happiness. To have even one more hour in his arms, I knew I would do almost anything.

We were perhaps halfway to Solio when I began to smell water. Soon I could hear the river, too, just ahead. Pegasus and I approached it slowly, having only a little moonlight to steer by. As we came nearer, I could see the swirling movement of the current, ghost shadows twisting and eddying. The banks were steep and sheer. There was no way even Pegasus would make it down safely, and then how deep would the river be? Could we swim or wade through? I couldn't even guess in the dark. We picked our way north instead, scouting the bank for a way across, and then doubled back to the south.

Finally I made out the faintest sketching of a bridge. As we came closer, I saw it was fashioned of bamboo and thick twisted rope, only a few feet across, the kind local tribes built and tended for their own use. I didn't know how strong it was, but these things usually held small carts and oxen. It would probably do.

I dismounted and took his reins, and we began our descent, Pegasus sliding a little in the pebbled gravel. He whinnied, then startled. The bridge felt solid but loose on its ropes, so that it swung under our movement. I had a swaying, seasick feeling and knew Pegasus wasn't any happier.

Yard by yard, we crossed it. I could hear the water roaring maybe twenty feet below. White foam shifted in the moonlight, looking alive, and darker water jumped, silvered on its edges. When I spotted the pale bank I felt pure relief. I'd begun to have the feeling that we'd come too far and were risking too much, but we were nearly there. Nearly on solid ground.

The ropes groaned, making a sawing and ripping sound, and then the bamboo began to snap. Pegasus dropped with a lurch. He cried out, falling, and for a moment I was sure I'd lost him, then the bridge shuddered as he stopped. His legs had punched right through the bamboo bracings. He was up to his chest, the slats holding him, just. Below us, the river roiled and sent up a terrible sound. I was probably in danger of crashing through myself, but I could only think of Pegasus and the mess I'd got him into.

Thoroughbreds are as skittish as they come, but Pegasus had always had a wonderful head on him. He was brave and cool even then, fixing his great eyes on me in the dark, trusting me to find a way. Because he believed I could do it, I believed I could, too, and started working on a plan. I had a rope tied to the saddle, which just might be long enough to pull him out if I could anchor it well.

I felt the bridge give and twist like bedsprings as I inched forward, too aware of adrenaline and my own ragged breath. Finally I reached the far bank and found a wattle tree wedged in well and angled into the side. It was a young tree, but it was all I had, and I hoped it would do. I worked my way back towards Pegasus, who waited with epic patience. I made a running knot across the bridge of his nose and another going round his head in a makeshift halter. The rope wouldn't work if it slipped off. My thought was only to anchor him until morning. There was no way he could clamber out of the slats, not without leverage, and it would be too dangerous to try on my own in the blackness. I could lose him, and I would never chance that.

Just as I got the halter secured and the other end tied to the wattle tree, I leaned against his neck, resting. "This is going to make quite a story," I told him in the dark, his velvety ears coming forward, listening. Tying a wool blanket over my shoulders into a cape, I settled along his side for warmth. But just as I thought I might be able to snatch a little sleep, I heard the smacking of brush and a rumbling crash. A herd of elephants had got our scent and come around. Now they wheeled and thundered on the bank, terrifying Pegasus. I didn't know they wouldn't rattle the bridge to pieces with us on it. By instinct, I stood. Pegasus struggled, lunging against the slats, shifting his weight in a rolling motion. I was full of pure fear, thinking he'd crash through, but somehow he got one leg out, then two. He stretched for the bit of the bank he could reach, pulling forward as the bridge gave and shifted around us. It was like trying to walk on a raft of shifting toothpicks, or crumbling burnt sugar, or nothing at all.

Somehow, like a hero, Pegasus gained his footing and pulled through the remaining slats. But we were at a terrible angle. His weight dropped down the bank behind him, steeply, and he was exhausted. The sandy loam gave like water, and I thought I might lose him anyway. The elephants weren't far off. I could hear them groaning their warnings, and the unmistakable trumpeting of a bull.

Urging Pegasus on, I stood by the tree and grabbed the rope with both hands, wedging my full weight, bent in two, pulling with everything I had. Finally we were both on the ridge. I could see deep lines cut into Pegasus's chest from the bamboo, and there were great strips of flesh torn from his legs. We were both lucky to be standing there, but we weren't safe yet. The elephants were still nearby and heaven knew what else. Pegasus smelled like blood, and we were both tired. That made us an easy target for anything on the prowl. We would have to keep going.

When we finally made it to Solio it was nearly dawn. Berkeley's loyal Somali servants still had run of the place until the family could find a buyer. They knew me, and though it was an ungodly hour they welcomed me in and readied a dry stall for Pegasus.

I carefully cleaned and bandaged his wounds and found they weren't as awful as I had feared. The slats had gouged shallow trenches into the skin of his chest and legs, but there were no signs of infection and no fresh blood. He would heal well—thank God. In the meantime, where was Denys? Perhaps the rain had stalled him too? I had no idea what conditions were like and I hoped for the best as I settled down to sleep.

When I woke a few hours later, I had coffee and a light breakfast, all the time keeping one ear cocked for the sounds of Denys. He was coming in his noisy wagon. I would hear him half a mile away, and then we would be alone for six days. We'd never had anything near that much time, and I felt dizzy with the idea of his closeness, his smell, his hands, and his laughter. He would show me places and things he loved, and we would live right to the edges of every moment we had together. If only he would come.

Finally, after lunch I saw one of Denys's Kikuyu boys come running up the road towards the house, loping steadily along as if he could run for ever. My stomach lurched watching him, for I knew what he meant.

"Bedar says he won't be coming, *msabu,*" the boy said when he reached me. He had likely covered twenty steep miles that day. His bare feet were thickly padded with leathery calluses. He wasn't winded.

"Not coming at all?"

"They've found no ivory."

Denys was still working, then. His days didn't belong to him, and he couldn't have come if he'd wanted. That didn't mean I wasn't crushed. I watched as Berkeley's man gave the boy water and food, and then watched him set out again after Denys, heading fearlessly to the north, tracing the bend in the road. When he was finally out of sight, I felt my spirits sag. Pegasus and I could have died on that mountain in the dark, and for nothing. I wouldn't be seeing Denys. We wouldn't have our days at all, and I had risked so much to get them, to be here. I was almost sick with it.

I packed up my things, and then threaded my way down to the river to the site of Berkeley's grave. Months had passed, and the mounded-up earth had begun to sink here and there. I groomed the plot with my hands and the tip of my boots, wanting to do something for him and to feel close to him again. Above me, a pair of starlings scissored the air, calling out to each other in an elaborate system of chits and replies. Iridescence bloomed along their chests and heads in jewel-like green and blue and copper. The leaves quaked around them, but the rest of the forest was still.

"Oh, Berkeley, I've got myself in deep this time," I said. "What am I going to do?"

Nothing, not even the birds, answered.

42

When Karen returned from Denmark, I tried not to hear news of her, but that was impossible. Colony life was too narrow and too bent on exposing every turn and gambit. She'd been ill and in bed for a time. That year's coffee crop wasn't good, and her debts were mounting perilously. I'd also learned that Denys had set off for Europe with almost no warning, but since he hadn't sent word to me directly, I didn't know why. I finally ran into Karen at the Muthaiga Club at the end of March. She was there having tea with Blix, and seeing them, I nearly fell on them both. That's how things were in the colony. You needed friends, no matter how complicated those ties were, or what they cost you.

"Beryl," Blix said, squeezing my shoulders. "Everyone's talking about how your horses might just win everything. Wouldn't that be something?"

Karen and I kissed hello tentatively. She looked thinner. The skin around her eyes was drawn, and her cheekbones were hollowed with shadows. "Denys has gone back to London," she said almost immediately, as if she couldn't keep her mind on anything else. "We had two weeks. Two weeks together after eleven months apart. And yet I'm supposed to be grateful. I'm supposed to be brave and carry on."

Part of me wanted to shout *Yes* at her, loud and strong. She'd had a long string of days alone with him when my time with Denys had been stolen outright. And yet I also knew the grief she felt. I had it, too. Now he'd left the continent again. "Why London this time?"

"His father is fading. He and his brothers will need to find a buyer for Haverholme. The estate has been in Denys's family for several hundred years. I can't imagine how difficult this will be for them all." She shook her head and short curls tumbled. Her shingle had grown out roughly. "I know I should be thinking only of Denys's family at a time like this, but I want him home."

Blix coughed lightly, a warning or reminder.

"You're tired of hearing this song, I know," she snapped. "But what am I supposed to do? Honestly, Bror, what?"

I could see that he wasn't going to tangle with her if he didn't have to. "Excuse me." He pushed back his chair. "I've spotted a friend on the other side of the room."

When Blix had gone, Karen sighed deeply. "I've finally agreed to give him a divorce. You'd think he'd be more grateful."

"Why now? He's been asking for years, hasn't he?"

"I don't know. I started to feel terrible about fighting so hard to hold him. I've just wanted *someone,* don't you see? There was a time I thought Denys would marry me, but that seems a fool's scheme more and more."

I swallowed to steady my voice, determined to appear at ease with her. "Will things be more difficult on the farm, now, with Blix moving on?"

"What, do you mean with money?" She laughed darkly. "Bror has always managed to spend twice what's in his purse. Then he asks for another loan . . . as if I actually have it."

"I'm sorry. You deserve more."

"I suppose part of me knew what I was getting into with him.

Maybe we always know." She made a soft clucking noise, as if swallowing air, or immovable fact. "Bror was never any good at feelings, but Denys isn't any better, God help me. What can I do? He's ruined me for life without him. That's the thing of it."

The colour must have rinsed from my face as she talked. I was losing the battle with normalcy and found it hard to balance my cup or quieten my hands. "He always seems so happy to be on the farm."

"Why wouldn't he be? He only comes when he wants to come. It never costs him anything. My struggles matter, yes, but they're not his."

She was speaking of commitment—she wanted all of him, and for life—but she seemed not to understand how this would be a stranglehold for Denys. She couldn't force a promise. He would have to enter her life freely or not at all. After what I'd been through with Jock, Denys and I very much agreed on this. "Why do you keep trying?"

"Because when he's here, I'm happier than at any other time. It makes everything else endurable. I'll walk across the lawn and hear music from his gramophone, or come through my door and see his hat on the peg, and my heart lurches to life. All the other times, I'm sleeping."

"You feel very much alive to me."

"Only because you don't know me. Not the way Denys does."

I sat and listened to Karen's sad, beautiful words, wanting to hate her—her good chairs and carpets. Her rare white lilies and face powder and overdramatic kohl. She was wrong for trying to keep Denys on a chain, but didn't I want him, too? We were kindred in this respect, closer than sisters, and irrevocably estranged at the same time.

Before I left the hotel, I found Blix at the bar to say goodbye.

"How are you really?" he asked. Something in his tone was more delicate than I'd ever heard him be.

"Still standing." I straightened my shoulders for him so he would worry less about me. "You know, Cockie was a lifesaver to me in London."

"She's a wonderful girl."

"She's marvellous. If you don't marry her, I will."

"Right." He laughed and his eyes crinkled. "The plan is to do the deed when she returns. If she hasn't come to her senses by then." He laughed again, looking past the rim of his glass. "I'll be the one wearing white."

"And Dr. Turvy? He'll be there, I suppose."

"Yes. He's promised to give away the bride."

43

I trained Wrack in a fever. The St. Leger was in early August—there were only a few precious months left to get him on top form—and then the worst happened. Wrack's recent successes should have made Ogilvie feel confident in his horse, but his friends had begun to whisper to him. How could he trust a girl to bring Wrack into his sharpest glory? For any old race at Nakuru, certainly, but for the St. Leger? Did he really want to risk it?

And so it was that less than three months before the race of my life, I had no horse. I could barely think or see straight. In the year I'd had Wrack, I'd put everything into him. His skill and prowess and moments of glory were me—mine—with my stamp on every reach and thundering turn. Now his loss had left me nothing. I was hollowed out.

"What will we do?" I asked Ruta. We were sitting on hay bales up in the stands, the sun and the day's labours gone. Velvet night pushed in, soft and deadly.

"We still have half-a-dozen horses to run at the meeting."

"In the smaller races, yes. I know we can take some of those, but for the classic, the one race that matters?"

"We must think on this," he said, looking out at the night. "There is much we don't yet know."

"All the other owners will see that Ogilvie has pulled Wrack. And if he wins anyway, without us, they'll clap him on the back saying how clever he was, how forward-looking." I sighed and stewed, tugging at my hair, until Ruta left for home and his wife.

When I was alone again, I listened to the pulsing thrum of insects and the more distant noises of the stable, knowing that if Denys were anywhere on the continent, anywhere at all, I would have run to him, just to feel his arms around me, to feel centred there and know I could go on somehow, finding strength and courage along the way. But he wasn't. He was nowhere I could find him.

A few days later, Ruta was out on breezes with Melton Pie when Eric Gooch came into the stable. He was an owner I didn't know very well—tall and nervous-looking, with a tic of straightening his tie every few minutes. I was familiar with one of his fillies, though. Wise Child was out of one of my father's best brood mares, Ask Papa. Like Pegasus, she'd been delivered into my hands, a bundle of slick warmth and promise. She had the right blood in her to be a serious contender for prize money, but early on another trainer had run her too hard. Her fragile tendons had been jarred severely on the wrong sort of track, concussing them. Now, no matter how perfect her pedigree was, she could barely carry a rider.

"Her legs could be built back up again," Eric said. "With the right care."

"Maybe they could," I agreed. "But in twelve weeks?"

"She's a fighter. And I don't know." He straightened his tie again while, above it, his Adam's apple bobbed preposterously. "I have a hunch you'd know what to do with her."

He was referring to my success years before with D's horse, Ringleader, who'd had a similar injury. I'd trained him on the shores of Elmenteita, and he'd come back to run and win. But there hadn't been the urgency then, and my career wasn't at stake. "I don't want to make crazy promises," I said. "The truth is she might never live up to her potential now, let alone win classics. But the chance is there."

"You'll take her then?"

"I'll try. It's all I can do."

The next day, Wise Child came to us with her soft lovely muzzle and her fighter's spirit and those legs that nearly broke my heart. She'd been done terrible wrong and needed painstaking care now. Over the next twelve weeks, we couldn't make the smallest mistake with her.

Like Elmenteita, Lake Nakuru had a rich and muddy fringe at its edge, which gave well. That's where we brought Wise Child to run her paces. Sometimes Ruta rode her and sometimes I did—easing her from a trot to a canter to a gallop. A rose-pink tide of flamingos startled around us, making their wooden sound. Tens of thousands of birds climbed as one and then receded, settling with a clamour only to startle again. They became our timekeepers. They alone saw a kind of magic begin to happen as Wise Child grew stronger and surer of herself. She had been wounded, nearly broken. You could still see her fear each morning as she tested those first few steps gingerly, as if the mud might hold knives. But she had a warrior's courage. When she opened up now, we could see trust and willingness in her, and something more than speed.

"This muscle," Ruta said in her stall, as he groomed her silky and compact bay body. "This muscle can move a mountain."

"I think you're right, Ruta, but it also scares me. She's in top shape. She'll never be more ready, but even so it would take almost nothing for those legs to fail. It could happen on race day. It could happen tomorrow."

Ruta continued his grooming, the dandy brush skimming her gleaming, liquid-looking coat. "All this is true, but God is inside her. Her heart is like a spear. Like a leopard."

I smiled at him. "Which one is it, Ruta? A spear or a leopard? You know, sometimes you sound just like you did when we were children, boasting how much higher you could jump than me."

"I still can jump, Beru." He laughed. "Even today."

"I believe you, my friend. Have I told you lately how very glad I am that you're here?"

I knew Ruta and I would be together always, until the very end. But no matter how close loyalty or God or magic crept into the weeks we trained Wise Child, human frailty and fear were stronger. Three days before the race, Eric came to see me. His wife had seen our heads pressed a little too close together at the club one evening, talking of Wise Child and her possibilities, and now she had given him an ultimatum.

"It's you or her," he said, in a near-strangled way, clutching at that tie until I wanted to rip it from his neck.

"But there's nothing going on between us! Can't you tell her that?"

"It won't matter. She's got to mean more than the horse, or anything else."

"Don't be stupid! We're nearly there. Pull her after the race if you must."

He shook his head, swallowing. "You don't know my wife."

"This is going to ruin me, Eric. I've killed myself for your horse. This is my race. You damned well know you owe me that."

He went red to the tips of his ears, and then slunk away like a coward, muttering words of remorse.

When Sonny Bumpus came with a groom later that morning to take Wise Child, I was beside myself. I'd used Sonny as a jockey before, and we'd known each other since we were children, all the way back to my terrible years at boarding school in town. We'd lined up desks to play at steeplechasing then. Now he was one of the best riders in the colony, and it didn't take much work to guess that Eric had asked him to ride Wise Child, and that both Sonny and my horse were being handed cleanly over to the new trainer.

"Tell me why this is happening, Sonny. You know how hard I've worked."

"It's the worst sort of shame, Beryl. If I had any choice, I wouldn't take her. I was all set to ride Wrack, but now he's broken down. He'll run again, but not this time."

"Wrack's out?"

"For now, yes."

"Then Wise Child's sure to win. Goddamn it, Sonny. I have to have this!"

"I don't know what to say, kid. Gooch isn't likely to change his mind." He pressed his teeth together hard, making the muscles in his jaw jump. "I'll tell you one thing, though, everyone on the track will know what's what. You've done the work with her. All I'm getting is the ride."

When he'd gone I stared at the wall, my heart shuddering in place. There had been times in my life when I might have deserved this sort of comeuppance. I couldn't pretend otherwise. Eric's wife had no doubt heard an earful of gossip about me, but I hadn't so much as put a finger on him. I had worried over Wise Child, nurtured and babied her, loved her. Now she'd been taken from my stables, my hands.

Not even Ruta could talk to me.

44

At the post, ten horses ripple and stamp, their jockeys light, brilliant as feathers. They're poised to run, dying to run, and when the starter gives his signal, they do. Ruta stands behind me in Delamere's box. We both feel Wise Child in the field, quivering like music. Every horse is glorious. Each has a story and a magnificent will, blood and muscle, clean legs and flying tail—but none of them is like her. They none of them have her strength.

Sonny knows how to get everything from our filly, but little by little. One pulsing beat at a time. He intuits when to coax her or hold her back, or inch her into a waiting, almost infinitesimal gap. She has speed and smoothness, and a reserve of something else, something undefined—but will it be enough?

Soon, everyone in the grandstand comes to their feet, craning to see bits of coloured silk above churning legs, the stakes high or negligible. None of that matters. The money is an afterthought, something to play at, shells on a table. The horses, though. The horses live, and Wise Child is more soulful and alive than she has ever been or ever will be. She gains on a black stallion, then a chestnut, and a creamy filly. Flank and rail, shadow and silky animal grace. At the final turn she has the lead. A nose at first, then a body length. Two.

Ruta puts a hand on my shoulder. My stomach leaps into my throat, my ears. There isn't a sound in the crowd of thousands, none that I can hear. Somewhere Eric Gooch is watching with his wife, dying a little to see his horse in front. But he won't see what I see. No one knows what to look for except me and Ruta, and Sonny. How Wise Child lists from the rail. A snag, a falter, a flickering sway that amounts to less than a fraction of a moment. Her legs are going. They've done all they can for her.

The field closes on her as I lurch backwards, into Ruta's chest. I feel his steady drumming heart with my whole body, the beating of a long-ago *ngoma,* the pounding of *arap* Maina's fist against the taut hide of his shield, and that's how I can bear the rest of it, when I want to cry and scream and go to her, stopping the race. Everything. Can't the world see that she's thrown all of herself on that track, and that it isn't enough?

Then, somehow, from a place beyond sense or strategy, she breaks forward, unpinned from her body's flaws and marvels. It's only courage that takes her the final distance. Only grit. When her muzzle hits the tape, the crowd releases the flare of a single collective cheer. Even the losers have triumphed with her, for she has shown them something more than a race.

There is a bright blur of thrown tickets, bodies crowding the rails and gate. The band begins to play. Only Ruta and I are still. Our girl has done more than win. With those legs, with not much more than her heart, she's broken the St. Leger record.

45

*E*ven when he was very old, and horses were behind him, and Africa, too, Sonny Bumpus would keep a silver cigarette case in his pocket that I'd engraved for him with Wise Child's name and the date of our St. Leger. He was fond of taking it out and stroking the warm and gleaming top with his thumb, ready to tell anyone who would listen about the ride of his life, and how I'd brought back Wise Child from a near-crippled state to produce one of the greatest victories in the history of racing.

Sonny was a good egg. He had had that moment of perfect flight, but he gave the greater part of the glory to me. And though Eric Gooch never came crawling to give Wise Child back, or even thank me, most of the colony was ready to praise my accomplishments. Later that season, Ruta and I had a string of validating wins. Welsh Guard triumphed at Eldoret, Melton Pie took the Christmas Handicap, and our own Pegasus won gold at three gymkhanas running.

In February, I began to train Dovedale, a horse of Ben Birkbeck's, and when I met him at D's hotel in Nakuru to talk over our strategy, Ginger Mayer was on his arm. I hadn't seen very much of her since Karen's shooting party, but she looked lovely and content now, her bright red hair pulled back on one side with a jewelled clip, her pale skin flawless. On her left hand sat a fat pearl ring. Apparently, she and Ben were engaged. She'd made quick work of it, too; his divorce from Cockie had been finalized only months before.

"The wedding will be here at the hotel," Ginger said, tapping her fingertips on her collarbone, just above the teal silk collar of her dress.

I shouldn't have been surprised by any of it. Colony life was so small and confined the same people kept popping up in different combinations. Of course Ginger was marrying Ben. Who else was there, after all? But if I'd ever had any patience for the way things worked here, I was losing it. It was like watching fortune's wheel spinning over and over—spilling bodies that struggled to climb on again, clinging for dear life. I had done my fair share of falling, and I felt exhausted now. I also wasn't entirely myself. The weather had been so dry lately that it had got into my throat, stinging whenever I swallowed. My ears felt as if they were padded with searing cotton. My eyes burned.

"You should see my doctor in Nairobi," Ginger insisted later.

"Nonsense," I told her. "I'll be all right when it rains again."

"You work for me now." She laughed, only pretending to be serious. "Just promise me you'll see him."

By the time I got to Nairobi, fever had taken me over. I shook with chills, wondering if malaria had finally got its hooks into me, or typhus, or black water fever, or any of the other deathly ailments that had plagued settlers in Kenya for fifty years. Ginger's doctor wanted to plunge me into an ice bath straight away. Apparently I had tonsillitis, and he wanted to operate.

"I don't like doctors," I told him, reaching for my jacket. "I'll keep my own blood, thank you very much."

"The infection's not going away. You'll go septic if you keep this up. You wouldn't want to be the girl who died from bum tonsils, would you?"

And so he operated. I fought only a little as the paper cone soaked with ether was pushed over my nose. Everything spun and hollowed with blackness, and when I finally came to again, climbing into consciousness as through a dense fog, I saw Denys's familiar face, the light through spotty shades making a smeary sort of halo around him.

"You're back," I croaked.

He patted his own throat, pantomiming that I shouldn't try to speak. "Ginger made me swear to come and see you. I think she was worried her doctor might do you in." He smiled ruefully. "Glad to see he didn't."

Behind him, a nurse in a prim tricornered hat fussed with another patient's bedding. I wished she would go away and leave us alone. I wanted to ask how he'd been, and if he'd missed me, and what would happen now. As it was, I could barely swallow.

"Tania would have come, but she hasn't been well," he said. "The farm is desperate and she's been so low I'm afraid she might hurt herself." He saw my eyes widen and explained, "She's threatened it before. Her father went that way, you know." He paused, thinking, and I could see how he struggled with every word. Denys didn't easily discuss matters of the heart, and then there was the complex puzzle of connection between us three. He clearly didn't want to be speaking of Karen with me, and yet I was deeply involved on both sides.

"I've arranged for a neighbour, Ingrid Lindstrom, to stay with her when I go away on safari," he went on. "Tania shouldn't be alone now, and she shouldn't worry about anything."

"She can't know about us." I risked a whisper. "I understand that." Of course I did.

He looked away to where the shadow of my bedrails stood sketched on the bumpy wall. The dark slanted lines were like the bars of a prison cell. "I never seem to know what to say to you, Beryl."

"This is goodbye then."

"For now."

I closed my eyes, feeling the tendrils of exhaustion wanting to pull me under, into medicine-thick sleep. I had always known I couldn't have Denys—he wasn't *for* having. His spirit was too free for that. I understood that too well, and yet I'd believed we could go on as we had, stealing what time we could, living each marvellous moment as it came. But that was finished. It had to be.

"Beryl," I heard him say, but I didn't answer. When I awoke again later, the room was dark and he was gone.

Ginger picked me up the next week and drove me back to my lodgings in Nakuru so I wouldn't have to suffer the train. My throat ached, and my encounter with Denys had left me saddened and raw. Whether or not he married Karen, the bond they had was too complicated and too gripping for either of them ever to separate. Somehow, I would have to find a way to wish them happiness. I did care for them both, as confusing as that was.

"You're still not up to snuff, are you?" Ginger asked. I'd been quiet, watching the road rise and fall in front of the car, the wheels dipping into ruts so deep they sometimes made my teeth jar. "I shouldn't get involved," she went on delicately. "Denys is such a lovable person, isn't he?"

I looked at her slantwise, wondering what she might know, and from what source. "We're good friends, of course."

"He tries so hard with Tania." She clenched the wheel with pale-yellow kidskin gloves. "But I'm not sure he can really put anyone else at the centre."

Frankly, Ginger was surprising me. I had only ever heard her chatter about shallow things: lace and waistlines, engagements and puddings. I preferred this real talk. "Many people can't," I said. "Does love really have to look one way for it to count?"

"You're far more understanding of the whole thing than I'd ever be."

"Really? You and Ben haven't exactly had a conventional courtship." I swallowed and felt small knives, wishing I had ice or chilled custard for my throat, or that the dust would settle. "I'm sorry. I don't mean to be a bitch. I really do wish you two the best."

"It's all right. I waited a long time for him without knowing if he would ever be free. Is that stupidity or courage?"

"I don't know," I told her. "Maybe it's both."

46

After Ginger and Ben were married, she began to play hostess at their farm, Mgunga, and seemed particularly keen on new guests or visitors to Africa. She loved to throw dinner parties, always perfect in a silk frock with a string of pearls that nearly swept her knees. I had a few things I could dust off for polite company but generally wore slacks, instead, and a crisp man's shirt. That's what I chose for a dinner party she threw in June, thinking more about how odd it was to be invited back to Njoro as a guest. Their property was less than a mile from Green Hills, and as I traced the familiar road in my new car, nostalgia rose up to meet me. Little had changed and also everything.

Sir Charles and Mansfield Markham were brothers. They had come to Kenya looking for a winter home for their well-to-do mother, who'd had her fill of London's icy damp. They'd found a suitable villa very nearby in the Rongai Valley, which was where Ginger had stumbled on them. Once she'd finished fêting them properly, they were going to go off on safari, hunting elephant with Blix.

Mansfield was twenty-two, well shaved, and genteel. His skin was as smooth as butter, his hands milky, without the slightest sign of wear. At dinner, I noticed him watching me while his brother seemed distracted by the full platter of gazelle steaks. I didn't have the heart to tell Charles there was little variety here, and that he'd likely be eating nothing else for months and months.

"My people are from Nottinghamshire," Mansfield told me, his trimmed nails tracing the heavy base of his water glass. "Like Robin Hood."

"You don't look very swashbuckling."

"No? I keep trying." He smiled and his nice teeth showed. "Ginger tells me you train horses. That's unusual."

"Is that a polite way of saying *masculine*?"

"Er, no." He blushed.

Later I found myself facing him over brandy in the low, broad sitting room, where he began to explain what he had said before. "I'm not all that masculine myself, actually. When I was a boy I was sickly and spent too much time with the gardener, learning the Latin names of plants. I garden for sport. My mother gives me sets of white handkerchiefs at Christmas when she gives Charles rifles."

"Handkerchiefs are useful."

"Yes." His eyes crinkled. "Though perhaps not in Kenya."

"What would you choose instead?"

"For myself? I don't know. Maybe what you all have here. This is marvellous country. I have a feeling it could bring out the best in anyone."

"I've never wanted to be anywhere else. I grew up just the other side of the hill. My father had the most wonderful horse farm. It was my whole life."

"What happened to it?"

"Money trouble. It's crass to talk about such things, though, isn't it?"

"It's real. That's my feeling."

I didn't know what it was about Mansfield that put me at ease, but before long I found myself telling him a story about how once an enraged stallion had attacked Wee MacGregor while I sat atop him.

278 · PAULA McLAIN

The two of them had gone at it as if I didn't exist. It seemed like a matter of life or death, and then just as suddenly they backed away from each other.

"Weren't you afraid?"

"Of course . . . but also fascinated. I felt as if I was witnessing something private and rare. The animals had forgotten about me."

"You're much closer to Robin Hood than I am, aren't you?" he asked after listening keenly.

"Would white handkerchiefs save me?"

"I hope not."

The next day, when the Markham brothers had gone off to join Blix, I drove to Nairobi for a few days to take care of some business. I'd arranged to stay at the club and returned there, that first night, to find Mansfield at the bar with the best bottle of wine he could find.

"There you are," he said, clearly relieved. "I thought I'd missed you."

"I thought *you* were off to find elephant."

"I was. But we only got as far as Kampi ya Moto before I told Blix to turn the lorry round. I had to see about a girl."

I felt myself flush. "Did you read that in a book?"

"Sorry. I don't mean to be presumptuous. I just couldn't stop thinking about you. Do you have other plans for dinner?"

"I should lie and say I do. That would teach you."

"It might." He smiled. "Or I might hang around for another day and ask you again."

Presumptuous as he was, I found myself liking Mansfield. He set us up in the darkest corner of the dining room, and as the courses came and went, he refilled my glass before it was half empty, and leaned over to light my cigarette as soon as I thought to reach for one. His solicitousness reminded me of Frank, but he didn't have a whit of Frank's coarseness.

"I loved your stories from the other night. I think I would have been another person entirely if I'd grown up here, as you did."

"What was the matter with your lot?"

"I was too coddled, for one thing. Too cared for, if that makes any sense."

I nodded. "I've sometimes thought that being loved a little less than others can actually make a person, rather than ruin them."

"I can hardly imagine someone not loving you. When I move to Kenya we're going to be great friends."

"What? You'll pick up and settle here, just like that?"

"Why not? I've been drifting for years, wondering what on earth to do with my inheritance. This seems such a clear direction."

The word *inheritance* seemed to flutter over the table. "I've never known how to handle money," I told him. "I'm not sure I understand it."

"Nor do I. Maybe that's why it sticks to me like glue."

I picked up my brandy and rolled the globe of the glass in my palms. "Only trouble sticks to me with any regularity . . . but I'm learning to think that can shape a person, too."

"You're going to force me to say it, aren't you?"

"What?"

"That you have a wonderful shape."

After dinner he trailed me to the veranda and lit my cigarette with a heavy silver lighter that bore his initials, MM, in a deeply stamped scroll. This was obviously part of the spoils of being a Markham from Nottinghamshire. But I could tell he'd grown up with beauty, too. And culture. He had perfect manners and the kind of optimism that came when you knew that if life didn't go exactly your way one moment, you could change its mind the next.

As he bent to light his own cigarette, I watched the smooth movement of his hands, feeling there was something awfully familiar about him. Then it struck me. It was Berkeley he reminded me of, in his compactness and dark, slim composure. His easy cultured manner. They were cut from the same cloth.

He looked up. "What?"

"Nothing. You have lovely hands."

"Do I?" He smiled.

Beyond the pink terrace, the veranda flared out, flat and cool and dark. Fireflies skimmed its surface with plaintive, flickering pulses of desire. "I love it so much here. It's one of my special places."

"I have a room," he said, looking not at me but at the winking tip of his cigarette. "It's the most charming thing you've ever seen. A separate little bungalow with someone's nice books everywhere and a table made of ivory tusks. Would you like to come for a nightcap?"

Denys's cottage. He was never there any more, but it made my throat tighten to think the place could belong to anyone else, even for a night.

"That's sweet of you, but I'm afraid I have to say no. At least for now."

"I'm being presumptuous again, aren't I?"

"Maybe so," I told him. "Sleep well."

The next afternoon Markham asked me to ride out to Njoro with him by car.

"The roads are terrible," I warned him. "It will take all day."

"Even better then."

He didn't lose his sunny quality even when one of the tyres on the auto blew out on the road with a sharp report, loud as a shotgun. He'd clearly never changed a tyre, so I did it while he watched, as amazed as if I'd pulled the spare from my pocket instead of the boot.

"You're a remarkable woman," he said.

"It's really quite easy." I poked around for something to wipe my grimy hands on, and finally had to settle for the knees of my slacks.

"Honestly, Beryl. I've never met anyone like you. It makes me want to do something rash."

"Like learn to change a tyre," I teased.

"Like buy a farm for you."

"What? You've got to be joking."

"Not at all. We should all get back what we've lost if we can. And anyway, it wouldn't only be for you. I'd love to have that sort of life."

"We've only just met."

"I told you I was feeling rash," he said. "But I should also warn you I'm quite serious. I'm not the sort of fellow who minces around when he sees something he wants."

We got back into the car and drove for several miles more in silence. I didn't know what to make of what he'd said, and that soon became obvious.

"I've made you uncomfortable," he said after a while.

"Please don't misunderstand. I really am flattered."

"And yet?" He smiled sideways at me from behind the wheel. "I feel a large qualification coming. I've a special sense for them."

"I'm just a very proud person. No matter how much I'd love to have a farm like Green Hills, I couldn't accept such a large gift from you, or from anyone."

"I'm proud, too," he said, "and stubborn as well. But it seems obvious to me that we want the same thing. We could be partners in a grand venture. Equally independent, equally *stubborn* partners."

I had to smile at that, but didn't say anything more until we came to Kampi ya Moto Station and began to climb the steep grade. There wasn't anything left of our farm but a few now-derelict outbuildings and listing paddock fences—but the view from our hill was the same.

"It's so lovely," he said, stopping the car and shutting off the motor. "And all this was yours?"

There were my Aberdares, unfurled in blue against the fresher, paler blue of the sky. And the sharp lip of the Menengai Crater, and the darkly fringed Mau Forest humming with life. Even the ruin of my father's old house didn't make me sad when I took in everything else. "Yes, it was."

"Oh, I nearly forgot," Mansfield said suddenly. He stretched behind him and pulled out an ice bucket he'd hidden well, wedging it against the rear seat. It was half full of tepid water and the curving bottle that had lost any hope of chilling long before. "It will probably be terrible now," he said as he popped the cork.

"It doesn't matter," I told him. "A dear friend once told me that champagne is absolutely compulsory in Kenya. You must belong here after all."

"You see, then?" He poured for us, into the simple glasses he'd brought along. "What shall we toast?"

I looked past him, through the window glass at the view that had forever been stitched into my heart. "I'll never forget this place, you know, even if one day it forgets me. I'm glad you wanted to come."

"Green Hills is a lovely name. What shall we call our farm?"

"You're going to keep at it until you wear me down, aren't you?"

"That's the plan, yes."

I looked at him, so like Berkeley with his fine smooth hands and his beautiful haircut, and suddenly had a strong urge to kiss him. When I did, his lips were feather-soft. His tongue tasted like champagne.

$\mathcal{T}$rue to his word, over the next few months Mansfield wore down my doubts and my defences little by little. The farm was one thing—I had always longed for a way to replace Green Hills in my mind and heart after all—but soon I realized he was set on marrying me.

"My divorce from Jock has only just come through. You can't really think I'm mad enough to try matrimony again?"

"Everything will be different," he assured me. "*We're* different."

Mansfield did seem to be a rare sort of man. He was nothing like Jock or Frank or Boy Long, and also listened to every tale about my thorny past without batting an eyelash. I'd decided not to keep a single thing from him—not even about Denys and Karen. I couldn't if our relationship was going to have a prayer. That much I'd learned, and painfully.

"Are you still in love with Denys?" he had wanted to know.

"He chose Karen. There's nothing I can do to change that." I watched a small cloud pass over Mansfield's expression and his mood. "Are you sure you want to get involved with me? My heart's always been restless, and I can't promise I'll be good at any of the dull stuff, the cooking and whatnot."

"I could have guessed that part." He smiled. "I'm looking for a companion as much as a lover. Life has been awfully lonely at times. Tell me, do you like me, Beryl?"

"I do. Honestly. I like you so much."

"I like you, too. And that's where we'll begin."

We married four months after Ginger introduced us, in September of 1927. My bouquet was a cluster of lilies and white carnations, which Karen helped select as a gift, but the choice of my dress was mine—a slim crêpe de chine with sleeves that clung to my arms and a long silver fringe that lay over the skirt like a net of stars. I'd cut my hair for the day in a tightly cropped shingle I had done on impulse, liking immediately how free and cool my neck felt without the weight.

D stood in for my father to give me away and cried doing it, dabbing at his face with damp sleeves. Afterwards there was a fine lunch at the Muthaiga, and through it all I tried not to linger overlong on thoughts of Denys. He was off in Tsavo, then Uganda. I had cabled him with an invitation and got no response. I wanted to believe it was jealousy that kept him silent and absent, but it was just as likely that my news hadn't reached him at all.

I put my horses on the ease list, said goodbye to Ruta, and we then left for several months' honeymoon in Europe. In Rome we stayed near the Spanish Steps, at the Hassler Hotel, which looked like a nineteenth-century palace to me. Our bed was enormous and draped with gold velvet. The bathtub was Italian marble. The parquet floors had been polished to shine like mirrors. I couldn't stop wanting to pinch myself to see if it was all some sort of dream.

"The George the Fifth in Paris is even finer," Mansfield said. When we were there, and I stood gaping at our private view of the Eiffel Tower and the Champs-Elysées, he said I should wait until I'd seen Claridge's in London. He was right about that, too. We arrived in Mansfield's Rolls-Royce, a car beautiful enough to get all the doormen hopping. The attention and the gleaming marble, the vases full of flowers and the draping silk, helped to dispel the ghost of my previous trip to London and how knocked sideways I'd been. This wasn't that. Whenever I started to drift and the past came back too clearly, I watched the trail of our Louis Vuitton trunks.

We had escargot in Paris. Choucroute garnie with sprigs of fresh rosemary. Spaghetti with mussels and black squid ink in Rome. Even better than the meals were the cultural highlights in every city: the opera, the architecture, the views, and the museums. And with every new sight or incomparable view, when I thought, *Denys should be here,* I tried to ignore that voice. It was disloyal, for a start, and also impossible. Denys had made his choice and I'd made mine—and Mansfield was a good man. I respected and admired him through and through, and if the love I felt for him wasn't exactly the kind that could send me over the top of a mountain on horseback in the middle of the night, it was quietly solid. He stayed by my side. He held my hand and kissed me over and over, saying, "I'm so happy we've found each other. I can hardly believe it's real."

Mansfield had always been close to his mother, a relationship I was trying to understand, but how could I really? He was keen for her to like me, and thought it important that we get off on the right foot.

"She'll have certain expectations of what you're supposed to be," he told me.

"What do you mean?"

"Africa is Africa. When we've finished here we can hide away and behave however we like. But Mother and her friends aren't very advanced in their views."

I thought he was speaking of politics until we arrived at Elizabeth Arden. He'd booked me in for a full day of beautification and dropped me at the red door before I had time to protest. He took himself to Bond Street, and then to Harrods, while I was prodded and primped to within an inch of my life. My brows were plucked bare and drawn on with kohl. My upper lip and legs were waxed and buffed and my lips stained the deepest red I'd ever seen.

"How is this meant to please your mother?" I asked him at the end of the process. I felt naked with so much paint on. I wanted to hide behind my hands.

"It's perfect. You're exquisite. She won't be able to resist you, don't you see?"

"I'm worried . . . not that she won't like me, but that it matters so much to you. The whole scenario."

"Everything's going to be fine," he assured me. "You'll see."

Off we went to Swiftsden, the manor house where Mansfield's mother lived with her second husband, Colonel O'Hea. He was fifteen years younger than she, and neither of the Markham boys had much patience with him. I found him plump and silent, whereas Mrs. O'Hea was plump and full of opinions about everything. When I tried to shake her hand, she accepted only the tips of my fingers.

"Enchantée," she murmured—though she didn't seem remotely enchanted—and settled herself in the best chair to lecture me on the accomplishments of her prizewinning hounds.

At that first tea, I couldn't stop imagining how Mansfield's mother would have reacted to me as I was the day I turned up at Cockie's door with no coat at all, my hands chapped and blue, and my toes nearly frozen off. In Paris and then Milan, Mansfield had taken me to the best couturiers. I had all the right clothes now. Silk stockings, a fur stole, a diamond bracelet that slid up and down my arm like Bishon Singh's long-ago *kara*. Mansfield had been so generous. I thought he wanted to buy me beautiful things *because* they were beautiful, but now that I'd run the gauntlet of Elizabeth Arden and stood in his mother's jewel box of a parlour, I had to wonder if every gift had in fact been for her.

"She can hardly think I'm a society type," I told him when we were alone in our room. He sat on the edge of the burnished-looking silk bedspread, while at a long vanity table I swatted roughly at the back of my shingle with a silver-handled brush. "What's the point of all this fuss? My poor eyebrows will never grow back."

"Don't be cross, darling. It's only for a short while, and then we'll wear our old clothes again and have a lovely new life."

"I feel like an impostor."

"But you're not, don't you see? This isn't dressing-up. You *are* elegant under everything."

"And what if I wore my slacks? And behaved like myself? Would she throw me out?"

"Please be patient, Beryl. Mother isn't modern like you."

I didn't want to quarrel, so I told Mansfield I would try. But in the end, the only way we could survive our time at Swiftsden was to divide and conquer. Mansfield looked after his mother, and the chauffeur looked after me. I was driven to London for long excursions, and taken round all the tourists' haunts: London Bridge and Westminster Abbey and Big Ben. I saw the changing of the guard at Buckingham Palace, the red-suited sentries filing in and out as if they had cogs and wheels. Afterwards, I went to the cinema to see *The Battle of the Somme,* the projector and illusion of life transfixing me the way so much about London did—electric lights and electric kettles, music streaming out onto Oxford Street from a Magnavox loudspeaker. But the film's images of war were terrible. Men crouched in ditches, cowering in pain and terror that made me think of *arap* Maina, hoping to God he hadn't died that way. I missed Ruta, and wished he could have been there beside me in the dark theatre, though undoubtedly he would have been just as waylaid by it all, or even more so.

A few days later, Mansfield left his mother's side long enough to take me to Newmarket to look at a stallion. Mansfield thought we might want some new blood for our fresh start.

"I want us to be true partners in this," he said. "We'll find land wherever you like, and stock our stables with the finest horses we can find. You'll show me everything. I want to learn it all and to be a part of the big decisions."

I was relieved to hear it. Our shared dream of a horse farm had cemented us from the beginning—but at Swiftsden, under his mother's imperious gaze, I'd begun to have my doubts. Her opinion seemed to matter far too much to him there. The spine went right out of him when she was around, almost as if she were a grand puppeteer, and he made only of cloth and string. But in Newmarket, he squeezed my hand hard as we moved towards the stables. Of course he wanted a new life in Kenya just as much as I wanted Green Hills back. He meant to be his own man, to claim new territory, and to do it all with me by his side. Until that day, I would have to trust him and myself, too.

Messenger Boy was a towering red roan with a flaxen tail and mane, and a bright kind of fire whipping through him. He was the biggest stallion I'd ever seen and one of the most beautiful. His dame, Fifinella, was a derby and steeplechase winner; his father, Hurry On, was unbeaten, and one of the greatest sires of racehorses in the world. But though Mansfield and I were thrilled by him instantly, his trainer, Fred Darling, had a sobering story to tell.

"He's not going to make anything easy for you," Fred said. "I can't lie about that."

The full truth was he'd put Fred in hospital once. Not long after that, he'd killed a groom, trapping him in the stable and attacking him with his powerful hoofs and teeth. It was murder, pure and simple. If Messenger Boy had been a man, he would have got the chop for it; as it was, he'd been banned from racing in England. Kenya could give him a second chance, though.

"Can he be tamed?" Mansfield wanted to know.

"That's hard to say. I wouldn't do it."

"I want a go at him," I said, watching the way the sun glinted flame red through the stud's flared nostrils.

"You're not afraid?" Mansfield asked, reaching for my hand.

"I am. But we can't leave him here to be chained up like a dog."
For some reason, Messenger Boy made me think of Paddy, of the dif-

ficult line between wild, natural things and the civilized world. "He's still got something good in him. Anyone can see that."

Mansfield's hand clenched mine. I knew he was rattled by what we'd learned. "Will he win derbies?"

"If Ruta were here, he would say *His legs are powerful as a leopard's* or *His heart is like a wildebeest's,*" I said, trying to lighten the mood.

"All right then, how much for leopard legs?" Mansfield said to Darling, drawing out his chequebook.

48

$\mathcal{D}$enys and Mansfield had never met. When we drove out to Mbogani on a bright, dry afternoon, just after we'd returned from England, I was a little out of breath thinking about how they might size each other up. We'd brought back the new buttercup-yellow Rolls-Royce. My dress was from Worth, my rope of pearls from Asprey. Perversely, I wanted both Denys and Karen to see all of it— and me—to full advantage. I wasn't a waif any longer, or a child. But when we arrived only Karen's majordomo, Farah, was on hand.

"They are out walking, *msabu*," he said cordially. "Up to Lamwia, to the site of their graves."

"They're still very much alive," I said to Mansfield, when he gave me a curious look. "They're just overly romantic that way."

"That's fine," he said. "I love romance." He opened the rear door, and the three dogs we'd been travelling with rolled out onto the lawn, a borzoi, a pretty red setter, and a young blue deerhound that we'd brought back as a gift for Karen. The dogs leaped and yelped, happy to be free, while I couldn't stop looking up into the hills, wondering if Karen and Denys could see us, and when they'd come.

———

"You look well, Beryl," Denys said later on the veranda. My dress had been crushed from sitting by then, and I was feeling tired and a little nervous at seeing him. He kissed me quickly. "Congratulations."

Mansfield was a full head shorter, but so had Berkeley been. I found myself hoping that Denys saw what I did in Mansfield, and also what Mansfield saw in me.

"We went to the National Gallery," I said, feeling myself flush crimson, "and the Bolshoi Ballet in Rome." I was bursting to tell him all we'd done and how I was changed.

"How marvellous," he said several times, evenly, as I talked and talked. "Good for you both," but there was no real feeling behind his words. He seemed politely indifferent to everything.

Karen was clearly taken with her new hound, which had rich grey eyes and a ruff of wiry whiskers around her long nose. "She's delicious. You were a dear to think of me, especially since I've been lonely without Minerva." Apparently, just the month before, the pretty house owl had flown into the wooden blinds and got tangled in the cords and strangled to death. "We shouldn't care so much about animals," she said. "It's dangerous."

"I can tell you the animals aren't overconcerned about us," Denys said, settling back into his chair.

"Of course they are," she countered, reaching for the hound's damp soft muzzle. "Minerva was awfully fond of me, and so are my dogs."

"We ring the dinner gong and they run to us. That's common sense, not love. Not loyalty, either."

"He's in one of his black moods," she explained to us, as if he weren't there.

"Where are you off to next?" I asked Denys, dying to change the subject.

"To Rejaf. I'm taking some clients down the Nile."

"How exotic," Mansfield said, drawing on his cigar. "It sounds like a Hollywood film."

"The mosquitoes would tell you otherwise."

"I've always wanted to see the Nile," I said.

"It's hardly a moving target," he said, and then got up to see about something inside the house.

Karen raised her eyebrows at me. *Black mood,* her look said, but I felt slapped. I'd played out this encounter dozens of times on the ship back to Kenya, wondering how it would feel to see Denys again now that my situation had changed. I was married, and altered in other ways, too. I very much meant to be happy and wanted him to realize that—but he was behaving so oddly and being cold to everyone. Nothing was going as planned.

"You're going to buy land then?" Karen asked us. Her voice sounded strained.

"Yes, perhaps up near Elburgon."

"So far up-country?"

"The price is right, and there's a beautiful garden. Mansfield loves a good garden."

"That I do." He smiled and got up to pour brandy for us from a crystal decanter, looking at home with Karen's lovely things. "I'll just go and see about Denys. He probably needs a drink."

"You're well situated now, aren't you?" Karen said when he'd gone. I could feel something new in her gaze, maybe an unspoken question about whether my marriage to Mansfield was the real article or a sham. Whatever it meant, it made me uncomfortable. "You look awfully well."

"It's the pearls," I said.

"You've worn pearls before."

She meant when I'd been with Frank Greswolde, not that she would ever have had the bad taste to mention it. But surely she could see that Mansfield wasn't just any man ready to pay my way. He wasn't a *sponsor*—Cockie's terrible word—but my husband.

The dog whimpered in a dream at Karen's feet, flinching and twitching her paws. "We strike such dark bargains for love, don't we?"

Do we? I thought as Karen settled the hound with one hand, like a mother and her babe. But I didn't answer her.

49

One hundred and twenty miles north of Nairobi, Elburgon was cool in the morning, with sparkling, crisp skies and high, white flat-bottomed clouds. After a rain, mist settled in rifts along the hillsides, and I would take all of it in, walking to gallops in the early mornings, reminding myself that none of it was borrowed or tainted. That no one could try to ruin it for me, or take it away.

Our farm was called Melela, with a house that stood on stilts, dripping with blue bougainvillaea and flame vine. Purple passion fruit covered the back fence, and morning glories heaped over the veranda and arbour. Everywhere you looked there was a new splash of colour, and the air smelled alive. I had a heavy brass bell installed outside the main stable door, not long after we moved in, and Ruta rang it to wake the farm every morning before dawn, as our head groom, Wainina, had once done at Green Hills. Ruta and his family had a cottage near the stables, and he had his own office next to mine, though usually we found ourselves at the same desk, staring into the same ledger, side by side.

"What if we brought Clutt back from Cape Town to train for us?" I asked Mansfield in bed one night. I had been thinking about it for weeks, growing more excited by the idea and what it would mean. Money had kept my father away, and also the tarnishing of his reputation. But I was in a position to offer him a job and a prestigious place in the colony, one worthy of him and his talents.

"Would he consider an offer?"

"I think so. If it was sweet enough."

"With two Clutterbucks in one stable, I don't think the rest of Kenya could touch us."

"You don't know how happy that would make me, how right this feels."

I sent off a cable immediately, and before two months passed, I had my father back. He'd aged, and his hair had grown grey and thin, his face more careworn—but the very sight of him seemed to heal something in me. I had been so young when he left, hopelessly overwhelmed by my marriage, and the terrible loss of the farm. Nearly eight years had passed, and more heartbreak than I could properly chart for him, or even myself. But there wasn't any need to tell him my sad stories, or even the happy ones. I only wanted to stand by him at the paddock gate and watch one of our stallions run for all he was worth. To work by his side for a common goal. To be his daughter again—yes, that would do it.

Emma looked older, too, of course, and she seemed subdued if not any softer. But I found she didn't unsettle me as she used to. I'd become the mistress of a household. She was our guest at Melela, so what did it matter if she found me too coarse or headstrong now? Her opinion didn't mean as much as my own, or Mansfield's.

As it turned out, Mansfield and Emma got on well. They both liked gardening and soon could be seen kneeling together in domed sun hats, talking about root fungus or leaf blight, while I escaped to the stable where I belonged.

"What was Cape Town like?" I asked my father on one of the first mornings he was back. We leaned against the fencing along our gallops, watching one of our grooms exercise Clemency, a pretty new filly.

"Hot." He kicked dust from his boots, squinting into the flaring sun. "Competitive, too. The wins didn't come often."

"If we hadn't asked you back, would you have stayed?"

"I suppose so. I'm glad to be here, though. This is grand."

As ever my father hoarded his words and his feelings, but I didn't care. I knew he was proud of me and how far I'd come. I could feel it as we stood side by side, looking out over the green bowl of the spreading valley.

"It's the same view that we had at Njoro," I told him. "A little further north, but everything else is the same."

"I suppose it is," he said. "You've done well for yourself."

"After a fashion. It hasn't always been easy."

"I know." In his look were all the years we'd spent apart, the decisions we'd made, the difficult past we didn't need to name—all of it rolled up and pushed away like a heavy stone as he sighed once and said, "Shall we get to work then?"

In short order, the name Mrs. Beryl Markham began to appear in the racing columns, as a trainer and as an owner, too. That was utterly new. Clutt and I planned and schemed, building our operation by buying up the progeny of horses from the old farm at Njoro, animals that he'd overseen the beginnings of. It was a wonderful feeling to reclaim and realize seeds sown way back. There was a rightness, too, to the evenings when all our heads would cluster over the thick black studbook, dreaming of greatness, daring to predict the future: Clutt's and Ruta's and Mansfield's and mine.

Every morning, even before the gallops started, I rode Messenger Boy. I went off alone with him, though this made Mansfield nervous. Messenger Boy wasn't just any animal. He didn't trust me yet. Anyone could see that in the bold swing of his head and in the way he glared at the grooms who dared to touch him. He knew he was a king. Who were we?

One morning, I was only across the yard before Messenger Boy spooked. Whatever it was, I never saw it, only felt the muscular tremor as he bucked, twisting sharply sideways. Even startled, I sat him, but he wouldn't settle. I weathered three more violent twists before he sheered along the cedar-wood fencing and peeled me off forcibly. Thankfully I landed on the other side of the fence. Otherwise, he might have stamped me to death without even trying. It took four grooms to restrain him. My nose and chin streamed blood, so I left the grooms to care for him and went into the house to rinse and bandage myself. My hip ached, and I knew I'd have a massive bruise there, but it was Mansfield I really needed to worry about.

"My God, Beryl," he said the moment he caught sight of me. "What if he'd killed you?"

"It wasn't that bad. Really. I've fallen off horses all my life."

"He's too much of a loose cannon, that one. What if he really did hurt you? I know you want to be the one to tame him, but can that be worth the risk?"

"You think it's pride keeping me on Messenger Boy?"

"Isn't it?"

"This is what I'm best at. I know what he can be and how to get him there. I can see it, and I've no intention of giving up on him."

"All right, but why does it have to be you? School one of the grooms, or even Ruta."

"But it's *my* work. I really can manage him, Mansfield, and I will."

He stormed away unhappily while I finished tending to my wounds. When I returned to the barn, the grooms had Messenger Boy hobbled and tied between two thick posts. They'd hooded him and his eyes looked wild and murderous. *You'll never tame me* is what they said.

I could have ordered the grooms to free him, but I did it myself instead, working to be quiet in all my movements while they looked on anxiously. My father didn't challenge me and neither did Ruta, but they both trailed me at a distance while I returned Messenger Boy to his loose box. All the way there, the horse stamped warningly, and strained hard against the lead, and even when he was behind the stall door, he paced a tight line, whirling and glaring, challenging me. He

298 · PAULA McLAIN

seemed arrogant and full of hatred, but I guessed that beneath it all was sharp fear and self-protection. He didn't want me to change him or make him something he wasn't. He wouldn't be coerced into giving himself away.

"You're going to mount him again," I heard Mansfield say. He'd been watching from the house and had come into the stable without my knowing it.

"Tomorrow I will. He's still angry with me today."

"Why aren't you angry with *him*? Honestly, Beryl. It's almost as if you want him to hurt you."

"That's absurd. I just don't blame him for following his nature."

"And my feelings don't count?"

"Of course they do. But I have to get on with his training. This really is what farm life is about, Mansfield. It's not all window dressing and pretty flowerpots."

With that he stormed off again, and it was several days before I could convince him that I really wasn't just being obstinate but following my nature, too—because I had to. Nothing else felt quite right.

"I didn't think it would be so hard to watch you work," he confessed after his mood had softened. "What about when we have children one day? Surely you'll slow down then?"

"I don't see why I should. It was good for me to grow up on a farm. It made me."

"I suppose I'm more conventional than I thought," he said.

"And more stubborn even than you warned me about." Then I kissed him, wanting to make up.

In March, Mansfield and I went into Nairobi and found everyone at the club talking about Maia Carberry. Just two days before, JC's beautiful young wife had been giving a flying lesson to a young student, Dudley Cowie, when her plane spun in at low altitude, crashing at the edge of the Ngong Road, near Nairobi's Dagoretti Airfield. Dudley's twin brother, Mervyn, had just finished his own lesson and saw everything, the impact and explosion, the wall of flames that left nothing identifiable of either victim. Dudley was only twenty-two. Maia was twenty-four and had left behind a three-year-old daughter, Juanita. JC was with the child now, at the Carberrys' farm in Nyeri, apparently too heartsick to speak to anyone or even get out of bed.

When we ran into Denys and Karen at the club, they both seemed stunned. They were also worried about what could be done for the family.

"That poor girl will never know her mother," Karen said. She tugged worriedly on the cotton shawl around her shoulders. "She won't even remember her, will she?"

"That might be the biggest blessing," Denys replied grimly. "It's JC who's in real trouble."

"I'm surprised she wanted to fly when she had so much to live for, so many people counting on her," Mansfield said, looking at me directly, as if I could possibly miss his meaning. But I wasn't going to row with him on such a sad day. Our small tensions were hardly the point.

"Aeroplanes might be safer than automobiles," Denys said. "I don't think she saw flying as terribly rash."

"Your views aren't really the standard, Denys," Mansfield answered flatly. "Tell me, are you off down the Nile again soon?"

"Not exactly," Denys said.

"You haven't heard then," Karen said. "Elburgon *is* far north, isn't it?"

What she meant, we soon learned, was that a royal visit was in the making. The heir to the throne, Edward, Prince of Wales, was set to visit Kenya in late September with his brother, Henry, Duke of Gloucester. Denys had been charged to take them hunting.

"A royal safari?" I asked.

"A royal fiasco, most likely. You've no idea the number of preparations."

"It's the opportunity of a lifetime," Karen said sharply. Her shawl was crimson and deep blue with threads in a pattern that overlapped.

She held it firmly in front of her chest like a shield. "If you really don't want the work, give it to Bror instead."

Mansfield plucked at an invisible bit of lint on his trousers, still clearly disturbed by the news about Maia Carberry. Denys had his mouth set. Karen was feeling spurned in some way I could only guess at until Mansfield and Denys went inside to book us a table for lunch.

"It's one of the most significant moments in our history, and he won't take it seriously."

"He's never liked fuss or pomp," I said. "I'm guessing there are ten different committees or subcommittees who'll want to sort every detail down to the commode."

"It's not just the safari that matters. It's the social event of the decade. Perhaps the century."

"You know he's never going to care about parties." But I'd missed the larger point.

"Bror is newly remarried. I always worried there would be another Baroness Blixen, and it's happening at the direst moment. Divorced women aren't going to be welcome at Government House for the principal fêting. You see how impossible it all is." She clenched and unclenched her hands. Her knuckles were white.

"You want Denys to marry you," I said quietly, finally putting it all together.

"He refuses." She laughed icily, a terrible sound. "If he won't now, for this, for me, he never will."

50

*F*or the next several months, I tried to think only about our horses—
particularly Messenger Boy, who seemed to be resisting me a little less
each day. No one would have called him tame, but some mornings
when I rode him I felt something in the rounded smoothness of his
back that felt very nearly like forbearance. He might not have liked
me yet or even accepted me, but I was beginning to think he understood what I wanted from him, and that he might soon begin to want
those things for himself.

One morning I had just handed Messenger Boy to his groom for
cooling down when I met Emma in a sun hat as wide as a parasol.
"Are you feeling well?" she asked, a strange look on her face. So like
Emma. She hadn't even said good morning.

"Of course," I told her, but that night, when Mansfield was away
in town on errands, I felt a rocking wave of nausea and barely made
it out of bed before I vomited. When Mansfield came home, he found
me bent in two on the floor, too weak to stand.

"Should we go and see the doctor in town?" he fretted.

"No. It's just a touch of something I ate. I only need to lie down."

He got me back to bed, draped cool cloths over my forehead, and pulled the curtains closed so I could rest. But after he planted a sweet kiss in my palm and backed out of the room, I stared at the wall for a long time, thinking. I was pregnant, of course. The feeling was the same as it had been before, in London. Somehow Emma had suspected before I had come to the truth myself.

I knew I needed to tell Mansfield, but after the business with Messenger Boy and the way he'd reacted to Maia Carberry's death, I was terrified to bring it up. The pregnancy would only intensify his concerns about me. That was clear. What if he wanted not just to swaddle me but to curb me? What then?

While I was still stuck in a cycle of worry and doubt, Mansfield finally guessed. "Aren't you happy, darling?" He clasped my hands and gazed into my eyes.

"We're just getting started here," I tried to explain. "There's so much to do to make a farm run smoothly and get the horses in line."

"How terrible would it really be to take a little time off? When you're ready to get back to it, the horses will be here."

We were lying in our bed in the dark. His white pyjama shirt seemed to float and jump in front of my eyes. "I don't want to stop working, Mansfield. Please don't ask me to."

"Surely you'll stop riding . . . at least until the baby is born. You have to take care of yourself."

"This *is* how I take care of myself, don't you see? If we have this baby, I'll need to do my work just as before. I don't know any other way to live."

"*If* we have this baby?" He pulled back and his eyes hardened. "Surely there's no question."

I backpedalled. "I'm only afraid of how things will change."

"They *will,* of course. We're talking about a child, Beryl. Some dear small boy or girl who will look to us for everything."

His voice had taken on an intensity that sent me spinning. He didn't seem to understand that the very idea of throwing off the life I knew best for any other terrified me. There were women who never thought twice about giving themselves over to domestic life, the needs of their husbands and children. Some actually craved that role, but I'd never seen more than a hint of this sort of home life. Could I even do it?

"You'll learn to be a good mother," he said after I'd been silent for a long time. "People can learn all sorts of things."

"I hope you're right." I closed my eyes and lay my hand on his chest, feeling along the slick buttons of his shirt and the perfect piped edge of the cotton, the hem made so carefully and so well it wouldn't, couldn't, ever unravel.

51

The whole world would read about the royal visit—how the train station in Nairobi was festooned with roses and painted welcome banners. Hundreds of flapping flags. Thousands of people from every possible race in peacock-hued ceremonial robes and headdresses, fezzes and toques and velvet slippers. Our new governor, Sir Edward Grigg, bellowed his speech into a megaphone before the two young princes were whisked away to Government House on the hill, for the first of many grand fêtes and supper parties and sweeping, exclusive balls.

For a month, every white woman within a hundred miles had been practising her curtsy and wringing her hands over what to wear. It was a lottery of entitlement—all the honourables and baronets, and first or third earls of where-have-you rolled out in their finest form. I was four months pregnant and too distracted to be concerned about any of it—and I also wasn't nearly ready to share my news with others. To buy time, I'd begun to wear loose blouses and forgiving skirts—me, who was never out of slacks. I saw it as my only solution, along with hiding out as much as possible, but Mansfield was insisting we be present for everything. "Let's just tell people, darling. They'll all know soon enough anyway."

"I know . . . but it just seems so personal."

"What?" His forehead wrinkled. "It's happy news, silly."

"Can't you go to the parties alone? I don't feel like myself."

"You can't honestly think of begging off. It's an *honour* to be invited, Beryl."

"You're sounding like Karen."

"Am I?" He gave me a strange look. "I suppose that must mean you sound like Finch Hatton."

"What?" I met his eyes. "What are you suggesting?"

"Nothing," he said coolly, and strode away.

In the end, I went along to keep the peace. For the first elaborate dinner, Prince Henry was seated to my left. Down the far end sat Edward Albert Christian George Andrew Patrick David, dashing heir to the monarchy. Informally he was called David, and his brother Henry, Duke of Gloucester, was Harry, and both were keen to be shown a good time.

"I saw you riding to hounds in Leicestershire last year," Harry said to me over bowls of chilled lemon soup. He meant during our stay in Swiftsden with Mansfield's mother—though there hadn't been a formal introduction. He was taller and darker than his brother David, and only slightly less handsome. "You look marvellous on a horse, particularly in slacks. I think all women should wear slacks."

"Coco Chanel might be interested to hear you say it," the very done-up Lady Grigg chimed in from Harry's elbow, trying to insert herself. Harry ignored her.

"You nearly caused a riot that day at Melton," he said. "That was my favourite part."

I couldn't help but smile. "Yes, it seems high Leicestershire had never seen a woman astride a horse instead of side saddle."

"So refreshing to see the old birds get a shock. But they stopped talking as soon as they saw you take the fences so boldly. A beautiful woman with a good seat is her own argument."

I thanked him, laughing, while Lady Grigg craned our way again. She was the dignified wife of our governor, and yet there, with Prince Harry, she was transfixed by every word we were saying. I had the feeling she thought he was flirting with me. It was possible he was.

"Maybe you could break away before the safari and see our horses up in Elburgon," I suggested. "We have the best bloodstock around."

"Sounds wonderful." He smiled easily beneath his clipped dark brown moustache. He had grey eyes, and they looked at me clearly. "If it were up to me we wouldn't hunt at all. David's the one who wants to bag a lion. I'd rather ride to the top of the highest hill I can find and see everything, in every direction."

"Then do it," I said. "Who'd stop *you*?"

"You'd think that, wouldn't you? But I don't run the show here. I'm not much more than window dressing, really."

"You're a prince."

"I'm down the line." He smiled. "It's fine by me, really. Poor David's got his head in the noose."

"Well, even if you don't care for hunting, you've found the right fellow to take you out."

"Finch Hatton. Yes. He seems a splendid fellow."

"He's the very best there is." I glanced down to where Denys sat near Prince David, both of them flanked by admirers. Karen hadn't been invited, as she'd suspected. There would be hell to pay for Denys when he finally returned to Mbogani, though who knew when that would be. He'd been so preoccupied by safari preparations that I hadn't seen him, even briefly, in months.

In some respects, Denys and I were both in a period of suspension. There was no way this safari wouldn't change his life. The time and privacy he craved would be swallowed up by his new notoriety, and I knew some part of him dreaded it: the purest part, which only wanted to live simply, by his own code. How I understood that. Within a very short time, my belly would grow unmistakably round and my breasts tighten and swell. My body would transform first, and then every-thing else would follow. I still cared for Mansfield, but I also felt as if I'd boarded a train meant for one place that was now irrevocably going somewhere else entirely. The whole situation made me feel desperate.

With a stirring of passionate violins, the string quartet began to play Schubert. "Tell me, do you dance, Harry?" I asked him.

"Like a fool."

"Wonderful," I said. "Save one for me."

The next week, David and Harry came up to Melela as I'd suggested and raced on our exercise track. It wasn't much as races went. David was compact and athletic looking, but he wasn't a very able rider. He sat Cambrian and Harry sat Clemency, and for five furlongs the brothers were neck and neck while an entire entourage cheered them on. Cambrian was the much better racer; he was undefeated, in fact, until that day.

"You're nice not to say how bloody awful I am," David said as we walked back to the paddock, his blue eyes full of charisma. All along the fence, eligible women strained in a pose, ready to kill or drop their knickers for a whiff of his attention.

"You were lovely." I laughed. "Well, the stallion was, in any case."

"Who's this fellow?" he asked when we came near Messenger Boy. "Now there's a fine animal."

"He's had a bit of a chequered history, but he's starting to come round. Would you like to see him run?"

"I'll say."

I had one of the grooms ready Messenger Boy for me—thinking not just that he would make a magnificent impression on the prince, but also that it was a fitting opportunity to show Mansfield that I meant to keep handling our animals as before. It was probably obsti-nate of me, but I imagined I could easily explain how David had in-sisted on seeing Messenger Boy to his fullest advantage.

When that day was over, though, and the last vestiges of the entourage had trickled away, Mansfield let me know how unhappy I'd made him. "You're deliberately trying to put this child at risk, Beryl, and embarrassing me besides. They're famous playboys, both of them, and no one could have missed your flirtation."

"Don't be silly. I was only being friendly, and everyone knows I'm married."

"Marriage hasn't exactly kept you out of trouble before."

I felt slapped. "If you're angry about the horse, say that. Don't try to rub my nose in the past."

"You *are* being wilful about the riding, no doubt—but you also seem to have no idea of how you're prompting gossip."

"You're exaggerating."

"My mother reads every *word* of the society columns, Beryl. I would die if even a whisper of scandal made its way home. You know how difficult she is."

"Then why bow and scrape to mollify her?"

"Why deliberately fuel gossip and speculation?" He bit down hard on his lower lip, as he often did when he was angry. "I think we should go back to England until the baby is born," he went on. "It's a much safer place to be for many reasons."

"Why travel so far?" I bristled. "What would I do there?"

"Take care of yourself, for a start. Be my wife."

"Are you doubting that I love you on top of everything else?"

"You do care, I think . . . as much as you can. But sometimes I wonder if you're still waiting for Finch Hatton."

"Denys? Why are you saying all of this now?"

"I don't know. It almost seems as if we've been playing a kind of game lately." He looked at me closely. "Have we, Beryl?"

"Of course not," I said firmly. But later, as I tried to sleep, I felt a surge of guilt and awareness. I wasn't trying to toy with Mansfield exactly, but I *had* been flirting with the princes. In a way, I couldn't help myself. It felt marvellous to smile and make Harry smile, too, or to walk off in a particular way and know that David's eyes were on me. It was childish, and also futile, but for those moments, I could believe I was free-spirited and alluring again, as if I still had some measure of control in the world.

How had Mansfield and I come to a standoff so quickly? I wondered. We'd started off well, committed to being staunch allies and friends. It hadn't been perfect, but now this pregnancy was pressing us into separate corners. I had absolutely no desire to go to England to placate him, but what was the alternative? If things fell apart between us now, I'd be alone with a child to care for. I could also possibly lose the farm . . . and that seemed out of the question. Like it or not, I would have to bend.

52

The safari was set to depart, and Karen was throwing a royal dinner Denys had helped her secure—no doubt a peacekeeping concession. She couldn't go to Government House because of social protocol, but the princes could very well come to her. She made it worth their while, too, serving an incomparable meal with so many courses and small delicacies I quickly lost count. There was ham poached in champagne with tiny jewel-like strawberries and tart, plump pomegranate seeds, a mushroom croustade with truffles and cream. When Karen's cook, Kamante, came in bearing the dessert, a fat and perfectly browned rum baba, I thought he might float away with pride.

I watched Karen closely, too, certain she must be feeling this evening as one of her finest moments, but under the powder and jet-black kohl, her eyes were lined and exhausted looking. The safari plan had evolved, and Blix was now going along, too, as Denys's right-hand man. One safari had turned into several, beginning with a foray into Uganda, with other later trips into Tanganyika—and Cockie had been invited to go along as Blix's wife, and also safari hostess, making sure the water was hot for baths at the end of the day, and that Dr. Turvy had wired in prescriptions for plenty of gin. Karen was left in the lurch, and she was livid about it, I soon learned.

The culmination of the evening was a Kikuyu *ngoma,* the largest of these I had ever seen. Several thousand dancers gathered from tribes all over the area, their chiefs joining forces to give the princes a picture they'd never forget. The central bonfire licked up at the sky. Several smaller blazes encircled it, like brilliant spokes around a gleaming hub. The drum music rose and fell in great rippling crescendos, while male and female dancers flung themselves rhythmically in moves too ancient and complex ever to chart.

I watched it all remembering the *ngomas* of my childhood, when Kibii and I would sneak out together until dawn, transfixed and also confused by the sensual responses the dancers awoke in us, feelings we didn't yet have names for. I had changed many times since those days, my skin shed again and again. I would still know Lakwet if she crept out of the shadows to stand in the firelight, but would she recognize me?

On her veranda, Karen had hung two blazing beacons, ships' lanterns that she'd once brought back from Denmark for Berkeley, and which had been returned to her after his death. Watching the *ngoma* a distance away, Denys stood under one of these, his weight on one foot and his other foot cocked, his shoulder resting on a blue fieldstone pillar. Mansfield stood near the other—the two of them arranged as symmetrically as doorways into two different worlds. I couldn't help but be struck by the thought that fate might have lined things up differently. In some other time, or on another plane, Denys might have been my husband, and this child been his child. I'd have felt differently about everything then, happy and excited about the future instead of worried and sad. But here and now, the die was cast. Even, God help me, if some hidden part of me was still waiting for Denys to love me, to turn from Karen and claim me for his own, what did that matter? It wasn't to be.

I looked away from both men and back towards the fire, where the flames rose, copper and gold, blaze blue and white, the sparks thrown up and raining down again like the ashes of fallen stars.

A few days later, I found myself rapping at the door of Ruta and Kimaru's hut, after the day's work was done. Their kitchen smelled of spices and stewed meat. Asis was now four years old, with his father's high square forehead and his confidence, too. He liked to stand on the beaten-earth floor by the table and leap as high into the air as he possibly could, looking so like Kibii it could stop my heart.

"He will be an excellent *moran,* don't you think?" Kimaru asked.

"He'll be perfect," I agreed, and then finally confessed to Ruta that I would soon have a child, too.

"Yes, Beru," he said lightly. Of course he already knew. It had been ridiculous of me to think he hadn't. "And our sons will play together as we did, will they not?"

"They will," I agreed. "Maybe they'll even hunt. We both remember how . . . I do."

"A *moran* never forgets," he replied.

"You're my family, Ruta. You and Asis and Kimaru, too. I hope you know that."

He nodded, his eyes rich and black. I had the feeling that if I looked deeply enough into them I would see all the years of our childhood played out one marvellous day at a time. And in that moment, I felt the faintest stirrings of hope about this baby. None of it would be easy, but if Ruta was here to remind me of who I really was, it might be all right. I would still have to weather England and Mansfield's mother without him—but come the summer we'd bring the baby home. Melela would be my son's Green Hills. If I thought of it that way, the future wasn't nearly so terrifying.

"What does your father say?" Ruta asked.

"He doesn't know yet."

"Ah," he said, and then repeated a Swahili phrase he'd challenged me with years before, *"A new thing is good, though it be a sore place."*

"So I've heard," I said, and left him to his dinner.

53

Confinement is one of those funny old-fashioned words that say so much more than they mean to. I had mine in Swiftsden with Mansfield's mother, who made everything easy for me in one way, and a personalized piece of hell in another. I slept in a beautiful room and had a lady's maid, and didn't lift a finger, even to pour my own tea. It was obvious she meant to lavish this child with everything befitting a Markham. I wasn't really a Markham myself, and she made that expressly clear, all without saying a word.

I sailed from Mombasa alone, leaving Ruta and my father in charge of the horses. Mansfield joined me in January, and was there for the birth, on 25 February 1929, a day so bitterly cold the pipes clanged and threatened to burst in the nursing home in Eaton Square. The windows to the street had glazed over, blanketing out the world, and I found myself fixing on that opaque smear as I bore down. I had been given laughing gas and some sort of sedative. Both made me shake and believe I might snap into pieces. Clutching, strangling pains came in rhythms I had no control over. My knees shook. My hands quivered on the damp sheets.

Hours later, with a final sickening push, Gervase fell out of my body. I craned to see him, and won only the briefest glimpse of his puckered face, the tiny chest slick with blood, before the doctors took him away. I was still lurching in the grip of the drugs. I had no idea what was happening and could only lie there, prodded by the nurses to hold still.

No one was telling me anything—not why they'd taken my baby or if he was even alive. I struggled with the nurses, and then slapped one, and finally they sedated me. When I came to, Mansfield was in my room looking waxen and drawn. The baby wasn't right, he began to explain. He was dangerously small and he was missing things that should be there. The anus hadn't ever formed, nor the rectum.

"What?" I still felt thick and sedated. "How?"

"The doctors say it happens sometimes." He'd been biting at his lip again. I could see a pale lilac-coloured bruise blooming. "But what if the riding did it, Beryl?"

"Could it have? Is that what you think?"

"Mother's sure it couldn't have helped things."

"Oh." His words thudded at the back of my skull. "What can they do for him?"

"There's surgery. If he's strong enough, there might be several, actually. But he's not strong now. He's so small. His breathing isn't good. They're saying we should prepare for the worst."

When Mansfield left my room, I gathered the sheets and blankets around me, but couldn't begin to feel warm. Our son might die. The very thought had me shaking again—lost and sick and utterly helpless.

In my Lakwet days, I was at the Kip *shamba* once when a maimed child was born. It had a small stump where one of the legs should have been, the skin pink and raw, puzzle-stitched. No one tried to shield any of this tragedy from Kibii or me. The child would either live or it wouldn't—it was up to their god. That night the mother placed the babe just outside the door to her hut and slept, as the rest of the tribe did, without answering its cries. The theory went that if the oxen didn't trample it, the child was meant to live. But that night, a predator came and took it away—probably a leopard or hyena. That was thought to be the god's will, too.

Would Gervase make it through his surgery, or even his first night? Was some god going to punish me by taking him—or did everything that happened to us on earth come down to a blind roll of clicking dice, without any more reason or plan than chance? I wasn't sure what I believed and had never learned to pray. I didn't know how to surrender to fate, either—so I hummed an old African song under my breath as I waited, one full of thin courage . . . *Kali kama Simba, sisi Askari wote ni hodari.* Fierce like the lion are we, soldiers all are brave.

54

*A*stonishingly, Gervase survived his first precarious days of life. The doctors attached a strange sort of bag to his belly, and fed him through tiny snaking tubes in his nose. He gained an ounce, and then lost two. He came down with jaundice, and they put him under bright lamps. For the most part, we were kept from him because he couldn't be exposed to even the faintest risk of germs. I saw him only twice as I recuperated in the nursing home, and both times I felt punched in the heart. He was so frail and defenceless—like a broken bird.

On the day before Gervase's surgery, Mansfield came to my room looking pale and defeated. "I know it's too soon to be talking about all of this, but if he makes it, I want Gervase to go to Swiftsden for his recovery. Mother can make sure he gets the very best care."

"Of course, if the doctors approve it." For myself, I hated Swiftsden, but Gervase came first.

"And what will you do?" he went on. "When you're released from the hospital?"

"What do you mean? I want to be where Gervase is, obviously."

"I assumed you'd want to go back home."

"One day, yes. When we can all go together. What is this about, Mansfield?"

He turned and went to the window, pacing before it, his feet stitching the dark floorboards. The weather was still terrible, and all the panes were rimed over with greenish-looking ice that gave Mansfield's skin a ghostly cast. He looked different to me now that we'd come to England—not just more pallid, but weaker in spirit, too—almost as if he were reverting to his boyhood self, that invalid who'd spent most of his youth in bed, poring over the Latin names of flowers.

"I'm not sure I'll go back to Kenya," he said. "It seems more and more clear . . . how different we are. I feel a little foolish about it."

"Foolish to marry me? Why are you saying this now? We've made a life together. Do you mean to throw it away?"

"I wanted a new chance; I did. But maybe I was just playing a role. Or you were."

I felt the room lurch. "I don't understand. The farm is my whole life, and we have Gervase now. We're bound to him."

"I know that," he said wearily. Then he went to talk to the doctor while everything we'd said—and hadn't—hung in the room like a cold, crimped fog.

I could scarcely catch up. Mansfield and I had been at odds sometimes, and had never been an ideal match—but we'd wanted the same things and had been friends. Now any affection seemed to have dissolved as quickly as the sun had. It was a different season here, in more ways than one.

While I was still fretting over all of this, I heard a flurry of footsteps outside the door. I assumed Mansfield had returned with news from the doctor, but it was Prince Harry who'd come.

"You're supposed to be on safari," I said, taking in the shock of him. His fine grey suit looked as if it had been drawn onto his body. He didn't belong in a nursing home on Gerald Road.

"Everything was postponed. I imagine you've been too caught up here to know, but my father developed a lung infection. It was a door-die situation, but he's recovered. What of you? I didn't even know you were expecting, and then there you were in *The Times*. One son born to one Markham, Beryl, at Gerald Road. You're a wily one."

"I wasn't ready for anyone to know. Now the baby's in trouble, too." I felt my face crumpling and wondered if I were about to cry in front of royalty. Would that appear in *The Times,* too?

"I'm sorry. I heard. What can I do?"

"If you really want to help, you can make sure the surgeon is the very best. You must know who's good around here, and who can be trusted. He's still so small. Did you see him?"

Harry shook his head just as two nurses came in and pretended to busy themselves with linens. Obviously they were addled by having royalty in their midst and wanted a closer view.

"I'm happy to look into the surgeon," he said, ignoring them. "And please don't hesitate to ring me if you need anything else, anything at all."

"Thank you. I'm so worried."

"Of course you are." He reached for my hand and squeezed it, and then leaned over and pressed his lips to the back of my wrist. It was a harmless gesture, meant only to show concern, but the nurses turned and gaped. Their square caps tipped towards us like flowers, or like megaphones.

55

*W*eak as he was, Gervase had the heart of a young *moran*. He made it through that first surgery, in the middle of March, and was a little more whole afterwards. They created an opening in him where there'd been only a blank expanse of skin. The next month he had another operation to form a rectum out of tissue from his colon, and then yet another, to bring it all together, like dots connecting in a child's crude puzzle book. Each time we didn't know if he'd survive the procedure or the anaesthesia. There was always the risk of sepsis afterwards, and haemorrhage, and shock.

The doctors had said no to Swiftsden for the moment. He remained in hospital, while Mansfield and I stayed at the Grosvenor, though in separate suites. We weren't talking about the fate of our marriage for the moment. We were barely speaking at all.

One day Ginger Birkbeck came to visit me at the hotel. She and Ben were in London because she needed surgery for a benign tumour in some "female" region of her body she was far too delicate to name. But she didn't want to talk about that anyway . . . but about Harry.

"Tongues are wagging all over town about you two," she told me. "Word is that you're at the Grosvenor because it's across the road from Buckingham Palace, and that he comes and goes from your suite through a passageway along the basement."

"That's absurd. We're only good friends, and he's been awfully kind to me."

"Even so, you should take care. It's quite a serious thing. Forgive me for saying so, but your reputation hasn't exactly been spotless. And the gossip columns always jump to the easiest conclusion."

"Let them, then. I just don't care any more."

"So you *are* involved with Harry?"

"Whose *bloody* business is it if I am? Or if I'm not?" I paced the plush carpet—green tones and red tones all clashed together, in a muddle of Christmas and Sotheby's. My God, but I was tired.

Ginger's eyes widened. From her seat on my sofa, she asked, "You're not planning to say either way then?"

"You're missing the point! I'm trying to tell you it doesn't matter. No one's going to believe me if I deny the rumours anyway."

"You could be ruined, Beryl," she said. "Have you thought of that?"

I closed my eyes and opened them again. "Honestly, if I could have my life back and be left alone, I'm not sure I'd mind that much."

"I'm trying to help, you know. I only want what's best for you."

"Believe it or not, so do I."

There were a series of raps on the door, and Harry walked in with his lovely haircut and sharp, piney cologne and his knife-pleated trousers. "Hello," he said. "What's happening here? How's Gervase today?"

"Stronger by all accounts."

"That's excellent. Really excellent." He crossed the room swiftly and gave me a squeeze, and then he kissed me on the forehead while Ginger's cheeks went bright crimson.

Finally in early May the surgeons were poised to release Gervase to Swiftsden. Though I knew I was going to have a fight on my hands, I thought it was time to bring up Kenya, too.

"He would never survive the trip," Mansfield said plainly to me in his brother Charles's coldly lavish library in Connaught Square.

"Not now, obviously. But next year?"

"I'm not going back—not with the way things are. And Gervase will have a better life here."

"How can you uproot all of us without even considering another way?"

"You can do whatever you like," he said without emotion. "I'm only thinking of Gervase now. He'll have constant care from nurses, nannies, and the best surgeons on hand. He's never going to be a strong child. You heard the doctor."

"I have, actually. I've heard everything the doctors have been saying." I caught his eyes pointedly. "Do you know Gervase's illness could have happened to anyone? That my riding had nothing whatever to do with it?"

A muscle in his jaw convulsed, and he looked away. "It doesn't matter now, does it?"

"No. I don't suppose it does."

For weeks I had been tortured by guilt, thinking my actions had done Gervase harm—but in the end, placing blame on either side was pointless. His future would come down to power and resources. Mansfield's mother had never liked me. She would push to shut me out of my son's life, and Mansfield had grown so severe and closed to me. The door between us had become a wall, and Gervase was on the other side. "He's my child, too. How is it I have no rights, no say?"

He shrugged, pursing his lips. "You've brought everything on yourself. Now there are rumours this child is the duke's."

"But that's ludicrous. I was pregnant in June. Harry didn't even arrive in Kenya until October, when I was months gone."

"Harry? David? The rumours fly both ways. Honestly, Beryl. One prince wasn't enough for you? You had to try for two?"

I would have slapped him if I'd had any strength left for outrage. "This gossip disgusts me."

"So deny the claims."

"I shouldn't have to, especially not to you! And what does it matter what people think any more? Damn them all."

We went on in this way while the servants crouched, no doubt, just outside the door, ready to reveal everything to the *Tatler*. Mansfield was trying to strong-arm me into making a clearing statement to *The Times*. His mother was very nearly beside herself over the scandal. "Think of her good name," Mansfield implored. "Propriety means everything here."

"I'm so sick of things done in the name of propriety, I could die," I spat out. "I want to go home."

"Don't force my hand, Beryl. I can clear my own name by divorcing you and naming the duke as co-respondent. You'll lose any penny you ever thought you might get from me. You'll lose Gervase, too."

"Can you honestly say you're not planning to take him from me no matter what happens?"

He looked at me impassively. Tea things rattled just outside the door. I felt close to tears and also hollow, as if I'd lived all of this before, many times over, with different words laid out for the same horrible crimes, for being a woman, and daring to think I could be free. But now it wasn't only my fate that lay in the balance.

"Come after me with all you have then," I finally said. "Do your worst."

What transpired next would be whispered and tattled about for decades to come, and mostly bungled in the retelling, like the nursery game of telephone operator where even the most banal message turns tangled and foreign and unrecognizable. Some said Markham stormed the palace with a bundle of love letters from the duke. Some insisted that his mother went, begging an audience at the Royal Enclosure at Ascot. Queen Mary's solicitors were woken at daybreak, or perhaps it was Sir Ulick Alexander, Keeper of the Privy Purse. The old lady was outraged, terrified, dismissive, threatening. No one could cite a prince of the blood in a divorce petition, but she would pay to make sure it never happened all the same, ten thousand pounds or thirty thousand or fifty thousand in a capital sum that would generate an annuity for the rest of my life. If I would go the hell away.

Rumour and speculation took on a life of their own, and nothing that was ever said could begin to surprise me. I was too empty anyway. Gervase went to Swiftsden, as I'd always known he would, and he made progress there. His body healed. He babbled and cooed in his lovely cot, liking his own voice. Perhaps he would remember me standing over him, tracing the small crease of flesh beneath his chin. I hoped so. He had Mansfield's eyes, while I saw nothing of myself in him. Nothing except the way he had fought to be here, alive.

Through the years I would return to Swiftsden to visit him, always watched over by Mansfield's mother and various nannies, as if they were afraid I'd run off with him to Africa. I had certainly thought about it, if only so that he would know the colours of that place—the lion-gold grass and the snow-glazed summit of Kilimanjaro—and also more truly know me. Instead, I told him stories about Njoro—about Kibii and Buller and Wee MacGregor. Leopard nights, elephant nights, the flat forever sky. When I left I always said the same thing: "One day, we'll go there. I'll show you everything."

56

I stayed in England for the remainder of 1929, often going out to the Aero Club in Piccadilly. There was something soothing and even healing in watching aeroplanes stitch through the vacant blue over Shellbeach, glinting silver needles pulling thread. It was there that I ran into Denys, on a sheer October day. He had on a snug leather jacket and an aviator's scarf around his neck and was walking towards me across the terrace café, near one of the great hangars. I could scarcely believe it for a moment—as if I'd dreamed him. Then we rushed towards one another without any thought or awkwardness, like two people who had found each other at the end of the world.

"My God, it's good to see you." I gripped his hand, unable to let it go. "How are you here?"

"To get my flying hours in. The royal fiasco netted me the funds to finally buy the aeroplane I've always wanted. She's a lovely gold Gipsy Moth. I'll ship her back to Mombasa if we're both still standing in six months." He meant him and the plane. After Maia's tragedy, I was surprised to hear him be so bold, but that was Denys.

"They're beautiful machines." I looked up to where a bright

de Havilland waggled and straightened again. "They make me think of grace."

"You've been through the wringer, I know."

"You never liked Mansfield, did you?" I ventured. "You were always chilly near us."

"I wanted you to be happy. . . . I've always wanted that. But it surprised me when you married him. Honestly, I always thought you were too much of a free spirit for any sort of confinement. That we were alike in that way."

"Maybe that's what botched up things from the beginning. Who can say? But everything's tipped over now. I don't know what will happen to the farm or my horses, or even what to care about saving."

"You should learn to fly."

"Me?" I asked. "Does it feel as open up there as it looks from here?"

"Even more."

"Sounds like heaven then," I told him. "Save some of it for me."

Over the next few weeks, until I left for home, Denys and I met every day for lunch at the aerodrome, in sun or rain. I was as drawn to him as I'd ever been, and though part of me was longing to kiss and hold him near, it also felt wrong to have these desires when Gervase was still so vulnerable, and the wreckage of my marriage smoked in pieces around me. But Denys was my friend, too, and I needed one. He told me everything he was learning in the air, and I fell on each detail, happy to have something new to think about.

"It does seem like pure freedom," I told him. "If you can forget about the risk, that is."

"The fear never completely goes away. It makes everything sharper."

I nodded, understanding exactly what he meant. Even as a child I'd had it in me to test and challenge myself. Though I had sometimes forgotten that girl, she came back clearly when I looked into the sky, so sharp and blue it was a sort of window. Maybe I *would* fly, too. Maybe that's why Denys and I had had these days together at the aerodrome, and why I had begun to feel less low and desperate. The idea of it—of a future with wings—made the truest sort of sense, and began to cure me. Denys did, too. Just sitting near him helped me remember who I was in better times, stronger and surer, ready to look ahead, to face what came next without fear.

"Have you ever imagined us together," I asked him one day. "A time or place . . . a world, even, where we could be together? Simply, I mean, without trying to ruin one another, or wanting more than the other could give?"

His smile came slowly. His hazel eyes, when I looked into them, were bottomless. "What about this place? This moment?" He reached for my hand and we sat like that, side by side, for a few more precious minutes, while over our heads a silver Moth glinted like star fire and dipped its wings sideways, and passed behind a cloud.

57

*A*t the end of March 1930 I sailed home. I went briefly to Melela, to see my father and Ruta and our horses. It was harder than I ever imagined to find words to explain that Gervase was still in England, that they might never even meet him. My father wanted to go after Mansfield, as if we could spar across an ocean and change anything. Ruta was quieter, and also terribly sad for me, I knew. He seemed to guess immediately that the farm had lost its bloom.

"I don't have the heart for racing just now," I told him. "I can't seem to think about anything from the old days. I don't want to sit on a horse, and I don't want to smell the paddock. I'm going to learn to fly."

"I see," he said, and was quiet for a moment. "And where will we go for this flying?"

The word *we* nearly did me in, filling me full of tender holes. "How about Nairobi?"

We moved to the Muthaiga Club, where I rented Denys's old cottage, and Ruta and his family found a house in the native quarter nearby. The sight of Asis running alongside his mother or clambering into

Ruta's arms had me missing Gervase so much it was often almost enough to double me over. According to Mansfield's letters, he was still fragile but getting stronger all the time. Along with news, Mansfield had also begun sending a small allowance. Though he had been aggressive with threats of divorce when I was still in London, now he dragged his heels on the actual proceedings. But it didn't matter. He would see things through when he was ready, and I found I didn't champ at the bit to be fully free of him the way I had when things were so impossible with Jock. I was a mother, but couldn't hold my child in my arms. Freedom didn't mean the same thing that it had before. Nothing did.

One day Karen came to my cottage for drinks, and I was surprised to learn she'd been in England, too, just past the time of my well-publicized tangle with the Markhams and the monarchy.

"I can't imagine how awful it all was," she said. I'd told her a little about Mansfield and Gervase, but kept the most painful details to myself.

"I'm not the only supposed courtesan on Fleet Street. Some other girl will come along soon, and everyone will forget about me."

"If that was a wager, I wouldn't take it." She sighed and touched her drink to her lips, her gaze turning inwards for a moment. "While you were away, I had locusts at the farm, and then frost. Everything withered. It's why I went over, to see if there was any way Denys could help save me from my debts."

"And was there?"

"No," she said quietly. "He's promised to take me flying, though, when he returns. The princes are coming back for more safaris, too, though no doubt you already know that."

"David needs his lion."

"Naturally," she said bitterly.

"It's not all terrible. You know how much Denys has wanted his plane."

"Yes. And now there are more clients grovelling to throw in with him than he could ever accommodate. I should be happy for him, shouldn't I? And yet I'm afraid it will ruin us." Her eyes were lined and impenetrable. I had no idea if she was sharing the truth with me—that she and Denys were near the end—or spinning out a dramatic story. I wasn't sure how their unfolding drama affected me, either. But it did.

Denys returned a few months later and began to make arrangements for the princes' next visit. I didn't see him at first but heard from Cockie that he was planning to move into town from Ngong.

"Tania has given back his ring," she told me when we met in town for lunch. "Apparently the separation is mutual, but that doesn't mean it's not killing her."

"What do you suppose finally broke them?"

"She wanted more than he is capable of."

"That's no one's fault. They both tried as hard as they could, didn't they?" I paused, trying to find words for my tangled feelings. "We can only go to the limits of ourselves—I've learned that if nothing else. Anything more and we give too much away. Then we're not good for anyone."

"She may have to sell the farm, you know. After everything, and all her fighting for it. She's been undeniably brave."

"She's been a warrior," I agreed. And she had. For nearly two decades, Karen had set her complete self on the line, gambling against impossible odds, mortgaging everything, loving her land too much to let it fail. And yet it would fail. I could scarcely imagine Ngong—or Kenya—without her. "The only happy thing I can think of is that you have Blix finally. Was it worth everything you went through to win him?"

"I don't know." She twisted the ring on her finger, a square yellow diamond bright as the sun. "I'm not sure it matters anyway. I couldn't have made any other choice. He is my heart. Do you know what I mean?"

"Yes," I told her. "I think I do."

———

I was reading in bed a few nights later, in my cottage, when Denys came rapping on the door. I knew it was him before I answered. I'd been waiting for weeks—for years. But this time I knew he'd come.

Throwing on my dressing gown, I turned up the lamp and poured us each a generous glass of scotch. Even tired and unshaven, with a nasty scrape along the back of one arm, he looked like a piece of heaven to me. We sat without speaking for a long time, until I thought that it almost didn't matter what we found words for or didn't. His breathing steadied me. The rise and fall of his chest, the soft creaking of the chair under his weight, and his fine rounded fingers locking around the base of the glass.

"How's your aeroplane?" I finally asked.

"Perfect. I'd no idea I'd love it so much. And it could help business, too. The last time I was up I spotted three different herds of elephants, four massive bulls. For numbers like that, I could be out for weeks, drive hundreds of miles."

"What? Scout for them from the air then, and wire ahead to camp?"

He nodded. "Not bad, right?"

"Not bad." I smiled.

We fell quiet again, listening to the sounds of the insects in the grass and the jacaranda. "I heard Karen may have to sell her farm," I told him.

"She's looking at the very darkest side of things. I'm worried about her, but she's asked me not to visit. If we don't keep our distance now, we might just lose everything. Even our lovely memories."

I set down my drink and went to him, resting my knees in front of his chair and taking his hands. "I have so much respect for her, you know. She's the most remarkable woman."

"Yes." He looked at me carefully, almost solemnly, as if he were trying to read my features like an ancient text. The lamp threw a dark wand over part of his face, but his eyes gleamed, soft and amber coloured. They reminded me of Berkeley's Falernian wine. Of lions in the grass.

"Will you teach me to fly?"

"I couldn't take your life in my hands. Not when I've just got the hang of this myself." He said nothing of his own life, or of Maia Carberry's, how her plane had smoked and steamed on the Ngong Road for hours, keeping the authorities from even trying to recover her and Dudley's remains. I wouldn't have expected him to.

"I'm going to do it anyway."

"Good. I'll be back in three months," he said. "We'll go up and you can show me everything you've learned. We'll head over to the coast, or out on safari together. We never did get those six days, did we?"

I thought of Pegasus and the elephants and the dissolving bridge, of Denys's boy running twenty miles in bare feet to break my heart. "No, we didn't."

58

A great deal had happened to Tom Campbell Black since the day we met by the side of the road in Molo. He'd got the aeroplane he'd dreamed of and learned to master it, becoming the managing director and chief pilot at Wilson Airways in Nairobi, a spanking-new flying operation that ferried paying passengers and did courier work. He had also recently made the headlines by rescuing a world-famous German war pilot, Ernst Udet, whose plane had gone down in the desert. When I searched him out to ask about lessons, he didn't seem at all surprised to see me again, saying, "I always knew you were going to fly. I could see it in the stars."

"I see. So that's why you made a long, grand speech about aeroplanes and freedom and the clouds and nothing holding you back? That was all for me?"

"What? Don't I look like a mystic?"

"As long as you agree to teach me," I said, laughing, "you can be as mysterious as you like."

We began in the early morning over a peacefully sleeping Nairobi. The aerodrome was as ramshackle then as the town of Nairobi had been only thirty years before, tin and glass and hope standing tiptoe at the edge of emptiness.

Tom had never had a student before, but in a way, that didn't matter. Most of flying was instinct and intuition, with a few do-or-die rules thrown in on top. "Trust your compass" was one of these. "Your own judgement will go haywire sometimes. The horizon will lie to you, too, when you can see it. It's bound to. But this needle"—he pointed with no small drama—"this will tell you where you *should* be going. Not where you are. Put your faith there, and you'll catch up eventually."

The plane we used was set up for dual instruction. I could learn the instruments and the feel of the rudder bar with him on hand to catch my mistakes. There were earphones we could use to talk to each other, but soon Tom stopped wanting to use them. "You're going to have to find out where you're misstepping on your own," he told me. "I can keep correcting you, but what would be the point?"

He was right, of course. The throttle, the angle of the joystick, the tail skid and wing flaps and elevators—each element needed to become something I could feel and know—and even fail at occasionally, especially at the beginning. Sometimes the Moth's weight sagged, and she lost altitude, dropping towards the sun-bleached grass and the rocks, everything hurtling at great speed. There were unpredictable downdraughts near the mountains. The propeller could sputter out as quick as a breath, or weather could come up from nowhere. You could land in sansevieria, ripping your wings to tatters, or sideslip and crack the undercarriage. You could hit buried roots or clods or the deep snag of a pig hole and bust the struts, grounding yourself or worse. You could practise and practise and read all the signs correctly, and still founder. And yet the challenges felt exactly right to me. They brought me alive in a way I hadn't felt in a very long time.

"I want my B-class licence," I told Denys when he came back to town. "I could be the only professional female pilot in Africa."

"You don't want much." He laughed. "But you broke the same sort of new territory as a trainer, didn't you?"

"I suppose so. This feels different, though. It's just you and your instincts up there, isn't it? The challenge of that feels new every time." I was quiet for a while and then felt my way towards something I'd only just begun to realize. "After what happened with Gervase, I began to wonder if I'd ever find my way again."

"You'll see your son soon," he said softly. "Mansfield can't fend you off for ever."

"I won't let him. I would never give up on Gervase the way my mother did me. I couldn't."

"Sometimes when you're hurting, it helps to throw yourself at something that will take your weight."

I nodded.

"Just promise me you'll be careful when you fly."

"I promise," I said. "You know, Ruta has made the leap without a hitch somehow. He seems as exhilarated by the whole business as I am, and Tom says he has the makings of a damned fine mechanic."

The sun had set and I lit the hurricane lamp while Denys dug a book out of his satchel and then stretched out in a chair, his long legs crossed. He read aloud to me as I curled next to him, both of our bodies in a warm arc of light. For nearly ten years I'd wanted this . . . this exactly. *Is he really here?* I thought. *Am I?* Denys read on, his voice rising and falling, while a leopard moth that had got caught in the curtains stopped struggling for a moment, and realized it was free.

59

$\mathcal{D}$enys was between safaris, and there was a window, a very small one, for the two of us to go out alone. We made for southern Masailand, aiming at the Mara River with a team of Africans including Denys's man, Billea, and a Kikuyu boy, Kamau, he often travelled with. It was impossibly dry, and yet past Lake Province we saw countless animals—buffalo and rhino and shaggy lion, gazelles of every shade and variety. The golden slopes and shimmering flatlands swarmed with life.

Denys was most himself in wild places. Through a pair of smudgy field glasses, he could gauge a set of kudu horns, or the weight of still hanging ivory. He knew how to shoot anything, with no miscalculation, and could skin an animal so quickly and with such precision there was almost no blood in it. But he was just as keen not to shoot or kill, not if he didn't have to, using his camera instead. Photographic safaris were a new idea then, and he believed cameras had the power to change hunting, the sporting idea of it. Hunters could *have* Africa without taking any of it away—without ruining it.

On safari, I saw Denys in sharper relief than I ever had. He had an infallible compass, and a way of seeing everything as if he knew it would never be there exactly the same again. More than anyone I'd known, Denys understood how nothing ever holds still for us, or should. The trick is learning to take things as they come and fully, too, with no resistance or fear, not trying to grip them too tightly or make them bend. I knew all this from my Lakwet days, but being with him helped me remember it, and feel it all again powerfully.

For most of a day we walked through alkali flats, the white crust like a frosted layer of salt that rose in a powder when your boots punched through. We wore the chalk on us everywhere—up to our knees, in the creases of our fingers clenching the rifle strap, down in the cavity between my breasts, and in my mouth, too. I couldn't keep it out and stopped trying. I couldn't keep anything out, I realized, and that was something I loved about Africa. The way it got at you from the outside in and never let up, and never let you go.

Denys was happy and cheerful all day, though he'd drunk most of the fifth of gin we'd shared the night before. It was a mystery to me, how he threw it off. His blood must have been thick indeed, for it carried enough malaria to sink an ox, and yet he never fevered and never went down. The sun was an anvil on the top of my head, shoulders, and neck, where fresh sweat poured and wetted my collar. My clothes hung on me, the wet salt from my body drying in rings. I was breathing hard, and hearing my own breath rise raggedly. But we had our distance to cover. What was tiredness? The porters moved ahead in a line, and when my vision blurred, the slim lines of their bodies against the great whiteness of the plain looked like human geometry. Limbs became sticks and sharp dashes, an equation of simple perseverance.

Just past midday, we stopped and rested in the muddled shade beneath a great baobab tree. It was squat and wide, with ribboning, undulating bark like a skirt of some sort, or like wings. This one hung with fruit in pale-brown drooping pods, and with the baboons feasting on them. Several sat on a branch over our heads, and we could hear them cracking open the fruit, a musical rattle, like maracas. A rain of the powdery meat fell on the ground around us, into the short yellow grass, and stray spat seeds, too, and baboon droppings, which smelled foul.

"We could move off," Denys said when I grimaced, "or shoot them."

I knew he wasn't serious about the shooting, and joked, "Not on my account. I could probably lie down in the shit and drop off to sleep this minute."

He laughed. "The physical effort changes you. You grow a tougher skin."

"Mine was pretty tough to begin with."

"Yes, I knew that straight away."

I looked at him, wondering what else he'd felt when we first met—if he had sensed a jangling of recognition as I had, the sharp and familiar tolling of a bell, as if we were meant to know each other. "Did you ever imagine we might somehow end up here?"

"Under this terrible tree?" He laughed. "I'm not sure," he said, as more dusty powder fell around us from above. "But I could grow to like it."

By evening we'd reached the river and set up camp. We ate a young kudu that Denys had shot and skinned that morning, and then drank our coffee, staring into the fire as it snapped and spiralled, purplish smoke rising.

"Tania chased off a pair of lions once with only a rawhide whip," he said. "She and Blix were on a cattle drive. He'd gone off to shoot something for their dinner when there was a loud commotion among the cattle. The porters scattered like mice, and it was only poor Tania standing there while each of the lions climbed up on the backs of their quarry. The rifles were packed away in the trunks, ridiculously enough."

"So she whipped them away? That was brave of her."

"Yes, she has even more courage than you'd think."

We had been careful lately not to speak too much of Karen, for the farm had been sold, and it was clear she was going away. "You have plenty of reasons to love her," I ventured.

"And admire her," he said.

"Even better, for my money."

"I would never have made her a good husband, though. She must have known that deep down."

"It's funny what we fight for, even when we know it's impossible. Did she manage to save the oxen?"

"One, yes. The other they ate for dinner when Blix came back empty-handed."

"It all worked out neatly then."

"That time, yes."

From far off, we heard the high monkeylike chirping of hyenas, the laughing you hear tell of, though it's always sounded slightly mournful to me. The smoke billowed in a surge, as if it were trying to call out, too, to the horizon perhaps, or the just-stirring stars.

"It wouldn't be such a bad life, you know, to be a lion," Denys said. "The whole of Africa is his buffet. He takes what he wants, when he wants, without over-exerting himself."

"He has a wife, too, though, doesn't he." It wasn't a question.

"One wife at a time," he clarified.

Then, while the fire rose and smoked and threatened to singe our feet, he spoke out Walt Whitman, because I asked him to. He said the words to me and to the stars while I grew more and more still. I was thinking about how I had struggled and strained for years, as Karen had, and towards things that were disastrous for me. And yet maybe that was unavoidable. The pilgrims and the lost often did look the same, as Denys had once told me, and it was possible everyone ended up in the same place no matter which path we took or how often we fell to our knees, undoubtedly wiser for all of it.

Barely seeming to move, Denys reached for my hand. With aching slowness he traced the fine bones and lines and ridges, the thickened flesh where I'd worked and worked. I thought of Karen with the rawhide whip. She was incomparably strong and courageous under her scarves and powder, her goblets and crystal and chintz. We had done a painful dance and lost a lot, we three, hurting one another and ourselves. But extraordinary things had happened, too. I would never forget any of them.

I think we sat like that for hours. Long enough for me to feel my own density settle more and more completely into the chalky dust. Aeons had made it, out of dissolving mountains, out of endlessly rocking metamorphosis. The things of the world knew so much more than we did and lived them more truly. The thorn trees had no grief or fear. The constellations didn't fight or hold themselves back, nor did the translucent hook of the moon. Everything was momentary and endless. This time with Denys would fade, and it would last for ever.

"What are you thinking?" he asked me.

"Just of how much you've changed me." I felt his lips on my neck, his breath. "This is why there is poetry," I said, so softly I wasn't sure he could hear me. "For days like these."

60

$\mathcal{T}$hough I knew full well to expect it, I felt my stomach twist and my knees go soft to see Karen's lovely furniture on the lawn and her books in crates. She was selling nearly everything, or giving it away— and I wrestled with the deep physical memory of watching Green Hills go piece by piece, just like this, while I looked on helplessly. Now that her land would go to others, she was trying to find a protected parcel for the Kikuyu who had been squatting on her property, so that they would have something for themselves that wouldn't be taken away later. I found her wringing her hands over them and smoking, pacing a circle around her things.

"Now you have come, too," she said. "So many visits and farewells, I don't have any tears left for them." Her white dress was loose around her breasts and legs, her straw hat abandoned on a chair. She looked young to me, suddenly.

"I could cry *for* you," I said. "It wouldn't take much."

"Did you hear they're going to hold a *ngoma* in my honour?" She waved away blue smoke. "Won't that be something? There won't be a dinner, though, like the one we had when the princes were here. All my things are crated."

"I'm sure it will be wonderful all the same. They mean to celebrate you. You've made such an impression, and no one will soon forget you."

"I've been dreaming about Denmark lately, and of standing on the bow of a great hulking ship, watching Africa grow smaller and smaller."

"I hope you can come back one day."

"Who has the privilege of knowing what's possible, or the burden, for that matter? I can tell you, though, that I never thought I *could* leave. I think that's what the dreams mean. I'm not leaving Africa, but slowly, ever so slowly, Africa has begun to seep out of me."

I felt my throat constrict and swallowed against the knot. Her millstone table had been pulled out to the edge of the veranda. I'd always thought of it as the heart of Mbogani. The old granite was freckled and pitted and had borne how many brandy snifters or cups of tea, all her finery, the Sèvres and Limoges, Denys's large feet, and his books and his hands. It was where she'd sat a thousand times, lighting a cigarette, shaking the match, and looking off into a middle distance, collecting herself. Gathering her wool scarf around her shoulders, preparing to speak.

It felt strange to be here with Karen and her vanishing farm, after all that had happened, the things that had drawn us together and pushed us apart. But the truth was it would have been even stranger not to come.

We sat down in two low rattan chairs, looking up at the five knuckled hills of the Ngong. "They say you're learning to fly," Karen said.

"Yes, it's been such an important thing—and it's made me so happy."

"You're twenty-eight?"

I nodded.

"That's the age I was when I sailed for Kenya to marry Bror. How our lives turn and turn. Things come that we never would have predicted for ourselves or even guessed at. And yet they change us for ever." She trailed her fingers in the grass, back and forth lightly and soundlessly. "I always wanted wings myself, you know . . . perhaps more than anything else. When Denys took me up the first time, we skimmed down over my hills, and then on to Lake Nakuru where thousands of zebras scattered under the shadow we made."

"It's the clearest feeling of freedom, isn't it?" I asked her.

"Yes, but real clarity, too. I thought, *Now I see. Only now.* From that great height all sorts of things that have been hidden show themselves. Even terrible things have a beauty and a shape." She caught my gaze with her black, black irises and held it. "You know, Beryl, you'll never truly have Denys. Not any more than I did. He can't belong to anyone."

My heart dropped then. "Oh, Karen . . ." I reached for words, but they weren't anywhere to be found.

"I suppose I always knew you loved him, but kept it from myself for a long time. Perhaps you did, too."

It felt so awful, hearing her strip the veil from years and years— and yet also necessary. *We should be telling the truth to each other,* I thought. *We've earned that, if nothing else.* "I didn't mean to take anything from you," I finally said.

"And you haven't. No, it's the gods who are punishing me for wanting too much." She looked up at her hills again and then around at her things on the lawn. "Such happiness always comes with a price, and yet I would pay it all again and more. I wouldn't take a single moment back, not even to save myself pain."

"You're the strongest woman I know," I told her. "I'm going to miss you." Then I leaned to kiss her on her cheek, just where her tears had come to blur the powder.

61

*H*ow our lives turn and turn.

Denys was meant to come for me and fly us down the coast to Takaungu. On the way home, we'd test his theory and try to spot a few herds of elephants near Voi and alert some waiting hunting friends with a cable. It was early May. I told Ruta I was going, and then Tom, whom I found at the Wilson Airways hangar, scribbling figures into his flight log.

"But we have a lesson tomorrow."

"Can't we postpone?"

He looked at me and then out through the door of the hangar, where scudding clouds tatted the pale blue of the sky. "Don't go, all right?"

"What is it? Do you have one of your mysterious feelings?"

"Maybe I do. There's always another day, isn't there?"

I didn't want to give up the trip for a vague premonition, but Tom was a wonderful teacher and I trusted him. He also rarely asked anything of me. So I went back to my cottage at the Muthaiga, and Denys left for Voi. I learned later that he'd also asked Karen to go with him, before he'd asked me, but that morning his only passenger was his

Kikuyu boy, Kamau. They took off in glorious weather and were out for several days before flying to the foot of Mbolo Hill, where his friend Vernon Cole lived. Vernon was the district commissioner. He had a young son, John, who was transfixed by Denys, and his wife, Hilda, was newly pregnant with a second child. They made Denys a lavish dinner and listened to him talk about the elephants he'd scouted from above, just as he'd suspected.

"There they were, bold as you please, just *browsing* along the river. Weeks of scouting cut out in moments. Only moments."

The next morning at dawn, Denys and Kamau took off again, this time for home. Hilda gave them a bushel of thick-skinned Kenyan oranges to take along. Kamau held them in his lap as the propeller swung to life, and the Moth's engine fluttered, coaxed by Denys's fingertips on the throttle. He took her up quickly, and circled twice before sailing out of sight.

In Denys's cottage, I was sleeping, dreaming of nothing. Ruta woke me with a knock at my door. "Have you heard from Bedar?"

"No," I answered sleepily. "Why would I?"

"I don't know," he said. But he had guessed at something. Felt it, as Tom had.

Waving once, the Moth's custard-yellow wings sheared away and dropped out of sight. Denys had named his plane *Nzige*, which meant "locust," light as the wind, agile and imperturbable. The wonderful machine should have gone on for ever, and Denys, too, but a mile north, for no reason that anyone would ever be able to confirm, his plane spun in at low altitude. He may have broken a crucial cable, or mishandled the wind shear somehow. Perhaps he manoeuvred too sharply at too low a speed, or lost control of her in any number of ways. All anyone would know was that he met the earth almost vertically, hurtling into the rocky soil near Mwakangale Hill and exploding on impact. Bursting into flame. When the Coles traced Denys's smoke to the site, there was almost nothing left of his body, or the boy's. The Moth was a ruin. Only a handful of blackened oranges spilled over the charred ground, and a slim volume of poetry that had been thrown from the wreckage, fluttering with bits of ash.

In shock, Hilda Cole dropped to her knees and bent double. Later that afternoon she would miscarry her baby, and that's how three came to die that day at Voi. Three souls perished, and none of them mine.

62

*K*aren buried Denys on the farm, as she knew he wanted it, at the crest of Lamwia, along the Ngong ridge. The spot lay at the top of a steep incline, and the coffin bearers struggled to get there, stumbling with the heavy box. Karen walked ahead and stood nearest the open hole, red as a wound, when they lowered him in. I was entirely numb from the inside out, unable to speak to her or anyone.

The day was shockingly clear. Below the ridge, the coppery slope rolled onto the plains. A pale stretch of road stood out like rope that had been tossed down from the clouds, or like a snake that went on ceaselessly, all the way to Kilimanjaro. Around the site of Denys's grave, the grasses were lush and living. Plaited through them were two dark forms, the shadows of a pair of eagles drifting above us in ever-widening circles.

Mourners had come from Nairobi and Gilgil, Eldoret and Naivasha—Somalis and Kikuyus and White Highlanders, hunters and gun bearers, pilgrims and poets. No one there hadn't seen something to love and admire in Denys. He had always been unflinchingly himself, and honourable for that in the way these eagles were honourable, and the grass, too.

During the brief service, Karen's head sagged to her chest, and I felt a strong urge to go to her. I was the one person there who knew precisely what she'd lost in Denys; she was the only one who could have understood the weight and colour of my sorrow, too. But a shift had taken place, and it held me back. She was his publicly acknowledged widow now. The gods may have stolen him from her, but with his death she had won him back. No one could challenge their bond, or doubt how she had loved him. Or how truly he'd been hers. One day she was going to write about him—write *him* in such a way that would seal the two of them together for ever. And from those pages, I would be absent.

I didn't think I could weep any more, that, like Karen, I had spent a lifetime's worth of tears, but somehow my grief found a way to open wider that day. When the service was over, and the mourners had gone down over the hill to Mbogani, I lingered long enough to reach for a handful of dust from Denys's gravesite, red as life's blood and older than time. I closed my fingers around its powdery coolness and then let it go. In a way, it didn't matter if there was something proprietary in Karen's sadness, or in how she had loved Denys. I hadn't loved him any more perfectly—and I understood that, finally. We had both tried for the sun, and had fallen, lurching to earth again, tasting melted wax and sorrow. Denys wasn't hers, or mine.

He belonged to no one and never had.

After Denys's funeral I went back to his cottage, where I'd been living, but the sight of his books nearly undid me. It was shocking to think how his mind simply wasn't in the world any longer. I would never hear his laugh, or touch his fine strong hands or trace the crinkles around his eyes. When he fell out of the sky, everything he was and would yet do had vanished. And he'd taken my heart with him, too. How would I get it back again?

I couldn't think of what I might do with my days or where I might go, but somehow found myself back in Elburgon, at Melela. My father seemed surprised to see me but didn't ask any terrible questions.

I couldn't have begun to answer them if he had. I only wanted to be alone, and to be near horses, two things that had always soothed my soul in the past. For weeks I stayed, waking before dawn and striding out into the cold morning to think. The colours of the country were beautifully the same. Mist hung stretched over the towering cedars in the forest, and the ragged curve of the escarpment rose and receded off towards forever. But something was missing. For all its beauty, Melela now seemed to mock me. I'd pinned so many dreams on it, believing that if Mansfield and I could rebuild Green Hills here, re-writing the sad changes of the past, some part of me would feel re-claimed and strong in a way it hadn't, not really, since I was a young girl—hunting with *arap* Maina, running with Kibii through the tall bleached grasses, slipping out of the window of my hut with Buller at my heels, both of us unafraid of the night.

But all Mansfield and I had truly managed to do was humiliate each other and ourselves, and to carve great big holes in one another. Gervase was a world away. Some days I could barely stand to think of him—and now Denys was gone, too. One crushing loss lay like a black stamp over the other. A shadow smothering a shadow, empti-ness and more emptiness, and what could be done?

My father was worried about me, I could see that, but nothing seemed to help until one day, when I heard a familiar sputtering sound echoing through the hills, and there was Tom's Moth, wag-gling its way towards the farm through pure and cloudless blue. Using our long paddock as a makeshift runway, he set it down like a feather.

"How have you been?" he asked after he'd cut the engine and clambered out over the wing.

"Oh, you know." I felt myself give way, and couldn't manage an-other word. But I didn't have to. Tom handed me a flight helmet, and I lowered myself into the rear cockpit, grateful for the sound of the engine rattling to life, the vibration of my small seat, everything shudderingly present as we came to speed. When we roared up over the hills, and the landscape slid sideways and reeled away, my head began to clear for the first time in weeks. Cold air swept against my face and filled my lungs. It was so much easier to breathe up there, and even with the constant noise of the prop and the wind, it was peaceful in a way my wounded spirit had been craving. I remembered how once a native boy had asked me if I could see God from the aeroplane. Tom was there and we had both laughed and shook our heads.

"Perhaps you should go higher then," he said.

Tom kept us up for a good long time, tracing a wide circle over our valley, towards Njoro to the east and Molo to the north. The tip of the wing was like a bright, silvering wand. Watching it, I felt a whisper of hope and something like redemption. It wasn't God I saw at this height, but my Rift Valley. It stretched in every direction like a map of my own life. Here were Karen's hills, the flat shimmer of Nakuru in the distance, the high ragged lip of the escarpment. White-bellied birds and red dust. Everything I'd lived through lay unfurled below me, every secret and scar—where I'd learned to hunt and jump and ride like the wind; where I had been devoured a little by a good lion; where *arap* Maina had stooped to point at a cloverleaf-shaped print in drying mud, saying, "Tell me what you see, Lakwet."

This valley was more than my home. It beat in me like the drum of my own heart.

Only when we needed fuel did we make our way back to Melela. Tom stayed to dinner and, because he would fly out again at dawn, took himself off to bed early while my father and I stayed up with hot, bitter coffee. There wasn't any sound in the room—just low light stretching out against the wall and the feeling of something important coming towards me.

"I'm going back to Nairobi," I told him after we'd been quiet for a long time. "I'll leave with Tom in the morning. I'm going to take up flying again."

"I wish I saw the point in it," my father said.

I'd obviously surprised him—and though I didn't know if "it" meant aeroplanes or leaving Melela, I said, "Come up in Tom's plane one day. Maybe then you'll see."

He'd been reading the black studbook, his longtime bible. His fingers caressed the spine for a moment, and then he shook his head. "I know where I'm meant to be."

"I do, too," I told him, and the minute the words left my mouth I knew they were true.

"What shall we do with the horses?"

"I'm not sure at the moment. They're Mansfield's, too, after all. It might be years before our divorce is settled. But however all of that turns out, I want to earn my own living. I *need* to know I can take care of myself."

"You can do that flying?" He sounded incredulous.

"Maybe. Tom says one day aeroplanes will ferry people far and wide, as ships do now. I could be part of that. Or transport mail and parcels, or I don't know. Denys had a scheme about scouting for hunters from above." It was the first time I'd said his name aloud since the day of his funeral. Even though my throat ached, it also felt right to call Denys into this room. He was the reason I'd thought of flying for myself at all.

"It's awfully dangerous. I know I don't have to tell you that." He stared into his coffee, thinking quietly. "But you've never been afraid of anything, have you?"

"I *have,* though," I said, surprised at my own emotion. "I've been terrified . . . I just haven't let it stop me."

It was quite late by that point, and we were both too tired to say anything more. I kissed him on the forehead, wishing him good night. But as I settled myself in bed, no matter how drained and exhausted I felt, there was a strange kind of energy pulsing through me, too. Thoughts appearing more plainly than they had in many years. Melela wasn't safe. It would more than likely dissolve one day as Green Hills had. Pegasus would die as Buller had, both of them my earliest heroes. My father would drift away little by little or all at once. Great rocking changes would come again and again . . . and I would survive them the way I had long ago, when my mother had boarded a train and become smoke. The tribe had found me then, and given me my true name, but Lakwet was only a name after all. I had forged her myself, out of brokenness, learning to love wildness instead of fearing it. To thrive on the exhilaration of the hunt, charging headlong into the world even—or especially—when it hurt to do it.

Now I stood at the threshold of another great turning, perhaps the most important of my life. The sky had taken Denys, but I knew there was life up there, too—a combination of forces suited to me, to how I was made, in powerful ways. That great soaring freedom and unimaginable grace came fully tethered to risk and to fear. Flying demanded more courage and faith than I actually possessed, and it wanted my best, my whole self. I would have to work very hard to be any good at it at all, and be more than a little mad to be great, to give my life over to it. But that's just what I meant to do.

The next morning, I was awake even before Tom was. I packed my few things quickly and waited for him in the dark. When he saw me he smiled, understanding immediately the decision I'd come to and what would happen now.

When we returned to Nairobi, I clocked through hours of instruction like a possessed woman, taking every moment Tom could give me. Four weeks after Denys's accident, nearly to the day, Tom and I finished a short run and seamless landing at the aerodrome in Nairobi. Most of the town was yet asleep, and the Ngong Hills were draped over with mist and stillness, but the morning wasn't over. Tom had a secret in his pocket. Instead of taking her back to the hangar, where Ruta waited, he had me spin the Moth around for another take-off. This one would be mine, though. My first solo.

"Just once around the paddock." He smiled. "Nice and steady." He took off his helmet and scrambled out casually, as if this were something we always did—me alone behind the controls, and him on the ground.

Nice and steady would certainly do it, but adrenaline tumbled through me so crazily, I felt dizzy. Could I remember everything Tom had said over the last months and put it to use? Could I quiet the clamouring in my head, the vision of the ten thousand things that could go wrong? Only one had taken Denys's life, and that was still an utter mystery.

Willing my hands still, I gave Tom a thumbs-up. Ruta came out of the hangar and stood beside Tom, and I waved to them both, taxi-ing the Moth to the end of the murram strip, where I pointed her nose at the implacable hills and opened the throttle.

I thought about the tug of altitude and the Moth's weight. I thought about speed and wind, the hundreds of adjustments Tom made without thinking, but that I was still learning. He had faith in me, though. I felt that solidly, and Ruta's belief in me, too, as he raised his hand once. *Kwaheri.* Farewell.

Gunning hard, I sped along the hard-packed runway, my heart in my throat, every nerve alive. I waited until the last possible moment to pull back on the stick, and then the Moth inched up, bobbling a little, and gradually steadied, finding the wind and her centre. Behind me I felt Tom and Ruta, and Denys, too. Before me lay everything, an entire world opening moment by moment under my own strong wings.

I was off.

EPILOGUE

4 September 1936

There is no way of knowing how close I have come to the clawing reach of the Atlantic when my engine finally kicks and thrashes to life again. The sound of it is jarring. It startles me as if I've been asleep for years and years—and it's possible I have been. I push the throttle forward to full power and ease back on the stick, away from the icy waves. The Gull's nose tips upwards again, finally responsive. She climbs, scrabbling her way up, tooth and claw, scaling the face of the storm. I am climbing with her, out of an inner fog. A tangling blindness.

It's only when I'm level again and my hands have stopped trembling that I let myself think about how long my engine might have been silent, and how ready I was to give in to the stall, to plummet when I felt the bottom go. I've always had that in me, but also a sound inner compass. There are things we find only at our lowest depths. The idea of wings and then wings themselves. An ocean worth crossing one dark mile at a time. The whole of the sky. And whatever suffering has come is the necessary cost of such wonders, as Karen once said, the beautiful thrashing we do when we live.

———

For several more hours the black rain doesn't give way. I follow the rim of the long night, almost delirious with exhaustion, and also more awake than I have ever been. Finally, I spot the ghostly beginnings of daybreak—or are those hints of land? The window glass has a mantle of ice, and fog shifts in front of my eyes, but soon I know I'm not imagining it. The grey-black canvas becomes water, and then clear waves, and then the growing form of a cliff's edge like swept-up cloud ledges. I have reached North America, the Gulf of St. Lawrence and Newfoundland. Flickering smudges becoming more real by the minute. This is the place I'm meant to go.

My plan is to stop in Sydney, on Cape Breton, and refuel, then go on from there—south by southwest over land this time, New Brunswick and the tip of Maine, and finally to New York. But I am still fifty miles from land when my engine begins to sputter in a sick way, a hiccuping, lurching stall. My final fuel tank is three-quarters full, so it can only be an airlock. As before, I flip the toggle to the petcock on and off, and the engine answers with wheezing. I'm dropping now, and my hopes are crashing, too. Three thousand miles and darkness and near death to fail now, when I'm so close? It's a terrible thought, a dimming one. Again and again, I flip the sharp petcock switch, my fingers bleeding. The Gull coughs to life, climbing, only to falter once more, my propeller windmilling, my window glazed, glinting back the sun in a pitiless mirror.

For ten or fifteen minutes, I limp this way, in the wounded glide of fuel starvation, nearing the rough lip of landfall. Soon I can see muddy-looking boulders and a bog that's like black pudding. When I try to bank one final time, my wheels catch and sink, the nose sticking fast, throwing me forward. I smack the glass hard, wetting my forehead with blood. I am only three hundred yards from the water's edge, nowhere near New York. And yet I have done it.

I am so tired and can barely move, but I do move. I push open the heavy door, and force my feet to the ground. The bog tugs hard at my boots and I sink, blood streaming into my eyes. I drop lower and am half crawling soon, as if after so many hours in the clouds, I have to remember all over again how to walk. As if I must relearn just where I am going, and where—impossibly—I have been.

AUTHOR'S NOTE

*A*fter her first solo, in June of 1931, Beryl Markham quickly went on to become one of the first women ever granted a professional B licence. Though she never fully stopped training racehorses, or winning derbies, she also became a bush pilot, working for Bror Blixen on numerous safaris, and pioneered the practice of scouting elephants from the air, fulfilling Denys's vision.

When in 1936, after twenty-one hours of flying, she succeeded in her record-breaking voyage across the Atlantic, she made every significant headline in the States. A crowd of five thousand cheered her arrival in New York, at Floyd Bennett Field. When she returned to England, however, she got no formal reception. Instead, she was greeted by the terrible news that her friend and flying mentor, Tom Campbell Black, had been killed in a plane crash while she was away.

Scandal and speculation followed Beryl for much of her life. In 1942, she published a memoir, *West with the Night*. It sold only modestly, though many believed it deserved greater accolades, including Ernest Hemingway, who said, in a letter to his editor, Maxwell Perkins, "Did you read Beryl Markham's book . . . she has written so

358 • AUTHOR'S NOTE

well, and marvelously well, that I was simply ashamed of myself as a writer . . . it really is a bloody wonderful book."

Hemingway met Beryl on safari in Kenya, in 1934, when he was traveling with his second wife, Pauline Pfeiffer. Reportedly, Hemingway made a pass at Beryl and was rebuffed. Nearly fifty years later, his eldest son, Jack, showed some of his father's published letters to a friend, the restaurateur George Gutekunst, including the description of *West with the Night.* Gutekunst was driven to search out Markham's book and then convinced a small California press to reissue it. It became a surprise bestseller and allowed Beryl, who was then eighty and living in poverty in Africa, to spend the remainder of her days in relative comfort and even some notoriety.

Since then, the book's reputation—like its author's—has been marred by gossip and speculation. It's been suggested that she didn't write it at all, but instead that her third husband, Raoul Schumacher, a Hollywood ghostwriter, did. I can't say I'm surprised by the public's doubt in her. Beryl was so reluctant to talk about herself, even people who believed they knew her quite well in later life were often surprised to learn she knew anything about flying or horse racing or could write more than a postcard. But the overwhelming evidence attests that Beryl had shown her publisher a large portion of the book (eighteen chapters out of twenty-four) before she ever met Raoul.

Though they depict the same place and time, and house many of the same characters, Beryl's book hasn't found as wide an audience or had the same impact as Isak Dinesen's *Out of Africa,* but I believe it has the potential to. From the moment I read even a few sentences, *West with the Night* took powerful hold of my imagination. Beryl's descriptions of her African childhood, colonial Kenya in all its seasons, and her extraordinary adventures fairly leap off the page—but more striking to me is the spirit behind the words. She had so much nerve and pluck, plunging fearlessly into vast gaps between the sexes, and at a time when such feats were nearly unthinkable. I hadn't ever encountered anyone quite like her—a woman who lived by her own code instead of society's, though that cost her much. Who would have fit perfectly into Hemingway's muscular fiction, but she actually lived!

Beryl was undoubtedly complicated—a riddle, a libertine, a maverick. A sphinx. But strangely, as I was writing her character and pitching myself deeply into her world, she became more knowable and familiar to me in some ways than Hadley Hemingway in my novel *The Paris Wife*. Beryl and I share at least one profound piece of emotional genealogy: My mother also vanished from my life when I was four and returned when I was twenty. I felt a bone-deep jolt when I discovered that link—and it became one reliable way to get close to Beryl, and gain important insight into some of her more difficult choices. The loss of her son, for instance, is utterly heartbreaking to me. Though she would never be very close to Gervase, who remained in England with Mansfield's mother, apparently he inherited Beryl's willfulness and her stoicism. He was proud of his mother's adventurous spirit and accomplishments, and felt more fondness for her than for his father, it appears, who was even more distant and unavailable.

Beryl's relationship with Ruta spanned her lifetime, as their shared childhood experiences grew into mutual respect and unshakable trust. Though they were separated for a time in the 1930s when she moved to England, after the Second World War, she was able to track him down, and they were never again out of touch. Though Beryl kept her heart closed to most, and her secrets locked up tightly, her friends and confidants agree that, after Ruta and her father, Denys Finch Hatton was very probably the only man she ever truly loved. She died in Nairobi, in 1986, at the age of eighty-three, near the fiftieth anniversary of her record-breaking flight, and perhaps thinking of the moment she climbed into her Gull, tucking a hip flask of brandy into her flight jumpsuit.

"*Twende tu,*" she called out in Swahili as she buckled her helmet.

I am going.

Paula McLain—Cleveland, Ohio

ACKNOWLEDGMENTS

$\mathcal{B}$ooks are intricately collaborative efforts. I might slave away at my desk in isolation, but I'm hardly alone. Many, many amazing folks have had a hand in the making of *Circling the Sun,* and though I hope I've expressed my gratitude to them individually at many points along the way, they certainly deserve formal props and my humble thanks here. My agent, Julie Barer, is quite simply the best there is. With heart and grit and wonderful instincts to spare, she's become my first and most important reader, and also a dear friend. I wouldn't want to do any of this without her. Susanna Porter is the kind of editor other writers rightfully covet. She read (and read!) innumerable drafts—but never stopped believing in what this book could be. Her sharp eye and insight and unshakable commitment live on every page.

I have found the best possible home at Ballantine Books and Penguin Random House, and have come to rely on many crucial, crucial players there who do their jobs so well. Bottomless thanks to the completely lovely and brilliant Libby McGuire; also Kim Hovey, Jennifer Hershey, Susan Corcoran, Jennifer Garza, Theresa Zoro, Quinne Rogers, Deborah Foley, Paolo Pepe, Benjamin Dreyer, Steve Messina,

Kristin Fassler, Kate Childs, Toby Ernst, Anna Bauer, Mark Ma-guire, Carolyn Meers, Lisa Barnes, and, of course, the indispensable Priyanka Krishnan. Thanks to Sue Betz, who was so thoughtful and thorough in her copyediting; to Dana Blanchette for her beautiful design of the interior elements; and to Robbin Schiff for the abso-lutely stunning cover. I'm grateful to the amazing Gina Centrello, who weighed in with an essential read when the stakes were high, and also have to thank the incredible sales force for their passionate commitment to books, for knowing their accounts so thoroughly, for getting my work into the hands of booksellers and readers, and for doing their jobs so tirelessly and well.

The home team at Barer Literary is incomparable and I owe them much: Gemma Purdy, Anna Geller, and William Boggess. Many thanks as well to Ursula Doyle, Susan de Soissons, and David Bam-ford at Virago; Caspian Dennis at Abner Stein; and Lynn Henry, Kristin Cochrane, and Sharon Klein at Doubleday Canada and Pen-guin Random House Canada.

The MacDowell Colony supported me with a generous writing residency, where I had the impossible gift of uninterrupted time and space, and was able to work on a critical draft of this book. Steve Reed provided helpful notes on piloting and flight, and also was the person who first put *West with the Night* into my hands. Though he would most assuredly rather have cash or a vintage biplane, he'll have to accept my eternal gratitude! Stacey Giere of Maple Crest Farm was key in helping me flesh out the world of horses and horse train-ing. I owe her much for her time and expertise.

My heartfelt thanks goes to the amazing team at Micato Safaris for making my trip to Kenya so memorable and magical: Felix, Jane, and Dennis Pinto; Melissa Hordych; Marty Von Neudegg; Liz Wheeler; Philip Rono, Wesley Korir, and Jessica Brida. Mark Ross was won-derfully helpful, as was Cheryl de Souza of Airkenya. Thanks also to Fairmont Hotels & Resorts, particularly Mike Taylor, Alka Winter, and Mary Wanjohi, and to all of my gracious hosts and contacts in Kenya: The Norfolk Hotel; Segera Retreat; Jens Kozany and the

Zeitz Foundation; the Craig family and Lewa Wilderness; Andrew, Zoe, and Bruce Nightingale of Kembu Cottages in Njoro; and Jacqueline Damon and Sleeping Warrior Eco Lodge at Soysambu Conservancy.

Brian Groh was the frontman in researching my trip to Africa to follow in the footsteps of Beryl Markham. He also gave early feedback on the manuscript, and has been a lionhearted friend for many years. Other key early reads and crucial support came from Lori Keene, David French, Jim Harms, Malena Morling, and Greg D'Alessio. Other dear friends have given me unflagging support and love for many years and must be thanked: Sharon Day and Mr. Chuck, Brad Bedortha, the phenomenal O'Hara family, Becky Gaylord, Lynda Montgomery, Denise Machado and John Sargent, Heather Greene, and Karen Rosenberg. Chris Pavone talked me down from a ledge or two. Big thanks to the East Side Writers— Terry Dubow, Sarah Willis, Toni Thayer, Charlie Oberndorf, Karen Sandstrom, Neal Chandler, and Justin Glanville—who are always on my side.

Special appreciation and a big kiss goes to Terry Sullivan for his boundless confidence in this book and me, for the phenomenal dinners, and for making my life a lot more fun! And finally, I have to thank my mother, Rita Hinken; my incredible children, Beckett, Fiona, and Connor, for sharing me (sort of!) with my work; and my sisters, who are everything.

A NOTE ON SOURCES

*W*riting fiction about people who actually lived is somewhat like skydiving. All sorts of things have me flinging myself out into space toward my story—curiosity, imagination, an ineffable connection to my characters, and, let's face it, some strange love of the sensation of falling. But it's the research that gives me my parachute. Concrete sources anchor and ground me and make my process possible. They tell me what I need to know in order to invent what I must as a novelist—and for this I am thankful and humbled. *West with the Night,* Beryl's own account of her incredible life, compelled me to learn more about her, was the source of ignition for my novel, and is a phenomenal work in its own right.

Mary Lovell's *Straight On Till Morning: The Life of Beryl Markham* was the first biography to bring Beryl to light, in 1987, and her pioneering efforts and careful research have been crucial to my own and other writers' abilities to imagine Beryl's life. Mary Lovell also compiled Beryl Markham's stories in *The Splendid Outcast,* a collection that wouldn't have been available otherwise, and for that we should all be grateful. Finally, Lovell's sympathetic view of Beryl was an important touchstone for me as I worked.

Other important sources were *Out of Africa* and *Shadows on the Grass*, by Isak Dinesen; *African Hunter*, by Baron Bror von Blixen-Finecke; *The Lives of Beryl Markham* and *Silence Will Speak*, by Errol Trzebinski; *Never Turn Back*, by Catherine Gourley; *Too Close to the Sun: The Audacious Life and Times of Denys Finch Hatton*, by Sara Wheeler; *Isak Dinsesen: The Life of a Storyteller*, by Judith Thurman; and Isak Dinesen's *Letters from Africa, 1914–1931*, translated by Anne Born.

Incredibly beneficial in helping me conjure both colonial Kenya and the lives of these British expats were *The Flame Trees of Thika* and *Nine Faces of Kenya: Portrait of a Nation*, by Elspeth Huxley; *The Bolter*, by Frances Osborne; *The Ghosts of Happy Valley*, by Juliet Barnes; *The Tree Where Man Was Born*, by Peter Matthiessen; *Swahili Tales*, by Edward Steere; and *Kenya: A Country in the Making, 1880–1940*, by Nigel Pavitt.

CIRCLING THE SUN

Paula McLain

A READER'S GUIDE

A CONVERSATION BETWEEN PAULA McLAIN AND LILY KING, AUTHOR OF *EUPHORIA* AND *FATHER OF THE RAIN*

Lily King: How did the idea for this novel find you?

Paula McLain: Ideas are so interesting, aren't they? Sometimes they're skittish as hummingbirds—but other times they storm into your life and steal your car keys and simply will not take no for an answer! I know from previous conversations that the concept for *Euphoria* completely hijacked you when you happened on a biography of Margaret Mead—though you'd never, ever thought you'd tackle a historical novel. For me, I was deep into another story when I was given a copy of Beryl Markham's memoir, *West with the Night.* The minute I let the book fall open, I was riveted to Beryl's amazing life, but also swept away by some quality in her voice—a unique blend of toughness, daring, and nostalgia. She's so tender when she addresses her memories of Africa, and so aware of how the place brought her most alive. I was hooked hard and instantaneously.

I should mention that in Cleveland it was January and freezing. *I want to go to Africa,* I found myself thinking. *I want to go to Africa NOW.* The quickest way to get there was to give in to the world of the book. And I did—in a big way. The first draft flew out of me in just a few months, faster than I'd written anything before.

LK: Did you feel a connection to Beryl Markham even before you began writing the story? In what way?

PM: It was almost eerie how quickly Beryl took hold of my imagination and drew me in. As I tried to explain, her voice got my immediate attention, and the fierce contours of her personality, too. But for a book to work for me, I have to be more than *interested* in my subject. I have to feel deeply bound to them—and that our lives are somehow twisted up together. It's mysterious, and incredibly intimate. The first time I felt this way was when I began to write *The Paris Wife*, about Ernest Hemingway's first marriage to Hadley Richardson. Writing from her point of view was like channeling her. Becoming her. With Beryl the intensity was even greater, because I was discovering that we had a surprising lot in common—we both grew up with horses, we both married young, to men considerably older. And we both grew up without our mothers. These parallels in our lives definitely made me feel I had access to her as a subject in a really singular way— and had me wondering if I haven't always been meant to find and write about her.

LK: When you write historical fiction, you have to accept the fact that you are inventing dialogue and scenes and emotions for people who really lived. How does that feel? Does your responsibility to the facts as you have learned them ever come into conflict with your responsibility to the novel you are trying to create? Have you ever had to violate one in favor of the other?

PM: What a wonderful question, Lily. In one respect I think it's an incredible privilege to be fleshing out the lives of these remarkable people, illuminating the hidden particulars, and bringing history to life in an intimate, *human* way. But the terrain does get tricky at times. Through the reach of imagination, we presume to know all kinds of things that can't *be* known. And then there are the times, as you mention, when the facts either don't jibe with or can't support a moment that feels right for the story, or for the emotional arc of a character. For example, I've never come across any piece of evidence that suggests Karen Blixen knew Beryl was in love with Denys Finch Hatton. Nor is there any record of the two women confronting each other about Denys, acknowledging their rivalry. But as I drew toward the end of my last draft, I just kept thinking there *should* be such a moment, because the story needed it, but also because the characters—and their real-life counterparts—deserved it. These were strong, smart women—not pushovers or shrinking violets by any means, and not inclined to hide their heads when the truth came knocking. When I was still stewing about my authority to invent such a moment, my editor brought it up as well, wanting the scene, and feeling it demanded to be there. And now it is.

LK: Have you always loved history?

PM: I've always loved biography, to be sure. One the first books that ever really touched me as a young reader was the story of Annie Oakley. I think I checked it out of the library ten times when I was a second or third grader, feeling obsessed with her. But history . . . well, history was boring! All those survey classes I took as an undergraduate, memorizing the names of generals and dates of important battles, put me in a coma. Then I took a class in graduate school that sort of blew me away. It was social history, focusing very specifically on women's stories from Colonial times through the Industrial Revolution. We read the diaries of factory workers, and housewives living in the Massachusetts Bay Colony—and suddenly the real business of what it meant to live in those time periods came alive for me. That's the feeling I'm trying to replicate when I research a time and place for a new book: being totally sucked into that world in a visceral way. A reader once told me she thought historical fiction was like a living wax museum. Isn't that a wonderful way of thinking about it?

LK: Which part is more thrilling to you, the discovery of all the details of your subject's life or the creation of your own story out of these details?

PM: I think it has to be the threshold place between those two things—when in the sifting through of facts and materials I come upon a detail that gels the story for me. For *The Paris Wife,* it was when I arrived at the end of Hemingway's memoir, *A Moveable Feast,* at the line where he says of Hadley, "I wished I had died before I ever loved anyone but her." I believed him, believed he regretted betraying her (with her friend Pauline Pfeiffer, who would become his second wife) for the rest of his life. And that broke my heart. Right then, I knew the novel was, more than anything else, about the rise and fall of a marriage.

Similarly, when I was researching Beryl's life, I found myself wanting to know how she became such a bold and fearless woman, aeons ahead of her time, ready to take on all sorts of things women simply didn't do. Part of the recipe, it seemed to me, was Africa itself, how she came of age in such a wild and expansive place. But just as consequential was her mother's leaving. That early loss forced her to toughen her skin, and to thrust herself toward the people and things that might do her harm, rather than running from them. That's when her character fully materialized for me, and I knew I wanted to explore her childhood and early adulthood more than her adventures, later in life, as a famous aviator.

LK: Before I read your novel, when I thought of Denys Finch Hatton and Karen Blixen, I saw Robert Redford (who didn't even try to be British) and Meryl Streep. I read somewhere that you loved that movie, too, and maybe have watched it as many times as I have. How did you get them out of your head to create your own version of these two?

PM: It was no short order—let me tell you! I've watched that movie countless times and have whole chunks of it memorized. And some of the scenes are burned indelibly into my brain—like when they go up in the vintage biplane, and Meryl Streep reaches back and touches Robert Redford's hand, and the flamingos are flying, and the musical score is swelling. Seriously, if that doesn't make you cry, something in you is broken!

But the further along I got in my research, the more a switch seemed to flip. The real Finch Hatton—though he looked nothing like Redford, and was almost completely bald!—became so compelling and irresistible for me, I couldn't help falling for him. At one point, Karen Blixen's letters and photographs covered my desk. Her voice and face filled my head. . . . Meryl couldn't compete after that, no matter how great she is at accents!

LK: It's daunting, taking on another culture and time period. What was most challenging?

PM: Maybe the most challenging thing was taking on colonialism, which—politically speaking—is sort of abhorrent to me. But Beryl did grow up in that world. I didn't want to give her my opinions and a stump to shout them from, but rather to represent her enmeshed, insider point of view as accurately as possible.

LK: What was most surprising?

PM: I think the greatest surprise is just how wild and irreverent those folks were back then. Cocaine, opium, wife-swapping: You name it, they did it! It makes us seem terribly conservative now, nearly a hundred years later.

LK: How did you decide which part of Beryl's life to tell?

PM: I imagine that if you gave ten writers the same facts and sheaves of research material, they'd tell ten different stories. It's so individual, what we respond to in someone else's life. For me, what came alive first and most plaintively was Beryl's African childhood. I'd always loved frontier stories—the Little House books, *The Swiss Family Robinson*—and was transfixed by the idea of what it must have been like to grow up at the edge of absolute wilderness, in a place so new "you could feel the future of it under your feet," as Beryl writes in *West with the Night*. I grew up with horses, so that's another bit of her life that really spoke to me. Oh my goodness, but the horse training and racing was fun to write!

LK: Did you go to Kenya for your research, and if so, how was that trip? Where did you go? What did you discover?

PM: I did indeed go to Kenya, and it was easily the coolest thing I've ever done. I started in Nairobi, visiting the places the meant a lot to Beryl and that, believe it or not, still stand almost a hundred years later. I saw the Muthaiga Club, Karen Blixen's farm (now a museum), Denys Finch Hatton's grave. I spent time in Njoro, where she spent her girlhood. The land that was her father's horse farm still is a horse farm, and the current owner has refurbished the storybook cottage Beryl's father built for her when she was fourteen. I stayed there! I also went horseback riding in the bush, slept in a tent (though a pretty fancy one) in the Masai Mara, and flew in an open-air vintage bi-plane. Every moment of my trip was absolutely incredible, mostly because of how privileged I felt to be stepping, as if through a time machine, into her world.

LK: One of the relationships Beryl had that most intrigued me was her friendship with Kibii, her best friend from childhood. Did that relationship ever go further than a friendship? It seemed like it was often teetering on the verge of something more.

PM: Several of Beryl's biographers have suggested that left to their own devices, as they often were, Beryl and Kibii were probably each other's first sweethearts, experimenting with one another as adolescents do . . . the out-in-the-bush version of playing doctor. That seems likely to me as well, though Beryl never confirmed or denied it in an interview. What strikes me in their alliance even more is how they grew from being the fiercest of competitors to the most loyal of friends over the course of their lives. They knew each other so well, and trusted and valued each other for many decades. I find that quite moving.

LK: Toward the end of the novel, Beryl says, "I've sometimes thought that being loved a little less than others can actually make a person rather than ruin them." Is this your thought, or did Markham ever say or write something like this? Can you explain further what she means?

PM: In that line, I'm actually extrapolating something Beryl said of her father in an interview toward the end of her life: "I admire my father for the way he raised me. People go around kissing and fussing over their children. I didn't get anything like that. I had to look after myself. . . . Funnily enough it made me." Her independence and undeniable resilience were born out of her unconventional upbringing, to be sure. Though we might see the circumstances of her girlhood as heartbreaking—the disappearance of her mother, the benign neglect of her father—I wanted to call attention to the fact that Beryl never played the victim or felt sorry for herself, but in fact sharpened herself on those losses, becoming stronger. Becoming herself.

LK: The dreaded final question: What's next?

PM: There *is* more than a smidgen of dread in that question! It's not always obvious, when I think about something new, what's going to swim up from the deep to activate my imagination, or even that something *will*. I'll bet you have that fear too—that one of these days the muse might hang up a "Gone Fishing" sign and vanish? But I'd very much like to get to a place where I can fight back against the panic and uncertainty, and simply be at rest, waiting for the spark of inspiration.

For today at least, that seems doable. I'm sitting at my desk, looking at my yard full of barren, skeletal trees. Nothing seems alive out there, but spring is going to come soon. It always does eventually!

QUESTIONS FOR DISCUSSION

1. At the beginning of the book, Beryl reflects that her father's farm in Njoro is "the one place in the world I'd been made for." Do you feel this is a fitting way to describe Beryl's relationship with Kenya, too? Does she seem more suited—more made for—life there than the others in her circle? Is there a place in your life that you would describe the same way?

2. While it is clear he loves his daughter, do you feel Beryl's father is a good parent? Do you think Beryl would have said he was? Did you sympathize with him at any point?

3. Beryl is forced to be independent from a very young age. How do you think this shapes her personality (for better or for worse)?

4. After Jock's drunken attack, D fires Beryl and sends her away. Do you understand his decision? Despite all the philandering and indulgent behaviors of the community, do you feel it's fair that Beryl is judged so harshly for the incident?

5. How would you describe Beryl and Denys's relationship? In what ways are they similar souls? How does their first encounter—outside, under the stars at her coming-out party—encapsulate the nature of their connection?

6. Karen and Beryl are two strong, iconoclastic women drawn to the same unobtainable man. Do you understand how Beryl could pursue Denys even though he was involved with Karen? Did you view the friendship between the women as a true one, despite its complications?

7. Why do you believe the author chose the title *Circling the Sun*? Does it bring to mind a particular moment from the novel or an aspect of Beryl's character?

8. When Beryl is quite young, she reflects that "softness and helplessness got you nothing in this place." Do you agree with her? Or do you think Beryl places too much value on strength and independence?

9. When Beryl becomes a mother herself, she is determined not to act as her own mother did. Do you feel she succeeds? How does motherhood spur her decision to exchange horse training for flying? Could you identify with this choice?

10. After Paddy the lion attacks Beryl, Bishon Singh says, "perhaps you weren't ever meant for him." Do you think that Beryl truly discovers what she is meant for by the end of the novel?

PHOTO: © NINA SUBIN

PAULA McLAIN is the author of the novels *The Paris Wife* and *A Ticket to Ride,* the memoir *Like Family: Growing Up in Other People's Houses,* and two collections of poetry. She has received fellowships from Yaddo, the MacDowell Colony, and the National Endowment for the Arts. She lives in Cleveland with her family.

paulamclain.com
Facebook.com/paulamclainauthor
Instagram.com/paula_mclain

To inquire about booking Paula McLain for a speaking engagement, please contact the Penguin Random House Speakers Bureau at speakers@penguinrandomhouse.com.

About the Type

This book was set in Granjon, a modern recutting of a typeface produced under the direction of George W. Jones (1860–1942), who based Granjon's design upon the letterforms of Claude Garamond (1480–1561). The name was given to the typeface as a tribute to the typographic designer Robert Granjon (1513–89).